Northern Destinies

Lilli Babits

Northern Destinies

A PageMaster Publishing book

~~~

Published by arrangement with the author

This is a work of fiction. Names, characters, and incidents are products of the author's imagination and are not to be construed as real. Any resemblance to actual events or persons is purely coincidental.

Copyright © 2007 by Lilli Babits
ISBN: 978-0-9797759-0-1

All rights reserved. No part of this book may be used or reproduced in any manner without written permission from the publisher.

PageMaster Publishing Co.
Perry, Michigan
www.pagemasterpublishing.com
Printed in the U.S.A.
2nd printing - October 2007

*To God,
creator of the master roadmap and
designer of the adventures that fill our lives.*

Northern Destinies

Prologue ~ 1986

Sitting cross-legged on the cabin floor near the hearth, three women held sticks with marshmallows over the fire. A beagle snored on the couch. They'd spent the afternoon packing items that Esther would take to her new home in the morning. One sturdy box was full of pastel beach rocks. Although she hadn't lived in the cabin long it seemed that her easy smile and felicitous words had always been a part of Arcadia.

"It's not a real good-bye. You'll be at the library twice a month and we can meet for lunch." Cindy's life took a positive turn after meeting her friend in the laundromat two years ago. She had welcomed Esther's conscientious tendencies as a respite to her own flamboyant personality and in just a few months' time, the friendship had become golden.

Karen leaned into Esther, "You're a blessing in my life and have taught me so much about faith. You were wise to accept that fate put you here. The good-bye tomorrow won't be a farewell. It'll simply mark an end to one of many visits, Es."

Sporadic murmurs eventually replaced the conversation. By midnight only a trickle of whispers broke the dark silence. When the fire's glow subsided beneath brittle ashes, the women finally retired to their sleeping spots. Tranquility and love had combined to create a string of unique moments; the evening would become a cherished memory. Esther sighed placidly as her thoughts wandered far away and into the room of her first memory...

Spring 1965

The baby was finally home and they were now a family of four. Ken was back to work, a repertoire of lullabies reigned the forefront of Agatha's mind, and Esther's dolls were lined up in birth order on her bed. She'd picked up her crayons and paper in the kitchen and was now lying on her bedroom floor. Gazing at the towering elm tree outside her window, Esther listened to the hallway fan circulating a breeze through the already warm house. She was certain that she'd never forget this day. Mommy had called it May16th and daddy circled the date on the calendar. It was the first morning baby Joseph's crying wakened her. Now focused on a pair of quarreling sparrows, she fought the urge to tiptoe into her parents' room and touch the wonderful blessing in the bassinet. She explored beneath her bed to find a puzzle instead.

The doorbell chimed in the hallway.

"Honey, please get the door for me! It's probably the nurse."

Esther dashed down the hallway to execute her mother's request. After pressing the button to release the lock and wrapping her little fists around the knob, she yanked with all of her might to pull the door open. This simple accomplishment instilled a small sense of pride; she liked to be a helper.

"Good morning. Are you the big sister? Your hair is magnificent, darling."

Esther peered down to her bare toes and blushed from a sense of shame that fluttered in her chest. A word like that probably wasn't good; she couldn't fix her hair with a comb. Mom said she had hair like a lion and that only finger combing would do. And this morning with the new baby home and her elaborate art project in the kitchen, mom hadn't the time to braid her hair.

"I'm Nurse Constance. What's your name?" The dark-haired woman wore a white dress and a sweater of such light blue color that, on second glance, one might not see the bluish tint after all.

The shameful knot dissolved when the youngster looked up to meet the nurse's warm grin. "Esther. I'm four. Are you here to see our Joseph?"

"Yes, I am, Miss Esther. Your mom and I have a visit scheduled for today."

Making a come-on-in gesture with her delicate hand, Esther led the nurse into the kitchen where her mother was stacking dishes to drain. The coffee brewing on the stove mingled with the other household odors to provide a comforting aroma. The yellow kitchen lined with maple cabinets boasted a southern window that offered a backyard view to the sunny day. A dozen folded cotton diapers were stacked in a wicker basket on the floor beside the table. Constance guessed Agatha Gardener to be around twenty-eight years old. Although she appeared fatigued, as are all mothers with newborns, she seemed to be content.

Agatha's soft blue eyes and wide smile offered a genuine welcome that immediately put Constance at ease. "Thanks for coming so early. The baby is sleeping now but I expect him up shortly. Would you like some coffee or tea?" Suddenly self conscious of her disheveled attire and lack of make-up, she checked her feet to see that she'd at least slipped on her good pair of sandals this morning instead of the usual rubber flip-flops.

The nurse extended her hand and Agatha shook it softly, "I'm Constance Nelson and a cup of coffee would be great; just black, please. Your neighborhood is lovely and I passed a new elementary school; that's a real plus with two young children." She sat down as Agatha grabbed cups from the rack and poured the steaming brew.

"Yes, it is. The school was built just two years ago so we're quite pleased." She turned her attention to her daughter, "Esther, I hid a package of pecan rolls from daddy last night—could you please get them from the pan cupboard? You may have a roll and then go back to your bedroom or the living room while I talk to the nurse. Did you get all of your dolls dressed?"

"Yup. Now I'm gonna do the Humpty Dumpty puzzle all by myself." After retrieving the package and accepting a roll and napkin from her mother she skipped atop tiny feet back to her room to tackle the job.

The women settled at the small table. Constance inquired how Joseph had fared overnight, writing Agatha's responses to her specific questions. The nurse shrugged off her sweater as she spoke, "The doctors aren't positive yet what's causing his digestive and breathing troubles. The respiratory specialist is reviewing the chest x-rays this afternoon and we'll have results from the initial sweat test and blood tests back this week. They hope the blood tests reveal nothing more than a virus or bacterial infection. However, if they cannot make a diagnosis from the first round, they'll test aggressively for other diseases or allergies that can cause the symptoms he's experiencing."

Constance paused briefly to check Agatha's reaction and was relieved to see her composed. "If the doctors decide that further testing is necessary, someone will call you later this week. But until they pinpoint the cause we need to make sure you're treating his congestion. Your first line of defense is a bronchodilator medication; I understand he was given breathing treatments in the hospital. I have a nebulizer in my car, so if you'll excuse me just a moment, I'll be right back with it."

When she heard Constance depart, Esther scurried into the kitchen. "I think our baby is fine."

Agatha's heart swelled at the sight of her young lioness still in bare feet and unbraided hair. "C'mere, sunshine." Esther ran into her mother's arms to offer a whole-body hug, unaware of the nourishing affect her innocence and charm provided.

The nurse returned with a large canvas bag on her shoulder just as Joseph awoke. Agatha sent Esther into her bedroom to find a pair of socks, then nursed the baby while Constance withdrew the medical equipment from the bag. She disliked the idea of Joseph being further inspected, but self-pity wasn't an option; the baby's health was her top priority.

Constance rubbed the cool stethoscope before placing it on the infant's chest. With eyes closed and body tense, she remarked quietly, "Lungs are congested but the heartbeat is strong. He does need the medication." She plugged the nebulizer into an outlet and added a dose of medicine into the chamber beneath the mask. While performing these tasks, she wrote each step for Agatha. "You'll keep this nebulizer at home. If his cough returns or he's exhibiting breathing difficulties, you'll administer this medication every four to six hours." Constance swirled the medicine in the chamber, and continued, "Keep track of the breathing treatments. If you find that he requires more than four doses in a twenty-four hour period, call your pediatrician. If he has a fever, call your pediatrician. If his coughing doesn't improve after a breathing treatment, take him to the hospital."

Constance strapped the rubber mask over Joseph's face and wisps of steamy medicine billowed around his cheeks. The women watched it flow into the baby's mouth and nose with each breath he drew. With eyes closed and tiny inchworm fingers wrapped around her index finger he sat quietly in his mother's arms. His big sister returned, curious. Agatha began a slow back-and-forth-rocking motion, more to assuage her nerves than to calm the baby.

"How long does he have to smell the fog?" Esther's large and inquisitive brown eyes begged a response.

"This fog makes his breathing easier; it takes about six minutes."

Esther pondered the answer for a moment and posed another question, "When will he get better?"

Constance offered an explanation in terms that the young child could understand. "The doctors aren't sure yet. Perhaps it's a cold in his throat or maybe a bad germ. Your brother also has tummy problems and he might need some extra tests at the hospital before the doctors can help him."

Esther shut her eyes briefly to dispel the frightening words that spilled around her, and she immediately chose to simply love her brother and let no worries inside.

Pleased with the subsequent lung check and normal temperature reading, Constance described the cleaning and sterilization procedure for the nebulizer and then rose to depart. "I need to get back to the office. It was a pleasure meeting both of you. You have enough medication for twenty breathing treatments. If you have any questions, be sure to call your pediatrician's office on that card. You should hear from either the hospital lab or your doctor in a couple of days. Good luck!"

With her lightly freckled nose pressed against the window, Esther silently watched the nurse disappear down Lavender Lane. Agatha uttered a pleading prayer, *Dear Lord, Please heal this precious child.*

~~~~~~

Two days had passed since the nurse's visit. With Joseph swaddled and snuggled on her shoulder, Agatha watered the zinnias along the back porch and relished the breezy morning. The fluttering poplar leaves in the yard next door played a rhythmic melody and pulled her back in time: she saw tiny Esther toddling around the backyard on a warm and windy day three years ago.

Esther now played in the sandbox, building mountains and humming the resident melody that stirred the hearts of all precocious four-year old girls. The demanding ring from the kitchen startled Agatha and she dropped the hose. Striding into the house with Esther on her heels she knew instinctively who the caller would be.

Except for the greeting, the conversation was one-sided; Agatha offered only monosyllabic responses to indicate comprehension. There were no bacterial infections, the x-rays didn't show pneumonia, and the sweat test was inconclusive. The attending doctors agreed that the distal intestinal obstruction Joseph had suffered in the hospital was cause for concern. A second sweat test was scheduled for the following Wednesday. She numbly returned the phone back into its cradle and inhaled a deep breath. She pulled a strand of long blond hair behind her ear. *The mystery will be solved soon; Joseph will receive appropriate treatment and we'll move forward with our new lives.*

After brushing tiny kisses across Joseph's downy hair, she turned to watch her daughter sort crayons at the kitchen table, skinny legs swinging from the chair's edge. Esther was creating a book for her brother. Agatha hoped that she'd continue adding pages to it because the book would be a cute keepsake.

The first page was Joseph: a big happy face with stick hands and legs. Ken had written the May 16th date below the picture. The next page contained a large square with several oval windows drawn inside; this, Esther had explained, was the hospital where he was born. And so her work continued. Esther faithfully added pictures as she felt necessary. Today's page displayed a big yellow circle to represent the sun because it had been such a warm May.

Hoping it might diminish her fear somewhat to share the news with the one person who could help carry the emotional burden, Agatha dialed Ken's office number. As she waited for him to answer the phone, a trickle of gut-wrenching terror jarred her spine. But the sound of his voice eased the tension from her face and she greeted him with the most courageous voice she could muster, "Hi, honey. How's your day been?"

"It's hectic but we're making great progress. We've nailed down the Jennings counter-offer already. What's up, babe?"

"The hospital called this morning. The doctor wants to see Joseph for another sweat test next week. There's no bacterial infection and the pneumonia check was negative; the intestinal blockage he had in the hospital might be an indication of a serious underlying condition. I'll fill you in tonight." She breathed deeply then, "Good luck this afternoon—love you, Ken."

"It'll be okay, Agatha. Relax and give the kids a hug for me. I'll be home early this afternoon. I love you, too." Tall and slim with a bashful smile, firm handshake, and dark chocolate eyes, Ken's gentle voice subdued her plaguing anxieties. She counted the hours until his arrival home; she'd lean into his strong frame and absorb comfort from his embrace.

The baby had fallen asleep on her shoulder; Agatha clung to him. After tucking his tiny feet into the blue plaid blanket, she quietly returned to the backyard to turn off the water spigot and save the zinnias from drowning.

~~~~~

Saturday brought rain, but the clear and bright Sunday would more than make up for it. Despite her recent lack of sleep, Agatha was upbeat and looked forward to the baptism. She was up at five o'clock with Joseph and, after feeding and tucking him back into the bassinet, decided to shower early. After drying her long blond hair and clipping it into a single ponytail, she brewed a pot of coffee and ambled to the backyard with a warm mug clasped tightly between her palms. Perched on the fence post, a wren warbled its song. Ken's spot for meditation was his workbench downstairs. In warm weather, the rickety bench on the porch was hers.

Shutting her eyes, Agatha recalled an April evening with Ken. The air had been damp and smelled of fresh earth. The daffodils and hyacinths were blooming and Ken had mowed the grass that day, which made the yard appear especially tidy. She was very pregnant and they were choosing baby names while snuggled beneath their Mexican blanket on the bench. She couldn't imagine her world without Ken in it. Although married for six years, a wistful smile from her husband still ignited a desire that only his touch could fulfill. He was her rock with strong roaming hands and he possessed the logic and charm of an old-fashioned kind of lawyer. She smiled at the pink and orange sky as it unwrapped itself from around the sun rising higher in the east. After a final sip of coffee she hopped off the bench and returned to the kitchen.

While Agatha arranged meat and cheese slices on a large serving tray, Esther snuck up from behind and wrapped her arms around her mother's waist.

"I'm starving today."

"Well, hello there big girl. I'll pour a bowl of cereal and

juice for you in just a minute. Let's be quiet so Joseph stays asleep a little longer. He's got a big day." Agatha pressed her cheek against her daughter's head to breathe in the sleepy fragrance of her just-awake hair.

Excited about the baptism, Esther chattered ceaselessly between mouthfuls of Cheerios. "Will grandma and grandpa be at the church? How about Aunt Gail and Uncle Ed? I hope they bring Charlie because he's good at pushing me on the swing."

"Yes, dear. They'll all be there." Agatha gently pulled her fingers through her daughter's unruly hair to bring the frizzy ringlets to life. "Finish your breakfast and bring me the pink barrettes for your hair."

The Gardener family arrived at the church in plenty of time and sat in the front row pew with their attending relatives. Joseph cried out and fussed briefly but Agatha wasn't concerned. Despite the congestion and erratic digestive problems, he had a marvelous disposition. And he'd been sleeping better at night since Constance had delivered the mist tent a few days ago.

After the first hymn ended, Pastor Evans directed the family to the baptismal font. The ceremony was brief and the children remained silent throughout as if tiny church angels had gently nudged them. Joseph's godparents, Gail and Ed, made the trip from Flint; as usual, Agatha's father was the event photographer.

Sharing the day with family members gave it added meaning. It had always been Agatha's belief that a day's purpose ballooned with importance when loved ones joined together. An emotional wave descended upon her as the baby slept on her shoulder. *Dear Lord, Take special care of this family. Lead us to do what is right and good. Give us strength and courage to endure whatever illness we encounter. And help Joseph breathe freely today.*

~~~~~~

Ken left the office early on Wednesday. Agatha hadn't called and he couldn't wait a minute longer for details from the hospital trip. After parking in the driveway he jogged nervously into the house. "How'd the test go, honey?" He wandered through the kitchen. "Agatha? Esther?"

He tiptoed down the hallway to inspect the bedrooms and found them asleep on Esther's bed—it was a precious image. His daughter wore her princess gown and lay in a curled-up position surrounded by her favorite dolls. Agatha and Joseph were entwined on a stack of pillows that Esther had apparently dragged in from the living room; Agatha's long hair draped over her shoulders in straight strands like a picket fence. He decided to let them sleep and crept to the kitchen to make dinner.

The aroma of simmering marinara sauce awakened Esther first, who boisterously jumped off the bed, which woke her brother, who woke their mother. "Daddy's home!"

"Hey, sunshine. How was the hospital visit? Did you behave well for mommy?"

"The trip was good, but Joseph cried and we had lots of waiting. I colored eight pages in my shape book already."

After Ken's harried workday, stirring the contents of the saucepan had subdued his nerves. Now seeing his doe-eyed daughter in the costume dress lifted the weight almost entirely from his shoulders. He bent down to exchange hugs with her and then straightened as Agatha and Joseph entered the kitchen. It appeared that her day had been much rougher than his had. He knew in an instant that the news wasn't good and spoke quickly to initiate a light-hearted conversation.

"I think the sauce has just the right amount of basil. I'll take the baby so you can cook the noodles." Ken reached for him and felt his stomach tighten as tears clouded her dismayed blue eyes. He wrapped his arms around his wife and son. Although she wept like a tiny kitten he knew the pain was immense. Agatha never let Esther see her upset—it was a rare occasion when she let tears fall in their daughter's presence. After a minute she dried her cheeks on her shirtsleeve and forced a smile.

Agatha whispered into her husband's ear, "We'll talk after the kids are in bed. I'd like us to have a regular sort of evening until then, okay?"

"Let's talk while Esther's in the bath after supper. I can't sit on pins and needles until her bedtime, Ag. What'd the doctors say?" The whisper came through clenched teeth; Ken wasn't about to let her dilly dally around. In fact, he wanted an answer immediately.

She squeezed her eyes tightly to keep them dry and then peered up at him imploringly, "I need a few hours of normalcy before spilling everything out and making it all real. Please."

He looked to the floor, ran his fingers through his wavy brown hair, and counted to ten. Nodding angrily, he pulled Joseph into his arms, set the baby's head into the crook of his neck, and quietly set plates and forks around the kitchen table.

With the pasta cooked and a salad made, the family sat down to share the meal. Ken held Joseph as he picked at the food on his plate, Esther prattled nonstop about the day's adventure, and Agatha solemnly nibbled at the supper she couldn't taste.

~~~~~~

By eight o'clock the evening's darkness had crept into the house to fill its corners with deep, gray shadows. The porch light illuminated the geraniums beneath the front window. Inside the kitchen, the stovetop light glowed above the Philco radio on the counter where Ernie Harwell announced the final plays of the Tigers' game. Seated at the small maple table, Agatha was sipping tea when Ken entered the room with trepidation and sat down beside her.

"The doctors suspect cystic fibrosis. The pediatrician and respiratory specialist have discounted asthma; Joseph's mucus sample is uncharacteristically thick and sticky. Digestive problems are another CF symptom because the pancreas is usually plugged as well. And we both know about Joseph's problems in that area. The salty taste of his skin is another strong indicator. It's a serious and incurable disease, and that's not the worst part." Her reddened eyes stung him with fear.

"What is it?" Ken removed his glasses and set them onto the table; the plastic frame tapped the wood to break the eerie pause. He wished they were reviewing credit card bills or his father's recent gallbladder surgery—topics that were tough to discuss last month but now seemed stratospheres away from worrisome.

"Joseph will be lucky to see his tenth birthday." The sentence was barely audible but it boomed and resonated in his mind. Tears streamed down her precious face and she trembled in agony.

He remained stoic and calm, "What do we do next?" Ken captured her eyes with the question and saw an intense anguish, yet he gleaned strength and determination from her expression as he reached for her hand.

"Today's sweat test will check Joseph's sodium and chloride levels again. He apparently was unable to produce a sufficient amount of perspiration during the first test to provide a conclusive result. The doctor will call in three days; it's likely the test result will be positive. Our lives are about to take on a whole new meaning, Ken. We'll walk down the path that God has set forth for us. We'll keep our faith during this journey. And we'll love and care for our little boy for as long as we have him." Her tear-filled cheeks wretched his heart.

Ken reached across the table to clasp Agatha's other hand into a firm grip. With fingers laced and eyes aligned he could think of only one response, "I love you, Agatha, and we've been blessed with a delightful family. We'll cherish every minute of every day, do our best not to fret, and we'll do whatever it takes to keep him healthy and happy."

He sullenly gathered her into his arms and carried her to bed. They'd need plenty of sleep before tomorrow's minutes arrived.

Autumn 1966

Early September in Michigan meant that the petunias and marigolds clung to their color while the sounds and smells of summer waned. The wind carried the scent of tired tomato vines and withering chicory stalks whose blue button flowers had shriveled into crispy cocoons full of tiny seeds. The doorway that led to the autumn season hadn't yet opened but a person might see it just around the corner if he squinted. The daytime sky was still brilliant and warm, while dusk brought a subtle chill to the air that drove a person to the closet for his jacket in the evening.

"It'll be a fabulous day, Es. Let's get a picture by the maple tree before we leave." Agatha retrieved her camera from the pantry and pulled Joseph up from the floor and onto her hip as they strode out the front door. Across the street Mrs. Thielman was washing her Volkswagen again. Imagine, a car with an engine where the trunk ought to be.

"Maybe I should stay home, Mom. You're already crying and we're not even at school yet." Esther was torn. She was wearing her brand-new uniform *and* new shoes, and she was anxious to meet her new classmates. But who would color pictures for Joseph or dust the coffee table while she was gone every morning? "Will Joseph be in the picture so I always remember how sad I am to leave and how happy I am for my first day of school?"

Although nearly seventeen months old, Joseph had been walking on his own for a only month. Like many CF patients, his pancreatic function wasn't optimum, even with the enzyme medicine. And chronic lung congestion kept him from sleeping well at night. Thus, his height and weight were below average.

Agatha set down her blue-eyed toddler and backed several steps away before clicking the picture. She knew the resulting photo would neither give justice to the moment nor recreate the feeling that made her throat feel swollen but it was all she'd have a decade from now. Joseph grinned as she reached for him; he had Ken's wistful smile and it was a powerful antidote to the sadness that sometimes crept into her otherwise vibrant spirit. His hair was brown like Esther's but not nearly as curly; it swept around his temples and neck like tiny bird wings.

"Okay kids. Into the car we go. The bell rings in ten minutes so we need to leave now if we're going to make it on time." Agatha turned the radio dial to WDLV as she backed the Impala out of the driveway. Diana Ross and the Supremes were crooning with gusto; Agatha donned her white-framed sunglasses and rocked her head to the beat with shoulder length hair bouncing in time to the music.

Esther enjoyed watching her mom sing in the car because she wasn't thinking about all the stuff that she had to do for everyone. She was just a nice lady who was driving and singing and mostly smiling. If Esther knew how to use that camera she'd take a picture of her mom at this very moment.

Joseph began to cough—his usual reaction to a sinus infection.

"Esther, will you please clap his back for me?"

The young girl knew the drill and scooted closer to her brother. "Lean up with me and cough now." Baby blue eyes met her brown while Esther's soothing voice calmed his fear. She tapped his back several times just as Nurse Constance had taught her; she was confident and effective. The toddler responded with loud and hard coughs that cleared his airways. He took it in stride as part of their routine.

"Good job. Feel better?" She wiped his nose with a tissue from the box beside her and then peered into his reddened face.

He rewarded her with a smile and favorite response, "Hi!"

They arrived at the school in time to see teachers take their positions on the classroom numbers painted on the asphalt. Esther kissed Joseph's forehead and quickly slid from the car.

Agatha stepped out briefly for a final hug and kiss before releasing her precious girl into the world of Formica desks and crayon-scented classrooms.

"Bye-bye, Esther. See you at one o'clock." The sunglasses hid the tears but the crack in her voice revealed her emotions. Letting go of Esther was torture.

Mrs. Young, standing in front of number 127, recited the names of her new kindergartners. Esther was the eighth student called and she ran to take the spot behind a boy named Tony. The ninth student was another girl.

As the teacher called the remaining eleven students, a girl named Linda tapped Esther's shoulder to strike up a conversation. "I have a new uniform and my knee socks match. It looks like yours is new, too."

She beamed above her new saddle shoes, "Yeah. It came in the mail last week and this is my first time wearing it. My mom sewed up the bottom to make it fit. I'm Esther Gardener. What's your whole name?"

"I'm Linda Harrison and I have two brothers. Tom is in the second grade and Steve is in the fifth grade. Do you have a brother or sister?"

"My brother is Joseph and he still wears diapers, but he's a blessing from God."

Mrs. Young clapped her hands twice to get the children's attention, "Follow me to our classroom, students." As she waddled across the walkway leading her line of five-year old ducklings to the west entrance, Esther felt like a soldier. She heard a lot about soldiers on TV because a war was happening far away and Dad said that President Johnson was doing a piss-poor job handling the whole thing.

Full of fun projects and storytelling, the day for the kindergartners passed quickly. After a brief recess, the children colored apples in the shape of an *A* and bananas in the shape of a *B*. A few homesick students had trouble coping in the noisy classroom, while others were vibrant and content to be a part of the busy environment. Esther belonged in the latter bunch.

Tony eyed Esther's drawings and couldn't resist giving his opinion. "Those bananas look bad because they're green and not yellow."

"That's because bananas come from a place that's fifty hundred miles away and the men pick them green at first so they won't rot on the long boat ride."

Reflecting on her first day of school, Esther peered around at the faces of her classmates. Some had freckles, some had lost a tooth, and a few cried too much. She was glad to have her hair in braids today because she didn't see anyone else with hair like a lion. Linda was nice and Esther thought that she might be a great friend someday. But she'd wait to show her the lion hair.

~~~~~~

September stepped aside for a breezy October. The leaves had lost their green luster and the trees danced with their brilliant new colors. Most of the maples were already yellow and orange while the poplars were nearly bare at this point. The big oak tree on Lavender Lane was wearing its grand sienna dress. It was Esther's favorite because the roots had pushed up the sidewalk to make a tiny hill for her wagon to glide down.

"Can we go for a wagon walk, Mom? I bet Joseph wants some of that fresh air outside. We could go to Mrs. Warren's house and back." Esther pulled open the coat closet, stepped atop the canister vacuum, and grabbed her red jacket with the white softness inside. She retrieved Joseph's blue jacket and knit hat as well.

With elbows deep in dish water, Agatha responded, "I think dad is downstairs; ask if he'll help you get the wagon out and put the farm blanket inside."

After retrieving the blanket covered in pigs and cows, Esther bolted to the basement to find her dad whistling beside his workbench. She believed that this was his daydream spot. The concrete floor held a constant layer of sawdust, providing a large space where she drew shapes with her fingertips while her dad executed important tasks. Ken had recently cut several dozen pine cubes that ranged from three to five inches square. They were stacked in rows across the bench waiting to be sanded. Joseph would especially enjoy the extra-large blocks.

"Dad? Mom said you have to come upstairs and help me get the wagon out to ride Joseph right now."

Ken turned on the stool to see his gregarious daughter bound to him; he quickly extended his arms to catch her. "Hey there, sunshine. Is it warm enough already?" He removed his eyeglasses to better squeeze her into his chest and tickle her skinny tummy. Before Esther could respond he plopped her onto his shoulder and trotted up the steps. She was pleased that she hadn't spent an extra minute convincing her dad a wagon ride was a great idea. They were on their way.

Mrs. Warren's house had a birdbath in the front yard and was an entire seven houses away, which meant a fourteen-house walk. That suited Esther just fine because pushing Joseph up the hill by Bentley's oak tree was tough.

Agatha hollered out the front door, "Wait a second, honey. I want to get a picture. The colors are so pretty and you both look cute in your jackets." CF would snatch away her son far too soon and she wanted as much of him on film as was physically possible. After snapping the picture she gave each child a kiss and a tender hug, "You be careful by the Bentley tree, Esther. Understand?"

"Yup. See you later." And down the sidewalk they strolled into the neighborhood's Saturday morning. Her head was full of important thoughts. *I wonder what I'll be for Halloween. Maybe Joseph can go trick-or-treating if dad takes him in the wagon. Linda said she's gonna be a princess, but that's what everyone's gonna be. I'd like to be Dorothy's scarecrow.*

"Hello, little lady and Joseph. How're you this fine morning?" Mr. Bentley was raking leaves. He always smoked a pipe and Esther thought it smelled nice.

"We're doing good. Next week in school we're painting pumpkin faces on big paper. And Mrs. Young is making applesauce on a little stove that she's bringing to school. She said applesauce takes a lot of patience and stirring."

"That sounds like fun. I have some great leaf piles here and you're welcome to do some jumping."

"Thanks, Mr. Bentley. Maybe after lunch."

She carefully pulled the wagon down the sidewalk hill and ran to Mrs. Warren's house. Almost there, she turned and spoke to her brother, "Let's stop at this house and get pretty leaves for mom and dad."

Esther settled the wagon onto the edge of the lawn and helped Joseph out. He collected random samples from the confetti of leaves beneath their feet and tossed them into the wagon. She chose only the smoothest orange ones.

After gathering what seemed to be hundreds of leaves, she led him back into the wagon. She then tucked the blanket beneath his legs and scattered the autumn treasures all around him. "Don't throw any of these out, okay?"

Joseph met her eyes and grinned crookedly before offering a simple reply, "No."

Now breathless, Esther parked the wagon in front of her own porch. She led her brother up the steps, opened the screen door and hollered in, "Mom, we're back with a surprise."

Agatha hoisted the grinning toddler up into her arms. "A surprise?"

"They're outside. C'mon and I'll show you."

Agatha donned an expression of sheer delight, "These are beautiful. Where'd you find them?"

"We got 'em from the lawn by Mrs. Warren's house but the people won't mind because they have millions."

"Put them into the blanket and bring them inside. We'll press the prettiest ones with wax paper in between the encyclopedia pages." Agatha would save a leaf for Esther's memory book. She made a mental note to mark a date on the December calendar to check the preserved leaves; it'd be a fun winter activity.

After pressing the best ones, Esther queried how long their colors would last.

"I'm not sure, sweetie. Perhaps for a few months. But that's all right; God sends new leaves every October."

~~~~~~

Struggling to breathe, Joseph awoke from his nap. Agatha tapped his back to loosen the mucus while Ken set up the nebulizer in the living room. Although Esther was fully accustomed to seeing her brother wear the medicine mask, her heart still wrenched when she thought of his suffering. To give Agatha a break from the duty she performed during the week, Ken administered Joseph's breathing treatments on the weekends. Joseph coughed and shuddered. Ken patted his back and caressed his wavy hair to soothe his rigid body. Not once did Esther sense her parents were angry at the disease; they loved Joseph intensely. And it was their job to protect him and seek the best possible medical treatment he could get. So far, they were faring well in their battle and little Joseph's life was, for the most part, normal.

Agatha was fully adjusted to sleeping in three-hour increments during the night now and she realized that it wasn't her body growing accustomed to the frequent lung clearing sessions, but her spirit. She had finally accepted CF as part of her life because she knew that as long as she had her family and a strong faith, there was nothing she couldn't conquer.

~~~~~~

The turkey and sage stuffing had been roasting since early morning and now the mouth-watering aroma had wafted throughout the house. Esther played checkers with grandpa while Uncle Ed, Charlie, and her dad were glued to the football game on TV.

Aunt Gail found it necessary to step into the living room occasionally and shush the loud men, "For goodness sake, it's just a game, Ed."

"Esther, please come into the kitchen!" Agatha had read her daughter's mind.

"Coming!"

"Downstairs on the dryer is a stack of white cloth napkins. Please bring them upstairs and then wash your hands and set the table with Grandma Gardener."

Steam billowed from the stovetop, messy spoons were scattered across the counters, dishtowels hung from shoulders, aprons were covered in greasy smears, and lovely serving bowls that she'd never seen out of the cupboard were being filled. It was magic. She bravely trotted downstairs, strode cautiously through the stale basement air, grabbed the napkins, dashed back up the wooden steps, and re-entered the warm kitchen with relief.

The large table for six people wore a yellow tablecloth and displayed tall white candlesticks set in crystal holders. Four yellow placemats and a fragrant bouquet of flowers covered the small one; this table had the metal chairs around it, including one with a booster seat. And, of course, beside Joseph's plate was a small cup of applesauce. (Stirred into this fruit was the enzyme medicine he ate with every meal.)

The table-setting team proceeded around the tables arranging silverware at their proper positions, followed by the cooks, one right after the other, with bowls and platters full of November delicacies.

Esther shouted into the living room, "Dinner is ready!"

As tradition dictated in the Gardener family, names were put into a bowl before dinner. The person whose name was drawn gave the Thanksgiving prayer. This year was Ken's turn.

"Dear Lord, We thank you for this bountiful meal and the love of our family and friends. Thank you for the blessings you continue to bestow upon us and for the freedom to praise your name. We pray for peace in Vietnam so that our dear brothers can be home with their families. Amen"

Sharing their meals at the small table were Esther, Charlie, Joseph and Aunt Gail. The older children chatted about school events and Christmas lists. Like a mother hen, Esther efficiently assisted Joseph by helping him scoop food onto his spoon, making sure he ate all the applesauce, and wiping his messy face with the napkin. She lovingly tended to him, hardly realizing that she was serving his needs first before taking bites from her own plate. As Gail watched the siblings she grasped how much one needed and loved the other. Their lives would forever be entwined as long as this little boy lived, and perhaps beyond. And she understood how lucky they were to have each other, to have this symbiosis, just the way God had planned.

Spring ~ Summer 1968

Daniel trembled with anticipation as he tore the wrapping paper from his parents' gift. The junior drafting kit contained graph paper, vellum, pencils, a T-square, rulers, triangles, a compass, and a protractor. The other gift, from his grandparents, was a large box of eighth-inch thick rectangles, squares, rods, and triangles in assorted sizes made from scrap hardwood. Daniel knew for certain that these would beat any present he'd receive for the rest of his life. After shrugging off the momentary bout of speechlessness he uttered a boisterous thank-you and boldly embraced the gift givers.

By late summer he had designed and built two 3-foot skyscraper models. To create a realistic visual effect, he'd glued pieces of pale blue tissue paper behind each window frame inside of the models. Living in a Chicago suburb had its drawbacks but Daniel couldn't imagine growing up without the inspirational buildings and their imposing skyline nearby. Someday he'd be an architect and display the models in his office. And his friends would visit and say, "I can't believe you built those when you were only nine years old, man."

Daniel's hands were itching to assemble the next model. He couldn't dispel from his mind the medieval design he'd recently finished, and wouldn't sleep until the frame was built. Certain that everyone else in the house was asleep, he held his breath before shimmying down the ladder on the bunk bed he shared with Dennis. Once his feet touched the floor he silently emptied his lungs and retrieved the glue from his bottom dresser drawer. From under the bookshelf, he withdrew a shoebox full of wooden building pieces that he'd sorted earlier in the day.

With just the beam from a flashlight and his design sketch on the floor, he glued the base sections onto a sturdy piece of cardboard in a few minutes. It wasn't a skyscraper this time, but a castle. He designed it with a drawbridge; this would be the only uncovered wood section of the finished structure and he'd use roughly sanded sticks to ensure a realistic appearance. The castle itself would be covered in flat stones that he'd collected from around the neighborhood during the past few weeks. (After washing the stones, Daniel had suffered a stern lecture from his mother as to why filthy rocks don't belong in the kitchen sink.)

Piece by piece he worked, with a sliver of light and a lot of gumption. Daniel was thrilled to be building and grateful that he was able to keep steady hands throughout the gluing process. Two hours later, most of the frame was built. It had to be sturdy enough to hold the small stones that he'd place onto it later. He figured that the lookout tower at the back of the castle would be difficult to cover because it was tall with a relatively small circumference; he'd have to make sure that each layer of stones, starting at the bottom, was completely dry before placing the next layer. He wondered for a moment how the English and Scots built castles without concrete. *What'd they use for mortar? Mud? Clay? That's it. I'll wrap a thin layer of clay around the main structure, and then press the stones into it.*

Daniel examined the frame closely and decided to check its corners tomorrow using the Pythagorean formula his grandpa had taught him. Without perfectly squared corners a structure was useless. He put away the shoebox and glue, and then slid the castle frame against the wall so it wouldn't get bumped in the morning. Dennis snored beneath rumpled blankets while his compulsive brother crept back up to the top bunk.

His neck and back ached from crouching—the cool sheets were a welcome caress to his tired muscles as he nestled into the pillow and drew the blanket beneath his chin. Closing his eyes, Daniel recited a prayer before falling into a velvety sort of slumber, "Thank you for my life. Bless my family and friends, bring peace to Vietnam, and help me to be a great architect."

~~~~~~

A not-too-warm summer persuaded the wildflowers and gardens to burst into a glorious array of color and offer abundant harvests. Beach outings, baseball games, bicycle rides, and neighborhood picnics filled the long days of June and July. August crept into the Jacobson household without notice. Well, almost. The smiley-face sticker on Dennis' calendar reminded everyone that it was time for the trip to Indiana.

"Can I bring my new mitt to show grandpa? I'm real good at catching air balls now." When he tilted his head at just the right angle to reflect a charming innocence, Dennis usually got his way. His enthusiasm was unstoppable; perhaps because it was propelled by such loud and robustious behavior.

"Oh, all right. Bring your mitt and ball, but hurry. We don't want to run into traffic." And it was usually mom who gave in.

The Jacobson family, along with the mitt and ball, were packed into the Chevy in anticipation of a resplendent drive to Carbondale, Indiana. Although the trip would take just three or four hours, John Jacobson refused to linger in Chicago while the freeway filled with cars. This meant a departure time of seven o'clock in the morning.

Genuinely fond of John's parents, Sandra enjoyed the visits with her in-laws, but it was a tiring chore to pack for the family and prepare the picnic basket for the road trip. And it was always during the rushed laundry loads that she lost socks.

She'd convinced John to take Interstate 94 through the city so the children could see the skyline. Traffic was light enough to enjoy the view and, as usual, Daniel's palms and nose were pressed against the glass to absorb the details from his distant vantage point. As the space between the buildings and boy grew wider he mentally stripped a building of its bricks to visualize the girders. An excited shiver tickled his neck as if he himself had designed the structure that jutted into the sky.

The Jacobson family had been downtown on many occasions. Daniel was often appalled to see the city dwellers and businessmen strolling down the street completely unaware of the majestic miracles that stood all around them. He knew that each building was the result of thousands of man-hours and untold amounts of blood and sweat. The structures had begun as mere sketches on a drafting table and were now alive in their own right. He'd give anything to accelerate his life about ten years and get his hands on a stack of college-level architectural design books. Someday he'd design something real important.

Seven-year old Dennis wasn't impelled to gawk at the magnificent skyline. He'd seen the city, declared that it looked cool, and moved forward with his young life. The differences between the brothers didn't stop at their interests. Dennis had inherited his father's curly dark hair and eyes while Daniel resembled his mother, with blue eyes and honey-blond hair. Dennis relished a stormy Lake Michigan shoreline; his older brother preferred the sound of cicadas buzzing in August. Dennis was clutter and chaos, an unacceptable combination in the bedroom he shared with his tidy brother. John and Sandra had broken apart more than one fight between the pair during the past year, but knew the boys would eventually learn to co-exist and appreciate each other.

"Is it time for our picnic?" Four-year old Amy was an impatient traveler and Mr. Jacobson reminded her that they had to get farther into Indiana first.

"We'll stop in about an hour, Amy. Ask Daniel to make a picture of a house for you to color." Sandra grinned at her husband. It was a typical comment from John, who endeavored to smooth out the rough spots and disappointments for his kids.

Daniel opened his notebook and quickly drew a basic box house with a triangle roof, square windows, and rectangular door. On each side of the house he drew a simple tree that comprised a long, thin rectangle with an oval shape on top.

"How do you make that so fast?" Her tiny brow furrowed as she posed the query.

He smiled and set the notebook on her lap, "Piece of cake, kiddo."

Dennis shuffled through his box of baseball cards while Daniel pondered the upcoming weekend. He loved his grandparents but there wasn't much to do outside except climb the maple tree and explore the vacant field beside their house. Maybe they'd find a snake or large bird nest. Or maybe grandpa would take them up to the attic and dig around for old treasures. Mom mentioned they might tour the Indianapolis Zoo this weekend; that'd be fun.

Minutes crept by slowly as the Chevy rambled south through rolling hills and cornfields.

While Amy announced the appearance of every grazing farm animal, Sandra remarked on the quaint personalities of the white farmhouses that speckled the corn and wheat fields. Posted near several homes were clotheslines that flashed rows of colorful sheets and shirts billowing in the Midwest breeze. Tractors, balers, split-rail fences, red barns, and billboard signs added visual interest to the otherwise tedious landscape along Highway 41.

"Aha! There's our Lake Village sign; only twelve miles to the picnic stop." John Jacobson looked forward to the halfway point of these trips so he could stretch his back and legs. This was a task he would noisily perform while stepping from the car with a long, low growl. After the children used the smelly outhouses and cleaned their hands with soapy washcloths that Sandra prepared for the occasion, John would pour himself a dose of coffee into the silver thermos cap. And he never failed to declare, "Good coffee—it seems to me that your brew was made to be drunk in this very spot, Sandra."

Seconds after their arrival in the tiny park, the three children clamored from the Chevy and ran to the hill. The family discovered Lake Village Park purely by accident five years ago when John turned west out of Sunoco instead of east towards the freeway. The park entrance happened to be the first spot where he was able to turn the car around. And there it was. An emerald patch of grass with ancient maple and oak trees, a scattering of picnic tables, a pair of horseshoe pits, and a hill designed specifically for children who'd been cooped up in an automobile for two hours and needed to burn energy.

Onto a lopsided picnic table bleached gray from sun exposure, Sandra unpacked the egg sandwiches, fruit, orange juice, and precious coffee thermos. She removed her sunglasses, ran her fingers through her creamy blond hair, and reached up to the sky in a catlike stretch.

After removing the clip-on shades from his glasses, John pressed against his attractive wife to envelop her in his arms from behind. "I love this life, Sandra. Thank you for sharing it with me."

She turned around to embrace and kiss him gently; her response to the statement put a smile on his rugged face, "If the brass bed is too squeaky tonight, let's move our blankets onto the floor."

Piling back into the car atop hot vinyl seats put sour expressions on the children's faces. Sensitive to their feelings of martyrdom, John and Sandra rolled down their windows until the glass disappeared fully into the car doors. The wind whipped around the kids' heads to swirl their hair in every direction. As tradition dictated, Sandra passed a stick of Trident to each child. The powdery texture and minty fragrance of the gum were realized for just a moment before being popped into their small mouths. Once the gum chewing began in earnest, time would certainly accelerate.

Sandra kept busy switching between radio stations in search of her favorite Joni Mitchell song. Dennis sorted his baseball cards by team and player positions (with pitchers on top). Daniel daydreamed a walk through Chicago, and Amy brushed her ragged Fluffer bunny with a pink comb.

~~~~~~

"Where's baby Amy? You've brought along a big girl."

Amy leapt around Grandpa Jacobson until he picked her up and twirled her into the air. "I _am_ Amy but I growed lately." Bashful around strangers and in new places, dark-haired Amy was the epitome of vivaciousness among friends and family. She never had to be prodded for her opinion or an idea; she poured out whatever happened to cross her mind, and often without warning. She inherited this trait directly from Grandma Jacobson, a woman full of wisdom and common knowledge who was far too opinionated to keep it to herself.

After a gleeful exchange of hugs and hellos, suitcases were shuffled into their appropriate places, shoes got kicked aside, and molasses cookies were placed into the hands of three merry children. As the grown-ups assembled around the kitchen table to chat about the Cub's baseball season and exorbitant price of a new car, the children ventured into the yard in search of outdoor entertainment.

Dennis monkeyed into the maple tree while Amy lounged on the back porch to stroke the grumpy cat. Daniel strolled the perimeter of the yard and stopped dead in his tracks when he encountered several large stacks of sticks piled in the southeast corner. He dashed into the house.

"Grandpa! What're you gonna do with those stick piles?"

"Bert had his old elm tree taken down a week ago and grandma and I helped clean up the debris. I brought the large branches and sticks over here and figured you might think of something to do with 'em. Any ideas?"

Daniel sauntered to his grandfather and leaned into him, "How about I build a playhouse for Amy?"

"Sure enough. I wrestled up some string and twine from the basement; thought you might be able to use that as well." He winked at Daniel and tossed him the bag of string before the boy skipped back out with a plan already hatching in his head.

Dennis and Amy were more than happy to sort the sticks into three piles based on their lengths. Once sorted, Daniel arranged the longest sticks into a frame for the dome-shaped playhouse. He planned the diameter of the small house to be seven feet wide and its height to be four feet. Dennis stood in the center of the frame holding the sticks in place while Daniel wove the twine in and around the frame top. Once sturdy, the three children, under Daniel's direction, wove the smaller sticks to fill in the frame and create walls and a ceiling. Because he was such a perfectionist, the younger children quickly decided their tasks were complete and headed into the house in search of an extra cookie or two.

Working tirelessly on the dome-shaped playhouse, Daniel wove cotton string in and around the sides, parallel to the ground at six-inch intervals. He wanted the structure sturdy enough to block both wind and rain. Once the sticks were all in place he pulled up clumps of tall grass from the field next door, then wove and pressed them all around the dome for added wind protection. Finally taking a few paces back from the structure, he eyed it critically. Although slightly misshapen on one side, it was a good playhouse, considering his raw materials.

Dennis bolted from the house with a mitt in one hand and a ball in the other. The grown-ups gradually appeared in the yard, one by one; the guys would play a few rounds of catch before supper. Mom and grandma gathered folding chairs from the garage; they'd sit beneath the maple tree while Amy napped inside with Fluffer bunny.

"Holy smokes, Daniel! Nice structure." Grandpa was a builder at heart and always appreciated Daniel's efforts. John and Sandra beamed with pride yet again as they surveyed his newest creation; Daniel's ingenuity never ceased to amaze them.

Grandma chimed in, "I have an old brown blanket that you can put on the ground to make a floor. You may get it from the top shelf of the hall closet, Daniel."

With a few finishing touches and the flooring in place, the playhouse was complete by late afternoon. After supper, Amy arranged Fluffer and two of grandma's baby dolls around a tray filled with plastic cups, plates, and Ritz crackers. She adored her Daniel for making such a fine house.

~~~~~~

Darkness finally cloaked Indiana and grandma drew the shades. The children drifted into sleep while recollections of the day swayed like tall wild grass through their thoughts. Dennis relived his climb up the maple tree to enjoy the exhilarating view from its top branches. Contentment filled Amy's thoughts as she recalled the bubble bath she'd taken tonight in the giant claw-foot tub. And the clever mind of irrepressible Daniel was busy designing a different sort of structure from the giant pile of sticks. The hallway clock eventually chimed ten times and the grown-ups shuffled into their own beds.

~~~~~~

Amy awoke at daybreak but remained on the small cot in the den to relish the sounds and smells of the Saturday morning. Breathing deeply to gather the aroma of cinnamon rolls, she could hear the hushed voices of grandma and grandpa in the kitchen. Grandma was probably at the stove in her checkered apron while grandpa sat at the table working his crossword puzzle. She heard the oven door close and leapt from the cot. Amy offered a good-morning hug to grandma before seeking out a spot on grandpa's lap; she snuggled blissfully against his arm. The rest of the family rolled from their beds and wandered into the kitchen to begin the day as Amy finished her breakfast beneath grandpa's prickly chin.

The grown-ups agreed, after coffee and breakfast, that a zoo trip would be the best way to spend the day. They hadn't seen the Indianapolis Zoo in several years and it was a good day for the excursion. John promised to rent a stroller for Amy and buy a round of steamed hotdogs and milkshakes for everyone. The children jogged outside to inspect the playhouse before departing for the trip. The impressive little structure was still intact and Daniel smiled inwardly.

~~~~~~

In with string, out again. In with straw, out again. In with sticks, out again. Fidgeting and fussing throughout the day, the little bird swiftly built her nest in the ceiling of the playhouse. Exhausted by nightfall, she tucked herself into the nest and immediately fell asleep. In the autumn, she'd fill the crevices of the nest with feathers and other insulating material from the nearby field. This would be her winter home.

Teary good-byes and promises of a Thanksgiving visit preceded the return drive to Chicago. Settled into the Chevy and heading north now, each family member pondered a different moment from the Indiana weekend and held it close to his or her heart to relive and cherish during the ride home. Sandra understood that these trips would provide the children with nostalgic moments to uncover and explore on a melancholy day during their regular routines in Chicago. And a few of those memories might even be carried into adulthood. She herself kept a basket full of such childhood moments—now more than twenty years old. The scent of petunias frequently stirred her favorite childhood memory back to life. Happiness, Sandra believed, most certainly came from within.

"I wish we coulda stayed at grandpa's for another day," whined Dennis. "We only got to play catch two times."

"But we saw monkeys and elephants and ostriches. That's way better than dumb ol' catch, Dennis." Splayed above her mischievous brown eyes, Amy's furrowed brows projected frustration with her silly brother.

The drive back to Chicago seemed shorter somehow, and again, the Jacobson family drove up Interstate 94 to catch a view of the skyline. Skirting the edge of the city after dusk, the children were mesmerized by the thousands of tiny square lights that glowed like candles behind the towers' windows. John looked forward to a night in his own bed while Sandra made a mental note of the groceries she'd need to pick up in the morning. Real life and real work would resume tomorrow.

Stepping into the house ahead of the others, John flicked on the kitchen light. The family members blinked at each other as if awakening from a dream and then dashed into their respective bedrooms to drop pillows and suitcases. As was usually the case after returning home from a trip, the children ambled through the house to gather up its familiarity and let the arms of the walls wrap around them. Slow smiles crossed their young faces as they rediscovered the blessings on Pine Haven Road.

With the kids bathed and a load of laundry started downstairs, Sandra called her in-laws to thank them for hosting the fun weekend.

"It's so cute, Sandra, and she's the tiniest sparrow I've ever seen. She made herself right at home in Daniel's playhouse as if it were just the thing she'd been waiting for."

"I'll have to let Daniel know that he's built a birdhouse. Thanks again, Mom. We'll call in a week or two."

While tucking her young architect into bed that night, Sandra told Daniel about the bird.

"A sparrow? Aw jeesh."

Spring 1971

"Pencils down!" Mrs. Harrington bellowed.

Esther dropped hers abruptly and cringed as it fell to the floor where Mary stepped on it with her well-polished shoe. Esther secretly envied the shoes of several classmates; her mother insisted that ten-year old girls wear only flat, leather soles on their feet. And her saddle shoes were most certainly the plainest and flattest in the school. She nervously tucked her crisp blouse into her wool skirt; the uniform constantly irritated her and she felt strongly that God wasn't concerned at all about clothing styles. *If I can convince Father Patrick to change the uniform policy then I bet more people would like me.*

With the geography test over, her thoughts returned to Joseph. Although he'd crawled out of the mist tent this morning coughing much less, the overnight dose of steam left him looking like a drowned rat. In spite of the drenching night, he was cleaned up and ready for school by 8:30. *Dear Lord, help him breathe freely today.*

Esther now looked forward to the lunch bell, and then recess. Because she was so tiny she could easily squeeze into her hiding spot between the two forsythia bushes on the south side of the school building and never be found by her classmates. She was such a great hider that she hadn't yet been *it* this spring. And that wasn't even the best part about her spot. A mother robin had built a nest in one of the bushes and laid three blue eggs a week ago. She had to frequently bite her tongue to keep the nest a secret.

"Hey, Esther!" Linda called out as the children lined up before returning to their classrooms. Esther grinned as her friend approached, all sweaty and smiles. "How's Joey doing?"

"He's fine with some extra coughing. Wanna come over after school?"

"Okay. I got fifty cents for the market. How about we get a freeze pop on the way home?" As she chatted, Linda jerked her arm until the silver MIA bracelet slid onto her wrist. Footage from the Vietnam War frequently appeared on the TV news and Esther wanted a connection to that distant reality with a bracelet of her own. All those men fighting and getting hurt. She just hated that. But to have a soldier's name on her wrist to pray for—that was a good thing. Linda said she'd get a letter from the government when her soldier was found. Esther thought he must be very brave.

Mrs. Harrington's whistle blew twice. That meant mouths closed and hands down. Esther had been a great soldier all year long. It was the 16th of April and she hadn't stayed after school to clap erasers for misconduct, not even once.

Back in their seats the students practiced multiplication facts. Esther checked the clock; only seventy minutes until the final bell. Signs of the upcoming summer break were obvious in the classroom. The cursive alphabet that hung cheerfully above the chalkboard in September now drooped from exhaustion. The floor's spattering of dark skids and scuffs would require hours of buffing in June. And as any teacher will testify, rising temperatures outside had a direct effect on the attention spans inside.

Walking past rows of antsy students, Mrs. Harrington approached Esther's desk and whispered, "Your mom picked up Joseph an hour ago because he wasn't feeling well. You may walk straight home today without waiting for him at the kindergarten door." Mrs. Harrington patted Esther's arm and shuffled to the next row of students.

~~~~~~

"I don't get why a nun has to wear a dark dress all the time. It makes them look scary. And why can't they have a baby? Girls are made to have babies so why doesn't God give them a baby?" Esther frequently pondered the doctrine.

"My mom said it's because nuns are sort of married to God. And they help other people all the time and pray. And if they had a baby then they wouldn't be able to love God as much." In Linda's opinion there wasn't any point in asking the questions. That's just how it was.

"Baloney. I don't think the nuns love God any more than I do. They know all the Bible verses real well but I pray a lot myself. And I'm named after a hero in the Bible, too."

"Let's stop worrying about this. What else do you wanna talk about?"

"Joseph turns six next month and we're having a big party for him. I saved up my money to get an Etch-A-Sketch; my mom and I are gonna buy one at K-Mart next weekend. I know he coughs a lot but he's so smart that he teaches me how to play chess."

The prattling stopped as they rounded the corner to Lavender Lane; Linda would continue down Woodbine Drive to her own house. Because Joseph was ill, the girls agreed to play another day.

Esther turned onto Lavender and contemplated the weather for a moment. She offered her face to the sun and squeezed her eyes tightly until it warmed her lightly freckled cheeks. Clamoring up the porch steps she thought of graham crackers and milk—her favorite after-school snack. She'd barely set her lunchbox on the kitchen counter when she heard the racking cough and sensed an impending trip to the doctor.

"Esther, could you please get my rosary?" Agatha frantically searched her purse for keys while slipping blue Keds onto her feet. "How was your day, sweetie?"

She ran to her parent's bedroom to fetch the rosary from the corner of the dresser mirror. Its beads were purple and the crucifix was silver; she sometimes wore it as a necklace when her mom wasn't looking. With the rosary clutched in her fist, Esther returned to the kitchen, "The geography test was pretty easy. Is Joseph okay?"

She followed her mom into his room. Agatha drew the limp and sweaty boy into her arms and carried him to the car with her daughter in tow. Esther knew the routine and assumed her spot beside Joseph in the back seat of the car. The Children's Hospital was twenty minutes away and it was her job to keep him calm and alert. She offered her hand to him, which he immediately clutched with trembling fingertips. She clapped his back but he shook his head.

"It's not coming out," Joseph whispered to his sister with great effort. Esther kept a small flat box beneath the front seat that she carefully retrieved and placed onto her lap. She removed the top to expose a few thin storybooks and her illustrated Bible.

"I'll read you the Daniel story today. He was very brave and had great faith, and when he was put into the lion's den the beasts didn't take a single bite."

Esther leaned into Joseph and began to read the story. Her voice, a sound that he'd heard every day since birth, eased his mind and body into a comfort zone that only she could create. She was always there for him with unlimited patience and no trace of panic. While straining to breathe he pressed his head onto hers and felt the story come to life. She spoke slowly at first and then animated her voice during exciting parts of the tale. Once finished, she soothed her brother's arm with soft caresses and whispered gentle reassurances near his ear.

In the front seat, Agatha pushed an eight-track tape into the car stereo and pressed PLAY to hear the voices that would alleviate her anxiety. Peter, Paul and Mary sang the ballad of Puff, the Magic Dragon. Agatha quietly sang along as tears threatened to tumble beneath her sunglasses. *Will there ever be a trip to the hospital that doesn't terrify me?*

As Esther clutched Joseph's arm in a firmer grip he set his smaller hand over hers to acknowledge her empathy. They'd both come to love the folk-singing trio for reasons unknown. After all, it was during times of emotional dilemma that their mother played the music; one might think they'd cringe to hear it. Rather, the opposite was true. The music kept them glued together during the crises that cystic fibrosis sometimes forced upon them.

As the car pulled into the hospital parking lot, Esther placed her palms over Joseph's pale cheeks and gazed into his fearful blue eyes. "You'll feel much better in a little while. Stay calm and trust that Dr. Reynolds will help you."

Joseph absorbed her advice and for that moment he loved his curly-haired Esther more than anything else in the world.

~~~~~~

Sitting among several strangers in the white and chrome waiting room, Esther wished she'd brought along her *Little House on the Prairie* book. Agatha had lovingly remembered to bring a snack for her daughter and set the apple and bag of pretzels onto Esther's lap before being shuttled into an examination room with Joseph. Esther desperately hoped that Joseph wouldn't have to stay. He'd already spent dozens of nights in a hospital bed over the past few years and each time had been hard on the family. Mom didn't sleep, dad had to keep the household running, and Joseph suffered. She didn't care that Joseph coughed or that he sometimes woke her during the night. That didn't matter. She wanted them all together on his birthday.

Tilting her head against the back of the rigid chair, she slid into a forlorn and foggy daydream. Shadows of a healthy Joseph and a sick Joseph wove in and around the edges of her thoughts. She was staggering between laughter and tears when her mother's voice startled her back into the day.

"Hey, Es. They have to admit him to the hospital. His fever is bad and the doctor is worried about an infection. Joseph needs some strong medicine and the doctors have to watch him."

"Will he come home tomorrow?" She ambled to Joseph and possessively draped her arms around his frail shoulders.

"If the medicine works well he'll be home in two weeks. That will be plenty of time for his birthday. It won't be so bad." Agatha asserted the last opinion more as a reassurance to herself than to pacify her children.

Ken arrived at the hospital in time to see Joseph being settled into his room. A nurse was inserting an IV while an aid wheeled in a portable oxygen tank. Esther ran to greet her father and Ken immediately wrapped his arms around her. Standing beside the petite girl made his six-foot stature appear giant-like; his broad chest and shoulders completely covered her. "You're a wonderful daughter and an amazing sister; your mom and I appreciate you very, very much."

The nurse returned with a nasal cannula and blood pressure cuff. Although the routine was familiar to Esther, it still twisted her heart to see her brother endure such pain without so much as a whimper. And as precedent dictated, Agatha would spend the night and Ken would take Esther home. A loudspeaker announced that the visiting hours would end in fifteen minutes.

Esther climbed onto the bed with Joseph and laid down beside his IV-free arm.

"I plan to beat you in chess when you come back home. I'll practice with Dad and you'll be impressed when I take your queen."

"I can beat you without my queen." Joseph asserted in a strained voice, and then smirked until the cannula slid deeper into his nostrils. He relaxed into the pillow and tilted his chin forward while straining to take a breath that would only partially fill his infected lungs.

"See you tomorrow after school. I'll bring Play-Doh and coloring books."

"I'll be here."

~~~~~~

The night and day seemed to pass in a finger snap. The house on Lavender Lane was immensely quiet as Esther walked softly through the kitchen and into the living room after school to find her father. She discovered him reclined in his favorite chair, newspaper draped over his stomach and eyes closed.

She whispered into his ear, "I'm home, Dad. How are you?"

He responded in a scratchy voice, "Oh, well, not so bad I guess. We started jury selection this morning and it's a mind-wringing task. How was school, sunshine?"

She clamored onto his lap and tucked her head against his throat. "Too long but we had a fun science experiment today about condensation. How's he doing?"

"I talked to mom this morning and Joseph has a lung infection. The medicine he's taking will be effective; his fever is lower today and if he does well through the next several days, he should be home a few days before his birthday. The party is set for May 8th so I think everything will work out fine, Es." Ken knew that his daughter's blissful nature would be darkened until Joseph was safely home. The buoyancy that she typically exuded became subdued whenever Joseph fell ill.

"Can we go see him right now? We could have a sandwich when we get home, and then practice chess. Maybe mom will come home for a night, too."

~~~~~~

While her father prepared for the hospital trip, Esther worked on the memory book she'd started when Joseph was a baby. It now held more than thirty pages. She enjoyed perusing the pictures, especially the ones she drew when she was just four. Today she drew a lovely blue cake with six red candles.

At the hospital, she was pleased with her leather-soled shoes; heels would definitely click-clack down the corridor and make too much noise. She carried a canvas bag with crayons, dinosaur coloring books, and Play-Doh. Also in the bag were a banana and sandwich for her mom, whom she hoped to convince to come home for the night because leaving for school in the morning without her hugs was tough. When Joseph's illnesses necessitated lengthy hospital stays, Esther grew tired of wearing her brave face and pretending that she didn't mind going to bed without her mother's nighttime prayer. But she carried no resentment against her brother; it was the disease she despised.

"There's our other half." Agatha wearily rose from the vinyl chair with open arms to Ken and Esther. The three united for a brief hug before Esther climbed onto the bed beside Joseph.

"You look better today. Can you clear everything out easier?" She wasn't being polite; she saw that he wasn't quite so pale and she wanted to know if he was coughing productively.

"I can't sleep but breathing doesn't hurt so bad. What's in the bag?"

While the children rolled doughy snakes on the bed tray, Ken and Agatha snuggled in the turquoise chair beside the bed. He gently rubbed her neck and shoulders while she leaned forward to receive his caresses. They were a loving couple and openly expressed their commitment to each other often. During walks through the park, Ken always reached for her hand; in movie theatres Agatha rested her head on his shoulder; and when one spoke, the other was attentive and patient. They meshed beautifully together; where one ended, the other began.

Nurse Kay marched in with Joseph's food tray, prompting Esther to quickly wad up the Play-Doh. "How's our big boy doing?" Kay glanced at the family with a cheerful wink.

"Tired. Is it supper?"

"Yes. I have a fine entree tonight. Chicken soup, mashed potatoes, and cooked carrots. Do you want to eat with your family now?"

"Okay."

The nurse set his tray onto the table, checked the IV, guided Joseph higher upon his pillows, and then waved good-bye.

Ken tugged at Agatha to walk with him down the hallway. Once they disappeared from the room, Joseph was glad to have Esther alone because she'd be honest. "How many more years will I live?" He wanted an answer that was real without capricious reassurance.

"The grown-ups always say you're doing better than the doctors thought you ever could. So if you get well from this sickness you can probably live for a lot of years. You're sort of smaller than other kids but that doesn't matter because you're way smarter. Everyone says that your Lego robots are amazing. You're basically even if you consider everything. Once people know you they don't care about your coughing. Eat your enzymes and then eat all of that food."

Ken and Agatha stood at the end of the hallway peering out the window to watch the commuters crawl down Beaubien Street before spilling onto the freeway. Captivated by the scenario of cars and pedestrians bustling through busy intersections, their minds were numbed momentarily as though they'd been swiped with a dab of Novocain.

Agatha spoke first, "It's definitely pseudomonas aeruginosa, but the doctors say that the steroid and antibiotic will beat it down; we should see a great improvement in six or seven days." She sighed with tearful eyes and pressed her cheek onto Ken's chest. "Nancy Neuberg from church stopped by the hospital today. She and several other women from the ladies' group want to throw a birthday bash for Joseph in the church hall once he's recovered. Balloons, games, potluck, Sunday school classmates, and a big cake. It'd be a delightful day and I think Joseph would really enjoy that. I told her I'd call next week to let her know. What do you think, Ken?"

"Let's do it. I'll call family members to let them know the change of plans; they'll definitely want to be a part of it. And how about we keep it a surprise? We'll tell neither Joseph nor Esther about the party."

"Great idea. And Ken, I'm staying here tonight."

~~~~~~

After sixteen days of medicine, oxygen, loving touches, family visits, plenty of stories, and bucketfuls of prayer, Joseph recovered from the infection and was home in time for his sixth birthday. And the May 8th party date arrived not a minute too soon. Esther loved a birthday celebration even if it wasn't hers. She yanked off her pajamas, slipped into her pink skirt and blouse, and pulled handfuls of wavy hair into a giant clip at the back of her head. She was surprised there wasn't yet a cake in the oven when she sat down to eat her cereal and toast.

"Are you baking the cake after breakfast, Mom?"

"Dad and I decided to have a small family dinner at the Black Forest Restaurant; they'll provide a cake. We don't want too much excitement so soon after Joseph's recovery."

"You're joking, right?" Esther was horrified. This was definitely not the kind of birthday she had in mind and angrily chewed her toast.

"Nope. We're leaving around three o'clock so he has ample time to rest today."

"Are you sure dad thinks it's a good idea, too? He likes birthday parties." She waited for a response but the room was quiet. Mom wasn't going to budge. She ran into her brother's room.

"Hey, how're you feeling?" Esther moved cautiously to avoid stepping on the army guys he was setting up for battle.

"Pretty okay, I guess. I heard you talking to mom about a party or something. I think going to a restaurant is a good idea so you don't have to worry." Joseph concentrated on his battlefield as he spoke.

"Oh, that's just darn stupid. Old people go to restaurants for their birthdays, not kids."

"Drop it, Es." Joseph was officially closing the debate.

She stormed from his room in a huff and headed to the backyard. She'd go to the dumb restaurant and put on a happy face for Joseph. But she refused to speak to her parents unless absolutely necessary. She ran onto the lawn and spun around a dozen times to gather up a bunch of dizzy and then fell to the ground to watch the world spin around her. *Dear Lord, Let him breathe without pain today.*

~~~~~~

"This is the church. Why are we here, Dad?" Esther had a mighty urge to push steam from her ears—she was certainly angry enough.

Ken smiled and chuckled loudly, "Let's go inside." The children exchanged confused glances and frowned before scooting out of the car. Ken swept Joseph into his arms and rushed to the side door while Agatha gripped Esther's hand and ran behind the guys. When they reached the entrance, Ken opened the doors wide.

"SURPRISE!"

Joseph hopped down to the floor and stared at the people who had gathered for the celebration. A brightly decorated table was filled with snacks, presents, party favors, and a huge sheet cake. Streamers and balloons hung everywhere. All of his Sunday school pals wore Batman cone caps. He was overcome with joy and laughed so long and loud that he nearly choked.

"Thank you." Joseph exclaimed with tearful eyes.

Esther was equally overjoyed and beamed with delight. She hugged Agatha tightly, "Great idea, Mom. I can't believe you kept it a secret . . ."

"I think this party celebrates much more than Joseph's birthday, don't you?" Agatha captured her daughter's grateful eyes.

"Yeah. We have lots of blessings."

Summer 1971

A radio blared a Beatles song into the breezy July afternoon on the lake. Long-haired girls wearing denim shorts jauntily strolled through the park towards the beach. And shirtless boys with hair nearly as long followed closely behind. Karen Holsten opened her small umbrella and set it on the table to shield her syrup from the sun. A sturdy forty-something woman dressed in a floral cotton dress and wearing sensible leather sandals, she looked forward to a sitting-down kind of morning. While driving into town she had decided not to fret over the number of syrup bottles she sold—or didn't sell—today. A few hours near the beach with her thermos of iced tea and *Reader's Digest* was time well spent in her mind.

It was July 17th, the first official Farmer's Market day in the Elberta Marina Pavilion Park, fifteen minutes north of her home in Arcadia. Only a handful of vendors brought their wares today, but the townspeople were pleased with the turnout. Quilts, jams, vegetables, crafts, honey and syrups, and tie-dyed shirts were displayed on rows of mismatched tables near Lake Michigan. The seagulls circling the scene were more curious than hungry today. Karen was initially perturbed that John was in Cadillac for the weekend. But now that she was here alone, it wasn't bad. She could think her own thoughts and set her own schedule.

John and Karen Holsten had moved from Ohio to Arcadia fifteen years ago. Brian was nine years old at the time and rapidly adjusted to small-town life. They were nature lovers before it became fashionable and had camped in many state parks across the Midwest. The family preferred open spaces and starry night skies to city congestion and monotonous workdays that droned on like a Bingo caller. On a mild spring evening in 1956 their neighbor in Toledo, Harold Baumers, mentioned that a thirty-acre orchard was for sale in Arcadia. John was sideswiped by the comment.

"Now, why are you tellin' this to me, Harry?" John offered a puzzled reaction to the odd piece of information while removing darts from the board behind his garage. He twitched his thin English nose before dropping the darts on the bench that held his beer. John was lanky and well-postured. His face, with high cheeks and close-set hazel eyes, resembled that of a fox. Having grown up in a large family on an Ohio farm, he'd had his fill of working the land, tending cows, and cleaning barns. He wasn't the least bit interested in hearing about an orchard today. Or so he thought.

"Well, I might take my family up to Arcadia in a few weeks to check the place out. I hear it's real nice up there by the great lake and dunes. I was figurin' that it'd be a good place to live."

And John hadn't been able to push the idea out of his head. Harry never did make the three-hundred-mile trek, but John did. He had to. He hadn't slept for days as thoughts of the orchard and strolls along the lakeshore stole his drowsiness. The following Saturday, Karen packed a basket full of chicken burritos and fruit, and the Holstens made the life-changing journey north to see the property.

The blueberry orchard and farmhouse were on the northeast edge of Arcadia on Joyfield Road. The Holsten family loved the place instantly; the current owners had meticulously maintained every square foot of the land. The interior of the 1904 white clapboard farmhouse proudly displayed hand-carved oak molding and oak-plank floors. A few updates would be necessary but the house itself had great character and potential. It offered only one bathroom, but with a large living room, dining room, three bedrooms and an enormous kitchen, the house was plenty large enough.

The kitchen cabinets were solid birch and the window above the sink faced westward to frame the sunsets descending into the fields. In the living room, built-in bookshelves stood on each side of the stone fireplace. Surrounding the outdoor flowerbeds were dozens more smooth fieldstones. Karen was overjoyed at the prospect of the new residence and lifestyle, and the tour left Brian with an imploring request, "Let's live here."

While guiding the property tour, the Arcadia realtor noted the sugar maple trees, "These are great sap producers. You could make some fine syrup with the right equipment." Karen loved the idea, and the more they saw, the more their hearts leapt. The property held two barns; two tractors and a large wagon would be included in the sale. An oak tree, perfect for a tire swing, shaded the front yard.

Two months later, John resigned from his purchasing job at the Toledo machine shop and moved his family to Arcadia. Karen still felt that it had been the best decision they'd ever made. She phoned her mother when the sale of the Arcadia house was final.

"Honey, that's an astounding coincidence. Your Aunt Velma and Uncle Darren built a cabin there a few years ago. You've always favored Velma. The Lord works in mysterious ways, doesn't He? They worked on that cabin for over a year; I think I have a picture of it somewhere."

When her mom finally paused to take a breath, Karen interjected a request for her Aunt Velma's phone number. As soon as they were settled into the Arcadia house, Karen made a silent promise to reconnect with her favorite aunt.

Northern farm life wasn't easy at first. Not at all. Making ends meet the first two years used up most of their savings, and the blueberry harvesting was tedious and time consuming work, even when they hired a pile of high school kids to help pick. Karen had the wisdom to plant a nine-hundred square-foot vegetable garden and canned dozens of jars of tomatoes, beans, pickles, and carrots. Without her foresight, and Aunt Velma dropping by with pots full of roast beef and trimmings, they might've gone hungry during their first winter. Oh, and their first Arcadian winter was nothing short of wicked. Bone chilling wind and snow that drifted seven feet high made them wonder whether moving north had been a good idea after all.

Brian thrived in this northern country years ago. Biking to school every day, working in the orchard, collecting sap, snowshoe walking, and playing little league baseball had turned their timid son into a strong and boisterous lad. They had joined the local church and enjoyed fellowship gatherings that included picnics, beach outings, and bountiful potlucks. This was home and Karen became quickly and deeply attached to the land and community.

"Hey Karen! How've you been these days?" It was Marilyn Lowry, a friend and administrator at the 1st National Bank in Frankfort, another small town less than a minute from Elberta.

"Hi, Marilyn. How are your girls? How's your mother's hip?" Karen's dark Mexican eyes widened at the sight of the woman who would surely offer generous tidbits of current events from around town.

"We're all fine. Samantha is spending the weekend in Grand Rapids with my sister; her daughter is Sam's age. Mom has been out of the hospital for a week now; she'll be fine but will probably need a walker and cane for a few months until she heals up."

"I have an extra chair. Take a seat. What do you hear in town these days?" Although Karen's complexion was dark, the sun today was too harsh even for her skin; a hat was required gear. She lifted the brim slightly to make better eye contact with her friend.

"You know the big news already, don't you?" Marilyn peered over her sunglasses.

"I've had my nose so deep into the garden and orchard that I barely have time to make supper in the evening. What big news?"

"I heard that Carl Williams will step down as the Frankfort Mayor in November. Word is out that the City Council members have their eyes on Jack Dawson for the job. I think he'd make a terrific leader, but that leaves the town with only one practicing attorney."

"I've yet to meet Jack, but I met his wife, Audrey, last May at the Garden Club meeting. She's a real nice woman."

"Audrey has the greenest thumb in the county and I can't think of a soul who'd do a better job running this town than

Jack. He spearheaded the committee to update the schools' textbooks two years ago. And he helped get a decent budget approved for the new gymnasium and local road maintenance. Really, Jack is someone who takes the future of this town seriously and he'll do right for us." Marilyn was eminently pleased with herself to impart such important information.

"Well, then I suppose that's good for Frankfort." Karen leaned back in her chair to catch a passing lakeshore breeze; she lifted her feet from the ground to cool the damp creases behind her knees.

"Did you leave John at home or is he over in Cadillac again?"

"He's in Cadillac. They have six boats at the shop now. I think it was a good move to partner up with Bill and Rob last year; it's really become a good business and the extra money helps so much." Karen inhaled a breath of summer before continuing, "They keep the boats rented for most of the summer weekends. Working away from the orchard a few days a month gives him something different to tinker with. You know my John—the man won't sit still for a moment."

Marilyn eyed the bottles of syrup, "How's this year's batch?"

Karen withdrew a miniature biscuit from her foil-lined box, poured syrup onto it, and handed it to Marilyn with a napkin. "You'll love the flavor. And this year we boiled down to twenty gallons."

Marilyn popped the syrup-covered biscuit into her mouth and closed her eyes to savor the taste, "Mmmm. Sensational."

~~~~~

July warmed into August. Sailboats dotted the horizon, ice cream sales peaked, mosquitoes shortened the town's blood supply, thousands of sandcastles were built on the beach, and the blueberries continued to ripen.

"A sprinkling of snow today would be a real treat." Karen eyed her angular husband as they poured buckets of berries into cardboard crates. She was glad to be immersed in the exhausting work and recalled how Brian had loved the blueberry season years ago. October 23rd would mark the second year since losing their son to the Vietnam War. He'd given his life with four other young men in the platoon. First a phone call, then the casket, then a letter from his commanding officer praising Brian's courage, strength, and character. *He didn't have to die for anyone to see that, Lord. We all saw that in our Brian. Why'd you take him?*

John climbed back onto the tractor seat and then hollered back to Karen, "The truck won't be here until Thursday so we need to store these in the cellar or they'll turn to mush in this heat. I'm going back to where the kids are picking and will send Keith and Ritchie up here to move the berries." Already peeling from last week's sunburn, John now wore a Tiger's baseball cap to protect his fair skin from further damage.

Karen nodded at John and waved him off to the task. She strode purposefully to the house to prepare lemonade for the boys. On her way, she filled the watering can and tended the thirsty flowerbeds nearest the front porch. She hated to waste steps in the heat.

Once in the kitchen she added ice to the pitcher of juice and stirred gently. Gloomy thoughts returned as she pulled her thick damp hair away from her forehead. It wasn't October 23rd that shred her heart into pieces, it was August 12th—his birthday. This day tormented Karen and nearly drove her to the brink of insanity at the thought of never, ever being able to touch him again. Not ever. Not once. The precious child she nurtured and adored. The little boy who'd grown up to be a kind and virtuous young man. He was gone. Today was only August 3rd, but the mourning was already creeping in. In nine days their son would've been twenty-four years old and in the prime of his life. She shook her head, cut several granola bars, filled the serving tray, and brought the refreshments onto the back porch.

"Hey Mrs. Holsten! We'll get those berries cooled down in no time." Ritchie and Keith had already begun hauling the fragile cargo into the cellar.

"I have lemonade. Come and take a five-minute break with me." They were happy to capture a moment in the shade and eagerly gulped down their drinks before wiping sweaty brows.

"Are those cookies?" Keith eyed the homemade granola bars before asking politely if he could have one. Ritchie's hand was directly behind Keith's as he grabbed for a treat from the tray.

"My Aunt Velma taught me to make these. They're healthier than cookies because the grains are left whole. They're supposed to be made with honey, but I used maple syrup. They've got oats, raisins, and nuts. What do you think?"

"These are excellent. Thanks." Each boy snatched another bar on his way off the porch to the cellar.

Well, now what? Vegetables need picking. Back in the kitchen, Karen retrieved two large colanders to fill with green beans and tomatoes. She'd be sure to rotate the pumpkins. This was her first year growing the darn things and she wasn't sure yet how they'd turn out. Marilyn mentioned in April that the elementary school would need large pumpkins to decorate the stage for the Pilgrim play in November. Karen planned to donate some and keep a few to put on the porch in October with her Indian corn.

Another memory struck like a branding iron. She closed her eyes tightly to halt the tears that threatened to flow. Brian was stirring and salting toasted pumpkin seeds at the oven. Talking animatedly about his Halloween costume, he rubbed his small palm across the seeds to check for doneness. She wished she'd hugged him more often or lingered longer beside his bed after tucking him in at night. A somber and peaceful feeling drifted through her then. *Life is full of joy; it's time to rediscover it.*

Autumn 1971

A bus full of sixth graders was something to be taken very seriously. These kids had energy levels that would put Muhammad Ali to shame, and the surge of testosterone and estrogen pulsing through their bloodstreams added teeth to the already unpredictable animals. It was imperative that Mr. Martin address the group in a stern and formidable tone.

"Heads up, students! I want your full attention while I make three important points. Can everyone hear me?" Mr. Martin intended for this field trip to proceed with minimal chaos.

A few rowdy boys in the back of the bus hollered back, "Yes, Sir!"

"First, you will remain quiet during the tour unless asked a question or given permission to speak. Second, you will not touch, push, shove, pinch, grab, or kick fellow students on the bus or during the tour. And third, you'll remain with the group at all times."

The four chaperones, already frazzled at ten o'clock, checked their purses to ensure an adequate aspirin supply while the teacher did a final head count before departure.

"Hey Daniel—it's a note from Ruth." Daniel secretively seized the paper square and unfolded it. Coping with the recent onslaught of female attention had him stumped; he didn't chat well. Besides, girls rarely talked about anything interesting. Embarrassment barely described how he felt when the giggling gender fluttered around him. Austin gave him an elbow poke before spinning around to find Ruth in the crowd.

"Hey Ruthie. Danny will be sure to find you in a dark corner of the library."

Daniel spoke angrily through clenched teeth, "You're a jerk, Austin. This could be a decent trip so quit screwing around." He banged his head onto the seatback and closed his eyes. *Five of my paper route customers haven't paid in four weeks and I'm paying for their newspapers. It comes out of my profit and that's a real drag. I have six years to save for college and the paper route isn't earning much. I know of at least ten yards I can rake for ten dollars each, and then snow shoveling. If the winter brings enough snow, then I might easily make over two hundred dollars.*

Despite the pep rally that raged on in the seats behind him, the driver managed to safely complete the expressway portion of the journey. The bus exited onto Milwaukee Avenue to begin its final lag of the trip downtown. Daniel bolted upright to catch the view of the astounding project progressing in the heart of his city. He pressed his face against the window as they turned onto Clinton Street. Once the driver made it to Monroe Avenue and drove eastward, the thrill overtook him as they passed the immense building site.

The arrangement and coordination of cranes, concrete trucks, bulldozers, scaffolding, workers, and other vehicles was an awesome engineering feat by itself. Daniel wanted to holler to the bus driver, Drop me off here! In three years this would be the Sears Tower and stand over fourteen hundred feet high. Two city blocks had been opened up for the monstrous skyscraper. He practically had the newspaper clippings memorized. *Designed by Skidmore, Owings, and Merrill, it will be completed in 1974. It'll be 1,454 feet tall and the estimated weight will exceed 400 million pounds. Twenty-eight acres of black anodized aluminum panels and 16,000 bronze tinted windows will form the tower's facade.*

Daniel couldn't fathom what its drawings and blueprints might look like. And the small towers of steel stacked around the site took his breath away. *Who inspected the steel for possible faults?* The tower was growing steadily. Hundreds of men worked like bees to create the reality of a designer's vision. *Who got to see the blueprints? How many of the guys simply managed other men? How many men were there to just move materials around? Who checked the structure's integrity as the workers made progress?* The questions rattled through his head so fast that he chuckled and turned away from the window. He couldn't contemplate any further; the thrill of the site had completely intoxicated him.

As the bus arrived at the parking structure entrance near the library Mr. Martin stood to make a final announcement, "Remember the rules, students, and we'll have an enjoyable visit."

~~~~~~

"Welcome Deerfield Middle School students to Chicago's Central Library building. I'm Rene Beckman and will be your tour guide today." She began the tour speech as the group passed the front desk, "Believe it or not, the Chicago fire in 1871 led to the establishment of Chicago's free public library. Mr. Burgess of London proposed the English book donation as a gesture of sympathy for the great loss. Several thousand titles representing works in the classics, fine arts, theology, philosophy, and natural science were enthusiastically donated. In January 1873, the library opened its doors to the public on the fourth floor of the City Hall building. The building we're inside now, which was designed to be practically incombustible, was opened in 1897. Any questions so far?"

Daniel could think of a dozen, but started with just one, "What architectural firm designed this building?"

"The building was designed by A.H. Coolidge, an associate of the firm Shepley, Rutan & Coolidge of Chicago."

"Are there blueprints we can see?"

"The blueprints are not currently on display, but I can tell you that it took twenty-five draftsmen one year to complete over a thousand drawings."

"What are those stones in the walls and arches?" He was wholly impressed by the beauty and detail of the interior design.

"You're looking at colored stone, mother of pearl, and favrile glass. The Preston-Bradley Hall is truly a masterpiece."

Daniel raised his hand again but Mr. Martin pushed it down. "We need to move on, Mr. Jacobson."

Miss Beckman led the class through the main sections of the library, pointing out interesting historical facts and architectural features. Daniel's mouth remained agape throughout the tour. *Why don't designers make buildings like this anymore? Someday I'll design one, and a hundred years from now, people might say, "That's a Jacobson building."*

As the class prepared to exit the library, Miss Beckman placed a card into Daniel's palm. "This is the address and phone number of the Chicago Historical Society. If you'd like to know more about this library, or any other historical building in Chicago, I bet they'd be happy to help."

~~~~~~

Residents of the windy city didn't have much time to enjoy the lovely fall foliage. Gusty October blasts that swept down from Minnesota and Wisconsin were quite effective in relocating the leaves from the tree branches to the ground.

Mr. Stewart requested that the boys rake his leaves into three large piles for burning later in the day. Daniel was seriously wiped out from the two hours of raking and turned on the spigot to gulp a few mouthfuls of water from the hose. He was glad he'd brought Dennis to help with the job this afternoon and appreciated how diligently his younger brother worked for two dollars. Dennis was a much more reliable worker than Austin, hands down. Daniel now watched his flamboyant brother leap around the yard with a long, straight stick. He appeared to be rowing over the grass and it looked like a lot of fun.

Daniel dashed into the garage to put his rake away and spotted a long aluminum pole. He guessed it to be about eight feet long. *Perfect.* He ran back into the yard with the pole and imitated Dennis' jumping motions. Carrying the pole upright and parallel to his body, he ran forward, stuck the pole into the ground, and then swung in a rowing motion across the grass. The boys traveled around the yard several times before Mr. Stewart stepped from the house to watch.

"Hey fellas—ever see a pole-vaulter?" The boys stopped jumping and walked to Mr. Stewart.

"What's a pole-vaulter?"

"Well, a good pole-vaulter in high school can jump about thirteen feet high. My grandson, Eric, is a vaulter at Wheeling High School. He uses a twelve-foot plastic pole. He runs on a short track, stabs the pole into the ground, and swings up over a crossbar that's set above a big foam pad. It's a lot of fun to watch and I bet you boys would make great vaulters. You've got speed and strength. Let's get some stuff from the garage for you to jump over."

After dragging out two small stepladders and a long PVC pipe, Mr. Stewart placed the ladders a few feet apart and set the pipe between them. The height was just four feet, but Dennis had a blast jumping over it. He eventually cleared five feet and was quite proud of the accomplishment. "Let Daniel try it."

Dennis and Mr. Stewart held the pipe for Daniel. By the end of the afternoon, he'd jumped over six feet. Mr. Stewart refused to let him attempt anything higher; the thought of a sprained ankle or busted leg in his yard irritated his stomach.

Dennis' excitement remained as the boys stowed away the ladders and poles, "Thanks Mr. Stewart. That was pretty cool."

Daniel relished the idea of jumping competitively instead of running races. His father had prodded him recently to begin thinking about the high school track team, and now Daniel was certain that he'd found a tolerable event.

~~~~~~

"This'll be the best Halloween ever. I got a creepy raincoat and hat from my grandpa. My brother gave me blood goop to put on my mouth. It'll be totally hideous. Meet me at my house at six o'clock." Pete's enthusiasm was contagious.

"I'll definitely be there." Daniel loved Halloween. Even more than Christmas. The candy was a mere bonus after a wild night of pranks and shenanigans. He stomped into the back door of the house and froze as if he'd hit a wall. The kitchen hadn't been in such utter disarray since Amy's tonsillectomy two years ago. His mom was practically famous for the spotless kitchen she kept.

"Mom?" No answer. Speaking with a higher pitch, Daniel yelled again as he dashed into the living room, "MOM?"

Empty. He raced to the hallway and found her in bed beneath skewed blankets.

"I'm glad you're home; I feel terrible. It's the flu and I can barely lift my head and arms." Sandra was weak and feverish.

"What should I do? Dad's in Detroit until Thursday."

"I called him this morning and he can't get a flight back until tomorrow. That means you'll have to help, honey. You need to wash dishes and put the clothes from the washer into the dryer. Then you'll put together a supper; canned soup and sandwiches will be fine. Do you think you can handle that?"

"Yeah. Will you be up for trick-or-treating tonight?" He feared her response but held fast to the remote possibility she'd be well enough to take Dennis and Amy out later.

"Just speaking with you hurts my head and throat; lifting myself out of this bed tonight would be impossible. I know how much you love Halloween, but just this one time you'll have to take Dennis and Amy trick-or-treating."

"Guess I don't have a choice." Irritated now, he shuffled from the bedroom and into the kitchen to make a phone call before starting the chores.

"Hey, Pete. Looks like I won't be going out with you guys tonight."

"WHAT?"

"My mom is real sick and dad's out of town so I'm stuck taking the kids out tonight." Daniel was experiencing disappointment on a very high level.

"Aw c'mon! Can you get a neighbor to take them out? This is gonna be one of our last Halloween nights ever. There's got to be another option."

"They're my brother and sister; I'm taking them out and it's cool. Maybe we'll see you guys in the neighborhood. Have a blast, okay?"

"Yeah, bummer you won't be with us though." Pete's response was heartfelt; it wouldn't be the same without Daniel.

~~~~~~

With dishes, laundry, and supper done, dress-up preparations began in earnest. Although Daniel initially resented the responsibility given to him a few hours ago, he cheered up considerably while pulling Amy's witch costume over her wiggly and excited seven-year old body.

"Mom said I could put on green make-up tonight. Can you help me?" Her precious brown eyes and exuberant request would not be ignored.

Daniel had trouble rubbing the colored ointment onto her cheeks because she kept babbling and giggling. *This is fun.* "You're looking real scary, little witch."

Dennis appeared wearing a long purple wizard cape. His hat, at least eighteen inches tall, was covered in silver stars and moons. "Help me put this white mustache on my face, Daniel."

Daniel searched for an adhesive in the Halloween make-up kit while Amy ran to Sandra and modeled her costume; the green-faced witch returned to the living room with a camera. "Hurry up Dennis! Daniel has to take our picture and then we can go."

Although he hadn't used the camera much, Daniel knew how to turn on the flash and advance the film. "You two look really great. Put your bags down and stand by the couch. Now say, SCREAM." He snapped a few photos then hurried back to Sandra.

"The kids are dressed and pictures are taken. We'll be back by eight o'clock. I'll leave the porch light off so kids don't come hollering at the door for candy. I'm sorry that you're sick; this will be a fun night. Do you need some water or anything?"

"I have plenty to drink in my big cup. Thank you for giving up your evening. It means a lot to them and I'm sure this will be a very memorable Halloween because they'll be walking with you tonight. A big brother is much more fun than a parent. But you're not wearing a costume. Run up to your room and get it, honey. The kids can wait."

"Nah, I'll wear it next year. They're hyped up and ready to go. We'll see you in a little while, Mom."

The house grew still and Sandra breathed a sigh of relief. Daniel had handled himself like a young man and assumed the responsibilities without a single complaint. She felt lucky to have such a good kid. She knew that environment played a big role in a child's attitude and behavior, but genes were much more important. The three children thrived in the same family environment and neighborhood, yet were so different from each other. Dennis was her carefree and spontaneous boy. Amy was her loving and nurturing child. Daniel was her serious and very intelligent child who was already striving to do the right thing in such a mixed up world. *Dear Lord, Thank you for these beautiful children. Bless them on their brief journey tonight through the zombies in the neighborhood.*

~~~~~~

Nearly tickling one's throat with every breath, there was something special about the Halloween air in Chicago. Perhaps the excitement permeating the neighborhood had made the airwaves fuzzy. A walk during any other dark autumn evening would be dreary and lonely. But tonight the dogs howled more eerily, costumes rustled, leaves crunched and scattered, and laughter echoed down the streets. It was magic. One only had to ask a grown-up about a favorite Halloween night to see a mischievous grin appear on his face.

"Are your feet tired, Amy?" Daniel checked his watch. He'd take them down two more blocks, and then head back home.

"Only a little bit, but my bag is getting real heavy. I bet I have about a hundred candies." The little witch's hat was now lopsided and flopped over her eyes. Dennis' purple cape had dragged through enough lawns and sidewalks to make it a challenge for even a bloodhound to decipher. Daniel was thoroughly enjoying himself as he watched his siblings dash up and down the porches surrounded by other costumed children wearing bizarre faces.

As Amy darted to the next house she was intercepted by a brutish vampire; he rammed directly into her. She dropped hard onto the walkway and the contents of her candy bag flew in every direction. It was her startled scream that brought Daniel to her side.

"It's okay, little witch. We'll have the candy back in your bag in no time. Did you bump anything?" Then the tears spilled onto her green cheeks and he completely lost control of his otherwise level temper.

He strode furiously to the vampire and mightily slammed both palms into the guy's back; the push nearly knocked the ghoul face down onto the lawn. "Mind your manners and watch yourself around the kids."

The vampire turned around to display canine teeth beneath a ferocious glare, and then boldly punched Daniel in the face. Daniel dropped hard and shook his head to clear the lights that burst around his eyes. He gathered his wits quickly, rose to his feet, and wrestled the caped bully to the ground. The boys rolled and punched until the homeowner rushed to the disturbance.

"Get outta here you hoodlums! You ain't fighting on this property!"

Amy and Dennis had observed the scuffle with eyes wide open and hearts beating madly. Holding his hand over his left cheek, Daniel marched back to his siblings and knelt before them. "You are <u>not</u> telling mom about this. She doesn't need to know that this fight happened or that I got punched. Understand?" The witch and wizard nodded in unison.

"You're the greatest brother in the world. Let's go." Amy proudly took Daniel's hand and led the way home.

Dennis looked up to his brother with a newfound respect as he strode beside him, "I'm giving all my Snickers bars to you."

Summer 1972

A shiny roller skate in each hand, Esther with attitude hobbled down Lavender Lane to her house. She'd skate in the 4th of July parade even if it meant wearing casts on her arms. There'd be dogs pulling decorated wagons, bicycles with streamers, and skating girls with ribbons flowing in their hair. Today, Esther's knees and elbows had paid dearly for her stubbornness. Agatha suggested that she wrap a winter scarf around each elbow to soften the blows during the training period. But Esther dismissed the idea immediately, declaring that it was totally out of the question; she'd look ridiculous and her arms would get too sweaty.

Joseph was finishing yet another puzzle when his sister stomped into the kitchen. "Chess beats skating hands down, Es. Mom is running out of bandages and you're gonna have scars all over. Ride a bike in the parade. That's what I'm doing."

"I'm not wimping out, Joseph. Some of the sidewalk bumps are really bad and if I don't time my jump right, then kabam! I'm actually skating pretty well, you know." Applying soapy water to her scraped knees caused a teeth-clenching grimace that added a growl to her response. She took a seat beside her brother at the kitchen table and wondered why he was inside.

"How come you're not playing with Will?" She hoped all was copasetic with the friendship. Will was a real rough-house sort of kid, while Joseph was a more laid back boy. Despite their personality differences they got along swell for the most part. But one never knows what might scorn a seven-year old boy on any given day.

"He went up to St. Ignace yesterday and won't be back until Saturday. His family goes there to visit his grandparents and take a boat ride to Mackinac Island. Will says it's a really neat place because only horses and bikes are allowed—no cars."

"It'd be fun to go north. Sherry goes to the Sleeping Bear Dunes every summer. She gets to see giant sand dunes, swim in Lake Michigan, and visit souvenir shops with Indian toys."

Their gazes locked and they grinned widely. Neither spoke a word, yet each knew precisely what the other was thinking.

~~~~~~

Just seven years old, Joseph understood the importance of putting himself on the good side of his mother before requesting a favor. "Whatever is cooking in that oven smells great, and I'm hungry."

Agatha peered over her shoulder, "Just your basic meatloaf with baked potatoes, kiddo. Since when did you begin to appreciate the aroma of ground beef and onions?"

Joseph blushed before pressing his hands onto the counter edge to noisily clear his lungs and brace for what would come next. Agatha clapped his back several times with such force that it nearly pushed all the wind out of him, but she knew exactly how hard and where to hit to loosen the sticky mucus. She, Ken, and Esther could all assist with Joseph's lung clearing whenever needed. Because the morning clearings were vital and intense, Ken was in charge of those.

With breathing back to a regular pace after several minutes, Joseph fished silverware from the drawer and began to set the table. Esther arrived to help, too. Now Agatha was perplexed.

"Does someone have something to tell me? Neither of you works in the kitchen without being told. Esther?"

Esther came clean, "The way you read our minds is so weird, Mom. Did grandma do that?" She swallowed hard, "Can we talk at suppertime when dad is home?"

Even though it meant extra clean-up, Agatha habitually served dinner in matching bowls, platters, and plates. She'd taught Esther and Joseph years ago how to properly set the utensils, ". . . the blade of the knife must always be placed so its sharp edge points away from the plate." Agatha hoped that her daughter would continue the tradition of setting a formal

English table. Formality seemed to be fading away with the chronic use of paper plates and busy schedules these days.

A half-hour later, the Gardeners were seated around the kitchen table with hands washed, milk poured, and the table prayer finished. Agatha raised her eyebrows to Esther and said simply, "Spill it."

"Have you ever been to the upper peninsula or Mackinac Island? Or a big lake with huge beaches?" Esther posed the questions and both children wore hopeful expressions as they awaited a response.

Ken answered, "As a matter of fact, your mom and I spent our honeymoon in Arcadia. It's a small town on Lake Michigan. Uncle Clem is an avid fisherman and he owns a cabin up there." He winked at Agatha and tapped her sandaled foot with his shoe. She blushed and scooped a spoonful of potatoes into her mouth to keep from giggling.

Joseph wanted more details, "Is it past the Mackinac Bridge? How far is it? Does he still have the cabin?"

Like a typical Michigan resident, Ken answered the map query by holding his left hand up in the shape of a mitten to represent the state. He then pointed to the top knuckle of his pinky finger. "Arcadia is right about there. It's a five-hour drive from Detroit, but I don't know if Uncle Clem still has that cabin. I do know, however, that he retired recently and lives in Frankfort, which is in Benzie County, just north of Arcadia. It's a beautiful area and hadn't yet been discovered by tourists when we were there a dozen years ago. There are some decent restaurants and marinas in both Arcadia and Elberta, and plenty of nice beaches."

Esther, the bolder child, came right to the point, "Can we go there?"

Agatha lit up to the idea immediately, "That sounds like fun, Ken. We've yet to take a week long family vacation. Our trips have always been spent either visiting family in Ohio or touring the local zoo or museum for a day. If there's a good medical facility in Benzie County, a week on the lake would be a superb vacation."

"My current caseload is hectic, but the two biggest items will wrap up by early August. I'll call grandma tonight and get Uncle Clem's phone number. If—and this is a big IF—Clem still has his cabin or knows of a decent place we can stay, I'm in. Spending a week up north this summer is a fine idea, and I'm certain there's a hospital in Frankfort." Ken winked at Joseph.

~~~~~~

Agatha leaned dreamily on Ken's shoulder as he drove through Grand Rapids. She'd had her long hair cut into a pageboy style last month; Ken dubbed her his blond Cleopatra. He'd let his beard grow out over the winter and now sported stylish wire-rimmed glasses. The Birkenstock sandals that he wore on his feet made him appear as though he'd stepped right off the Berkeley campus. Lying sideways on a pillow pressed against the car door, Joseph breathed noisily while he slept.

Esther was absolutely beside herself with anticipation and excitement. She had the map spread across her lap and was using her hair clip to measure miles; they'd driven halfway already. "Dad, tell me about the cabin again."

"It's in the tiny town of Arcadia, about a dozen miles south of Frankfort. The log cabin is a quarter-mile from the Lake Michigan beach. When your mom and I were there it had cream-colored linoleum flooring and a big orange rug in front of the stone fireplace. The kitchen stove has just two burners and the refrigerator is quite small. The dinner table is very heavy, walnut I think, and there's a bench on either side of it instead of chairs. The two bedrooms are quite small, with only enough room for a double bed and a small dresser. The bathroom has just a shower stall, no bathtub. But when you're on the lake in August the cabin has everything you need."

It sounded unique. Esther closed her eyes to imagine it. She'd never stepped foot inside of a cabin but was confident she'd love it.

~~~~~~

Uncle Clem was perched on the crooked porch of his cabin with a pipe clenched between his teeth and newspaper draped over his outstretched legs when Ken drove into the sandy driveway. Clem rose from his seat to greet the nephew he hadn't seen in more than a decade. A short and husky man in his early sixties, Clem was a typical northern outdoorsman with richly tanned skin and deep creases around his eyes and mouth. Today he sported an ancient short-sleeve oxford shirt and brown dungarees. Ken chuckled at the sight of his uncle and memories tumbled across his mind as he parked the car and slid out to exchange a handshake.

"Welcome to Arcadia." Clem beamed at Ken, "I must say that the hippie-lawyer look suits you." He turned to Agatha for a quick embrace, "How're you, Agatha? You look radiant. And I finally meet the real Esther and Joseph from the Christmas photos I get in December." Clem took each child by the hand and marched to the cabin, "C'mon inside and see where you'll be staying this week."

Ken set his arm atop Agatha's shoulder and led her into the cabin behind the children. "It's just like I remember it, Clem, except that the ugly rug is gone." Ken regretted not bringing his family to Arcadia years ago. He felt a twinge of guilt for letting himself get too wrapped up in his career and everyday life in the city.

"This is incredible! No white walls and it's all logs. And the fireplace is made of big rocks." Esther barely contained her astonishment and literally leapt for joy throughout the tiny cabin as she peeked into the bedrooms and switched on the light in the closet-size bathroom.

"I've never been in a cooler place." Joseph plopped onto a walnut bench, "This is gonna be a great week."

"I hope you have a wonderful stay. The weather is supposed to hold out pretty well. Daytime will hit eighty degrees and nights will be about sixty. The beds have wool blankets, so you'll be fine. I'm sure you want to unpack and run up to Frankfort for groceries, but first let me show you the path to the lake."

Clem wandered out the back door with the family behind

him to point out the trail that led down to the beach, "It's about three hundred yards from here; just follow that trail. Be sure to wear sandals because the sticks and rocks will tear up your feet. Do you remember how to get to the Red Owl market, Ken?"

"Yup. It's M-22 north past the Betsie Bay and then left onto Main Street. If my memory serves right there's a smoked fish shop on the corner." Ken was surprised he'd recalled the market's location after so many years.

"The fish shop is still there and now Tom's son, Josh, runs the place. The Blueberry Festival starts tomorrow morning in Frankfort. The girls would enjoy the crafts and homemade foods. Also be sure to visit the Cherry Hut in Benzonia for lunch or dinner this week." Clem continued with further instructions, "There's no phone in your cabin so I'll leave these directions to my house. I'll be home tomorrow—stop by for a cold drink. And let's plan a fishing trip."

Ken appreciated the invitation, "We brought poles and tackle in hopes that you'd ask. I'm sure you'll see us more than once this week."

Agatha grew giddy with excitement at the prospect of setting up housekeeping in the little cabin. After Clem's departure, the family worked together to unload the car, unpack suitcases, dig out beach gear, and stash into the kitchen the boxes of dry goods they brought for the week. They'd get perishable groceries tomorrow after the festival. Supper tonight would be tuna sandwiches, grapes, and graham crackers. Bagels with honey and bananas would be the morning fare.

"Hey Mom, do you have my inhaler?" Joseph coughed loudly and then pressed his hands onto the table's edge while he cleared his lungs. Ken approached quickly and asked if he needed a tapping; Joseph nodded. The young boy braced himself for the hits. Ken forcefully clapped his back for several minutes to help clear his lungs. Agatha brought the inhaler and gave Joseph two puffs of the medicine.

He took it all in stride, "Let's go!"

The trail meandered through a small pine forest, curved around clusters of lilac bushes and wildflowers, and finally ended at a small ledge with a lovely view of the sapphire lake.

Turning to Ken, Agatha offered a salubrious smile, "Isn't this perfect?"

The kids tossed their towels and sandals off the steep edge and plunged down the sand bank. Giggling with delight the pair dashed to the water's edge and twirled into the lapping waves.

"Whoa. This water is freezing, Dad." Joseph hurdled over the chilly waves to avoid contact; goose bumps covered his skinny torso and he gave in to a mighty shiver.

Ken ran to the children, pulled Joseph from the water, and drew him into his arms. "Should we walk out a little ways? I won't dunk you, promise. Paddle your legs while I hold you up."

Esther followed the boys deep into the lake while seagulls swooped over the group to investigate the commotion. Agatha clicked her camera wildly to capture the beloved moments before spreading a blanket and towels on the beach. She brought a book to read but realized her mistake immediately; she wouldn't dream of sticking her nose into it today because the lake and her family were all the entertainment she desired for now. She unwrapped the denim skirt that covered her swimsuit and lounged back on the blanket to absorb the sun's warmth and sounds of her children.

"Hi there. Haven't seen you around the lake this summer. Are you visiting?" The woman extended her hand and introduced herself, "I'm Karen Holsten."

Agatha removed her sunglasses to greet the stranger. "Hello. Yes, we're up from Detroit for the week. I'm Agatha and those are my children, Joseph and Esther, with my husband, Ken. We're staying in the cabin just up the road. Are you vacationing this week?"

"My husband and I are full-time residents. We've lived in Arcadia for fifteen years now. It's beautiful isn't it? Who owns the cabin you're renting?"

"It belongs to my husband's Uncle Clem. He lives in Frankfort."

"Oh yes. Clem Gardener. It's the cabin with the crooked front porch, right? The fishing king in these parts, that's Clem." Karen's dark eyes sparkled beneath the wide brim of her floppy denim hat.

"Won't you join me here, Karen? I'd love to hear about the town and get a few ideas on what we might do this week." Agatha patted a spot beside her on the blanket. The women basked in both sunshine and small talk while scanning the horizon for freighters and sailboats.

From the water's edge, Esther noticed the chatting stranger and waddled atop legs that ached from the cold water towards the two women. She wanted both a warm towel and an introduction.

"Karen, this is my daughter, Esther. And Esther, this is Mrs. Holsten."

"Pleased to meet you, Esther. How old are you?"

"Eleven, and going into the sixth grade. Do you live here?"

"My house is northeast just a few miles. I was telling your mom about our blueberry orchard. We're quite busy picking now; we'll have a table set up at the festival tomorrow. Do you plan to see the Blueberry Festival this weekend?"

"Are we going tomorrow, Mom?"

Agatha readily agreed, "We'll be in Frankfort to get groceries so I suppose we can explore the festivities and craft tables downtown while we're there."

Esther hugged her knees and pulled the towel over her head to warm up. She then rolled off the blanket to lie directly on the warm beach. Sliding her hands into the sand, it caressed her fingers as she curled them up. The sound of the waves flopping onto the shore, the voices of daddy and Joseph mingled with noisy seagulls, and mom and Karen's laughter lulled Esther into a dreamy mood. *How will I say good-bye to this place in just seven days?*

~~~~~~

Agatha and Esther wore straw sunhats to the festival while Ken and Joseph sported navy blue baseball caps. Because his small bedroom was musty and lacked a window, Joseph had survived a difficult night in the cabin. He'd spent much of it propped up on the couch where it was easier to breathe. Ken suggested that Agatha and Esther peruse the festivities while he and Joseph visit Clem; the young boy would need a quiet day to recover from the sleepless night. They agreed to meet in the park on Main Street at three o'clock and then do food shopping together.

"Look at those pretty t-shirts." Esther ran to the table that held stacks of tie-dyed shirts. After making a purchase they found other equally interesting tables to explore. They bought postcards, blueberry muffins, Indian moccasins, and a small cedar storage box shaped like a log cabin. Agatha declared that they couldn't hold another item so the girls meandered to a shady spot where tables and wagons were loaded with cartons of blueberries for sale.

Karen spotted the Gardeners, "Hi girls. Enjoying the festival today?" She wore a farcical floppy hat covered with plastic flowers; pink-framed sunglasses were perched on her nose.

Esther giggled and Agatha pinched her shoulder in a way that clearly conveyed the message, *Mind your manners*.

"We're having a great time. The guys are meeting us at the park shortly. These berries are beautiful; they'll be great for pancakes and lunches this week." Agatha gave Karen a dollar for a quart of berries.

"My husband is working in the orchard today—we're at the tail-end of the harvest. I've got the easy job for sure. Have you ever picked blueberries, Esther?"

"No, but I'd love to if you need help." This week was already turning out to be better than she could have imagined.

A vision of eleven-year old Brian leapt before Karen's eyes; his enthusiasm used to light up a room. And now she was at last meeting his equal. Karen blurted out the invitation, "Agatha, we'd enjoy seeing your family at the orchard tomorrow. There'll be a sizable group of high school kids picking for us, and families come and pick their own berries for fifty cents a quart. I can show you around the orchard and we'll take a walk through the maple trees that I tap every spring. Come any time during the day, we'll be there."

"That sounds like fun." Agatha wrote the address and directions to the orchard on the back of a receipt. "It's nice to have met you here; we'll see you tomorrow morning after breakfast then."

Juggling the treasures that filled their arms, Agatha and Esther jogged to the park. Joseph spotted the pair and his eyes widened when he saw the bags. "Got anything in there for me?"

"We have blueberries, muffins, shirts, and moccasins. And I got this especially for your agate collection." Esther withdrew the cedar cabin from the bag.

"Wow. Thank you." Joseph opened the roof of the cabin and inhaled the cedar scent. "Guess what? Uncle Clem is taking us fishing on his boat tomorrow. He said it's best if just us guys go, but we'll be back in the afternoon and then we can explore those dunes by our beach. Can I go fishing, Mom?"

"If you can rest reasonably well tonight, I think fishing will be an adventure." The ever-present prayer begged repeating as she ran her fingers through Joseph's light brown hair. *Dear Lord, Let him breathe freely tonight.*

~~~~~~

It was like she'd opened up a storybook. The rows of blueberry bushes seemed to cascade across the land for miles. The sky was so crisp and blue it appeared surreal; Esther sensed that if she could reach up and press her hand against it she'd feel cool paint dripping between her fingertips. And the white farmhouse surrounded by beds of marigolds and petunias beckoned a stranger to stop and rest on the porch step. Looking westward, wildflower seeds had found their way into patches around the barns and fields. They now blossomed in the summer sun, spattering the otherwise green landscape with orange, purple, and yellow strokes. *I can't go back to Detroit.*

Near the barn Karen was loading jugs of water onto a large

wagon for the pickers. Esther ran to her, still speechless from the idyllic scenery. Karen's guard dissipated at the sight of the buoyant girl; she opened her arms and drew Esther into a loving embrace. The sturdy Mexican woman and petite English girl shared a laugh and exhilaration that ignited a friendship. The bond would grow strong and deep in the years ahead.

"We'll help load the water. How do you pull this giant wagon, Mrs. Holsten?"

"John will be here shortly with the tractor and a wagon full of blueberries. He'll switch the berry wagon with this one. We'll load the berry crates into that small white barn; it has huge fans that keep the fruit cool. Tomorrow morning a freight truck will pick up the berry crates and take them to a packaging plant where they'll get sorted and packed into containers for grocery stores and such."

John arrived minutes later, red and perspiring from the sun. Karen made the round of introductions before switching wagons. As soon as John drove back to the fields, the girls began hauling crates from the wagon into the white barn. Within a half hour, the fruit was neatly stacked and the chore wouldn't need to be repeated for another few hours.

"C'mon inside the house. There's someone I'd like you to meet." Karen led the way into the farmhouse kitchen. "Velma, this is Agatha Gardener and her daughter, Esther."

"Oh, my goodness. Such beauty to behold. Karen told me how you met yesterday. Would you like to help make cinnamon bread for the pickers?" Velma's shoulder-length gray hair was pulled back into a soft French braid. She wore silver wire spectacles over a cherubic face with mischievous eyes; a yellow plaid blouse and navy blue Capri pants covered her slightly plump figure. Agatha guessed her to be near seventy-five but with a youthful spirit and zeal for life.

Agatha peeked into the large mixing bowls, "Smells good and looks like fun—count us in."

The four women, wearing aprons over their stomachs and flour up to their elbows, kneaded dough on the big kitchen table. Lightening could've struck the house without one of them taking notice. They chuckled and conferred as if they'd been performing this task together every Monday for centuries. Karen floated through the afternoon, content with what life had suddenly brought. Velma sensed the happiness and couldn't help but be grateful. *Thank you, Lord, for the blessings of this new friendship. May it be in your will to grow.*

~~~~~~

Comfortably situated on the beach blanket, Agatha and Ken were glad to do little more than dig their toes into the hot sand and watch the waves roll against the shore. It was an extravagance to be savored, a moment for safekeeping and then retrieved from memory during a hectic day back in Detroit. Esther and Joseph wandered to the sand dunes that rose up from the beach about a quarter mile from the blanket; their feet splashed and dodged the water as they traveled away from their parents.

The strolling pair were inexorably attached. It was a bond to be envied. Esther never lost patience with her younger brother. Incapable of hurting him in any manner, she hadn't the mind to even yell at him. Joseph was a resilient and energetic child despite the CF, and he somehow understood that Esther had much to do with his positive temperament. She had faith in his abilities, supported him during difficult days, and tended to him with hugs and stories when he fell ill.

"I can't wait to eat the trout we caught today. It was so much fun, Es. And Uncle Clem is funny and real smart. I wish we could see him more. Guess what he has?"

"A hat with hooks and lures stuck all over it?"

"Nope—way better than that. He has some really great baseball cards. He's got the 1971 Al Kaline card. He even has the 1971 American League home run card with Norm Cash on it. I shoulda brought my cards because maybe he'd trade with me. I told him that I played chess too, and he wants to challenge me later this week."

"That's great. I know you're tired of beating dad and me all the time. We had a good morning, too. The Holsten's orchard is really cool. We picked blueberries and I met Aunt Velma. We made cinnamon bread and she gave us a bunch to eat for snacks tonight. Mrs. Holsten said we could visit again this week. I hope we do."

Arriving at the base of the dunes, they came to a halt. The sand rose much higher than it had appeared from the blanket. It'd be a tortuous climb, especially for Joseph who had been coughing a little too regularly in Esther's opinion.

She knelt in front of her skinny brother, "Hop onto my back and I'll carry you up part of the way. I can climb like a cheetah. You don't weigh much, and besides, you might not make it to the top walking with your own legs because hills take your breath away."

Joseph willingly hopped onto Esther before she began pawing her way up the hill. She stopped every four or five yards to catch her breath, and with each stop they turned to face the lake and absorb the placid view. Near the top of the dune, their radiant moods merged to become ecstatic and they both laughed out loud with joy.

The breeze beckoned Joseph down to the lake, "Let's run!" The pair zoomed downward, legs pumping like pistons as they gained momentum. It was glorious to run so fast; on level ground he'd never reach such a speed.

At the bottom of the hill, he coughed hard to clear his lungs and Esther tapped his back. Once he caught his breath, she again insisted he let her carry him, at least for a little while.

He whispered in her ear, "I'm never gonna forget this trip. Are you?"

"No way. I love it here." Although severely short of breath from the weight she carried, Esther didn't mind. Her heart would return to a normal pace once she sat down. "I'm gonna write letters to Mrs. Holsten and we can be pen pals. And if Mrs. Holsten writes me back, then she can tell me about all the stuff that's happening here while we're gone. I hope we come back next summer, don't you?"

"Yeah. We just gotta come back."

Autumn ~ Winter 1974

Watching film clips of its construction and the opening day ceremony on the evening news were thrilling, to say the least. But nothing prepared Daniel for the awe and inspiration he felt while walking with his family for the first time towards the ominous structure at 233 South Wacker Blvd. Although they'd walked just three blocks, his neck ached from straining backwards to explore the beauty of the tower; unable to keep his eyes off of it, he bumped haphazardly into passersby as he stared into the sky.

Grabbing his grandfather's coat sleeve, Daniel pulled him forward, leaving the rest of the family several steps behind. "I want to walk into that building with you, Grandpa. You taught me to appreciate this city's architecture and how to be a builder."

Shaking with unbridled exhilaration, Daniel turned around to see Dennis and Amy making wisecracks. *They have to know, right now, the facts behind this breathtaking creation.* He shouted to them, "Please. Let me tell you more before we go inside. This building has nine framed tubes, and these tubes are actually nine skyscrapers incorporated into one structure. And because the tubes are all different heights, the tower displays a different visual aspect from various angles. This 110-story tower is revolutionary. Steel frames with glass walls cover the building. It took almost four years and cost one-hundred fifty million dollars to build."

"Be quiet and let's get inside, Daniel; the tour guide will tell us that stuff." Ten-year-old Amy lacked the patience today to tolerate another of her brother's frenzied look-at-that-incredible-building moods. Her mind was on the lunch they'd enjoy downtown this afternoon. Eating gourmet French fries from a silver plate—now that was exciting.

Strolling to the elevators with the tour group, the Jacobson family admired the floor their feet touched. It was brilliantly decorated with metal tiles in a design that seemed to reflect the bundled tube structure of the tower. The elevator hummed and jerked as they were pulled up to the 103rd floor of the Sears Tower, bringing them more than a thousand feet up from ground level. Ears popped and everyone swallowed. From the observation deck, the other downtown structures appeared surreal. And the expressways and roads were merely gray and black ribbons wrapped around the city. The view extended for miles, far beyond the southern edge of Lake Michigan.

Dennis finally dragged his brother from the window, "We live in Chicago okay? You and grandpa can come back another time. Let's go get our burgers."

The Tower was nothing short of a miracle. The grin on Daniel's face remained until he shoved a pricey French fry into his mouth and began to chew.

~~~~~~

A sophomore in high school now, Daniel's goal to become an architect frequently consumed his thoughts. Money was a key issue. *Two more years to save for college. If I can just make enough to pay for my first year at Penn State, then I'll be able to relax.* He refused to borrow money to cover all five years of college. His parents were pushing him to attend the University of Illinois; tuition would be far more reasonable as an Illinois resident. But his heart was set on Penn State and that meant a higher tuition plus room and board.

Daniel had expanded his paper route during the summer to include eighty houses in the surrounding neighborhoods, and he now wondered whether he'd ever be able to sleep in on Sundays. John drove him to the paper station at 4:30 every Sunday morning to pick up the newspapers for delivery by six o'clock. As he peddled his bicycle through the darkness and into his territory, the load felt more like a hundred-and-eighty papers. Next year he'd look for a restaurant job; it wouldn't be nearly as back-breaking and the paycheck would be about the same.

After delivering the papers and parking his bike in the garage, Daniel hung his coat and stepped into the kitchen. His stomach reacted with a growl to the smell of maple and butter. The combination was an olfactory celebration. A plate stacked with pancakes sat across the table from Dennis, and he knew it was his.

"What's up, Dennis? You look glum." Daniel sliced a healthy chuck of the warm cakes and ate lavishly.

"I woke up this morning and realized I have to plan a future. It's your fault, by the way. All the yakking you do about college tuition and a future income. Now I'm thinking about what to do with myself after high school. You're off to college in a couple of years and I need to make a game plan by the time I start my junior year." Dennis spoke in a woeful tone.

"Aw c'mon. You're only in the eighth grade. There's a big world to be conquered and plenty of room for you. Wanna go to the field and play a bit of catch or shoot a few baskets after church? The workout will do you good." Daniel was usually the sibling who assumed the cheerleading role. He was continually upbeat, which sometimes drove Dennis and Amy nuts.

~~~~~~

The Jacobson family arrived in the church parking lot with several minutes to spare before the service started. Sandra glimpsed around at the dozens of parked cars, "I remember when the lot was only half this size and it barely filled up on Sundays. Isn't it wonderful that the congregation has grown so much?"

The family proceeded inside and were greeted by several friends; a peppering of small talk ensued before everyone assumed their favorite pew seats. Amy waved to Rebecca as she watched her sneak past the back pews to the organ in her stocking feet. No one minded that Rebecca played without her shoes because she did such a fine job; the congregation kept this secret hidden from the Pastor, who might not approve.

Pastor Coleman was a very soft-spoken man and a newcomer might initially wonder how he maintained such rapt attention during his sermons. They soon discovered that the precision of his word choices and eloquent intonation kept everyone tuned in. Psalm 19 was preached today. And its message was to revel in God's creation. Glorify him and praise his name. Keep the attitudes of the heart and mouth pleasing to God—the obedience will be rewarded. Daniel thoughtfully considered the Sunday sermons; many of them fueled his soul with positive energy.

"Hi Daniel. Are you coming to the bonfire next week? After church clean-up they're burning all the sticks and stuff. I think it'll be fun." Lori attended the service each Sunday with just one thing on her mind: Daniel Jacobson.

"Yeah. I think my folks are planning on it; I hear there'll be cider and donuts too. That's worth a few hours of raking and stick gathering, don't you think?" Daniel either didn't realize the effect he had on girls or chose to ignore the ruckus he caused because the dating scene frightened him. He was a sturdy and strong young man with an easygoing nature. But it was his appearance that turned the girls' knees to wet sponges. He was fairly tall at fifteen, about five-foot nine, and already broad shouldered. His rich brown hair and sapphire blue eyes seemed to have been painted with a heavily tinted brush; there was nothing pastel about Daniel. And splayed above his blue eyes were long dark eyelashes. He was Hollywood material, no doubt about it.

"Where are you sitting for Bible study, Daniel?" Mindy would sit on his right side if Lori had already claimed his left. She tossed a lock of black hair over her shoulder in an exaggerated twist for maximum effect. He'd caught it and duly appreciated the feminine motion.

"Looks like a big group today, so I'm not really sure yet. I'll save you a seat Mindy." Daniel watched her sashay away, perplexed by the entire ritual.

"Let's shoot baskets. We'll dribble the ball to the court, okay?" Dennis enjoyed time with Daniel outside of the house because the brothers frequently bickered in the room they shared. Daniel insisted on precision and order while Dennis was far too laid back to worry whether his dirty socks were on the floor or in the hamper.

Dribbling, dodging, shooting. A little bit of roundabout and competitive play on the basketball court temporarily softened the rough edges of the hormonal teenagers.

"I just don't know what I'm supposed to do. The first time you built a Tinker Toy tower with grandpa you knew you'd be an architect. I'm not even sure which direction to turn career-wise." His dark eyes offered a forlorn look, like an exhausted Bassett hound who'd been taken on a walk that was much too far.

"Well, think about what you're good at. Start with that."

"Hockey, swimming, basketball . . . I'm good at the things no one will pay me to do." Dennis chuckled after reciting his talents.

"At school. Which subjects come easiest to you?"

"Art. I can draw anything from whatever perspective you want it drawn. You know that. Remember the award I got last spring for the chalk rendition of the table with all the weird bottles on it?" He swished the ball after posing the query and grinned unabashedly at his brother.

"You're right. You have great artistic ability and would be a great asset to a design firm with the proper training; perspective drawing can be tough if you don't have a knack for it. I have a lot of trouble with perspectives."

"I don't want to follow in your footsteps for crying out loud. I want to do MY thing."

"Cool your jets, Bozo. You're not getting it. That was just an example of how you might use that talent. And you're an excellent builder. A trade like carpentry might satisfy you and it can be sort of artistic as well."

"I like that idea. I don't think I want to be cooped up somewhere everyday doing the same thing. Carpentry would let me move around and be outdoors. But there's the winter factor to consider; maybe I'll move to Florida after high school."

"You should at least go to a trade school and get licensed. There's probably an exam you have to pass to become a registered carpenter." Daniel was kindly insisting that he extend his education past high school, at least somewhat. "My history teacher posts really neat quotes on her bulletin board. Some are pretty inspirational. Like the one by Lincoln, *Whatever you are, be a good one.* Or John Ruskin, who said, *The highest reward for a person's toil is not what they get for it, but what they become by it.* This is good stuff to think about."

"That's cool." Dennis whipped the ball fiercely at Daniel's gut. It was one thing to have an older brother who was smart and ambitious, but did the guy have to be good looking and kind-hearted as well? Good grief.

The boys played one-on-one until they were joined by another group of kids for a real game. It was a rough-and-tumble, knee-scraping sort of afternoon. But it was just what they had needed. Rain began to fall as the pair headed back home and by the time they reached their own garage both were drenched and absolutely famished.

~~~~~~

The pumpkins had been tarnished by frost months ago and were long gone, Thanksgiving was just a memory, and Christmas was a week away. Sandra's appetite for Christmas music seemed insatiable. She'd listen to Brenda Lee sing "Rockin' Around the Christmas Tree" until she was dizzy. And, of course, there was the Andy Williams Christmas album. Amy enjoyed watching her mom jig around the living room with candy canes and mistletoe dangling from her fingers. The family had just finished decorating the tree. As the afternoon deepened, each of the five Jacobsons assumed their favorite Sunday afternoon positions.

John and Dennis settled into the couch to watch the football game while Amy sat with Sandra in the kitchen stringing cranberries and popcorn to hang outside for the birds. This would be the first Christmas in several years that Amy wasn't missing a tooth. Still a little girl at heart and the apple of her daddy's eye, Amy was tall for her age and was usually a first-pick in gym class when they played team games. She and Dennis shared common physical traits, dark wavy hair and brown eyes; but Amy had a personality that more closely matched her oldest brother: she took life quite seriously and school was very important to her.

Daniel was stretched out on his bed; a book of historical building designs and skyscrapers lay in front of him. The description of the Yingxian Pagoda in China had his concentration locked. The amazing structure withstood the elements for nearly a thousand years. Built in the eleventh century, the one-hundred-eighty-foot building had been designed using the timber framing architectural method and contained fifty-six different structural variations. *This would be so cool to see.*

Amy answered the ringing telephone and hollered from the kitchen, "Daniel, it's Pete on the phone."

"Hey Dan, you busy?" Pete was psyched about something.

"Nah. What's up?"

"I finished my glider design—it has a six-foot wingspan. Instead of just one wing that I attach to the fuselage, I'm making it into two parts. A three-foot wing will attach on each side of the fuselage. We picked up the balsa wood today and I seriously need someone to help cut the ribs. You interested?"

"Definitely. I'll run over. See you in a few minutes."

"What's Peter doing today, Daniel?" Sandra liked Pete; he was a good kid from a nice family.

"He has the airplane design finished and wants some help with the rib cutting. Can I go over there for a little while?"

"Be home for supper."

~~~~~~

The design was indeed impressive. Pete had been working on it every weekend since early October. He hoped to finish the wings during winter break, which entailed cutting the ribs and leading edges, pinning and gluing the pieces together, and then covering the final assembly with monocoating. Daniel appreciated Pete's gumption and watching him fly the gliders was a blast. Not many words were exchanged by the teenage boys as they cut balsa-wood ribs. They were intent on making precise cuts to ensure maximum airflow over the wing; the whisper of x-acto blades moving down pencil lines on the wood created the only noise they needed.

The pair had been friends since the third grade; it was a solid friendship because they were so similar in personality and intelligence. No one would be surprised to see Daniel and Pete start a business somewhere together and become wildly successful. The problem was, Pete had his sights on law school and that had nothing to do with building skyscrapers. But each knew that they'd remain lifelong friends. Not that one ever mentioned it to the other. Guys didn't do that. They'd simply make sure that each had the other's phone number. When important events happened in their adult lives—like marriage, kids, or an extravagant voyage—they'd reconnect.

"What do you think about Mary Brenard?" Pete needed a sounding board and hoped his friend might volunteer a vote of confidence. An average looking guy who wore outdated eyeglasses, Pete was too smart to ever become one of the popular kids at school.

"I dunno. She seems a bit snobby. That's one girl who's gonna need a nice car and big house. She's real easy on the eyes though."

"Well, sitting beside her in biology class keeps me from even hearing what Mr. Pelman is saying. My brain dissolves when she looks at me. I wish I had the guts to say more than five words to her, but I'll need to do some serious weight training before I have that kind of confidence."

"You be careful about making contact with that girl. If you two ever go out and she lets you kiss her. . . BAM. She'll be wiggling her little finger and you'll be following her around like a puppy dog chasing a bacon strip. Girls scare me. They have a sort of power over us and I sometimes wonder whether we need them more than they need us."

"Who knows. I sure wouldn't mind spending some time with her outside of school."

Uncomfortable with the topic, Daniel decisively ended the conversation. "You just keep your head on straight, Romeo, that's my only advice."

With heads back down and knives poised, the friends finished the rib cutting, each with a different image in his mind. Mary in a swimsuit filled Pete's thoughts while Daniel mentally reviewed atomic structures for tomorrow's chemistry test.

~~~~~~

"Hey, Mom? Could you drop a few of us at Riverside Park on your way to the mall? Pete and I might sled this afternoon, and Dennis is calling Roger to see if he can go too." Daniel was digging through the winter-gear basket in search of his blue glove.

"Sure, we can do that. Amy and I plan to finish the Christmas shopping so we'll be at the mall for a while. Can you guys walk home?" Sandra wiped off sandwich crumbs from the kitchen counter as she spoke.

"Yeah, that's fine. We'll put the sleds into the trunk and then call the guys to make sure they're here in about twenty minutes, is that okay?"

"Sounds good. I'll get some laundry started downstairs and then we can head out." Sandra strode to the bottom of the stairway before hollering up, "Amy! We're leaving shortly so get yourself ready and find your boots."

~~~~~~

With six people and four sleds squished into the sedan, Sandra headed eastward to the park. "Are you boys okay to walk home this afternoon?"

"Yup. My dad said that a walk in the cold is a great character builder. My feet are going to be totally numb by three o'clock though." Pete wouldn't mind, really. The trek home with three buddies meant plenty of opportunities for adventure.

The park was fairly crowded with kids and sleds, and it appeared that the snow had packed into a smooth and solid layer so the hills were fast. Sandra paused for a moment as the gangly guys trampled out with their gear.

The salubrious laughter that echoed from the hill brought an avalanche of emotions to the surface. It seemed like just a few winters ago Amy was a toddler and Sandra held her in a purple snowsuit as they coasted down the hill together. Now here they were, prepared to traipse through the mall together and then enjoy a hot pretzel and Coke to celebrate the end of the shopping season. And next year, both boys would be in high school. *I don't feel old. Is forty old? I've plucked a few grays and fine print has been a challenge to read lately. . . Nah. Forty isn't old.*

"Okay kiddo. It's you and me against the crowds." Sandra tuned into the station that promised Christmas music all day just in time to hear jolly Burl Ives. Amy smirked at her whimsical mother.

~~~~~

The guys soared down the hill in every imaginable position. Feet-first, sideways, head first, backward, belly down, belly up. They chided and shoved in a way that only good friends dared. Parents called it horseplay, but to the four whom dared to be goofy for the afternoon, it was just plain F-U-N. The older guys knew that this would be their unofficial last year for sledding; next winter they'd have driver licenses and sledding would be out of the picture.

Between sled runs, they tackled and bombarded each other with snowballs, crammed snow down coat backs, and wrestled in the snow banks. They pushed the sleds down the hill with a mighty force that ensured the slickest rides of the season. Pete suggested making a train. He'd be the engine on the wooden sled; the remaining three guys would hold onto each other's aluminum saucers and the sled. They recruited a volunteer to give the caboose a strong boost to start the ride. Carrying its payload of four howling boys, the train sped downward like a racecar. It gained momentum way too fast and veered too far to the left. An ancient maple tree stood proudly on that side of the hill.

"JUMP OFF!" Pete screamed as the train approached the tree. He leapt from his sled while the other three boys leaned sideways to stop the descent. When Daniel and Dennis leapt from the train, it pushed Roger, riding in the caboose position, further in the direction of the tree. He didn't flip off quickly enough. Slamming into the tree, Roger's saucer slid out from under him and flew into the sky. His leg took the hardest impact before he smacked his chest and face against the tree trunk. He lay unconscious while the other three boys scrambled to his side.

"Oh, man!" Pete was frantic.

Daniel knelt beside Roger, "Are you okay? C'mon Roger!" Three young hearts began an adrenaline-crazed pounding.

It was Dennis who assumed a sensible and calm leadership role; he somehow knew exactly what to do and began shouting orders. "Pete! Run to a house over there and ask to use their phone. Call the emergency number and get an ambulance here now. Daniel, take the toboggan from that girl and bring it here. We'll put Roger onto it and get him up this hill if his back and neck are okay." He put his ear over Roger's mouth to listen for breathing. He then pinched his friend's face gently and clapped hard, "Wake up buddy. We're taking you up the hill."

Roger rolled his eyes and groaned. His breathing was shallow and he trembled with chattering teeth.

"Can you move your arms, Roger? Raise them up for me." Dennis watched Roger lift his arms from his sides. "Turn your head right and left; can you do it?" Again, Roger did as instructed.

"I can't move my leg!" Roger screamed in horror. He jerked his left leg, but the right one remained still. The accident had reduced the robust boy into a terrified child.

"We're gonna ease you onto this sled, okay? We'll be very careful with your leg. If you feel pain anywhere else while we're moving you, just yell and we'll stop. I don't want to worsen any injury."

Daniel set the toboggan down and the boys carefully slid Roger onto it. He screamed when the toboggan moved beneath his right leg; thankfully, his back and other limbs were all right.

Dennis removed his own coat and laid it over his friend, "I think he's in shock so let's keep him warm. Take off his wet mittens and start rubbing his hands."

With Roger settled in, Daniel picked up the toboggan rope and slowly began pulling him up the hill. Dennis was at the other end of the makeshift gurney pushing and steering to avoid bumps.

Pete ran from the house to meet his friends at the center of the hill. He breathed a sigh of relief when he saw Roger's eyes open and heard him moan in pain. "Oh man, I am so sorry you guys. I didn't know we'd run into that tree."

"Is an ambulance coming?" Dennis was clearly in charge of the situation.

"It'll be here soon. The lady at the house is coming to see if we need anything; she's sort of freaked out." Pete was nervous and frightened for his friend.

"He'll be okay once the doctor gets a dose of pain medicine into him. His right leg is broken. I'm freezing. Let me wear your coat for just a minute to warm up; I'll give it right back, Pete." Dennis trembled as he wrapped the large coat over his shoulders.

All sledding had ceased. The other children were red-cheeked statues watching the rescue mission ensue.

Daniel was the first to hear the sirens, "Here comes the ambulance, Roger. Bet you never thought you'd ride in one."

Roger swore as the toboggan crested the top of the hill to await the arrival of the emergency vehicle. The medical team took vital signs, checked head and limbs, and transferred him to the metal gurney for the drive to the hospital. Dennis recited Roger's phone number to the driver, who would contact the injured boy's parents.

Once the truck had departed with Roger safely inside, the three boys gathered the sledding gear and returned to the house of the helpful homeowner. Pete called his mom; she'd pick them up and drive them to the hospital. Daniel called his dad to let him know that they'd be home after supper.

~~~~~~

Roger was home by nine o'clock wearing a cast and carrying a bag of medical supplies. He had a broken tibia bone, hairline cracks on two ribs, and a mild concussion. Not bad considering the speed at which his body had slammed into the tree.

"Let this be a lesson to you guys. Horseplay is one thing but idiotic ideas are to be ignored. I understand you were a bit of a hero out there, Dennis. I'm not surprised, son. Nice job."

The Jacobson boys tossed around on their bunk beds well into the evening, unable to sleep. "You awake Daniel?"

"Uh huh."

"I'm gonna be a doctor."

"Hmm, Dennis Jacobson in medical school. I dunno. That's a special calling, kid. The life of a doctor is way beyond ordinary. But if you feel a pull in that direction, then go for it. And you know what? Northwestern has a great medical school."

"I'm pretty sure it's what I'm supposed to do."

"Serious?" Daniel felt that his goofy brother had just taken a giant leap into maturity; he smiled proudly at the thought of an adult Dennis in a lab coat.

"Yeah. Way serious."

Summer 1975

"How's your whitefish, Velma?"

Karen and her aunt were enjoying lunch on the deck of the Cabbage Shed restaurant. Both leaned back into the sun-bleached cushions to soak in the lakeshore breeze. The perpetual wind from the lake prohibited the use of table umbrellas; their arms and faces were warmed by the afternoon sun. Sailboats, fishermen, and seagulls populated the bay nearby. Families dined on picnic lunches in the nearby marina and park. A person didn't have to survive an Arcadian winter to fully appreciate the stunning beauty of the day, but it certainly helped. The ice and snow were a vague and distant memory.

"The chef did a nice job; it's well seasoned and not too dry. I like the almonds in the rice but these little celery pieces get stuck between my teeth."

"I think we should order dessert and then find a spot in the park to savor a slice of this lovely afternoon, don't you?" Karen had an agenda and kept the tone of her voice well-camouflaged from her aunt's keen ears.

"As long as we don't stay too long, I suppose. My petunias need watering and I want to take a nap before *Jeopardy*." After losing her husband to cancer five years ago, Velma was not easily deterred from the routine she'd spent years settling into. Her cat, flower garden, church and a few select TV shows were now the principal elements around which her world revolved.

After sharing a large piece of carrot cake the women ventured down to a bench near the lake.

"There's something I've wanted to discuss for a long time, Velma, and I must get it off my chest." Karen gazed up to the sky, perhaps listening for an angelic voice to echo downward and guide her through the conversation.

Velma took her niece's hand, "Well, I suppose you need to speak up then."

"Have you seen the new Bayview townhouses on Anchor Drive here in Frankfort? They're close to the beach and situated at the edge of a nice neighborhood. And all the conveniences of town are a short distance from Bayview." Karen swallowed the knot in her throat to settle her rapid respiration.

"You're telling me that I shouldn't be in the cabin alone and a townhouse in the city would be a good place for an old woman. I don't buy that scheme; not for a second."

"Please hear me out, Velma, because I've mulled it over for weeks. You're so isolated in the cabin; you may as well be living on a desert island. How many times did you tell me last winter that you awoke nearly frozen stiff from the drafts in that place? And remember when you fell asleep with the fire blazing in the hearth? What if a spark had shot out onto the rug? And don't tell me that you're not alone because you have Oscar. He's a cat and can't dial your phone in an emergency. In the townhouse you'd at least have neighbors nearby."

"I've been in the cabin for twenty years and I like the privacy. I can tend the flowers in my housecoat and slippers without neighbors peering out their windows at me. If that's where the Lord wants to take me, then so be it. Besides, you're just a few minutes away and you drop in nearly every day."

Velma pointed her index finger at Karen's chest, "I don't want an electric stove or linoleum floors. And I don't like carpeting either; I like wood floors. The walls in those townhouses are probably stark white too, and that's just too sterile for me. It'd feel like I had a foot in a nursing home if I moved into one of those places. You can't force me from my home." Velma rose from the bench after her petulant speech and retreated to the restaurant parking lot.

The pair drove back to Arcadia in silence. Karen relented and didn't force the issue; however, she was in a conundrum because she wanted her aunt in a safer place but didn't want to coerce her. She'd pray about it tonight and open her mind to His guidance. She pulled the car into the gravel driveway beside the cabin and hopped out to open Velma's door.

"Thank you for lunch, Karen. Are you stopping by tomorrow?" Velma forced a smile.

"I'll see you after breakfast. I'm making a batch of biscuits in the morning and will bring some over with a bag of blueberries." She was relieved that the sullen drive back home had somehow dissolved their disagreement. Velma slid out of the car and waved good-bye before shuffling up the cabin steps.

~~~~~~

A torrential rain had paused the blueberry harvest. A few years ago, John might've grumbled about the setback but today he was content to sit in his favorite chair and peruse his *Boating World* magazine. The harvest was difficult this year. Picking the fruit, hauling crates, loading trucks; it was arduous work for young men. But at fifty-five years old, the work was nearly tortuous some days. He had collapsed onto the bed at eight o'clock the past few nights utterly exhausted. Yet selling the fields or seeing the crop untended was unfathomable. *I might be able to afford a few more workers this year with the tractors finally paid off. I'll check the ledgers this afternoon; maybe our current financial position will allow employment of three more high school boys.*

Karen was writing a letter at the kitchen table. The Gardener family had vacationed in Arcadia three weeks ago and thirteen-year old Esther was blossoming into a wonderful girl. Gentle, unpretentious, and radiant. She was still a tiny thing but had boundless energy and an aura of joy about her. Again this year, Karen watched little Esther carry Joseph up the sand dunes to enjoy the lake view from high above the beach. Karen loved her little pen pal and hoped that she would remain in touch as time marched forward and hormones steered her to cosmetics and boys.

Once she sealed the letter into an envelope, Karen dug out the poster board from the pantry and made signs for the blueberry and maple syrup tables she'd set up at the Blueberry Festival this weekend. Profits from festival sales rarely topped one hundred dollars, but that's not what the weekend was about anyway. It was the opportunity to mingle with the townsfolk, greet tourists, and enjoy people's expressions when they tasted *real* maple syrup.

Although still overcast and damp, the rain clouds had moved eastward and away from town. A nice time for a walk on the beach.

"Hey John, wanna go to the lake?"

~~~~~~

He liked dragging a stick when they walked the shoreline. Something about making a mark in the sands of time. Yet the life of the line was so brief. In just a few seconds the waves tumbled over the mark and rearranged the sand into new contours. What was the point? Karen thought it akin to making a bed every morning. Sheets and blankets were pulled taut to make the bed appear as if a body hadn't just spent eight hours beneath its covers. Again, what was the point?

She preferred rock gathering. The smooth black stones were her favorites. They were irresistible, like a licorice lover who ate all of his black jellybeans from the Easter basket first. It just couldn't be helped. Atop her dresser sat two large pickle jars full of smooth stones she'd collected over the years. On the days she dusted Karen lifted the heavy jars and jiggled their contents. The rattling sound pierced her ears with lakeshore memories.

"I wish Velma would reconsider my suggestion about Bayview. That cabin is so desolate. She insists that the solitude is fine but I think she'd relish the idea of having neighbors to visit and taking short walks to the lake." Karen sighed deeply.

"I can see her point of view. It's hard for an older person to make such a drastic change. It can be frightening. I often think about the orchard and our future on this land. Will we be healthy and strong enough in ten years to maintain the place and harvest every summer? Should we sell the cropland but remain in the farmhouse? I don't like to think about it because that conversation eventually leads you to the end of your life. It's scary to go to the end. Let her contemplate for a while the idea of moving out of the cabin. She may realize before winter sets in that the quality of her final years might indeed be better in town. But that's up to her to decide; it doesn't matter what you think is best."

"You're probably right. I guess we maintain the status quo for now." Karen reached for John's hand as they finished their stroll. The beach was empty and from horizon to shore the waves were thunderous and white capped. The rhythmic drop and pull of the water lulled her worries to a different place.

~~~~~~

The telephone rang just as she finished tying the straw sombrero onto her head.

"Good morning, Karen. I'm glad you're not in the fields yet. I thought about what we discussed at the restaurant and I'm open to take a look at Bayview. Just a look, mind you. If I don't like what I see then I'm staying here and won't be budged." Although Velma had acquiesced to the idea she maintained a stern tone of voice.

"It's a deal. I'll call the property manager this afternoon and we'll go on Monday. John and I will be busy at the festival this weekend so Monday is best. Is that all right?" Karen wanted to scream with elation.

"That's soon enough for me. Are you bringing water with you to the fields? Don't get dehydrated out there. And put sunscreen on today—that skin of yours is becoming far too dark." Velma loved to mother her niece.

"I have my water stash and will bring a tube of sunscreen with me. I'll see you after supper today."

John was waiting for her on the tractor. He wore a Detroit Tigers cap on his head, a ragged white t-shirt on his back, and a patient smile on his face. When she sat beside him on the familiar seat Karen breathed in deeply the scents of the earth. Wild grasses, Queen Anne's lace, and a lingering odor from the barn that had housed sheep many years ago. Aside from a scattering of wispy cirrus clouds, the sky was a brilliant linen fabric draped over the fields with its edge ending at the horizon. She wished that painting were a talent she possessed because a camera couldn't possibly capture the remarkable sight and emotion it evoked.

"That was Velma on the phone. She wants to see a Bayview townhouse. I haven't seen the interiors myself so it'll be a fun excursion. We'll probably go on Monday."

"I'll keep my fingers crossed; Bayview would be a nice place for Velma. It looks like we can hire two more boys to help finish with the harvesting, by the way. Could you call the market and have them post something on the board?"

"Sure. I'll call Charlotte when we break for lunch. The berries I pick today will be our festival batch this year. I'm hoping to get twenty quarts today and ten tomorrow morning." Karen picked berries only for the festival, her freezer, and for homemade jam. She used her frozen berries during the winter for holiday pies and blueberry bread.

~~~~~~

Velma opened the cabin door after the first rap. Karen was surprised to see that she'd dressed up for the occasion. "I've always loved that color on you, Velma. You're brave to wear pantyhose in this heat."

"Don't be silly—I'm wearing a garter belt with nylons. Do these shoes look all right or should I wear my white sandals?"

Karen smiled at her beloved aunt, "The shoes are fine."

"I haven't been house hunting in thirty years so I wasn't sure what the appropriate attire might be these days. Might we have lunch at the Frankfort diner today? Phil is training his granddaughter to take over the business and I'd like to see how she's doing." Velma and Darren had been close to Phil and his wife, Peggy, for several years; lunch at the diner would give her an opportunity to catch up on local news through Phil's discerning eyes. "I still remember little Tracey in a diaper and sunbonnet sitting on her grandpa's knee." Velma was in a decidedly chipper mood.

"The agent is showing us two 2-bedroom townhouses. They have identical floor plans but one has a better view of the lake. They each have an attached one-car garage, which will give you plenty of storage. And you'll just love this—the stoves are gas. I don't recall whether the homes offer an area for planting flowers, but they do have private decks attached. Mr. Wilson said he'd be waiting for us at the 618 home." Karen hoped that Velma hadn't interpreted her enthusiasm as a sales pitch.

They found the first townhouse easily and parked across from it. Because only two units shared a building it didn't have the somber appearance of an apartment complex. It was professionally landscaped with evergreens, hostas, and a well-planned selection of begonias and impatiens. The owner of the 620 townhouse had placed large clay pots full of pink petunias on the front porch. Karen and Velma strolled up the walkway and rang the doorbell.

"Welcome, ladies. Please come in." Joe Wilson opened the door and gestured for them to enter.

Velma's initial reaction to the living room was delight. The room was spacious and well lit. The walls were a creamy yellow and the carpeting was taupe. A tidy fireplace and mantle filled a portion of the north wall and a large window opened to a view of the lake on the western side of the room. She shuffled to the window and peered out. *Oscar would love this view.* She liked the openness of the room and was glad it boasted a fireplace. The tour continued into the kitchen where new appliances made a good impression. Velma saw herself near the stove, mixing a batch of cinnamon bread or frying an egg. She saw her toaster on the counter and the perfect spot for her copper canisters that held flour, sugar, teabags, and cookies. *Karen is right. This is new and easy to manage. And the person next door grows petunias. . .*

They inspected the two bedrooms, which offered good closet space. Velma thought that perhaps she'd display her quilts in the second bedroom along with her two antique bookshelves and book collection. The tub in the bathroom was nice; its porcelain clean and unscratched. She hadn't realized how worn the cabin had become until she walked through this home. The terrace outside the kitchen had ample room for several chairs, a table, and flowerpots.

"Do you know who lives next door?" Velma was definitely interested at this point.

"I'd like to know that myself; let's go find out." A salesman at work, and doing a mighty fine job, Joe led the women over to the 620 door where he tapped a pleasant knock.

A gentleman answered the door promptly. "Yes?"

"Good morning. I'm Joe Wilson and this is Karen Holsten and Velma Richards. Ms. Richards is looking at the townhouse next door and has a few questions, if you don't mind."

"Glad to help. I'm Sam Kennedy and my wife is Dora. She's at the market but I can answer your questions." Sam appeared to be in his early seventies and displayed an easygoing manner.

Velma had only two questions. "How long have you grown petunias?"

"Um, well, I guess Dora has been planting petunias every spring for about thirty years now."

"Do you play cribbage?"

Sam smiled broadly, "Who doesn't?"

Velma offered her hand to Sam, "Thank you so much Mr. Kennedy. Have a wonderful day."

As the threesome descended the front porch, Joe Wilson scratched his head in bewilderment. "Now that was the strangest conversation I've ever witnessed."

"I'd like very much to live at 618 Anchor Drive, as long as I can bring my cat." Velma continued walking to Karen's sedan parked on the street. Lunch at the diner today would be especially good.

Karen was dumbfounded and exuberant at once, "I guess she'll be making an offer on the property. I'll call you this afternoon, Joe, and we can arrange a time to meet tomorrow or Wednesday to sign the documents you need to get this ball rolling."

Winter ~ Spring 1977

Unless a dire emergency dictated a venture outdoors most Detroit residents were inside their homes. This particular January day opened its door to a strong polar wind and the artic temperature had hitched a ride on its tail. Bundled in snow pants, parka, scarf, hat, mittens, and wool-lined boots, Esther felt certain she could take a brief stroll without threat of frostbite. The mercury hadn't risen above the zero-degree mark in several days and she was eager to taste a morsel of air that hadn't been recycled through a furnace.

She gingerly stepped onto the salty porch and opened her mouth to inhale the unfiltered oxygen. Although each breath made her lungs ache, she promised herself to walk around the yard so that she'd actually appreciate being inside. She quickly drummed up a few thoughts to keep her mind busy during the expedition. *How did Indians survive? Did they burn fires all day and all night long? And without cocoa. Were deerskins really warm enough?*

Once inside, it took her longer to undress and put away the winter gear than the time she'd actually spent outdoors. Joseph had obviously found her algebra book. He was a young man on a mission with the book opened to the first lesson and a stack of looseleaf paper beneath his right arm.

Esther sat beside him at the kitchen table, "Where'd you find my book?"

"In the basement with a bunch of dad's old law books. If I do a lesson every day then I'll know algebra in five months." Nearly a teenager now, Joseph still had the appearance of a younger adolescent. He remained small for his age but the disease had neither disabled his mental aptitude nor desire to learn. His appetite for math was voracious and the severity of his CF dictated indoor activities when the temperature dipped below twenty degrees. It was a perfect match.

"I'm making cocoa—want some?" Esther poured milk into a saucepan and swiftly stirred a few tablespoons of chocolate powder into it. She liked working at the stove and owed her cooking talents to many great teachers, including her mother, Karen, Velma, and both grandmothers. There wasn't a recipe or canning process that intimidated her. Although it required extensive vegetable chopping, her favorite dish to prepare and serve was minestrone soup. And she always looked forward to making strawberry jam in June.

"Is there some gingerbread left?" It seemed that Joseph ate nearly as much as he weighed everyday. Because of his pancreatic enzyme insufficiency, he consumed several hundred more calories each day than a normal child his age. And, of course, with each meal he took enzyme medication to ensure nutrient absorption and proper digestion of fats.

"There's roast beef left over from supper last night. I'll slice it for you to eat with this sweet stuff, Joseph." She wasn't even aware that she steered him into a balanced diet.

Beckoned by the chocolate aroma, Ken strolled into the kitchen. "Add a bit for me into the pan, Es, I could use a cup today."

The three sat in the kitchen with elbows on the table, chins in their palms, and eyes facing the southern window. They reveled in the tranquility of the backyard view framed in stark gray poplars and snowy pines. Except for Esther's footprints left by her recent traipse across it, the yard was covered in a pristine layer of snowy icing. Every tree limb and pine bough was cloaked in white. The bird feeder bobbled in the wind; its perches and tiny roof had been iced over and not even the bravest sparrows ventured to the seed banquet.

Agatha had been in the recliner for much of the afternoon; she couldn't be budged from her book; not even for chocolate. She'd started reading <u>Roots</u> a few days ago and the story had her captivated now.

This was the sort of Saturday that had been playing itself out in the Gardener house for many Januarys now. Their years together had unfolded into a predictable monotony and comfortable routine that urged contentment to take hold during the otherwise dreary month. The subtle pleasure that wrapped itself around each family member this afternoon was barely there, like a clean cotton sheet on a hot summer evening. The threesome knew that once they sipped down to the small chocolate circle at the bottom of their mugs, someone would suggest a game of chess or checkers. A familial clockwork, so to speak.

~~~~~~

Perhaps it was because the Christmas season was so chaotic. Or the frozen days of February demanded a spark of excitement. Regardless of the reason, Esther loved Valentine's Day. Adding splashes of reds and pinks to everything put a kick into her step. The grumpy Michiganders needed something to smile about and a heart-shaped box of chocolates usually did the trick. Today she was baking pink cupcakes. From the cassette player on the counter, John Denver sang one of his greatest hits; it blended nicely with the strawberry aroma. Belting out "Rocky Mountain High" into her spatula, she didn't hear the back door open.

Linda stood at the edge of the doorframe for just a minute, hand over her mouth, so the guffaws wouldn't tumble out. "Why do you listen to this stuff, Es?"

Esther tossed the makeshift microphone into the sink, "It's so much better than Zeppelin; I'm a country girl at heart."

"You're sixteen and this is folk music. You're supposed to be screaming along with rock-and-roll." Effervescent and trendy, Linda spent an inordinate amount of time each morning flipping and curling her hair so that it matched the popular Farrah Fawcett style. And she never left home without cherry lip-gloss.

"Wanna help me frost these cupcakes?" Esther raised her eyebrows in a pouty sort of way as she pled for her friend's aid.

"I'll frost if you do me a favor. Deal?" Linda winked.

"As long as it's nothing dangerous or stupid, I suppose."

"Cool. Tomorrow is Valentine's Day and I want to make you up in the morning. I'll be here at seven o'clock and bring my red skirt. My rear end has gotten too big for it; yours will look great though. I'm also bringing my make-up kit and a curling iron. I'd like to put a few people into shock, especially David Elder." Linda's eyes were wide with excitement.

Esther blushed at his name. She liked David, but he was a senior basketball star who'd never taken a second look at her. Nearly six feet tall with soft blond hair and dazzling blue eyes, his great-great grandfather probably captained a Viking ship. He'd dated at least a dozen girls, all curvy beauties, since his sophomore year. Linda obviously wanted to change that.

Esther assigned words to the nervous feeling in her stomach, "I don't know if I can pull this sort of thing off. I'm not a good flirt, you know that."

Linda was confident, "Once he sees you tomorrow you'll be in his dreams. Your best feature is that you don't even realize how pretty you are. The make-up will emphasize your beauty. You'll be lovely and shy—an unbeatable combination."

The girls finished the cupcakes and then ventured into Esther's closet to find the perfect white blouse to go with the perfect red skirt.

~~~~~~

Striding into the kitchen the next morning, she looked like a Valentine prize. The skirt was well above her knees and tied around her white collar was a pink silk scarf. Esther was dressed to kill and her friend had done magic with the curling iron and make-up. Linda beamed with pride.

Agatha wasn't so sure; the outfit certainly didn't reflect Esther's personality. And it was bound to fetch attention. Agatha didn't see the harm in it though, as long as Esther was aware, up front, that her school day would be different. "Honey, you look like a model that stepped out of a catalog. The boys will be distracted by you."

"I'll be fine, Mom. This might be my best Valentine's Day ever." The girls shrugged into their coats and mittens, grabbed book bags, and took off for the bus.

Ever vigilant Joseph scratched his head in dismay, "That skirt will get her into trouble. Mark my words, Mom. Nothing good can come of it."

~~~~~~

By fourth period, Esther was on the verge of an embarrassment overdose. The attention she'd been attracting was far more than what she bargained for and her cheeks were actually sore from blushing. In fifteen minutes she'd be sitting next to David Elder in Spanish class. She'd pay twenty bucks to change into her corduroys and sweater for the afternoon. Her only option now was to pray for a small fire in the building so they'd be sent home.

"That's a real fine dress; and you changed your hair." David leered with nothing short of primal lust. During the next forty minutes, he dropped his pencil a dozen times in order to catch an eyeful of legs as he bent down to retrieve the slippery writing instrument.

Reflecting on the morning she'd just experienced, and on David's obvious state of mind, Esther wondered whether it might actually be women who held the power of love. She almost felt badly for the male gender because it certainly seemed evident that these boys turned to mush at the sight of provocative legs, cleavage, or whatever. They were literally trapped inside of their hormone-driven bodies. She ground her teeth when she thought of the hundreds, no thousands, of women who abused this power to control the opposite sex. She made a vow that she'd neither tease nor tantalize again, and planned to bury the red skirt in the bottom of her closet tonight.

At the sound of the bell, he popped the question, "Do you want a ride home today?"

"Um, I usually take the bus with Linda." She was nervous and loathed the fact that it was the red skirt that had attracted his attention. But the thought of driving with David was a grand opportunity that she simply couldn't pass up. "I guess it'd be okay. I'll let her know during seventh period. Should I meet you by the front-lobby tree?"

"Where's your locker? I'll pick you up there." He flashed a bold smile that pushed her pulse into high gear.

"It's locker 467 near Mrs. Mason's biology lab." *Please don't let me throw up, God.*

~~~~~~

"David is driving me home today." Esther recited the fact out loud for the second time to make doubly sure it stuck in reality. She hated the red skirt now. It wasn't her brain or sense of humor that had earned the drive home with David. It had been legs and make-up.

"I told you that was an awesome skirt, didn't I?" Linda grinned with delight knowing her best friend might have a chance with a guy like David.

The medieval history class droned on for an eternity and when the final bell rang, Esther raced from the classroom to her locker. But David had somehow managed to beat her. Leaning sideways with his shoulder against the locker, it appeared as though he'd been waiting for hours. Their eyes locked and she nearly melted into the floor as his bold stare moved over her with an unhidden appreciation.

"Let me hold your books while you get your stuff." David juggled textbooks and then slipped her coat over her shoulders. His arm lingered for a moment and he brought her close to him in a swift hug.

"Thanks." She grabbed her purse and followed him down the hallway and out to the parking lot. The clouds had parted for the afternoon to offer a rare stream of sunshine; the couple lifted their cheeks up to the warm rays. His strides were long and she walked quickly to keep up. This was no easy task wearing Linda's two-inch heels but she managed in a miraculous sort of way. He opened her door first before taking his seat behind the steering wheel and starting the car.

"I need to warm up the engine because it sometimes stalls when it's real cold. C'mere, Esther." He pulled her across the seat beside him. "You're a very nice girl and I'm glad you're here. How about a Valentine kiss?"

Esther drew a sharp breath. She'd never kissed a boy and decided instantly that if she were going to kiss someone for the first time, then David Elder should definitely be the one.

"I guess so." She laced her fingers politely and turned to meet his stare.

David covered her cheeks with his palms and drew her into him. Pressing his mouth onto hers, his fingers caressed her throat. Her body acquiesced and she closed her eyes. His mouth opened for a long and lavish kiss as he pushed her beneath him. The kiss drained her of all thoughts before she trembled and gasped in response.

She scooted away tentatively, "Well, that was very nice. Thank you." She buckled her seatbelt and squeezed her fists to regain composure. She dare not look into his eyes again until they were safely in her own driveway.

"Tell me about yourself." David was calm and confident; this sort of adventure was nothing new and it was a scene he'd played many times.

"I'm sewing a quilt and I have a great brother. And if I could paint a picture of anything in the world, it'd be a blueberry orchard in Arcadia. And I started reading <u>Roots</u> a few days ago; it's really quite fascinating."

"You're very interesting, Esther Gardener. Where's your house?"

"It's on Lavender Lane. Take Spring Lake Road to Woodbine, and then right onto Lavender." Having recuperated from the mind-numbing kiss, Esther already looked forward to seeing him in class tomorrow.

"My dad is on a bowling league and has a bunch of free-game tickets that I need to use up before March 10th. If you're not doing anything Saturday would you be interested in bowling a few games?" David liked bowling on first dates because the environment provided ample opportunity to get to know a girl. And the view from the scorekeeping table wasn't bad.

"Sounds like fun. I've only bowled a few times so you can't laugh when I throw a gutter ball." Esther pinched herself.

~~~~~~

The loud coughing awoke her from a deep sleep. Esther stilled for a moment to listen for her mom's footsteps or voice. Nothing. More coughing, this time more strained. She hopped from her bed and hustled into Joseph's bedroom where she found him kneeling on the floor with arms pressed against the bed and head drooping to gasp for air between coughs.

"Where's your inhaler?"

"Dunno."

She didn't switch on the light because she hated seeing her brother in such a state of duress. Wrapped in darkness and the sound of Joseph's barking coughs, Esther clapped his back for several minutes as he worked to expel the mucus. She then quickly felt along the top of his dresser and ran her hands over the bookshelves until she found the inhaler. She shook it like a jackhammer, removed the cap and handed it to her brother.

After the inhalation, she felt his forehead and neck for a fever; he wasn't warm. She uttered a prayer. *Thank you dear Lord, please help him breathe now.* She shook the container again and gave him another dose of the medicine. The coughing continued for several more minutes while he worked to clear his lungs. Agatha finally appeared.

"Are you okay, babe?" Agatha sat near Joseph and checked him for fever; she too felt a normal temperature. "I dreamt that your cough was a bear growling. Isn't that strange?"

All three sat on Joseph's bed for a few minutes; a nightlight glow faintly illuminated a corner of the room. They appeared as mere shadows to each other, but each offered something to the other pair. Agatha was security and hope, Esther was strength and serenity, and Joseph was gratitude.

April meant pollen, which always triggered an allergic reaction in his already-sensitive lungs, despite the antihistamine he took every day. "I wake up in the middle of nearly every night lately; you'd think that it wouldn't bother me anymore. But it does. Just once I'd like to hit the pillow and not see my galaxy poster until sunrise. I'm sorry you're both awake now, although I hear that getting an eight-hour stretch of sleep is overrated." He grinned crookedly.

Esther drew him against her, "I love you and you're amazing." She yawned and stood to exit, "Your nighttime coughs don't bother me. They never did and never will. So find your shovel and scoop out the guilt you're carrying on that issue. You're the most incredible person in my life and you have enough gumption to fill our high school gym. G'night, nit-wit."

"Love you, honey. Get some rest and we'll see you in the morning." Agatha propped up his pillows and pulled the blankets around him before tiptoeing to her own bed.

~~~~~

The girls were on the bedroom floor sprawled against the bed. Esther sewed a new quilt block while Linda applied nail polish to her toes. "I float up to the clouds whenever I see him. And when he touches me nothing else in the world matters. Do you think it's love?"

"You two are a hot item. Mindy hates your guts because she's been after David since the Sadie Hawkins dance. I'm totally happy for you, Es, and I hope he appreciates what he has."

"David gets mad when I don't let him touch me you-know-where." Esther blushed.

Linda laughed at the admission, "He's not missing much; you don't have a lot in the boob department. Tell him to chill out."

"He says I'm being unreasonable—but if we venture into that territory then we might end up in a dangerous predicament because he's so hard to resist."

"If he cares about you then he won't push it. I don't think we're ready for sex yet anyway; I'm waiting until college." Linda was waving a paper fan over the wet polish on her feet.

"I'm waiting until I get married. That's what we're supposed to do, you know. But I don't think he wants to wait. And besides, I think he's already done it with someone." Esther's mood turned sullen.

"Well, he's very cute and a lot of girls would do it with him. Not everyone goes to church as often as you do, Es."

"I'll have to tell him that sex isn't happening until my wedding night." She hadn't yet mentioned to David that her vow of abstinence was inflexible.

~~~~~~

Karen phoned Esther a week before spring break to invite her north so she could assist with the maple syrup production. Agatha was infinitely amazed at the Lord's timing; she sensed trouble brewing between Esther and David. The trip would provide exactly what her daughter needed: time away.

At the bus station, Esther sat between her mother and brother. A brown leather suitcase rested against her leg.

"What algebra lesson are you on, Joseph? If I can help with anything let me know."

"Lesson forty-five. It's getting pretty tough but Dad helps me when he's got spare time. I'm adding abstract fractions, but the whole denominator-numerator same quantity rule is baffling me. I'll get through it." Joseph would miss Esther more than he dared to admit, but he reminded himself that she'd only be gone for five days. His recent tune-up at the CF center had been an eight-day session and they survived the separation. Of course, she and his parents had visited twice during the week to keep his loneliness at bay.

"Honey, I just heard them announce your bus number. Let's get your suitcase checked in. Do you have those snacks in your purse?" Agatha doubted that she'd ever be able to rein in the maternal instincts that prodded her to assist with every hurdle her children encountered. The thought of Esther taking driver's education this summer was horrifying so she focused on just one growing-up step at a time. Today's bus trip was plenty.

Esther embraced her teary-eyed mom and brother before boarding the bus.

"Call collect as soon as you get to Karen's house. We love you. Have a wonderful time and give the Holsten's a hug from all of us." *Thank you, Lord, for blessing me with such a fine family and good friends. Please take her bus safely to Arcadia.*

~~~~~~

It would've been easier driving a truck full of ornery cattle than hearing two women prattle and giggle for an hour from Cadillac to Arcadia. John now regretted making the offer to drive, but Karen was so happy to see Esther that he didn't have the heart to tell them they were giving him a headache.

"We have quite a few gallons done. Tomorrow morning we'll collect sap buckets while John boils the sap down in the evaporation shed. He expanded the shed last fall to make room for another person to skim froth and stoke the fire. I'll be sure to pack you a few bottles of syrup when you leave. Oh goodness—enough about syrup making. Tell me about David."

"He's nice and cute and a lot of fun. We've only been dating two months, but I totally adore him. He's a senior and plays on the basketball team; he has a younger sister and brother, and he's a great bowler. We sit next to each other in Spanish class; that's how we met." She withdrew his photo from her wallet.

"He's handsome; I'm very happy for you." Karen's enthusiasm was genuine. "How are your parents? How's Joseph?"

The conversation rambled on even after John parked beside the barn to end the journey. From the trunk he collected the suitcase and ambled to the house. A few mounds of snow lingered in the cool shadows beneath the thick fir trees.

Esther crept from the car. She mischievously made a snowball and walloped John in the back with it.

"Hey!" He dropped his cargo and began to rapid-fire his own snowballs. Karen joined in and laughter filled the yard.

"I give! No more!" Esther waved in a surrender motion. Breathless from the attacks, the threesome stomped off the snowy remnants from their coats and hair. John opened the door and the blueberry pie scent poured from the kitchen.

"You made pie this morning; thank you." Esther squeezed her friend's hand tightly, "It's so good to be here."

After supper the women played cribbage while John napped during the TV news. They popped corn after finishing their second game, and then Karen pulled down from the attic the trunk full of her mother's clothes and knick-knacks from the 1920s and 1930s. Hats, soft leather boots, a silk robe, pearl-handled combs, a music box, ancient teddy bears, and old-fashioned dresses.

"My mother was petite, like you, Es. Some people could hardly believe she was my mom because we looked nothing alike. My father's parents emigrated from Mexico and he was born in Texas; his family later moved to Ohio and bought a farm outside of Cleveland when he was just a little boy. Mom was a city girl who worked in the Cleveland bank. She met my dad there when he came in one day to apply for a college loan. He studied law for two years at Ohio State University in Columbus; dad and mom maintained a relationship through the mail and visited on weekends. He got fed up with their long-distance relationship, so he quit school, married her, and bought his own farm. And that's where I grew up with my two older brothers. Anyway, I'd imagine that some of these dresses would fit you quite nicely."

Esther spotted a splash of pink fabric and pulled out a fringe-covered flapper dress. "Oh, look at this one." She stood abruptly and held the dress in front of her, "This is beautiful."

"Go try it on." Karen couldn't remember the last time she'd had such fun; her mother would've loved Esther. She dug deeper into the trunk to find the small pink purse that matched the dress.

Esther bounced from the bedroom and back into the living room. She twirled around to shake the fringe on the dress, looking simultaneously adorable and ravishing. The sleeveless dress accentuated her lean shoulders; it hung just above her knees and didn't fit too tightly around her waist and hips. It was quite flattering against her light skin and sable-brown hair.

"That dress was made for you to wear. Take it home."

"No, I can't do that. This is too special to leave your house. But thank you for offering—it's truly wonderful." She waltzed back to the bedroom to change into her pajamas for the night.

~~~~~

"When we finish this batch of syrup we'll drive up to Frankfort and get Velma. She's excited about seeing you again and wants to teach you about granola. Would you mind if she spent the night with us?"

"That'd be terrific." Esther was glad to be in Arcadia, and although she saw Karen and Velma only once or twice a year, their frequent letter writing kept them close.

John, Karen and Esther worked steadily throughout the morning. He stayed in the evaporation shed stirring sap over the fire while the women hauled sap-filled buckets on the tractor. The work was especially uncomfortable for the women because a drizzling rain had made it a point to linger above Arcadia for the day. The chill in the air was hard to shake. By mid-afternoon they carried the last few sap buckets into the shed and poured their contents into the boiling pot.

Karen drove alone to Frankfort while Esther assisted with the evaporation and filtering stages. The syrup temperature had to be perfect before transfer to the finishing pot. A soggy Esther stoked the fire while John cooked the sap and skimmed froth accumulation from the top. Then they switched duties; John added wood to the fire while she stirred and skimmed.

The evaporation had created a sweet and sticky film that covered the small shed's interior. The maple steam permeated her senses, pores, and clothing. She wanted to remember this moment each time she poured the syrup onto her pancakes in Detroit. Closing her eyes tightly she inhaled the aroma of the boiling sap and fragrant burning wood to brand the feeling in her mind. Breathing the steamy air inside of the small shed, she now understood how Joseph felt after a night in the mist tent.

John constantly checked the thermometer until the sap temperature reading was precisely 218 degrees. "Okay. The mercury hit its mark and we're ready to filter." He handed a giant ladle to his helper and they took turns pouring the hot syrup through the filter-topped tube that led to the finishing pot where the syrup would cool before bottling.

"We must pour the syrup through this fabric to remove the sugar sand, which is a calcium compound that makes the syrup grainy. Work quickly—this syrup can't reach 225 degrees."

Esther raced against the mercury, and the faster she poured the more exciting the job became. And then, of course, she got the giggles. John couldn't help but be touched by her joy; it was contagious and in a few moments they were both laughing and pouring syrup, tears rolling down their cheeks. And this was how Karen and Velma had found them.

~~~~~~

Besides her small overnight suitcase, Velma brought a two-pound bag of fresh oats. Karen provided the other granola ingredients: raisins, walnuts, wheat germ, flour, brown sugar, and maple syrup. Velma's recipe from many years ago required honey as the conduit to hold the ingredients together. However, they now used maple syrup because it made economical sense.

Few words were spoken between the women as they worked in the kitchen. Their relationship had reached the point where polite conversation to stave off uncomfortable silence was unnecessary. Their subtle and quiet motions, nods, and nudges provided sufficient communication. They were content to merely share the kitchen space and take turns stirring the sticky batter. While the sun dropped into the hillside, sharply defined rays of light streamed into the kitchen window. The metal utensils scattered across the table glistened in the light to add further sparkle to the bright atmosphere.

John marched in loudly after he'd finished bottling the syrup. He was in good spirits and glad to be done with the springtime chore until next April. After hanging his coat and washing his sticky hands, he grabbed a plate and knife from the cupboard. He cut several bars of the warm snack. "Who's up for a few rounds of gin rummy while we eat this pan of granola?"

~~~~~~

She laid on her back in the grassy field, one leg pulled against her chest to stretch the hamstring muscle. The late April wind was strong and it rushed across her face and stung her eyes as she sat upright. Esther's experience on the track team thus far had been strenuous and exhilarating. After seven weeks of distance running and intense track workouts, her muscles were no longer sore or stiff.

During the first two weeks of the season, however, she had cringed in pain just stepping out of bed in the morning. Now she felt powerful and energetic from the training. Coach Rollings declared that her running technique and natural speed made her a good candidate for the 400-meter race. Esther agreed to train for that event and the coach gave her a workout schedule to follow. She was glad that her friend, Sharon, had convinced her to join the team.

Esther and several teammates had run a mile warm-up, six 200-yard sprints, and practiced a dozen block starts. After re-stretching muscles and resting their lungs, the group ran two 400-meter races while Coach Rollings observed technique and corrected errors.

Leaning against the fence to cool her legs after the practice, she checked her wristwatch. David was driving her home today; he'd be done with his chemistry make-up test by 4:30.

"Hello, Esther kitty." He came from behind and tugged her long braid.

"Hi. I'm just finishing up. Too bad we don't have a kite; the wind is fierce today."

"Do you have time to stop at my house before I take you home?" He slung her duffel bag over his shoulder.

"For a little while I suppose, especially if your mom baked cookies." Her stomach groaned from hunger.

"No one's home. I'd like to show you my room." He pulled her into him and lounged against the car. Taking her mouth in a kiss that stole her breath, he fit her lips to his own and she nearly melted. She pulled away, almost fearful.

"I don't trust us alone."

"Let me put it to you straight, Es. I'm not waiting anymore. We love each other, we're compatible, and you're beautiful. I think it's time to kick our relationship up a level. We've been steady for more than two months." David whispered along her jaw line as he kissed her throat roughly. She refused to let her body tell her conscience what was right.

"I won't have sex until I'm married. If you have to do it to continue this relationship, then I don't know what to say." Esther's throat tightened and she was desperately afraid she was about to lose him. But if he really cared then he'd respect her wishes without resentment.

"Well, then hop in and I'll drive you home." David clenched his jaw as the car tires screeched and spun against the pavement. Not a word was exchanged until they were parked in her driveway.

"It's been real, Esther. Have a great life. Nothing personal, I just need more from a relationship." There was neither remorse nor sadness in his voice.

Esther was forced to make one of two choices. The first would be to puke all over his lap. The second would be to exit from the car maturely, walk into her house, and puke in the privacy of her own bathroom. She chose the latter before drenching her bedroom pillow with sobs.

By the end of May she was over David but her heart wasn't any less broken.

Spring ~ Summer 1977

The final bell had rung two hours ago but the high school campus was still teeming with track athletes and coaches. Duffel bags were scattered randomly across the field as if a twister had recently paid a visit to this particular spot in Chicago. Although the temperature had barely topped sixty degrees, the necks and backs of the boys were wet with sweat after running intense workouts. A pair of discus throwers ambled into the gym to lift weights. While stacking hurdles at the north side of the track, Coach Atkins hollered at the pole-vaulters to cover the pits. The most important meet of the season was in two weeks and the team was determined to score well. Today's practice had been grueling.

"No way, Diane. I'm totally not going over there. I think he's dating Carrie." Liz could barely keep her eyes in their sockets and heart in her chest when she spoke to Daniel.

"We have as much right to use this track as they do, Liz. They're just hanging out and it looks like they're done jumping. Just casually jog by and say something." Diane was tired of hearing Liz babble over Danny and not do anything about it. Well, now was her chance.

Liz checked her shoelaces for the nineteenth time before jogging to the small group of athletes. She'd do it this time. Definitely.

"Hi, Dan. How's it goin'?"

"Oh hey, Liz. We're okay. What're you up to, besides cramming for the government test?" Daniel liked Liz; she was soft spoken and intelligent. Pretty too.

"There's a concert on the 14th so I've been practicing my solo. And definitely studying for the government exam." She paused then to catch her breath, "Great day isn't it?"

"An absolutely fine day. We're packing up here so I'll catch you tomorrow in class, okay?" He shot her a million-dollar smile and then opened his duffel bag to make sure he'd packed his tape and spikes.

Liz sighed dreamily and resumed her jog around the track.

"What is it with you, Jacobson? You could have your pick of any female in this school and you're not even dating. Liz is a great girl, you idiot." Austin jealously chided his buddy.

"I've dated, moron. I'm way too busy—track, exams, and my uncle's garage. Dealing with female complexities isn't on my current agenda. My grades are seriously important if I'm gonna get into Penn, so just back off. Why don't you ask her out?" Daniel felt huffy. The practice hadn't gone well; he'd barely cleared thirteen feet. He wanted to jump at least fourteen feet this spring to ensure a place on Penn State's track team next year. He knew there'd be no scholarship, but wanted the height under his belt anyway.

"No big deal; we're all feeling on edge." Austin slugged his teammate's shoulder as they sauntered off the track and into the parking lot.

~~~~~~

Mrs. Taylor's tone was neutral when she had asked Daniel to see her after class, but when the bell rang to signal the end of the period, his heart rate quickened. *Did I fail last week's assignment?*

She nodded pleasantly as he approached her desk, "I was very impressed with this report, Mr. Jacobson. I'd never heard of Louis Sullivan and found your report both thorough and intriguing. Aside from a dozen spelling errors, it's an *A* paper and I appreciate the work you put into it. Do you have access to a dictionary?"

"Yes, Ma'am, but I got pinched for time and didn't want to rewrite the whole paper. Sorry about that."

"Spelling errors aside, I sensed in your writing a real passion for architecture. You piqued my interest and I'd like to see a picture of the Wainwright building if you have one. Are you planning on college this fall?"

"I applied to Penn State; they have a great architectural design program. I've been interested in building design since the first grade. The Sullivan paper was a cinch to write because I suspect he and I were cut from the same mold."

"I wish you the best of luck. I'm sure you'll be accepted. Be sure to bring a dictionary with you to Pennsylvania, Daniel."

~~~~~~

She was practically sitting on top of him so he took another swig of milk to subdue his neon-bright nerve endings. Daniel would have much preferred lunch with Austin, but Carrie had hooked her arm into his and drawn him to a seat beside her in the noisy cafeteria. She purred into his ear, "Wanna come over tonight and study?" Her breast rubbed against his arm as she trailed her perfectly groomed index finger along the back of his neck.

"I'm not sure we'd get much studying done, Carrie." He chuckled nervously. He'd kissed a few girls but going further scared the wits out of him. Not that he didn't want to. He just didn't know how to go about the whole process—and he'd probably blow it.

"My thoughts exactly. How about 6:30?" She fluttered her eyelashes and leaned dangerously close to his lips while turning around to extract herself from the bench. Carrie made a grand exit from the cafeteria, passing Austin and Pete as they scrambled to Daniel for details.

Before his friends posed a single question, Daniel blurted out, "Yes, I might go to Carrie's tonight. Back off, guys."

"Dude, if her parents aren't home you got it made." Pete was wide-eyed over the opportunity in front of Daniel, "She likes you and I've heard great things about Carrie."

"I'm not doing anything with Carrie. If I mess around with every pretty face that comes on to me, I'll end up in a heap of trouble before graduation. I have big plans for my future that don't involve a bimbo yanking my chain."

"Suit yourself, chicken, but I think you're gonna get real tired of the chastity issue. See you at practice." Austin shook his head in dismay before the trio split in the hallway.

Daniel sorted through the tangle of thoughts as he pulled a physics book from his locker. *I don't have time for Carrie. I need to mind my own business, study for exams, get the garage built, and vault fourteen feet. Is that too much for a guy to ask?*

~~~~~~

Hank and Daniel had worked through plenty of rain showers but today the weather was cooperating, which was vastly appreciated by outdoor laborers during a northern Illinois springtime. Snow was uncommon, yet still a possibility in March. The sky was partly cloudy, the air was dry, and the temperature wouldn't exceed sixty degrees. Hank's backyard was strewn with nails, two sawhorses, ladders, and wood scraps. With the shingle packages open on the ground and the tarpaper nailed in place, Daniel and his uncle hoped to finish the roof today.

Weighted with measuring tape, nails, and a small nail extractor, Daniel liked the feel of the soft leather belt around his waist. Working from the pitch downward they'd made good progress on the roof by lunch, but his legs and back were stiff. He was relieved when Aunt Martha announced that lunch was ready. Stepping down from the ladder, he dropped the hammer, removed his belt and cap, and then stretched his arms above his head to work out the kinks. Just a bit over six feet tall with broad chest, wide shoulders, and well-defined leg muscles, he was an attractive young man. The training required to jump fourteen feet had sculpted his body into an athletic and brawny shape. It was no wonder that half the girls in school turned to mush at the sight of him.

"You're getting this garage done much quicker than I had expected. It'll be nice to have a place for the cars next winter, won't it, Hank?" Aunt Martha served up corned beef and cabbage on crusty rolls for the workers; the children enjoyed peanut butter sandwiches. A dish of potato salad and plate of brownies accompanied the entrees.

"Yup. We'll finish the roof today and then install the siding next week." Hank replied in between mouthfuls of corned beef.

"When did you and Uncle Hank meet?"

Martha arched her eyebrows in surprise, "That's a funny question, Daniel. What brought that on?"

"Oh, I dunno. You two get along so well and always seem happy. And Chad and Jamie are really good kids. Just wondering if you knew each other for a long time before you got married."

Hank answered first, "Martha was twenty-one when we met. I had just graduated from college and landed a job at Baxter & Company. It was in that little office complex next to the Book Warehouse in Deerfield. She was a waitress in the coffee shop and by about the third or fourth time she served my table, I knew I'd marry her. We went on just a few dates before I proposed."

Martha blushed like a young bride, "You pursued me until I gave in, Hank."

Daniel smiled. *How do you know when you love someone? To spend an entire life with one person is nearly unfathomable.* He pushed the issue to the back of his mind so he could focus on just one step at a time for now. *First get into college, then get the degree, and then complete AIA certification. Plenty to do without adding an unpredictable woman into the picture.*

~~~~~~

His dreams took flight during fourth period where he could design, draft, and create models. Daniel thrived on precision and it showed in his work. Mr. Crippen was a teacher who expected perfection from the students; not many kids met that expectation. In the past decade, only a few of his students had earned an *A* grade. The class was finishing their final project: Each student had to create a blueprint and scale model for a contemporary, two-story 1600 square-foot home. Daniel had finished his model earlier in the week and was assisting a classmate.

Mr. Crippen walked to the boys and tapped Daniel on the head with his mechanical pencil, "I need to talk to you, Jacobson."

"Yes, Sir." Daniel followed his teacher to the back of the room and took a seat beside the well-organized desk.

"I like your work. You've got the finest drafting skills I've seen in thirty years and it's a pleasure having you in the classroom. You're a natural. I have an offer that I'd like you to consider. Of course, you'll have to discuss it with your folks, so you can get back to me with an answer on Monday."

Daniel straightened in the chair and leaned forward in anticipation. "Thank you, Sir. My plans are to become an architect."

"My nephew, Mitch Smythe, is an architect in Grand Rapids, Michigan. He started his own firm about six months ago and is looking for a kid who can help with construction work and blueprint clean up. He's mentoring a young architect and has a draftsman, but needs a third guy to help keep loose ends tied. When he asked if I had anyone who might fit that bill, you came to mind. Interested?"

"I'll do it." Daniel was thrilled. The idea of working under the guidance of a practicing architect over the summer sent a triumphant tremor through his belly.

"Talk it over with your parents. You'd stay at Mitch's house over the summer. He converted his attic into a guest room about a year ago; I suppose that's where you'd camp out. Mitch has a wife and two kids, and they're a nice family. It would be a good summer for you. I'll give you my home phone number; have your dad call me for details this weekend. If your parents okay the deal, then I'll have Mitch contact your dad. Okay?"

"Yes, Mr. Crippen. Thank you very, very much." Daniel extended his hand and his teacher grasped it in a firm and proud handshake.

"You can't go so far away. I'll miss you for all those days." Amy was near tears; Daniel had just described the Grand Rapids opportunity. She poked her mashed potatoes in frustration because she knew a thirteen-year old sister had no say whatsoever in what her big brother did with his summer.

Sandra's mouth felt suddenly dry and she sipped her water quietly. She knew it was time to let him go, but darn it, that didn't mean it wasn't painful. He'd grown up so fast and she was proud of the diligent and respectful young man he'd become. He set such a good example for Dennis and Amy; it would, indeed, be hard to say good-bye in three weeks. But the opportunity was a dream come true for her son, and she wouldn't keep him from it for her own selfish reasons.

"We'll drive up to Grand Rapids and visit on a Saturday in July, Amy. I know you'll miss him but this is a great job for Daniel before he starts college." Sandra spoke in a perky voice to assert that she was fine with the idea.

"I'll have my own room this summer. How cool is that?" Nothing suppressed Dennis, the master of the *Life is grand—enjoy every day to the fullest* mantra. "I won't have time to miss you. I've got driver's ed, dude."

John directed stern statements to Daniel without batting an eye, "I'll call Mr. Crippen after dinner to discuss logistics. I'd like to know what Smythe will pay you, and I don't want you working more than forty-hour weeks. I'll get Smythe's phone number as well because I want to know the guy you'll be working for and living with for seven weeks." This was indeed a fine offer, but John needed more details before stamping his approval on the arrangement.

"I'll help with dishes tonight, Amy." Daniel tapped her arm and winked with a smile. He knew how to pacify his sister and would provide extra doses of attention before embarking on the Michigan adventure. "Baskin Robbins has a special on strawberry ice cream this week. Want to get a cone tonight?"

"I'm in." Dennis quickly estimated the number of days until he could leave clothes on the bedroom floor without reprimand from his tidy brother. Not many.

~~~~~~

Despite the diploma he held in his hand while posing for yet another photograph, Daniel didn't feel finished; this was only the beginning. Although he planned to whoop it up with his friends during the coming week, he was particularly anxious about June 9th. That's when he'd meet Mitch Smythe. While speaking with the architect a few weeks ago Daniel sensed him to be a direct and down-to-earth sort of guy. He was eager to learn what Mr. Smythe had to teach.

Amy approached Daniel and wrapped her arms around him ostentatiously. She disregarded the stir of embarrassment it caused her brother; he was very dear to her. He'd been her hero since punching the vampire all those years ago. If someone could define a perfect brother and friend, Daniel would be it. He gave her ample space during her moody days and cheered her on when junior high felt overwhelming and impossible. She was so proud of him. *This is a person who deserves the good things in life. Bless him, Lord, with happiness and love.*

Sandra strolled to her son tentatively and then clung to him fiercely, "I love you, sweetie. You're a beacon of comfort and joy to so many people. I pray that your life is full of blessings and love." Copious tears drenched her cheeks and the graduate did his best to soothe her.

Grasping her hands in his, he looked into her vigilant eyes, "Thanks, Mom, for all that you've done. I promise to make you proud."

~~~~~~

Although the room lacked artwork, it had charm and character. The walls were white to reflect light and open up the space. A simple pine dresser and queen-size bed were against one side of the guestroom; the other side offered a well-worn brown sofa with yellow and orange floral pillows. Beside the sofa sat a lopsided bookshelf full of classic hardcover and paperback books. A small crate with a tabletop radio had been placed near the bed. Daniel turned it on and searched for a decent station. Fleetwood Mac. That'd do just fine.

He unpacked his clothes into the dresser drawers and then plopped onto the bed. Tomorrow would be his first day on the job. Mitch had already explained that they'd spend the day at a building site where a foundation had recently been poured and framing would begin. Mitch hired a local building crew and Daniel would be their gopher. If he proved capable, then he'd assist with some actual carpentry work.

Content and drowsy, he grabbed hold of a thought that popped into his head: *Ask Angela about church.* The family had said a prayer before supper and he wondered whether they belonged to a church. If so, then he hoped to attend a Sunday service with the Smythe family because there were so many things to be grateful for. He drifted into a deep sleep and didn't flinch until morning.

~~~~~~

"Hey, Daniel! Up and at 'em fella! We're hitting the road in thirty minutes." Mitch hollered up the attic stairway.

Daniel leapt from the bed, pulled on a pair of jeans and ran downstairs. "Morning, everyone. Is it all right if I take a quick shower?" He was fuzzy headed but knew better than to spend ten minutes in a family bathroom without permission first.

"Get in there, kid. Then eat some cereal and eggs before we head out." Mitch was anxious to see the framework started and glad to have a willing helper.

The hammering, sawing, and drilling played a concerto in Daniel's ears. It represented men working together to create something that would stand for decades and be seen by thousands of people. A survival mechanism for man to build shelter had manifested itself into millions of carefully crafted and long-standing structures. From huts and caves to this. It didn't matter that this particular structure was merely a one-story restaurant. It would be a place where people worked every day, shared meals, and engaged in both ludicrous and serious conversation.

Mitch assigned Daniel's duty for the day, "You stand on this spot and you watch. I'll inform the crew that you exist to serve their construction needs today. When you hear someone shout your name, you go to that man and do as he says. Is that understood?"

"Yes, Sir. I intend to become irreplaceable by the end of the week." He meant it.

~~~~~~

The first ten days in Grand Rapids expired in a blur. Daniel fit into the crew as if he'd been with them for years, and Mitch still couldn't believe his luck. The prodigious high school kid lent an upbeat attitude and worked tirelessly to complete every task assigned. Mitch wasn't sure what he'd do in August when the kid was gone. But he did know one thing for certain: If Daniel would take the job, Mitch wanted him working in Grand Rapids during the next four summers. And once Daniel finished college, Mitch would mentor and guide him through AIA certification. He bet that this bright young man would finish all ten exams in seven or eight months' time.

~~~~~~

Saturday mornings at the Smythe residence were laid back and predictable, and this June 23rd was no exception. Mitch and Angela read the newspaper in the kitchen while Daniel and the kids ate pancakes in front of the TV.

"Daniel, you have a telephone call!" Angela shouted from the kitchen.

He stepped over the youngsters and trotted to the phone whose cord had been stretched taut to its limit. "Hello?"

"Good morning, son. How's life in Michigan these days?"

"Hey, Dad. It's real good. We started the interior work on

the restaurant, and I did a bit of detailing on an office-building design perspective. How's everything in Chicago?"

"It's been hectic, as you can probably imagine. Dennis is just three weeks from having a driving permit and Amy has earned a good bit of money babysitting the Saunder's twins. We expect a bumper crop of tomatoes from the garden this year. But that's not why I called. I'm holding in my hand a letter from Penn State."

"Really? Did you read it?"

"You're in, Daniel."

"All right!" Daniel whooped and spun in the kitchen before slapping Mitch on the back. "In the bottom drawer of my dresser there's an envelope full of Penn State papers and phone numbers. I need to call the student housing number and get my name on the list as a new dorm resident. If you could dig that out this weekend and call me with the number that'd be great. Thanks for calling, Dad. Give mom and the kids a hug."

Mitch tilted his chair back as he raised his coffee cup to toast the young builder, "I've heard good things about Penn State. What made you apply to a college that'll cost you an arm and a leg to attend?"

"Louis Kahn. Have you seen photographs of the Jonas Salk Institute in California? Or the Kimbell Art Museum in Texas? He was a Philadelphia man whose buildings have made him one of the most important figures in 20th Century architecture. He said that contemporary architects should produce buildings as spiritually inspiring as those created in ancient Greece and Egypt. Kahn graduated from the University of Pennsylvania decades ago—his influence undoubtedly reached professors at both Pennsylvania universities. I want to study architecture where Kahn's roots are. And my grandpa grew up in Pennsylvania and graduated from Penn State before moving to Chicago. So when I learned about Kahn, well, that pretty much clinched my decision."

"Will you stay in Pennsylvania during the summers?" Mitch wore a quizzical expression.

"Only if I can't find an architect or builder in the Midwest who needs an extra hand next summer." Daniel hoped his hint was strong enough.

"I could save a spot for you here." Mitch stood from the table and ambled to the sink.

"That all depends on how much you're willing to pay a proven good worker."

"We'll see how the rest of the summer goes, Mr. Jacobson."

Both men knew where Daniel would be after his first year in Pennsylvania.

Spring 1978

Still numb from the hospital trip yesterday, Esther didn't remember getting onto the bus. Her emotions were raw and her throat was tender from last night's unabashed crying. The bronchiectasis diagnosis was scary; permanently inflamed airways meant that lung clearing episodes would be more painful and future infections would be even more difficult to endure. She knew that cystic fibrosis would snatch away her brother soon and the tone of her prayers lately had become angry.

Each time Sharon turned to scan for Andy, her elbow bumped into Esther's shoulder. The distraction was good in a sense because a large rabbit hole had recently taken residence in her mind. During moments of utter despair she sometimes found herself in a frozen stupor. At other times she'd visualize herself climbing down the hole to save her brother. He was crying and frightened, and couldn't catch his breath. But the tunnel seemed endless and his voice grew softer and more distant the deeper she probed. Then the image would dissipate and she'd feel a jolt back to reality as if her psyche had just crossed a mirage in the neural network.

"Get focused, Esther. This is an important meet." Sharon was a long jumper, fast and strong and always so confident about herself in the world. She was right—Esther would win the race for Joseph. He often inspired her to push past the point of what felt like a complete lung collapse at the end of her races. His cheering drove her to great speeds and she'd miss him today. She wasn't the fastest runner in the division but consistently placed well in her races.

As she grappled with the reality of the day, Andy tapped her shoulder. "Switch seats with me, Es." Sharon's face was absolutely glowing; how could she refuse?

"I'll switch, but that means I've got to sit with the bozos back in your spot, doesn't it, tiger?" Andy flashed a flirtatious smile while she climbed over Sharon and shuffled back to the third seat.

"Hey, speedster. Ready for your race? Looks like you're running early and that's a real drag because the temp ain't gonna reach sixty degrees today." That was Scott, always looking on the bright side of things. The pole-vaulters were such an odd bunch; beautiful human specimens, but mentally light-years away from other athletes who were steeped in at least some sort of reality.

Esther replied jokingly, "The race time is fine with me, you guys. And it sure beats your competition time. While you're trying to hurl your skinny rear-end over fourteen feet at five o'clock, I'll have my feet on a bleacher seat and a bag of steaming French fries on my lap."

Jeff easily picked Esther up and plopped her onto his lap. A great guy—smart, athletic, and a lifesaver in her chemistry class. "How you doin', Es? I heard about what happened yesterday."

She knew he was referring to Joseph. "I'm okay; it helps to be focused on the meet." She replied with a rock in her throat. "He's on some pretty strong antibiotics and has super doctors looking out for him." She refused to cry here. Not on this trip. She didn't want to deflate the positive vibes on the bus. *Go Rosemont Tigers!* Feeling suddenly uncomfortable perched atop Jeff's legs, Esther cleared her throat and shifted herself to fall beside him onto the seat. A swell guy, but she didn't carry a flame for him.

Jeff clasped her hand and asked again for the umpteenth time, "When are we going out? Dinner and a movie; I'll take you to the park and engrave our names on the willow tree. We'll eat ice cream."

How could she refuse? Because her mom had a great story and it was true by all accounts. It was Esther's benchmark on how you really knew you were in love. When her parents first met in the orchard back in 1959, mom said she forgot to breathe. She said that he took her breath away, literally. The first time dad looked into mom's eyes her heart nearly leapt from her chest and she was bedazzled. After their first handshake she was completely in love, and they were married just three months later. It just wasn't there with Jeff.

"I'll think about it. Let's stay tuned into what's happening today."

"Esther! What're you doing at the back of the bus? The girls are NOT to be mixing with the guys. NOT today. Andy! Move your body now and switch places with Esther." Coach Rollings sensed a rise in hormones and he was intent on keeping the team in line. "Jeff and Andy! Do you have your tape today? If you didn't bring it I'm nailing your ears to this bus wall."

Andy replied solidly, "We got everything coach, and Jeff brought a tape measure for runway marks. I'm clearing fourteen feet today for sure."

~~~~~~

Esther's race was scheduled to start in fifteen minutes. "Hey Emily! Do you have spikes and a spike wrench? One of my spikes is bent and I need to switch it out." The girls ran to the bleachers where Emily had stashed her bag.

"Give me your shoe and I'll fix it. You stretch while I'm doing this. My race isn't for thirty minutes." Emily expertly replaced the spike while Esther pressed into the fence post, deeply extending her legs to stretch her calf muscles. She was ready. She wanted more than anything to tell Joseph she'd won. He needed good news right about now and she'd bring it to him.

"You're the best, Emily. Thanks." Esther deftly laced up her shoe and jogged to the 400-meter starting point. The Rosemont Tigers were competing against two other high school teams today. There were seven girls entered in the race—two were built like racehorses. Esther didn't flinch; she was puny but had innate speed and nearly perfect running technique. Besides, what mattered most, in the end, was the mind. And her mind was ready to fight and win. The runners paced in tiny circles around the starting area. Rubbing legs. Hopping. Twisting. Stretching. Praying. Keeping their bodies warm.

"Runners take your marks."

She set up at lane four, lead knee bent with push-off foot dug into the starting block. With arms taut against her sides and waist slightly bent, she bowed her head forward and waited for the sound of the gunshot.

"Set!" The starter raised his pistol. *BANG!*

The runners leapt from their blocks. The pack strode together for several seconds until three girls pulled away from the others. The runners jostled for a lead position. What Esther lacked in size she made up for in speed and agility. This was her race and a surge of power pumped through her chest and legs as she positioned herself into second place behind a racehorse. She let the runner pull her around the track, and then they were at the final eight yards. As she struggled for breath she saw Joseph in the hospital bed and drew energy from deep within. Esther flew past the racehorse and beat her by a full stride.

The Rosemont Tigers roared. Emily ran up to her and slammed her back. Sharon howled from the long-jump runway.

Wearing the biggest grin she'd ever seen, Jeff jogged to her from the vault area, "Little girl you might have yourself a PR; I clocked you on my stopwatch at fifty-nine seconds." He tugged her ponytail, "We're real proud of you, speedster."

As she jogged from the track to her teammates, Coach Rollings held up his hand for a high-five. "Beautiful job, Esther."

~~~~~~

Summer break was in full swing. Reading another Isaac Asimov book on the back porch, Joseph inhaled the smell of freshly cut grass while Ken pushed the mower. Esther picked vegetables in the garden. Now thirteen years old, Joseph knew that the summer days he'd experience were numbered. The lung infections were nothing short of debilitating and life threatening at this point; but his parents and sister somehow made them bearable. When he was stuck in bed, Esther read stories to him, shared the events of her day and mimicked the roles of her friends.

"Look at these cucumbers, Joseph. We have plenty for pickling this year." She was a simple and wholesome kind of beautiful; pretty even in a dirty t-shirt and faded denim shorts. She didn't bother with make-up; besides, covering her smooth and unblemished skin would be nearly sinful. Joseph wondered why a dozen guys weren't beating down the door for his sister. She'd be a prize to the man who won her. The guy had better be perfect.

"Hey folks. How's the world on Lavender Lane?" Jeff strode into the backyard for a visit en route to his summer job at the gas station.

Joseph smiled.

"What's up, Jeff?" Esther walked over to greet him, wavy brown hair billowing in the breeze.

"*Superman* is playing at the Twelve Oaks Theatre this weekend. Do you want to see it on Saturday night? We could get a bite to eat too, if you'd like."

"Sure. Sounds like fun. Call me tonight and we can set a time." She loved the movies and going with Jeff would mean an enjoyable evening.

"Cool. I'll call you after my shift tonight." Jeff latched onto her hand and squeezed it briefly before waving good-bye and jogging back to his car.

"That was mysterious. . . I've been wondering why the phone hasn't been ringing off the hook for you, Es, and then Jeff appears. Is he a nice guy?"

"Just a friend. And yes, he's a nice guy." Esther marched across the porch with the vegetables and tousled his hair as she passed.

He is a nice guy. What's wrong with me? She pondered her judgment while lining up tomatoes along the counter.

Sandra returned from her recent round of errands with a stack of mail in her hand. "There's a letter here from Karen."

Esther tore open the envelope.

```
Dear Esther,
     Hope you're enjoying summer so far. The lake
brought hundreds of beautiful stones onto the
beach during the winter. The spring thaw revealed
them lying about 200 yards from the area where
your family swims. Rabbits got into my garden last
week; I think they slipped under the fence. Half
of the bean plants are eaten up and several of my
cucumbers too. Live and learn I guess. We should
have staked the fencing down better.
     I look forward to seeing you in Arcadia next
month. Would you like to stay with us for an
extra week or two after your folks return to
Detroit? You could take a Greyhound bus back home.
John can drive you into Cadillac on the weekend he
works at the boat shop; you'd catch the bus from
there. We'd love to have your help in the orchard.
Has Joseph fully recovered from the recent lung
infection? Please give him our love. He remains
in my daily prayers.

                              Warmest regards,
                              Karen
```

"Karen wants help with blueberry harvesting." Esther squealed with delight and immediately pushed the letter into Sandra's hands.

"I'll talk to your dad about it after supper tonight, okay? It might be nice for you to get away for an extended time; Karen and Velma are good for you."

"YES!" Esther hoped desperately her father would approve of the visit. She dashed to the garage, hopped onto her bike, and pedaled to Linda's before she burst from all the news she had to share.

~~~~~~

Although she'd been working on it for two years now, it wasn't quite big enough. Esther wanted the quilt to be about sixty inches wide and eighty inches long, a good size to cover a twin bed or be draped across a couch. She'd spent hours last week searching for fabric around the house to use for quilt squares. Her mother suggested using material from a few childhood shirts and dresses that she and Joseph had outgrown years ago.

Esther even scavenged material from a few lightly used baby blankets. She loved sewing nearly as much as she loved to read. It was a soothing and rhythmic activity that produced a finished article, and she much preferred hand sewing to machine-sewing because it was more artistic and personal. While most of her friends took weekly trips to the mall, she was a quiet and content homebody.

"Wanna get some ice cream? Steve isn't home and there's no answer at Will's house, so you're my last-resort partner."

"Sure. Bring your enzyme pills."

Strolling down Lavender Lane to the Dairy Queen the siblings realized, almost simultaneously, that they hadn't walked through the neighborhood as a pair in years. Together they were besieged by nostalgia. As teenagers must do, they were blossoming and growing into their own separate identities, and forming different circles of friends.

"I remember when you taught me to ride your bike, Es. You used to ride it to the Bentley tree and then run back to get me so mom wouldn't see you putting me onto it. She was so afraid I'd hurt myself. I remember the look on her face the first time she saw me riding it down the sidewalk." Joseph chuckled.

"I remember a whole bunch of things. Stroller rides when you were a baby and wagon rides when you were a toddler. I was glad that you rode a bike in that 4th of July parade; I didn't want you to be pulled in a wagon when the other boys your age were on bikes."

"I appreciate everything you've done and the sacrifices you make. People say it's a miracle I've survived this far, but that's not true. Having you, mom and dad, my friends, and our church family gives me a lot of strength. Every day is a gift and I don't know how many more I'll have. So I just wanna say that you've been great."

"You're an amazing and prodigious intellect. Don't feel like you owe me anything or that I've ever suffered from your disease. It's from you that I learned the true value of persistence and faith." She stopped to embrace her brother where they stood. And he coughed.

"We have something pretty good, you and I. That'll never change, Joseph, regardless of where life takes us."

After supper that evening, Esther retrieved the thirteen-year old memory book from her closet shelf. She opened it to the next blank page and wrote an entry describing her walk with Joseph. She then withdrew the carefully folded Dairy Queen napkin from her pocket and taped it to the bottom of the page. *How many more ice creams will we share? How many more years will he be here?*

~~~~~~

Between streams of free-flowing dialogue they were concocting a new batch of granola.

"That's what I tell her all the time, Esther." Velma was pleased to have someone on her side of the debate.

"I don't mean to instigate anything, Karen, but Velma is a very strong and capable eighty-year-old woman. I've seen plenty of women her age that can't be bothered with much of anything." Esther spoke emphatically but with an apologetic undertone.

"But you must see it from my perspective, both of you. Velma is very dear to me and I didn't want her alone in that cabin so far away from civilization." Karen pled her case.

Although she'd been living in the townhouse for nearly four years now, Velma was still occasionally perturbed that her niece had convinced her to move up to Frankfort where neighbors and medical facilities were nearby. She was content in her new place, but sometimes longed for the tranquility that the cabin provided.

"Well, I haven't sold it; there's always an opportunity for me to move back if I think it's best." Velma knew that the townhouse was appropriate, considering her age, but she loved a good debate.

The women mixed new ingredients into the granola bars this summer. Toasted oatmeal with raisins and peanuts were fine, but how would the addition of pecans, wheat germ, and diced apples affect the taste? The timer beeped to announce that the final product was done. They'd let it cool before cutting samples.

"It smells better than cookies out of the oven." Velma couldn't wait to get her hands on it. She'd been upbeat since Esther's arrival a few days ago; the older woman adored the unpretentious girl.

"Have you thought about your major in college, Esther?" Karen removed her oven mitts and tossed them onto the counter.

"I'm going to be a librarian. I love to read and want to be a doorway into the world of books. And I like telling stories; there's no other profession more suitable for me."

"A librarian? Mercy heavens. You'll get awfully lonely. Those places are too darn quiet for my taste." Velma offered an exasperated and curious stare.

"Sharing information and knowledge is important to me. I'm choosing a career that lets me bring books into people's lives." Esther felt strongly about her decision and Velma wasn't going to budge her. "I'd like to get into Penn State."

Velma smiled and pinched Esther's chin, "You, little one, are a very unique child. A bright and wonderful creature, indeed. But you manage to baffle me far too often. Why not a Michigan university?" Velma continued with hands on her hips, "You'll be paying off an out-of-state student loan for a decade."

"I have lots of reasons. Of all the college packets I've read, Penn State beckons to me the most. The Library Science program is a good one and the campus is lovely with several grand libraries. I love American history and on weekends I'd be able to explore the historical East Coast cities, like Philadelphia and Boston, if I lived in University Park. And it's just a one-day drive from Detroit. Besides, I need to get out from under the constant influence of my parents. In Pennsylvania I'll be able to spread my wings and become my own self."

"Go for it, Es. You have the stamina to make it happen." Karen filled the mixing bowls with soap and water and then spun from the sink. "Let's take Esther to your cabin. We haven't inspected the place in months. Who knows—there might be a squirrel family living in the bedroom." She removed her apron, snatched her purse from the shelf near the back door, and wrote a note for John.

Esther slid into the back seat of Karen's sedan, excited to be a part of the capricious outing. Velma rolled down her window until the air blasted across Esther's face and hair. Carrying the scent of wild grasses, moisture from the lake, and laughter from the beach, the warm wind smelled delicious. The drive was just a quick jaunt to Glovers Lake Road, and then east a half mile.

"See that corn over there, Esther. Carl Edmund owns that farm. He inherited it from his father a few years ago. He's quite young, only about twenty-five years old and such a workhorse. If the sun kept itself up, he'd be out in the fields until ten o'clock tonight."

"He's a fine young man but needs to find a nice woman. A man can't keep up that kind of pace without a woman to take care of him, feed him right, and get him into church." Velma believed everyone should be married, and that living life to simply work a job or till the soil was empty without a partner. The car finally turned into the gravel driveway in front of the little cabin. Velma was the first to step out of the car.

"My goodness, the path to the porch is completely overgrown." Velma scanned the cabin and its property with a melancholy eye. She knew she'd never call it home again and it was like seeing a part of her life from a hundred years ago.

As Esther eased into the yard its surrounding scenery flashed around her in dozens of colors that had risen from the past. She pictured how it must have looked years ago with flowers planted in the rock-bordered beds and a garden full of thriving vegetable plants. Rakes would be propped against a tree to rest after having spent hours tidying up the yard. It was still a visual delight today. Velma unlocked the cabin door and beckoned the other two to follow inside. It was musty and stark, tinged with the odor of a long ago fire that had blazed in the hearth. A heavy layer of dust dulled the floor and countertops to a winter gray.

Karen was the first to speak, "Looks pretty much the way we left it, eh Velma? Should we check upstairs?"

Velma hadn't heard the query; her eye was on Esther's reaction to the rustic home. It reminded her of Snow White's response to the dwarves' tiny cottage—curious and charmed. Eminently pleased to see her so delighted, a smile grew on Velma's face.

"I'm nearly speechless, Velma. It's captivating. I was just imagining you here, baking in the kitchen or sweeping the floor. How lucky you were to call this home." Esther stood at the center of the living room, turning around slowly to capture its simple and natural beauty.

The women opened a few cupboard doors to check for mice, then ventured upstairs to see the large bedroom. Again, Esther's response was obviously positive. She loved the idea that the rustic structure served as a permanent residence, and quite easily pictured herself living in such a place surrounded by books and photos of her family and friends.

~~~~~~

Their backs were stiff, arms were aching, and feet were sore from standing all day in the orchard. Seated at the kitchen table, Karen, John, and Esther were eager to dig into the plates of spaghetti, salad, and slices of buttery garlic bread.

"This picking and hauling seems never-ending, and I've just been a part of it for a few days. There were five or six of us loading crates of blueberries onto Ben's truck. And by the time we finished, that entire truck was nearly full. Where do your blueberries go?"

John was glad to describe the berries' journey, "Only about thirty percent gets packaged into pint and quart containers for sale in the grocery stores. Another sixty percent gets processed into pie filling and jam, and about ten percent goes to bakery owners for fresh muffins and donuts. We sell our berries to a wholesaler and he in turn sells the fruit to grocery stores, food processing plants, like Del Monte, and to bakery owners. It's much easier for us to sell the fruit to one company that takes care of all the price negotiating and shipping logistics for us. I just want to grow the fruit."

"Do you like this work? Do you ever regret not staying in Toledo?"

"We're very happy here, Es. The work is strenuous, but only for three months. It's very satisfying, and Arcadia is a fine place." Karen's response was heartfelt.

"I believe that someday I'll live here. There's a pull to this community that won't let me settle anyplace else once I finish school."

Karen replied instantly, "It's good that you can hear your heart's desire. Listen to it but don't fear adjustments to your future plans, either. Life has a way of throwing curve balls before you can get a mitt onto your hand."

~~~~~

"Hi Joseph. How've you been?" Esther sorely missed him.

"You won't believe this. It's way cool. I'm a math tutor for a fifth grader and a sixth grader. I started last week after mom answered two ads at the grocery store. We're mostly working on decimal division and fractions; it feels great to teach. If I ever grow up, I'll be a teacher. "

"Of course you'll grow up, silly. It's fabulous that you're tutoring, Joseph. You have lots of patience. Do you teach at our house or in their homes?"

"The kids ride their bikes here because they live just a half-mile away. We work at the kitchen table and when we're done mom makes a snack. I tutor for thirty minutes and get paid five dollars. Mom has it scheduled so I only do it on Monday, Wednesday, and Friday mornings."

She pictured Joseph guiding a student through a problem-solving process, "I'm happy for you. How're you feeling? Any bad episodes?"

"I've been okay since we got back from vacation. But my pulmonary function test on Tuesday was bad so Dr. Reynolds wants me in for another tune-up at the CF center. Anyway, when you're back home you can meet the kids I'm teaching. I'll put mom on the phone. Bye."

"Hi Es. Are you enjoying Arcadia?"

Her mother was cheerful and Esther felt a small rush of relief. She knew that Joseph's tune-ups would become more frequent, but aside from that, all was well on Lavender Lane.

"I'm very happy here and have so much to tell you when I get back. Karen says she'll call tomorrow morning with my bus number and arrival time. Joseph sounds excited about the tutoring; that was a terrific idea. We're heading out to the market in Frankfort so I gotta run. Give dad a hug!"

Agatha sighed contentedly. It had been a decent week and Ken promised to get home from work early tonight. She went downstairs to find the old Mexican blanket. Snuggling with Ken on the back porch tonight would be a nice beginning to their weekend.

Autumn 1980

Karen hobbled down the stairs while fumbling with her bathrobe tie. The nights had cooled down considerably and she wasn't yet adjusted to the chilly air that billowed throughout the house. A phone in the bedroom would be a great home improvement, especially to receive calls that ring through at five o'clock in the morning. She finally reached the persistent device and feared the worst.

"Hello?"

"Is this Mrs. Holsten at 496 Joyfield Road?"

"Yes it is. Who's calling please?"

"This is Officer Mark MacMillan and I'm calling from the Paul Oliver Memorial Hospital in Frankfort, Ma'am. Are you Velma Johnson's niece?"

"Yes, Sir. Did something happen?"

"We'd like you to come to the hospital as early as possible today. Ms. Johnson passed away sometime during the evening. Her neighbor was in the front yard with his dog two hours ago and noticed her front door open. When he went inside to check on Ms. Johnson, he found her in the living room. We have some questions and a few items to discuss when you can get here. I apologize for waking you at such an early hour Ma'am, and I'm sorry you're hearing this news from a stranger. Can you come to the hospital reasonably soon? Do you have a ride?"

"Yes, officer. My husband and I will get there just as soon as we can. Thank you for contacting me." Karen placed the phone into its cradle with a resonating clunk. The darkness enveloped her as she put her head into her hands. The tiny nightlight in the kitchen illuminated the apple-shaped soap dish and row of glass jars full of dried beans and pasta. Invited by the small beacon, she shuffled to the kitchen table and sat down. The initial shock had left her with a numb sort of sensation; she didn't realize she'd been crying until she felt the tears drip onto the backs of her hands.

It didn't matter that Velma had lived a full eighty-seven years. She was irreplaceable and a one-of-a-kind woman. She'd been a vivacious and loving friend to the very end. Velma and Darren had no children. She nurtured, loved, and tended to so many little ones throughout her life that she more than made up for the fact that she hadn't left behind a son or daughter in this world. Karen wasn't ready to say good-bye. Another dark spot would settle into her heart without Velma in her life.

She put the kettle on the stove to boil water for tea and sat alone for a moment before waking John. She reveled in her memories and released them freely to dance hitherto around the dimly lit kitchen. Aunt Velma was the one who'd taught her to tie her shoes, who gave her the book *Pride and Prejudice* on her fifteenth birthday, who knew John was special before Karen herself knew, and who constantly praised her mothering skills.

When she and John moved to Arcadia back in 1956, Velma asserted that she was doing a fine job of raising Brian. It was Velma who frequently told Karen, "As Brian's mother, as the woman who bore him and tended to his needs as a baby and young child, you know your child better than anyone else. Your instincts are sound and you're doing a great job at listening to them." And this was a piece of advice that Karen cherished and clung to. And Brian had indeed grown into a virtuous young man who had a happy and positive outlook on life. And isn't that what a mother lives to see? *Dear Lord, Thank you for Velma. I pray that she is loved as much in heaven as she was here on earth.*

Staring out the kitchen window blackened by the night, Karen mourned the overwhelming loss as she silently wept over the cup of lukewarm tea.

~~~~~

As Velma's closest surviving relative in Michigan, Karen took charge of the funeral and burial arrangements. She was grateful that Pastor Wrigley had delivered such an eloquent eulogy. Nearly one hundred Arcadia and Frankfort residents paid their respects with heartfelt condolences and lovely flowers. Several members from Velma's family attended the service: Her youngest brother, Clyde, who'd traveled from Canada; his daughter, Marion (from Indiana); and a niece and nephew from southeast Michigan. Karen hadn't realized that Velma had touched so many lives and it eased her pain to be surrounded by others that shared her grief and realized the loss.

After the service, Karen and John welcomed everyone to their home for a buffet lunch and desserts. While the women stayed in the house tasting pastries and softly chatting up current events, John took the men and children outside where they toured the autumn-colored orchard and garden. The children loved the wagon ride behind his old tractor and their laughter brightened the otherwise dreary atmosphere. They were indeed the spoonful of sugar that coated life's bitter pill.

~~~~~~

Before taking a seat at the conference table, Samuel Sturman gestured to the tray holding two brown carafes and several mugs, "Coffee or tea?"

John poured himself a cup and returned to the upholstered chair beside Karen.

"As Velma Johnson's attorney, I called this meeting to read her final Will to you. Besides yourselves, two other individuals will receive a portion of her inheritance. These benefactors reside outside of Michigan; I'll contact them by phone this afternoon. They will each receive a copy of the Will by the end of the week. Additionally, Ms. Johnson left a considerable sum of money to the City of Frankfort for the sole purpose of renovating the library as the City Council and residents deem fit.

Now I'll continue with the portion of the Will as it relates to the two of you."

Mr. Sturman cleared his voice and recited the relevant text of the document, "I, Velma Johnson, being of sound mind and body, do hereby bequeath to Karen Holsten and John Holsten the following items: (1) the legal deed and title to my property at 618 Anchor Drive, Frankfort, Michigan; (2) all furniture, appliances, artwork, books, clothing, and household goods at 618 Anchor Drive; (3) ten percent of the balance on deposit in savings account 34-29877 at 1st National Bank in Frankfort, Michigan."

After describing the probate waiting period, Mr. Sturman gave instructions for procuring the real-estate deed and money from the 1st National Bank in sixty days. He passed the information and manila folder to John, who appeared to be more in tune with the oration. Karen and John then signed several documents to indicate their acceptance of the inheritance, as read by the attorney.

"What will happen to her cabin?" Karen couldn't imagine a stranger living there, or heaven forbid, someone purchasing the property and tearing it down.

"The cabin and its adjacent ten acres were left to a Miss Esther Gardener, who I've just learned is a student at Penn State University. Yesterday, I spoke with Miss Gardener's parents in Detroit about the inheritance."

"Praise the Lord!" Karen shot up from her seat, "Velma you are indeed a woman of wisdom." She reached over to John and hugged him tightly.

Autumn ~ Winter 1980

Leaning over a stack of books that belonged in the Schreyer business section, she grabbed the ringing telephone. "Pattee Library at Penn State, Esther speaking."

"Esther! You need to come home, pronto. There's a lawyer looking for you. What's going on?"

Esther held the phone away from her ear and stared at it in disbelief. She was an outstanding citizen, held a 3.7 grade-point average, and had yet to exceed the maximum speed limit while driving her Toyota. She'd never been in trouble and personally knew only three lawyers on a first name basis: her father and his two colleagues who practiced corporate and patent law.

"I dunno. I'll ask Mr. Brockman to let me out of here for an hour. I'll be there as soon as I can, Kelly." *Dear Lord, Please let Joseph be okay. Please let my parents be okay. Please let my friends be okay. I'm sorry for missing a lot of church lately, but I am scared now and need you. Amen.*

Esther dropped her bike at the Thompson Hall dormitory entrance and soared to the third floor. She was glad there hadn't been snow on the ground yet or she would've had to run home in her boots. Out of breath, she opened the door with a gasp.

Kelly waved a piece of paper with Samuel Sturman's phone number on it. "Call this guy. My partner will totally kill me but I'm skipping lab; I gotta know what this is about."

A demand from her tall and muscular roommate was not to be ignored. Kelly had been a basketball star in high school and was the toughest woman Esther had ever encountered. However, between her pair of burly shoulders beat a heart of pure gold. Kelly had grown up the only girl among four brothers and she wasn't easily intimidated. But she'd give you her last piece of Dentyne and sturdy shoulder to cry on in a heartbeat. There was one absolute truth that Esther had learned during her freshman year in college: never, ever judge a book by its cover. Kelly was a sweet girl living in the body of an athletic dynamo.

She nervously dialed the phone number and was greeted by a prim receptionist. "This is Esther Gardener; I'm returning Mr. Sturman's call."

"One moment, Ma'am. I'll put you through."

"Sam Sturman speaking."

"I'm Esther Gardener, Sir. Is there something wrong?"

"Good afternoon, Miss Gardener. On the contrary. I have good news to convey. Are you sitting down?"

"Yes, Sir."

"I understand that you were a dear friend of Mrs. Velma Johnson."

"Yes, and I was very upset when she passed away last month. She was an incredible woman; I wasn't able to attend the funeral service." Her eyes brimmed with tears at the thought of never baking granola with Velma again. She squeezed her eyes shut to squelch the tears and dispel the oatmeal and raisin aroma that had somehow traveled from her mind to her nose.

"Indeed, she was. Did you know she had a cabin on ten acres of property in Arcadia, Michigan?"

"Yes, Sir. Great place."

"Mrs. Johnson left that cabin and land to you in her Will. As soon as you can get to Frankfort to sign the necessary paperwork, the cabin is yours. I spoke with your mother yesterday and mailed a copy of Mrs. Johnson's Will to both of you; yours should arrive later this week. Your mother insisted I speak to you directly to convey the news."

"Are you serious, Mr. Sturman?"

"A hundred percent serious, Miss Gardener. When you can arrange a trip to Michigan, please call my office to set an appointment for signing the necessary transfer documents. Read the items that I sent and don't hesitate to call if you have any questions."

"Yes, Sir. I'll do that, thank you very much." She was stunned. Kelly grabbed Esther's arms and shook the facts from her.

"In a nutshell I just inherited a cabin on ten acres in Arcadia." Esther felt dizzy with shock as the reality of what just occurred sunk in.

"Whaddya?"

"A cabin in Arcadia, Michigan."

"Isn't that the lake place where your friend Karen lives?"

"Yup. And her Aunt Velma lived there too. Remember my bawling all over everyone about the woman who died last month? She left her cabin and ten acres to me in her Will."

"That is very, very cool Es. Sell it and you'll make a nice chunk of change. Then you can pay off your student loans and write a check for your last two years of school. You'll be able to start your post-college life debt free. This is so awesome."

"I'm not selling the cabin. I'm gonna live there."

Kelly hoisted up her backpack, shoved a textbook inside, and led the way out of the dorm room. "I'll walk back to the library with you. We need to talk."

The stroll down Frasier Road provided sufficient time for a cool-down and return to sensibilities. "Esther, my girl, you cannot live in a cabin in the middle of nowhere. If you don't want to sell it, that's fine. Take vacations up there, throw parties, and enjoy the lake on weekends. That's all peachy. But you're not living in Nowhereville. There are no men up there. If you stay in Arcadia you'll never have babies and you'll be the old woman who sketches seagulls on driftwood. I can picture you in a cabin forty years from now with nothing but perfectly groomed flowerbeds and a pair of hound dogs for company."

Esther stopped to set her hands on her hips and look sternly at her roommate, "This is in the Lord's hands, Kelly. It literally dropped out of the sky and thwacked me on the head. If this isn't somehow part of my destiny, then I don't know what is. When I graduate, I'm moving to Arcadia."

~~~~~~

"I'm good with *Canterbury Tales*. I can write an entire paper on why I prefer the Funk & Wagnall's dictionary to Webster's. Quote me a line from a Shakespearean work and I'll tell you who said it and the play it's from. But I cannot for the life of me get through this physics class without tons of studying every night." Esther was frustrated because she was struggling to maintain a seventy-seven percent average in the class. She hoped she could do an extra credit assignment to boost her grade up a few points.

"Sweetie Pie, look at you. You are a bookworm who's unrecognizable without a novel in your hand or textbook under your nose. You're a literary scholar and you're only a sophomore. This physics course simply rounds you out and expands your knowledge base. You don't have to ace it." Barry sympathized because he barely tolerated his World Literature course. An engineering student who spoke the languages of math, physics, and electronic circuitry, Barry was a good-looking geek who had an undeniably strong crush on Esther Gardener.

He'd just spent a half-hour explaining the inverse square law, using planetary orbits as an example. The orbits of the planets must be ellipses because gravity follows the inverse square law. If gravity depended on R^3 or R^4 or any power other than 2, the orbits of the planets would not be ellipses. It was as simple as that. But poor Esther was befuddled.

"Come sit with me."

She scooted closer to him and snuggled beneath his arm. She was dog-tired. But Barry had other plans and gently grazed his fingertips along her arms before dabbling her throat with kisses. He brushed his lips against hers in a gentle whisper. She gave in to the kiss while it grew deep and warm; he pulled her legs onto the couch and aligned their bodies. With hands gliding beneath her sweater, he continued to press alluring kisses along her cheeks and forehead. "I need you tonight, Es."

She bolted upright and swung her feet hard onto the floor. "You'd better get back to your place. It's late and I've got a rough day tomorrow." She saw the chagrin in his eyes and felt angry with herself for leading him on.

"Please let me stay, Es. You know that Kelly and Tom won't be back until at least eleven o'clock. Who are you waiting for?"

"A long time ago I made a promise to myself and to my future husband, whomever that will be, to remain a virgin until our wedding night. You're a wonderful man and a dear friend, but I'm not doing the casual sex thing. Please accept that."

"I won't push you into something we might regret in the morning. And getting married while we're both still in college is a bad idea." He scooped his book off the couch and pulled her up to him. They exchanged a fervent kiss before he departed for his apartment on Allen Street.

~~~~~~

"How's school, honey?" Agatha had rehearsed the discussion in her mind before placing the call; she felt certain her voice was calm and steady.

"It's okay. Physics is a real nightmare but I'm fine otherwise. Is everything okay, Mom? You sound upset."

"Well, we're pretty well settled down now. Joseph had to be hospitalized for nine days. He's stable and at home today, but the prognosis isn't one that I'd choose. The bronchiectasis is wearing him down. The walls of his bronchial tubes are weakening, which makes it real tough for him to clear his airways. The hemoptysis is chronic at this point, and the doctors are worried about his heart as well. We're taking him back to the hospital tomorrow where the pulmonary surgeon will examine him. I just wanted to fill you in on what's happening. Joseph might be weak when you're here for Thanksgiving, so this is a heads up, I suppose."

"Thanks for calling, Mom. Don't hesitate to call any time if you need me there, and please keep me apprised of his status; I want to know what's going on." Esther held back the tears that would fall when she hung up the phone. Tears for Joseph seemed to be a constant in her life lately.

"All right. I have to run. You won't believe who's stopping by for coffee this afternoon."

"I give up, Mom."

"Do you remember Nurse Constance? I happened to see her at the hospital the other day and invited her over on a whim. She's retired now and does volunteer work at the hospital. She asked about you and I told her you were in college; she just couldn't believe it."

"That's so cool—tell her I said 'hello', okay? And give Joseph a giant hug for me."

She paused for a moment to study the dorm room. Desks, a bulletin board, untidy beds, a small refrigerator, stacks of books, and posters of wildflowers. Her life continued on a normal course. Friends to enjoy, professors to loathe, books to read, and guys to kiss. But a few hundred miles away, Joseph's life was fading without hope for full recovery. The final months or years of his life might entail much sickness and suffering. She hated that. *Dear Lord, Let him breathe without pain today.*

She needed some cheering up before heading to class so phoned her number-one stabilizer. "Hi Karen, how've you been? Any snow there yet?"

"Hi! It's nice to hear your voice, Es. We're fine. We have a little bit of snow but not enough yet to get the plows running full time. How are you?"

"I'm okay and school is going well, for the most part. Joseph has been sick though and it's so hard to know that he's suffering without me there. I should postpone my degree and be home with my family. They need me now."

"Esther, I understand that you're feeling guilty. You're healthy, attending a fine college, and living a full and busy life. You're doing what you are supposed to. But from what I've gathered during the time I've spent with Joseph, I don't think he'd want you to put your life on hold. Your parents are there and he's got fine doctors in Detroit."

"It's so hard to live here while he needs comfort and support in Michigan. And I can give him those things better than anyone else."

"Honey, I certainly can't tell you what to do. This is something you pray about and you follow your heart. The answer will come so keep your mind open and hang onto that mitt for oncoming curve balls. Have you set a meeting with Mr. Sturman yet? You could come to Arcadia during Christmas break."

"Will you be home the weekend after Christmas?"

"Absolutely. Call when you know what day you're coming. I'll make some goodies, and perhaps bake a blueberry pie as well; we still have a few pounds of frozen berries left."

"Love you, Karen."

"I love you too, sweetie."

~~~~~~

Without her jacket, Esther crept slowly down the steps until she reached the main floor of the building. With teeth grinding and muscles tense, she angrily pushed open the door to burst into the cold and damp air outside. She was livid, frightened, lonely, and felt absolutely helpless about the disease that was literally strangling her brother to death. Inheriting the cabin was wonderful news, but Joseph was sick. Good fortune had fallen onto her lap, but in this instance she wanted nothing to do with it. She'd trade everything in her possession to give him just one week of life with pain-free breathing. It just wasn't fair.

The psalm she'd been reciting lately no longer eased her anxiety; she felt spiritually distressed. *The Lord will cover you with his feathers, and under his wings you will find refuge; his faithfulness will be your shield and rampart.* The rush of unabashed fury had consumed her clarity. And she wanted to cling to it now and scream in anguish because it felt good.

Wearing just a t-shirt and jeans in the cold wind she stood motionless. Her teeth chattered, goose bumps covered her skin, and her feet ached from the icy sidewalk. *Give the pain to me. It's my turn.* After nearly thirty minutes, she could no longer bear the frigid November air and traipsed back up to the dorm room to prepare for class. The anger had numbed the pain in her heart only temporarily. It'd be back.

~~~~~~

"You shouldn't display yourself like that, Heather. You're attractive enough without exposing so much skin. It's nearly winter for goodness sakes. Wear a sweater."

"Get over it, Esther. I'm twenty years old and there are a lot of fine men out there. Eric will be at this party tonight and I intend to get his attention. He's someone I want to spend some serious time with, if you know what I mean." Heather fluffed and teased her hair until her face appeared miniature beneath it. She then spritzed the coif full of hairspray.

"You should get to know him. I've got some questions that I personally don't want answered, but you need to think about them. Of the guys you've been with, how many of their middle names did you know? Does Eric have a brother or sister? Or a favorite holiday? Or a favorite ice cream flavor? It's my opinion that you're selling yourself short." Esther knew she was risking their friendship by digging into Heather's conscience without permission but she wanted her to ponder the consequences of her vicarious lifestyle.

"How you spend your Saturday nights is your business. If you're content with fuzzy slippers and a fat novel, then I'm happy for you. We're different women, Es. I came here to use your hair dryer, not for a lecture on morality. I happen to like men and a night of good sex makes my troubles disappear for a while. Have a great evening." She sashayed over the threshold and out into the world of beer parties and promiscuity without looking back.

Esther flopped onto the couch and reviewed her evening plans, realizing immediately that she had none. *I probably need to do something other than read tonight.* Kelly and Tom were at the movies. Many students were already celebrating the upcoming Thanksgiving holiday, despite the fact that it was a week away. She could walk to Barry's place tonight, although the students there were pretty rowdy; probably because the apartment complex was full of seniors. The decent parties typically offered gigantic bowls full of junk food, which sounded good tonight because her refrigerator was basically empty. *Take a chance.*

Esther had no trouble finding the party; the screeching music was literally shaking the Allen Street sidewalk. She was dressed down tonight in her favorite Levi jeans, bulky pink sweater, and Nike running shoes. She dabbed just a bit of blush onto her cheeks and left her hair to do its own thing. She hadn't been to a salon for a haircut in ages; her hair now fell down to the middle of her back and its natural texture and color were the envy of many women on campus.

Meandering around the building to find Barry or another familiar face, she finally encountered a group of people she knew.

"Hey, Es. Good to see you." Melissa held a beer in her right hand and clung to Greg's arm with her left. They'd obviously been imbibing. "Everything is up on the second floor, and I think Barry is there, too. See you later."

Esther wove through the packs of students hanging around the common area. She hiked up the steps and into the frenzy of loud music and partying students. *I'm a chipmunk in a monkey house; I don't belong here, except that I'm too hungry to leave. And tonight I'm going to fit in and have a little bit of fun. Where's Barry?* Approaching the apartment most likely to offer a decent banquet of junk food, she repressed the pulse of regret as she entered the room and stepped over the pile of shoes kicked off by fellow partiers.

A plate full of Cheese Whiz on crackers and one rum drink later, she had relaxed enough to blend into the atmosphere and connect with the sagacious students on the couch; their debate was captivating.

A group of engineer types exchanged thoughts on George Orwell's *1984*. "The Party oppresses the people and lies to them, just like the totalitarian governments of Orwell's time. I think he wrote the book to warn future generations what the world might be like if that kind of a government isn't opposed."

"The government would have to station police at every corner and install a camera in every house. It's just not feasible,

Mike. This country is huge. And what about the zillion acres of farmland in Kansas and Iowa? They couldn't police that territory."

"The government will soon be able to track your purchasing activities with a credit card number, and that tells them where you are, knucklehead. It's only the beginning."

She hadn't found Barry two hours later so Esther decided it was time to leave. The evening had cooled down considerably and she hugged herself while stepping out to start the long walk back home. She was pleased at having survived the excursion; the party hadn't been so bad and she'd met some interesting people tonight. But it was getting late and she liked to be in her pajamas by eleven o'clock, which meant she had to hustle. She was unaware of the student who'd followed her from the apartment.

"Hey, pretty girl. Where you going in such a hurry?"

"I'm heading back to my place. It's late and I've got a busy day tomorrow." Esther stopped in mid-stride and nervously eyed the large student.

The stranger linked his arm around hers and pulled her close, "I'm Joe. What's your name?"

"Esther. It's nice to meet you but I need to head home. Perhaps I'll see you again sometime. Do you live on Allen?"

"That's an odd name. You smell nice and you have a very pretty voice." Joe effortlessly led her off the sidewalk and into a dark parking lot. He probably outweighed her by ninety pounds and had a good grip on her.

She became a single-minded woman. *I'm going to kick you in the crotch and run like lightening, you scumbag.*

"I don't live in this direction, Joe." She peered up at him with a dose of doe eyes and delicately licked her upper lip. He relaxed his grip—just enough.

CRUNCH. He dropped to his knees, moaning.

Esther ran from her antagonist so quickly that she didn't see the couple on the sidewalk until it was too late. She rammed into the guy with the force of a linebacker. The impact lifted both of them into the air and then down onto their backs with a painful thud. She lay dazed for a moment on the grass.

The girl who'd witnessed the accident screamed, "Oh my gosh! Daniel, are you all right?"

The tackled student shook his head, squatted onto his knees and tapped Esther's shoulder. "Hello? Are you hurt?" He rubbed his shoulder as he leaned over to inspect the little runner. An odd emotion flickered through his chest as he sought out her eyes and then very nearly touched her cheek with his fingertips.

Stunned but uninjured, Esther shifted her eyes to his face. Her throat tightened to catch her voice as she met his blue eyes. She slid her gaze to his finely chiseled lips and drew a timid breath. *I'll never see a more handsome man as long as I live.*

"Um. I'm okay. I was running from a bad guy. Sorry about hitting you like that." Esther sat up slowly and brushed the leaves from her hair and sweater.

Daniel extended his hand to pull Esther onto her feet. "Do you want us to walk you home?"

Before she could place her hand into his, the other girl interrupted, "She doesn't need any help. C'mon, let's go." The girl pulled Daniel's arm and hurriedly led him away from the accident.

Esther stood motionless on the sidewalk as she watched the couple stroll away. His eyes had nearly stopped her heart a moment ago, but now it pounded furiously. He was breathtaking and her reaction to his gaze had turned her knees to Jell-O. Definitely red Jell-O because she was on fire. *Will I ever see you again, Daniel?*

Winter 1980

Facing the Environmental Control Systems class at eight o'clock in the morning was brutal. Daniel wondered sometimes whether Professor Nichols intentionally scheduled it at such an early hour to bruise the egos of his cocky Arch students. He saved a good chunk of money each month sharing an apartment a half-mile from the engineering building. Now he realized that his choice of residency last August lacked foresight. The winter sidewalks were riddled with deadly ice patches and navigating in the dark at 7:40 in the morning required a bit of guts. And to add insult to injury he'd left his gloves in the model shop yesterday. Landing a job with a design firm in Texas was a pleasant thought. Daniel made a solemn pact with himself that no person and no amount of money would keep him north of Kentucky once he graduated. He could intern and take the AIA exams anywhere. *Could I convince Mitch to move to Texas? Probably not.*

Trekking through the snow had its advantages, however. To keep his mind off the crushing pain in his lungs caused by the icy air he was breathing, Daniel let his thoughts wander into crevices he hadn't explored lately. He had to call Dennis. Mom mentioned that he'd been showing obvious signs of stress lately. Marijuana was a common sight on college campuses these days and he sorely hoped Dennis hadn't been tempted. And Amy was sixteen years old already. Good grief. His baby sister would actually be able to drive to Pennsylvania in a few months to visit, not that he'd approve of such a trip, but it nevertheless boggled his mind. And what about Kim? Did he love her? She was beautiful and had certainly broadened his sexual knowledge, but the relationship was lacking something.

The final three semesters of his education would start next month and he was eager to begin the race down the home stretch of his collegiate life. During the past month, Daniel made acquaintance with two of his future professors. He browsed through the *Principles of Construction Technology* text and wasn't intimidated by its contents. He looked forward to delving into the study of thermal performance, movement tolerances, weatherproofing, construction sequence, constraints of fabrication, and construction detailing. And learning to integrate mechanical, water, and electrical services within structures wouldn't be a struggle.

But he was anxious about his fifth year research paper; more specifically, he wasn't confident that his topic would be approved. He'd heard about green architecture from a visiting speaker and it struck a chord with him. Other students steered clear of such emergent topics because they lacked sufficient data and were prohibitive of in-depth research. That's precisely why he was attracted to it. He wanted to strike out in his own direction, and the goal of his paper would be to provide guidance for architects interested in designing structures that exist harmoniously with nature. Daniel would have to explore the influence of ecology on design philosophy and expression. To write such a leading edge paper would be extremely time consuming.

Plodding up the steps of the engineering building, he switched mental gears into data-absorption mode and hoped that note taking wouldn't be necessary for at least the first ten minutes of class. His darn fingers were numb from frostbite.

~~~~~~

Daniel had been enthusiastically welcomed to the Penn State track team in 1977. (During his senior year in high school he jumped fourteen-feet-six inches—a very respectable height.) Many college track coaches knew little about the pole vault and Coach Newman was pleased to meet Daniel three Septembers ago. At that time, the university's track team carried three vaulters; an athlete by the name of Don was their lead jumper.

Before graduating from Penn State in 1979, Don had jumped seventeen feet. Daniel proved himself worthy of a half-tuition scholarship by jumping sixteen feet twice and consistently earning points in key track meets that same year. He hoped to prove himself worthy of a full scholarship by jumping seventeen feet during the spring 1981 season. Hurling his body over a crossbar set at that height wouldn't come easy; it'd entail many hours of running, weight-lifting, pole-carry drills, and regular practices.

The air that circulated through the field house on this particular night was dry enough to scare away an iguana, but it beat pole-vaulting in the snow. Once again, the track team carried three vaulters. After clearing sixteen-feet-six inches in a meet last spring, Daniel was the leader. Vince was always good for fifteen-six and Mike was consistent at fifteen. The first 1981 indoor meet was scheduled for January 11th—less than four weeks away—and the guys were anxious to establish their marks. Daniel wanted to raise his grip a few inches on the pole today but was having trouble with his take-off step, due in most part to a foursome of loud and lanky guys on the basketball team.

To say that the basketball players and pole-vaulters didn't play well together would be a gross understatement. Daniel was a calm and rational young man until someone interfered with a jumping practice. Then those personality traits vanished into oblivion.

"The coach said we get the place on Tuesday and Thursday nights. We're not putting our gear away, Humphrey."

A pass was missed and the basketball bounced toward the vaulters; the ball players were obviously looking for trouble.

"If that basketball crosses this runway again it will give me great pleasure to shove this pole into your body and hang you from this ceiling. You guys are not supposed to be out here!" Vince didn't respond well to an interrupted practice, either.

As Daniel sat on the pit after bailing out of his jump, Vince hollered the same words of advice for the second time, "You're starting out too fast. Keep those first steps a little shorter, Dan."

Daniel returned to his starting point and stared to the end of his fiberglass pole. He then focused on the box at the end of the runway beneath the crossbar set at sixteen-feet-three inches.

He had to run tall, accelerate at the first mark, shift and plant the pole smoothly, stay tall, press forward, keep his trail leg long through the bottom, swing with the recoiling pole, and let his body strength and the laws of physics launch him over the bar. If his take-off step was right he'd clear it tonight.

One, two, three, go! Run, shift, plant, swing, up, pike, over, flop. Made it! Daniel let out a whoop and the guys cheered. They had just one more practice before Christmas break next week so it was imperative that their run rhythm and take-offs were precise.

Humphrey sauntered over to the pole-vault runway to stand beside the pit. He looked up to the crossbar then smiled at the vaulters, "That's cool, man." Dribbling the basketball back to the locker room, Humphrey flashed a peace sign to the vaulters.

Daniel grimaced and rubbed his shoulder before jumping off the pit. It was still sore from the little runner who had tackled him on Allen Street last month. By eight o'clock, the vaulters had each taken a dozen jumps. After putting the poles away, they jogged a half-mile around the track before heading back to the apartment for a shower and cold beer.

~~~~~~

Apparently eleven o'clock in the morning was early and Dennis wasn't wearing a happy face when he picked up the phone, "Hello!?"

"Hey Den, just calling to see what's up these days. How's the first semester winding down?"

"Oh hey. It ain't easy. I didn't think my freshman courses would be this tough. Chemistry is killing me; the professor is flying through the material before I can get a handle on it. And the lab work is absolutely neck breaking. I've wondered lately whether carpentry is my true calling."

"My freshman year was rough too; the dorms were barbarous and definitely not conducive to studying. Living at home is a huge advantage because you're sleeping well and able to study in a quiet environment. Cut yourself some slack once in a while because the mental breaks will do you good. Don't give up on your dream yet, okay? Stick it out for at least another two years because you might find yourself with some mental momentum by then."

"College might not be in my future, actually. I'm glad you called. I need to lay something down that's real heavy. Promise me you'll remain calm because I need someone thoughtful and intelligent right now. Are you with me?"

"Good grief man, spit it out."

"Do you remember Marcy, the girl I met at the football game in September? She's very sweet and pretty. We went to a few parties together and hit it off right away." Dennis was stuttering.

"Vaguely. I think you mentioned her the last time you called. What about her?"

"She's pregnant."

Daniel ran his fingers through his hair and swallowed hard. *Becoming a father at the age of nineteen is a rough way to start out in life.* "Has she seen a doctor? Does she have a due date?"

"She took a pregnancy test at the clinic last week; no due date was mentioned because Marcy hasn't decided whether she's keeping the baby yet." Dennis sighed heavily.

"Well, adoption is a great choice."

"There are actually three choices, and Marcy is struggling to make the one that's best for both of us: keep the baby, give it up for adoption, or terminate the pregnancy. She set a date for an abortion procedure in the event she chooses to terminate. It would happen on Friday, only six days from now. If she decides to keep the baby, that means I find a job somewhere to take care of a wife and baby. I won't let her raise the child alone."

"Has she totally ruled out adoption?" Daniel's heart pounded full of worry.

"We talked about it. She doesn't want to go through the hassle of pregnancy and childbirth, and then give up the baby. Marcy insisted it would be too traumatic." Dennis closed his eyes in anguish.

"Too traumatic? I may be overstepping the line when I say what I'm about to say, but you're gonna hear it." Daniel inhaled deeply and continued, "She can't end the baby's life because it doesn't fit into a schedule. The child was conceived in love and you're both healthy adults. If Marcy had been brutally raped, then I might understand the choice to terminate. And I'm pro choice when a child has a debilitating birth defect that would cause a lifetime of extreme pain and suffering. But not a baby that's likely to be healthy. Does anyone else know about this?"

"Nope. Just the three of us. She hasn't even told her roommate."

Daniel shuddered in fear, "Might you convince her to confide in her parents? She needs love and guidance to survive the week and make a good decision. Offer to go with her to see her folks, Dennis. Where do they live?"

"Over in Bloomington. That's where she grew up." Full of despair, Dennis sprawled back into his chair.

"That's not far. If Marcy decides to keep the baby or chooses adoption, then you'll want to meet her folks because you're in this together. Facing her mom and dad will be gut wrenching, I can promise you that, but Marcy will need everyone's support to get through the pregnancy." Daniel turned his eyes to the window and continued, "Personally, I hope that adoption is her choice; you're both too young to be raising a child. Give this baby a chance at life, Dennis. Thousands of childless couples want a baby."

"Okay. You've made your point. It certainly doesn't erase my panic and I know Marcy will continue walking around campus like a zombie until this is resolved. She needs to talk to someone else, but won't confide in her parents. I'm spending the afternoon with her and hope to cheer her up some. If she decides to continue with the pregnancy, then she'll probably tell her folks when she's in Bloomington next week during Christmas break. If she terminates it, well, that's a secret the three of us will share forever."

"Focus on making the right decision and not on what's most convenient. Your best bet is to love her and spend lots of time together this week. You two created a life at an inconvenient time and that's the bottom line here, Dennis. Maybe you should arrange a visit with Pastor Coleman and get his advice."

"When will you be in Chicago?"

"I'll be there from the 22nd through the 28th; I need a few days back at school after Christmas to finish my term paper. The driving eats up two days, so I have to limit the visit to six days. Do you know when grandpa will be in Chicago that week?"

"No, but mom knows for sure. She and dad are at a council meeting at church; they should be back around one o'clock. Do you want mom to call you?"

"Nah, I'll get a hold of her tonight. What's Amy up to?"

"She's making great grades but can't drive and dad says she's a Mr. Magoo. Apparently, Amy changes lanes without looking and can't figure out how to make a left turn. You should see dad's face when they walk through the door after he drives with her for a half hour; it's aged him a good ten years. It may take her six months to get a license at this rate." Dennis was chuckling now.

"Maybe I'll take her driving while I'm there." Daniel was serious; he'd be more than happy to replenish his dad's lifespan by taking the passenger seat with Amy once or twice. "I have to finish my Mamluk report; it's due in two days. Good luck, Dennis. Be sure to pray with Marcy when you see her. Call me anytime."

"I'm sorry about this and I know you're gonna fret over it. Thanks for not blowing a stack."

"A tirade over the telephone wouldn't have fixed a thing. Hang in there."

~~~~~~

Model building was intense for many architectural students, but Daniel worked on his project effortlessly in the noisy model shop. As a sophomore two years ago, the machinery had been intimidating. There were planers, table saws, band saws, miter saws, drill presses, lathes, a spindle sander, finishing machines, and more. He was grateful that the shop supervisors had been so patient while he learned to use the equipment. Tonight the sounds and smells were comforting and dispelled the troubles from his mind. He liked taking his paper designs to three dimensions and exploring the buildings in-depth.

This semester's assignment was to design and build a contoured site model for a Napa Valley winery. He drew the structure to include a three-hundred tonnes winery, a barrel store, three public tasting areas and a restaurant. Daniel chose colorbond steel and jarrah eucalyptus as the external building materials to enhance the structure's setting in a forest location. Once he assembled the wooden model, he'd paint it using colors to reflect his choices of dark blue steel and jarrah.

He checked the wall clock after cutting and sanding the structure's sections. The shop was closing in ten minutes so gluing and painting would have to wait until tomorrow night. Then he'd model the landscape surrounding the winery. He figured to be done by Thursday or Friday. While putting his project tray into the storage area he was rushed with a peaceful sensation and fondly recalled the skyscraper models that his dad kept stored away in the basement on Pine Haven Road. *Time flies. In two years I'll be halfway through the mentor program and taking AIA exams. In three years, I'll be designing elements for the architectural face of our country.*

~~~~~~

Ron pounded on the bathroom door to interrupt a perfectly good shower, "Dennis is on the phone!"

As he wrapped a towel around himself, Daniel desperately hoped for good news.

"She's going to the clinic on Friday. She won't tell her parents and there's nothing I can do or say to change her mind. Pastor Coleman said we can't tie her down for seven months. He's willing to talk with her anywhere and anytime, but she's got to make the choice to see him." Dennis was distraught.

"Today is only Tuesday. A lot can happen in three days.

Let's put this dilemma into God's hands." Emotionally drained from trying to come up with a solution on his own, Daniel realized now that they should've set the problem onto a larger pair of shoulders days ago.

"I dunno. She's mentally locked into terminating the pregnancy. And that's her choice. It really isn't ours to make. If she chooses adoption, she's the one who will endure the physical pain and discomfort of the pregnancy, she's the one who'll be gawked at by other students, and she's the one who'll have to emotionally break away from the baby. And then she'll have to spend the summer recuperating from both the birth and loss of the child. I love Marcy and will accept whatever decision she makes."

"Then I'll pray that the child's spirit will somehow speak to her conscience. Call me if you need to talk this week; I'll be here every evening." After hanging up the phone, Daniel stood in silence feeling utterly helpless while water dripped from his legs onto the kitchen floor. He shuddered then, not from his nakedness, but by a disturbing thought instead. *When a woman has an abortion does she ever forget about the child who might've been?*

~~~~~~

The promise of a white Christmas put smiles onto the faces of even the grinchiest Chicago residents. A four-inch snowfall was expected overnight, just three days away from the holiday. Amy was ice skating with her girlfriends; grandpa was reading in the den; and mom, dad, Dennis, and Marcy were seated around the breakfast table in the kitchen. The traditional holiday scents of pine and cinnamon filled the house but the mood was somber. Marcy clutched a tissue box on her lap; its contents nearly empty now. Dennis' arm was protectively draped across the back of her chair to provide a warm touch of comfort.

Marcy was spending a day and night with the Jacobson family before traveling to Bloomington for Christmas. She hadn't followed through with the abortion; a string of divine dreams had stopped her. The due date was June 7th. If the baby arrived as scheduled, she'd complete her first full year of college at Northwestern, deliver at Evanston Hospital, and place the baby into the arms of a woman who'd been wanting a child forever. Marcy had a strong stubborn streak and refused to give up her studies. Thus, as her belly grew during the next six months, she'd simply sit sideways in the student desks. And she'd schedule prenatal doctor visits around her coursework.

On the day that Marcy and Dennis drove past the clinic without stopping, he made a promise that her needs would supersede everything until the baby was born. Dennis made arrangements to meet Marcy's family in Bloomington the day after Christmas. He wasn't proud of their predicament but was willing to face the consequences and stand firmly beside the woman who carried his child.

"Hey everyone." Daniel waltzed into the house with gift bags and a brown woolen scarf wound around his neck. His younger brother met his stare with grateful eyes. Daniel set the packages down and walked around the table to distribute handshakes and hugs to his parents. He then sat beside Marcy and clutched her frightened hand. "I'm very pleased to meet you. It takes an incredibly brave and unselfish young woman to carry her baby knowing she'll say good-bye. If there's anything I can do to help, please let me know."

"Thank you. Dennis will help me through this." She leaned into Dennis and linked her arm into his. She was indeed a very pretty girl, probably Scandinavian descent, with proud cheekbones and a slender build. Daniel smiled to himself as he briefly envisioned what the baby might look like; the facial features of Dennis and Marcy were like night and day, and their combination would be quite interesting.

"Who's up for egg nog?" Sandra was still overwhelmed, but with her eldest son home a wave of anxiety evaporated. John stood from the table to reassure his wife with an embrace that the dilemma just thrown onto their laps could be managed.

"Please pour some for me, Mom." Daniel strode down the hallway to find his grandpa in the den.

"Hey—good to see you. Still interested in a quick trip downtown before the snow comes tonight? I left early from Austin's place in Columbus so we'd have a decent chunk of time before dark. We can grab a beer someplace."

"Absolutely. Let's ask the others if they'd like to tag along after our round of egg nog." Grandpa proudly patted his grandson's shoulder and followed him into the kitchen. John and Sandra chose to remain home so that Amy wouldn't return to an empty house after skating. Dennis and Marcy agreed to join the downtown excursion.

~~~~~

The foursome splurged on milkshakes, beer, and an assortment of light appetizers at Bergman's Restaurant.

"I can't get enough of the Chicago skyline. It's breathtaking to ponder the architectural phenomena of this city. It is far more than structure and construction; the color palette of the buildings and sky is exquisite as well. And the more I learn each semester, the more I can appreciate this grand city."

Dennis couldn't relate to his brother's uninhibited adoration of the buildings that appeared through the window of the restaurant; they were merely concrete and steel in his mind. "Sorry, Marcy. Daniel morphs into a driveling poet when he ventures into the city."

"Do you see yourself designing such a building someday, Daniel?" His grandpa was eager to hear Daniel's thoughts.

"I must earn the right to design something like this. I want to build well, create superb detail, and choose the best materials for the structure and its environment. It's not about magnitude alone; an architect must realize his responsibility for quality and weathering. The design must be visually appealing for a hundred years or more." Daniel smiled at his grandpa because he knew the older man understood.

"It's wonderful to have such a passion. My dream is to teach and ignite a fire in children's hearts that instills a desire for knowledge." Marcy finished her strawberry shake with a slurp.

She took delight in the loquacious Jacobson men and was glad she had accepted Dennis' invitation to stay with his family in lieu of her nearly empty dormitory tonight.

"Hold on tight to your dreams, Marcy. The next few months will be more challenging than you can imagine. Remember there will be professors, counselors, and family to help when you're feeling overwhelmed. Stay on your path and don't let anything deter you." Daniel gave Marcy a reassuring smile. Ever positive Daniel. The world needed more of his kind.

Grandpa rose from the bench to pull his coat and scarf around his shoulders. "I promised your parents we'd be home by six o'clock so we need to head out of here. I hope you're a Parcheesi player, Marcy. During Christmas season at the Jacobson household it's all about board games and popcorn, ain't that right fellas?" He winked at Dennis.

"Count me in." Marcy giggled and wrapped her arms around Dennis. The affectionate embrace caused a blush to rise on his cheeks.

~~~~~~

Four inches of snow were predicted, but when residents across Chicago opened the window shades their sleepy eyes blinked at eight. It appeared that a giant from another world had dropped a fluffy blanket across Pine Haven Road. The snow made the lawns, curbs, and road appear as a single, hilly layer. There were no visible sidewalks and the small shrubs were buried this morning. Kids squealed and parents groaned. Regardless of whether or not the Christmas shopping was done, a trip to the mall was out of the question today. And Marcy's drive down to Bloomington would have to wait until tomorrow.

"I can't take you driving today Amy, so let's make a snowman after breakfast." Daniel found a carrot in the refrigerator to use for its nose and then rummaged through the garage until he unearthed two pieces of charcoal so the fellow would have eyes.

"I haven't made a snowman in years." Amy was stirring a large pot of oatmeal on the stove. "Are you gonna help,

Dennis?" She found the box of brown sugar behind the cornstarch in the cupboard and set it onto the table. Amy was the early bird of the family and had showered, applied make-up, and styled her hair before everyone else finished their first cup of coffee. She was an efficient master of multi-tasking. It was no surprise that she was student council VP, a yearbook photographer, played first base on the girls' softball team, and was a member of the French Club.

"Yeah, I'm in. Let's get the stepladder and make a nine-foot guy today."

"Who's making a giant snowman?" John peered into the kitchen at the scheming kids and Sandra followed closely behind in her bathrobe.

"Morning. We're building a real monster. I found a carrot and charcoal. Do you have an extra big hat or scarf to wrap around its neck? The thing will need a personality if we make it tall enough for the entire neighborhood to see." A kid at heart when the need arose, Daniel was into details.

"I have a big straw hat downstairs that we could tie onto his head." Sandra sat beside John to delight in the playful mood that emanated from her grown children, regretting now that she chose to vacuum the living room ten years ago in lieu of building a snow fort with them. Once the oatmeal had been eaten and snow gear pulled on, the snowman project began in earnest.

The snowball rolling quickly made criss-cross swaths across the yard, and the busy Jacobson family was attracting a good deal of attention. The frosty enthusiasm was contagious and the other neighborhood lawns were soon filled with kids and parents building snowmen of every shape and size. By noon there wasn't a front lawn on Pine Haven Road without at least one frozen character to greet holiday travelers. The scene would've been a great opener to a horror movie, *When Ice Men Attack*. As Daniel carefully placed the head on top of the snowman's body, John judged its height to be nearly ten feet.

Marcy smiled up at the snowman and then shivered. Dennis rushed to his chilly girl, scooped her up, and carried her into the house for cocoa.

"Merry Christmas, Mr. Jacobson." Pete shook John's hand affectionately before striding through the kitchen and into the living room where everyone was enjoying cookies, rum drinks, and Bing Crosby's Christmas album.

"Hey there." Daniel raised his hand; he and Pete exchanged a high-fiver. The friends hadn't seen each other in several months and the reunion was long overdue. They scanned each other quickly and then nodded in unison as if to approve that all appeared in order.

"How's Michigan?" Daniel had been tempted to submit an application to The University of Michigan, but the tuition hurdle was too steep.

"Ann Arbor is a great city and I see myself settling there. The football season this year was a real blast. Bo Schembechler coached another spectacular team. And I found my dream girl." Pete was obviously proud of this latter piece of news.

"Oh no. You too? Dennis drove to Bloomington this morning to meet his girlfriend's parents; I'll have him fill you in on the current events in his life. Tell me about your girl."

"Minh is a junior and studying English and classic literature. She wants to be a teacher and then someday write her own book. Her parents came to Michigan from Vietnam; she was born here in the U.S. but speaks fluent Vietnamese. She's timid and funny and very smart. And I'm gonna marry her. Well, she doesn't know that yet, but I do."

"Congratulations—I'd like to meet her before the wedding."

Winter 1981

The colored lights were extravagantly strung across nearly every house on Lavender Lane. After hours of driving the interstate and Ohio Turnpike through the bland Midwest, Esther vastly appreciated the holiday scenery. Her street seemed so narrow and the houses so small this afternoon. *Have I grown or has my past become smaller?* A neighborhood built in the late 1950s, each house boasted a long front porch that easily accommodated a pair of lawn chairs in the summer and a row of jack-o-lanterns in the fall.

She idled slowly down the street to revel in the melancholy emotion that wrapped itself around her. Christmas trees twinkled in the windows, smoke blew from chimneys, and balsam wreaths donned many front doors. She laughed out loud as she parked in her parents' driveway. Joseph had built a fat snowman with a Spanish personality. It wore a sombrero and sported mom's Mexican blanket; a large black mustache hung beneath a frozen carrot nose.

Esther hugged her brother tightly; she was glad he'd finally grown past her own petite stature. He was thin but looked reasonably healthy. He'd recently had his wavy brown hair cut above his ears and it was neatly combed tonight. She turned around to meet Joseph's guest.

"Hello, I'm Sarah." She shook Esther's hand and smiled warmly. "Joseph has been kind enough to help me with geometry this semester; I'd fail it without him."

Esther winked and grinned at her blushing brother, "Did he tell you that he tutored two math students a few summers ago? He's a great teacher."

Ken and Agatha roamed into the kitchen to greet their daughter and a flurry of conversation ensued. In just minutes the group covered dozens of topics—ranging from Reagan's election, John Lennon's assassination, a new law firm partner, and the high school teachers who should retire—to Esther's current coursework.

"Do you really have to go to school for four years just to become a librarian?" Sarah didn't understand why eight semesters of college were required before one could officially manage a few dozen bookshelves.

"I was surprised myself at everything there was to learn. Principles and methods of classifying library materials, methods of descriptive and subject cataloging and classification of non-print materials, and organizing a library-media center in elementary and secondary schools. Plus electives like physics and European history. I'm enjoying it all and believe that this is exactly where I'm supposed to be."

Agatha served her Christmas favorites; pecan bars, shortbread cookies, and cinnamon bread, while the group huddled around the maple dinette to exchange small talk and reminisce about past holidays.

After Sarah's departure, Esther followed her brother into his bedroom. "Tell me about her, Joseph."

"Sarah is a charming person and I like her. She's in my history class and she asked me for geometry help. Satisfied Miss Nosey?" He grinned sheepishly before coughing.

"It's good to see there are girls in the world who've got great taste. Let me know if you want a ride to a movie or something. I heard that *The Shining* with Jack Nicholson is really scary." Esther plopped onto the bed beside her brother, "I'm driving to Arcadia after Christmas to sign the legal papers for the cabin and I plan to spend a night with Karen and John. I'd love for you to come, although I haven't yet asked mom and dad about your accompanying me. Interested?"

"When do we leave?" Joseph pulled an overnight bag down from his closet shelf and tossed it onto his bed. "I totally need a road trip."

~~~~~

Esther knew that posing the question she had in mind would put her onto thin ice. Time wasn't hers for the asking and Joseph's was limited, but she desperately wanted a slice of it for herself. Mom would balk, no doubt, but she had to ask. She smelled chili simmering as she entered the kitchen through the garage door and removed her boots. *Mmmm, cornbread, too.*

"Hey, Mom. I have a request that I'd like you to consider very carefully so don't jump to an answer right away, okay?"

"What's up?"

"You know I'm going to Arcadia this weekend, right?"

"Yes."

"I'd like to bring Joseph. The highways are salty and safe, and Arcadia hasn't seen a decent snow in a week, so even the back roads should be fairly clear. I wanna show him the cabin and spend a weekend together. Just us. He'd enjoy an evening with the Holstens; I know that John is a good chess player and would offer a great challenge. I'm well aware that Joseph's health is failing, but how many more northern trips will he get?" Esther started the discussion in a soft and persuading tone, but her voice was exasperated by the time she'd made her point.

"It's a bad idea. I know there's a hospital in Frankfort but I don't trust him being treated anywhere but the Children's Hospital or CF center in Detroit. His medical history and records are here and Dr. Reynolds and his staff have been taking care of Joseph for sixteen years. That's extremely important at this point. If something happened suddenly you'd be in the middle of a nightmare."

Now she was hot-under-the-collar angry at having been rejected and spoke without prevarication, "Something IS going to happen to him! He's dying and you're keeping him cooped up in the city limits no more than twenty minutes away from your favorite doctor. Oh, that's just a grand idea. . . There's an apartment complex just minutes away from Dr. Reynold's office. Why not keep him there under lock and key?" Esther cringed beneath her vehement exterior; she hadn't planned to blow up.

"There's no point in continuing this conversation. You're not a mother and you cannot possibly comprehend what I'm going through. He's my son and is precious beyond words; I want him here with me for as long as possible. Since developing bronchiectasis he's significantly weaker and tires more easily, Es. The trip would be far too strenuous."

"And you don't think he's precious to me? Joseph is my baby too, Mom. Stop and think for a moment how many thousands of hours of my life have been spent with my little brother. How many rides to the doctor? How many prayers at his bedside? How many games of go-fish and chess? How many wagon walks? How many hospital visits? I taught him to ride a bike. I could go on for days. Let him live before he dies. That's all I'm asking. Please trust me to spend a weekend with him. Just me and Joseph." Esther's chest was sore from jabbing her own index finger into it to make the point.

She leaned into her mother, tears spilling, as they shared the sorrow and anger that would surely become worse in the months ahead.

"Take him, Esther."

"I love you, Mom."

~~~~~~

As any Michigander will testify, December often provides a string of dreary and dark days. And this one was no exception. The clouds were so tightly meshed that they appeared as a gray, smothering fog that hung low and pressed the cold air deeper into the already frozen ground. Cars left out overnight were crisp with frost, and the drivers who ventured out to scrape the windows did so with ferocity and disgust. The cold temperatures didn't bother everyone, however; teenagers survived the dark days unscathed. And as long as he wrapped two scarves around his face, Joseph could endure the frigid temperatures for a short while. Esther and Joseph had every intention to make the coming weekend a great adventure, despite the ugly sky.

Esther slid a small duffel bag of snacks and medicines into the back seat of her Toyota. And, of course, Agatha's fastidiousness dictated that the trunk held blankets, flashlights, flares, and a dozen other emergency items.

"We'll stop at the Kroger near the freeway ramp and then switch places there. Mom will get hysterical if she finds out you're driving on your learner permit with me." Esther pulled her mittens off her hands and set them onto the dashboard.

"Before we get started, I want to say thanks, Es. My bet is that you twisted mom's arm backward to make this happen. That said and done, I've got a request: We need to find a place that makes great chocolate milkshakes." Beneath the skinny exterior, a chubby little boy lived inside of Joseph yearning to come out; but his pancreas guaranteed it'd never happen.

She slugged his shoulder lovingly, "We'll hit the Dairy Maid in Frankfort before we head back on Sunday. Promise to take extra enzymes before you eat the glop—you cannot get sick until we're safely back home."

They drove in silence for several miles; Joseph with hands at the two and ten o'clock positions while Esther observed the wintry landscape that offered banks of snow along exit ramps, a sunless sky, and trucks pulling trailers loaded with snowmobiles. They passed a family with such a trailer; three little ones were buckled in the back seat, each with a different colored hat. The boy in the bright orange hat waved to Esther and she returned the wave with a smile. *Will a snowmobile ride be pushing my luck? John could take Joseph for a quick jaunt around the orchard; they'd both love it.*

"I don't know that I'll ever get married. But I've thought a lot about how important that decision is. Just being sixteen you might not believe that I'd have any sort of clue about the whole thing. But I got an idea on how to pick the right person. Aside from physical attraction there should be a compatibility test you each take and then trade answers."

"That's interesting. What kinds of questions would it ask?"

"Really basic stuff. Like 'omelet or over-easy?' And 'sunrise or sunset?' And 'spring or fall?' I believe that preferences, those seemingly tiny decisions that you make everyday and the way you feel about simple stuff, are indicators of who you are underneath the daily rigors of life. There are questions that people don't contemplate before answering; the responses just pop into their heads. Grab a piece of paper and pencil and let's make some more questions. You might want to have these in mind when you date. I mean, you're in college and you're meeting people, right?"

Esther fished out the notebook their mother insisted she bring. It had notes of Joseph's medical history, current medications, and family doctor information; proof positive once again that Agatha always covered the bases. "Okay, shoot a few questions at me."

"Sledding or ice skating? Horror movies or adventure movies? Frisbee or volleyball? Dogs or cats? Elevators or escalators? Chocolate or vanilla? Describe your favorite shirt. What's your favorite movie? What's your favorite holiday? Hot dog or hamburger? French fries or onion rings?"

"You've certainly thought on this for a while. It's a great idea, but when you really love someone it doesn't matter that your preferences are different. I love you, Joseph, and our answers to those questions would probably match only half of the time, yet we're quite compatible."

"We've become compatible over time, there's a difference. We grew up together and experienced a lot of the same stuff. Same parents, same relatives, same school, same neighborhood. When you meet someone who's lived a separate life for two decades, you're joining together two different worlds. Get it?"

"I guess. But I wouldn't ditch a hunky boyfriend because he liked hot dogs better than hamburgers."

~~~~~~

"Welcome!" Karen fussed over the kids as she hung coats and shuffled them into the kitchen for desserts and cocoa. Pulling plates, silverware, and baked goods from the cupboard, she barely contained her excitement. Except for the sound of snowmobile engines, the Arcadia area was desolate from November through April. Having the young visitors during Christmas week brightened her world considerably, especially with Velma gone. She'd spent days baking holiday treats to prepare for the visit, and John had benefited from her baking spree after she insisted he sample everything twice.

"I understand you're a chess champ, Joseph." John had left the room and returned with a box that held an antique wooden chess set. "Interested?"

"Yes, Sir. Are we putting money on this game?" Joseph quickly opened his wallet to grab a ten-dollar bill.

"You're on."

After sampling the raspberry tarts and filling mugs full of tea, the guys wandered to the game table in the corner of the living room and set up the board in earnest. Joseph's chronic cough was imperceptible to the other three.

Esther leaned back into the oak chair, molding her shape into its seat cushion. "I can hardly imagine that I'll walk through Velma's cabin tomorrow and call it my own. I truly believe that destiny led me here and I'm supposed to be in the cabin. My friends declare that my choice to live in this town makes me a mad woman."

"I've thought a lot about your residency in Arcadia, Es. Having you here would be a dream come true because you're so dear. But it's selfish to have that desire; I want you in Arcadia only if you want to be here. You still have two years left of college. You might meet a young man or be offered a job in a grand library outside of Michigan entirely. Don't pass up other opportunities for this town. The cabin will be here for summer vacations and such; it doesn't have to be a permanent residence."

Esther offered a serious reply, "Destiny."

~~~~~~

Owning a snowmobile in Arcadia was a necessity if you resided on a street where the school buses didn't run. Because the plows cleared main roads and bus routes first, it wasn't unusual for Karen and John to be snowbound for a half day. A snowmobile could mean the difference between life and death if there was a medical emergency after a heavy snow. Today the machine would do no more than provide a thrill for a teenage boy.

"It's barely twenty-five degrees outside, Joseph. You need two scarves over your mouth and ski goggles on your eyes." As Karen prepared him to endure the weather, John offered snowmobile driving tips. After riding Joseph through the orchard trails, John would put him into the driver's seat and let him romp through the frozen terrain alone. The Lord had bestowed a brilliant day for the adventure. Snow sparkled beneath the rare December sunshine and magnificent white-cloaked evergreens bowed away from the wind gusts.

Esther was nervous. She knew full well that the cold air was hard on his lungs but didn't want another winter to pass without Joseph dashing through it recklessly. "You're to stay on the course he's designated, understand?"

"If this is as much fun as you claim then it'll be worth a trip to the hospital, Es." He probed into her eyes and then startled her with an assertion, "I'll do this only once before I die, and this is it."

The women bundled up and ventured out to stand on the east side of the barn where they'd catch glimpses of the guys as they sped around the course. After a few loops, John hopped off the snowmobile and motioned for Joseph to go ahead on his own for a few runs. With a thumbs-up, the boy took off after spraying a wake of snow at his audience's feet.

Several minutes passed without the sound of the humming motor. She didn't panic immediately because the north corner of the orchard was a fair distance. But when she saw John jog north into the field, she grew nearly hysterical.

"What if he fell? What if he's not breathing? Be ready to drive to the hospital, Karen. I'm going into the field."

Karen dashed into the house to get her car keys while Esther raced towards John.

The relief that pulsed through her body when Joseph crested the hill shook Esther from head to toe. The snowmobile was crawling and he held a huge brown animal on his lap.

Joseph shouted, "He's nearly frozen to death!" He coughed violently then. John reached her brother first and pulled the large dog from his lap.

"Hurry into the house Joseph, I'll bring the dog in. You shouldn't have left the course." John groaned with the load, "This dog is heavy. Speed up now!" Exhaling clouds of warm air with each step, John trudged slowly with the frozen animal.

"I'll ride back with Joseph. Can you handle the dog?" Esther panted from the adrenaline rush. *Lord, Please clear his lungs. Please help him recover from the cold. And please save the dog.*

"You two go on ahead. I'll be up in a few minutes." John marched forward on his mission.

"Karen! John is coming with a frozen dog. Do you have some blankets?" Esther's fright had simmered to a mere frenzy.

"A dog? Oh dear." Karen grabbed an armful of old towels and blankets from the closet and then assembled a makeshift dog bed near the fireplace. She started a fire in the hearth while John wrapped the dog.

Karen turned to Esther, "Does Joseph need to see a doctor?"

"We'll know in a few minutes." Esther knelt beside her brother at the kitchen table, closing her eyes as he spat into a handful of napkins. She soothed him urgently while he coughed. As he settled into the chair she saw blood in the napkins and caught a gasp in her throat. "Try not to cough too hard." She met his eyes, "Did you carry the dog far? More than a few steps?"

He nodded his head in a positive motion before releasing a lung-clearing cough. His chest felt constricted—almost like a hundred pound weight had been strapped onto him. Breathing was difficult and speech was impossible.

"Darn it, Joseph. An heroic effort in sub-freezing temperatures is a stupid idea." She yanked the boots from his feet and went into the kitchen to break ice cubes into chips for him to suck on. Next, she marched up to the guest bedroom and retrieved the nebulizer. He'd need the medication in mist form tonight because she knew he wouldn't be able to breathe deeply enough to draw a decent dose from the inhaler. But they first had to keep a careful eye on the bleeding because a large quantity of blood or prolonged bleeding would necessitate a hospital trip. In between coughs and napkin checks, they watched the dog and the bright orange fire that warmed him.

John and Karen worked together to massage the animal's chest, neck, and paws. The poor thing was barely alive. Karen strode to the kitchen, filled a large basting syringe with warm water, and brought it to the dog's mouth. He slurped some water and then lay his head down while a fierce trembling overtook his body. Karen cradled his head and John continued rubbing his body to stimulate circulation and accelerate warmth.

With the dog's shaking under control, Karen took a seat near Esther and offered a concerned look, "Can I get you anything? Does he need to get to the hospital?"

"I think he'll be all right. Exertion in the cold air often causes hemoptysis; if you could plug the nebulizer into an outlet near the recliner, it'd be a great help. He should probably spend the night in an upright position with his medication at arm's reach." Esther didn't bother hiding the look of worry from her friend.

After far too many minutes had passed, the bleeding finally became negligible. Joseph was drinking water easily and his coughing had subsided as well.

Karen and John kept an eye on the dog beside the now lukewarm fire. Although he wore a grumpy boxer expression with very dirty jowls, his eyes were loving and kind. His brown spotted tail wagged against the floor to make a gentle thudding sound. It appeared that he might have a chance at survival.

~~~~~~

After supper, Esther insisted that Joseph take a warm bath to relax. A trip to the hospital hadn't been necessary, and she was grateful beyond belief when her brother asked for something to eat. *Thank you God. Thank you God. Thank you God.* In lieu of a Scrabble game, the foursome chose instead to lounge in the living room; Karen, John, and Esther took turns rubbing the now warm dog. By late evening he'd recovered enough to hold up his head and drink water unassisted.

Karen saved meat scraps from the pot roast and fed them to the wide-jowled dog during the night. She fell asleep on the floor beside him and awoke the next morning with a stiff neck and slobbering licks against her chin. Esther had spent the night on the couch beside Joseph, who slept intermittently in the recliner. John had slept in his own bed, snoring freely without nudges from his wife.

~~~~~~

"Has Karen named him yet?" Joseph stood beside Esther in the kitchen as she scrambled a pan full of eggs. He popped two slices of bread into the old chrome toaster and smacked his lips while opening the lid on the blueberry jam.

"She won't give him a name until she knows for sure they can keep him. She called a few friends to spread the word this morning; apparently no one has seen a brown boxer mix in the area. I hope they can keep the big guy."

John stomped into the kitchen and removed his boots. He liked to start the tractors once a week during the winter months. "I'm hungry this morning. Is Karen in the shower?"

"Yup, then we're headed to Frankfort after breakfast to sign the cabin papers and pick up a few groceries." Esther patted the boxer's head as he plopped down beside the stove to better whiff the frying eggs and toast. "Looks like he's made himself at home here, John."

"I think Karen is already attached to him." John tapped Joseph's shoulder, "Your brother and I will give him a bath while you're gone this morning. Is dog food on the list?"

Esther liked how John and Karen thought so much alike. "Uh huh. That's the first thing she wrote down. She's also picking up a box of dog biscuits and two large food bowls."

~~~~~~

The law-office reception area was elegantly decorated with antique chairs and a contemporary loveseat. Business and scientific magazines were neatly stacked on a leather trunk that served as a coffee table. A brass spittoon held a potted fern; on the opposing wall hung oil reproductions of popular hunting scenes featuring Brittany spaniels and pheasants beneath cloudy autumn skies.

"Mr. Sturman is wrapping up a conference call so he'll be with you shortly. The paperwork is assembled in the conference room so follow me, please. Although Patricia spoke with precision and formality, her appearance was casual. "Would either of you like coffee or tea?"

"I'd like some coffee with milk, please." Esther sank into the roomy chair beside Karen, who also requested coffee.

"It doesn't seem possible that I was in this very room just three months ago in utter despair and disbelief." Karen's eyes brimmed with tears, "And I still miss her so much."

"Oh dear, I'm sorry—please don't cry. I miss her too. We can go home and do this in the summer when you've had more time to heal. How thoughtless of me to be here in Arcadia so soon." With sympathy tears flowing, Esther grasped her friend's hands and tugged at them gently.

"No, I'll be fine, honey. It was my idea that you come here in December. Sometimes I'm struck with waves of heartache, that's all. Let's get the paperwork done and then drive to the cabin after lunch. This is a special day for you." Karen wiped her eyes before Patricia entered with the coffee.

Sam Sturman finally appeared and sat across the table from the women. He succinctly explained the details of the real estate transaction and presented a small stack of papers for signing. "The property has no outstanding mortgage or liens. However, once you take ownership of this property, Miss Gardener, you are responsible for securing homeowner's insurance and paying the annual property tax to the City of Arcadia. Perhaps Mrs. Holsten has an insurance agent she can recommend."

Mr. Sturman handed a document to Esther, "You'll file this with the county so they have you on record as the homeowner. Be sure they have your current mailing address and your parents' address in Detroit for future correspondence and such." After she signed the small stack of documents, he presented to

Esther an envelope that held the cabin keys. He extended his hand to her, "Congratulations and best of luck to you."

Esther shook his hand eagerly, "Thank you so much, Sir. You've been very helpful."

~~~~~~

"Gosh Es, I can't picture you living here full time. Rural is great but this is no-man's land. What will you do all day?" Joseph knew his sister wasn't a socialite but he didn't think she'd make a good recluse, either.

"Phooey on you. Wait until you see the inside." Esther, Joseph, John, and Karen walked into the very cold and dark cabin. "There's an entire wall for books, a small dining table could be placed over there, a couch and table here, and look at the fireplace." Esther strode through the cabin and then stopped in the kitchen to lean against the counter. "It's not the same without Velma—the cabin feels strange. Yet I have a distinct feeling that she's with us somehow." She pulled open the cupboard to reveal stacks of old Corelle dishware rimmed with a gold geometric design.

"When Velma and I cleaned out the cabin years ago she refused to remove those dishes. Now I know why. If you open the drawers you'll find tableware as well. And the bottom cupboards are full of her old pots and pans. She bought new kitchen items for the townhouse and left these things for you." Karen walked to Esther and then clutched the girl to her. They stood together for several moments, shedding tears of both grief and elation.

"I understand now."

"Understand?" Karen was a tad unnerved by Esther's word choice.

"Her gift to me is much more than the cabin. It's about her unpretentious lifestyle. We all know she could've afforded much more but she certainly had her priorities straight, didn't she? I've been in too many homes where more time is spent matching draperies to a toss-pillow fabric than on making soulful connections with a friend or relative."

"That's your way, too, Esther. Velma didn't give that sensibility to you. She knew that you already possessed it and the two of you connected." Karen tugged at her friend's raggedy scarf, "What's this thing about?"

"Aunt Gail knitted it for me when I was in junior high." Esther rubbed it against her cheek affectionately.

"You could certainly afford a nicer and more stylish scarf, I'm sure. But you choose to keep that one."

Esther closed her eyes in thought before replying, "Possessions bog me down. When people get wrapped up in having the newest and the best they lose sight of what's truly valuable in life. Surrendering to materialism tends to bury God and our human relationships beneath earthly things." She scanned the room again, "I'll never tire of the raw beauty this cabin exudes."

Karen smiled, "You possess far too much wisdom, little one."

"Do you think she knows how grateful I am? Does she know that we miss her so much?"

"I think so. And remember that Velma lived a good life, and she was certainly very happy the day she put this cabin in your name."

John and Joseph tumbled down the steps from the upper floor.

"That's a great space and plenty big enough to be two bedrooms. I'll be your first houseguest!" Joseph's attitude had turned positive after exploring the cabin's interior.

"Is there a place in town where a guy can get a good milkshake?" Joseph checked his watch and discovered they had just a few hours before he and Esther had to depart for Detroit.

"The Dairy Maid is closed until May." John shrugged his shoulders in an apologetic gesture.

"Do you have ice cream, Karen?" Esther looked hopeful.

"Will chocolate suffice?"

Joseph tossed his head back and chuckled, "Perfect."

Winter ~ Summer 1982

It was too cold to snow. Ready to crack its next victim without warning, static electricity hovered over every doorknob and metal handle. The temperature in University Park hadn't exceeded eighteen degrees in nearly two weeks. Nice weather for the bookworms, but the frigid air threatened to dampen the spirits of even the hardiest social butterflies on campus, unless a special celebration had been planned.

"We'll drive to the bar, Es." Kelly was exasperated with her roommate, "It's your twenty-first birthday and we're going out tonight. I'm sure your mom wants every penny of the money she sent to be spent at the pub. Put on that red sweater and kick off the Nike shoes for an evening of fun."

"I'll go but won't get drunk—I'm no good at it. Two drinks is my limit and then it's Pepsi for me." Esther wandered to her room in search of a decent sweater and shoes. Once changed she pressed a smudge of color onto her lips from the only tube of lipstick she owned.

~~~~~~

"ESTHER!" The crowd of students roared as the women entered the pub.

Esther covered her gaping mouth when she caught sight of the large cake on the table where Tom, Heather, Laura, and Steve sat. Barry hauled Esther into his arms and twirled her in a bear hug. After Heather lit the candles, every patron in the bar sang "Happy Birthday" before toasting the librarian wanna-be.

"Thank you!" She blew out the flames after making the same wish she hoped would come true for sixteen years, *Remove CF from the face of the earth.*

The party group moved several tables into an L-shape while Kelly and Laura unpacked paper plates and plastic forks. Esther shut her eyes tightly to inundate her other senses; she locked the moment into a mental parking space. The odor of pretzels and stale beer, music blasting from the speakers, exuberant laughter, and the sticky wooden floor all wove together for compilation and storage in a special place. A stab of sadness chilled her when she realized that the coming September would be the beginning of her final collegiate year. She opened her eyes to erase the forlorn feeling.

Heather tapped Esther on the head and took a seat, "I bought a Bible last week and you're my inspiration to be a better person. But I need a push. Do I read it from the beginning?"

"You won't be sorry; it's a great book. The first Psalm is wonderful and Proverbs offers wise advice. You'll find the Ten Commandments in Exodus and the Sermon on the Mount is in Matthew. The words are powerful. Bring your Bible to the apartment the next time you drop by and I'll mark those pages if you have trouble finding them. The book of Esther is a must read; she was a hero." Esther embraced her friend.

"Hey, birthday girl. The DJ wants you to request a few songs. Hop to it and let's hear what he's got." Tom pushed her to the DJ station.

"Let's dance, sweet girl." Barry came from behind Esther and pressed his cheek against hers. He dated other girls but always returned to her as if she wore a spring that pulled him back. The couple frivolously swayed and bobbed around each other to *You're So Vain* until he picked her up like a baby doll. "I need to ask you something privately, Es."

They waltzed to a lone table.

He encased her small hands and pulled them onto his chest. "My heart pounds like this when I'm with you."

"That's because you were swinging me around, Tarzan." She didn't want a serious Barry tonight.

"My pulse goes haywire just sitting close to you. I love who you are. You're cheerful, careful, smart, funny, beautiful, and hundreds of other things. I love you." Barry locked onto her gaze.

She swallowed in a stunned sort of way. Such an admission was new to her ears and she wasn't sure how to respond. "You're wonderful too, Barry."

"What do you feel for me, Es? We've been friends a long time but is there something more?"

"I care about you and like being with you but can't say for sure if I love you."

"You'd know it, and I don't think you have the same feelings for me." Barry rose from his side of the table and sat on her bench. He pulled her head onto his shoulder and plucked his fingers through her hair. They stayed that way for a long while before returning to the L-shaped party.

~~~~~~

"How's Joseph today?"

"He seems to be improving but we saw Dr. Feinhold this morning and his diagnosis was very disheartening. Joseph's recent hemoptysis episode was horrendous and his pulmonary function is poor. And although the recent bronchial artery embolization was successful, the years of damage and trauma have substantially weakened his heart. The doctor wants him to finish his senior year at home to reduce exposure to infection and stress." Agatha's voice was choked with pain and fear.

"Aw jeesh. How does he feel about that?" Esther plopped onto a chair. She pressed her palm against her forehead to dispel the negative thoughts that threatened to take hold.

"Joseph accepts the doctor's order. He's weak and can't fight the reality of the situation. The vice principal is visiting tomorrow; she's bringing his textbooks and locker contents to the house. Each of his teachers will schedule an hour every week to review assignments here." Agatha cried as she spoke.

"Don't cry, Mom, especially around Joseph. Wait until he's in another room or sleeping. Cry in your pillow or go outside, but don't cry in front of him. Follow dad's lead and keep an upbeat attitude. And promise you won't groan when his coughs bleed." Esther wanted desperately to travel to Detroit the second she put down the phone, but knew it wouldn't do anyone a bit of good. She'd be home in seven weeks for the entire summer and would have to fret in Pennsylvania until then. *Why didn't I go to Michigan State? Why did I move four hundred miles away? Lord, please forgive my utter selfishness.*

"You're right, I promise. I'd have you talk to Joseph but he just settled down for a rest. I expect he'll be up and around after supper, perhaps seven o'clock tonight. Will you be home?" Agatha always saw an improvement in her son after he spoke with Esther.

"I'll be here. I love you, Mom. Stay strong."

Esther hung up the phone, grabbed the tissue box from the bathroom, pushed her *Peter, Paul, and Mary* cassette into the tape player, sat cross-legged on the floor, and wept through six songs.

~~~~~~

Chaos was a far cry from what actually occurred during the last two weeks of school. Days were filled with final exams, scheduling fall courses, packing apartments, and an avalanche of social commitments because everyone had to say good-bye to everyone before summer began. Ever organized and diligent Esther had most of her packing done and was on target in all of her courses. On a whim she decided that a hike through Black Moshannon Park was what she needed to unwind and freshen her spirit. It was a short drive to the park and she wouldn't hike for more than a couple hours. She jotted a note to Kelly and filled her canteen before changing her mind.

Stepping onto the gravel lot connecting two trails in the park, she was inspired by the beauty of the dark evergreens and lush deciduous trees filling the sky. Tiny wild violets and yellow buttercups speckled the edges of the woods while ferns speared through the earth to soften the bristly underbrush. She wore a watch but left her compass behind. *I need to keep a steady direction on a single trail so that backtracking is easy. It's four o'clock so I'll walk for forty or fifty minutes, and then turn around. I can be home well before dark.*

Strolling uphill, Esther passed a few hikers and waved the standard greeting. She'd grown fond of the park; her favorite trails were rugged and offered decently challenging inclines. She imagined Joseph walking beside her. *Dear Lord, deliver him from pain and ease his breathing.* She looked forward to time with her family in Arcadia this summer. Perhaps they'd do some sightseeing around Crystal Lake and Sleeping Bear Dunes. And pick blueberries with Karen, of course.

"Hi, do you walk here often?"

She stumbled at the sound of the voice, startled. A middle-aged man had approached from behind and assumed her stride length and speed.

"Um, just a few times. I like the trails and it's not far from campus."

"I'm Keith." He extended his hand to Esther, which she shook feebly before introducing herself as Ellen.

"A pleasure to meet you, Ellen. I used to come here with my family as a kid. Mom brought picnics and we'd hike for hours. Lot of great memories in this park, except for the poison ivy incident. Are you a Penn student?"

"Yup. A junior. Library science." Her skin prickled.

"I majored in history at the University of Pennsylvania; I teach at the high school now. You a resident?"

"No, I grew up in Indianapolis. I'm going home for the summer next week." *Get away from this guy.* She checked her watch, "Nice meeting you, Keith. This is my turnaround point. I'm meeting some friends this afternoon and shouldn't be late; see you around." Esther stepped solidly away from him and headed back to her car, which was at least a half hour away.

"Wait up. I'll walk back with you." Keith's voice deepened, "Hiking alone can be dangerous." He rammed his shoulder into Esther's side, forcing her off balance. Before she could dash away he snatched her arm into a vice-grip.

"Let me go or I'll scream!" Her heart beat wildly in terror.

He pulled her off the trail into a headlock, slammed her into the ground, and slapped her face. "If you scream you won't live through the night, Ellen."

I will not let him hurt me. I will get away. Protect me, dear Lord. Don't take me away from Joseph. Esther remained still waiting for the briefest moment when he might remove both hands from her body. *I'll kick him with the force of an explosion and run.*

"Please let me go, Keith. I'm sorry if I offended you. We can walk for a while if you'd like." Her voice was miraculously calm and composed.

"I got plans for you cupcake." He yanked her back up, scrunched her into his side, and dragged her farther into the woods.

"HELP! PLEASE!" She screamed with every ounce of energy she could muster through lungs compressed by the painful grip.

Keith released her shoulders to grab onto her head. The tiny second had come and she fled like a rabbit. The world flashed by on either side as she scrambled through the woods and hit the trail. She felt drugged with power and strength.

When I catch her I'll kill her. She won't get away. His heart beat in a pounding frenzy as he approached her heels in just a few seconds.

Esther had two advantages: high school track and a respiratory system that had just turned twenty-one. After two minutes of running, she had pulled away from him by twenty yards. After three minutes, she couldn't hear him panting behind her. After five minutes, she risked turning her head around to see if he was still running. He had stopped and was panting with palms on his knees and head drooped towards the ground. Esther slowed her pace but continued to run. She ran hard for another seven or eight minutes, and then jogged for another fifteen. She turned east onto a trail, jogged it for a while, then headed south onto yet another.

She eased into a walk, gasped for air, and swung her arms furiously while she uttered a prayer out loud, "Thank you Lord. Please get me home."

Did I go east and then north? Or east and then south? Why didn't I run to my car? I can't backtrack to the parking lot now.

He's probably looking for me. Esther decided to stay on the current trail and search out a hideaway spot to spend the night. She felt like a wolf's prey and trembled from the next thought that took root in her mind, *What if he finds me?*

~~~~~~

"When Esther says she'll be back at six-thirty, then she really means it. You guys know that. Has she ever in three years been late for anything? It's eight o'clock and I'm driving to Moshannon Park. If she got a flat tire or something we can help her out. Maybe her car overheated or she's been in a car accident." Kelly sensed something was amiss. "Are you coming with me?"

Tom and Laura immediately agreed to make the trip.

Dusk was settling into the area, which put Kelly further on edge. "Turn off the radio; I don't want any distraction." She peered out the windshield for a stranded motorist, but didn't see her roommate. They finally reached the park but were stopped by the ranger at the entrance gate.

"NO! I don't care that you're closing. We have to get in! My friend is here and she's hurt or lost. Can you help us find her?" Kelly was frantic.

"She probably left the park and went somewhere . . ."

"NO! Esther doesn't do that! Please let us in." The anguish in Kelly's eyes told the ranger that there'd be no turning her away.

"There are a dozen small parking lots throughout this park, Ma'am. If she's here then her car will be in one of them. I'll check the lots on this end with you and then radio the other rangers so they can check lots 7 through 12. What does she look like and what kind of car does she drive?"

"A 1980 blue Toyota Corolla, Sir." Tom answered coolly.

Laura volunteered Esther's physical description, "She's five-feet two-inches tall, weighs about one-hundred pounds, has long brown hair, and brown eyes. She's probably wearing her Nike running shoes."

After contacting the other park employees, the ranger locked the entrance booth, pulled his car from the space behind the gate, and led the students to the first lot. No cars. The second and third lots were empty as well. The Toyota was parked in the fourth lot. Kelly leapt from her car and ran to the empty Toyota.

"What do we do now?" Laura was in tears and Kelly stood in shock.

"I'll go to the main station and bring the guys back here to walk through the two trails that this lot connects. We won't penetrate the woods too far because it's dark; however, we can walk out a quarter-mile with flashlights and holler her name. If she's lost and hears us then she can yell until we reach her. If she's out too far or is injured and can't respond, we'll call the police." The ranger shouted as he jogged to his car, "Don't hit the trails without us!"

Kelly and Laura hopped onto the trunk of Tom's car. He voiced his concern. "If she had a boyfriend he'd talk her out of doing stupid stuff like this. But what's really irksome is that Esther isn't a girl who gets lost."

When the rangers returned the group hit the trails with lights and screaming voices. They searched well into the darkness, but heard no response. A host of bats darted overhead and put the girls into a frightened tizzy. They'd resume the search at dawn.

~~~~~~

Kelly had sipped coffee and paced the floor all night; Tom had crashed on the couch and Laura spent the night in Esther's bed. Kelly grabbed the phone on its first ring.

"I'm looking for a Kelly McGowan or Laura Bates. This is Detective Harmon."

"This is Kelly. Did they find Esther?"

"Not yet, Ma'am. I need to drop by your apartment to ask some questions and get a recent photo of her. I'll also need an article of clothing that she's worn in the last day or two; we're putting a dog onto the trails immediately. If you give me your address, I can be there in a few minutes."

"Yes, Sir. We'll be here." Esther's cuckoo clock chirped five times; nearly ten hours had transpired since she said she'd be home. Kelly was horrified.

"Who was that?" Tom rose from the couch in a wrinkled daze and scratched his groggy head.

"A detective will be here soon." Kelly poured herself more coffee and rubbed her eyes as Laura emerged from Esther's room wrapped in a Tweety Bird blanket.

"Should we call Esther's parents? Or maybe we should wait until the cop comes. He might want to talk to them. Jeesh, this is bad." Tom yawned and reached for the coffee cup that Kelly shoved in front of him.

Laura pushed a Pop-Tart into the toaster and began to cry.

~~~~~~

The hazy sun peeked through the evergreen umbrella to warm the face of the small runner. Esther opened her eyes hesitantly and surveyed the area. She remained still a moment longer to listen for suspicious sounds. Nothing. The log she had laid against all night was now smelly and damp with forest dew. Her clothes were wet and cold. She slowly sat upright to stretch her back and neck, and then moved into a crouching position before sitting on the log. Her legs were sore from the hard run and she was thirsty. Really thirsty.

She pressed her index fingers into her temples and began to churn numbers in her head. *I was roughly forty minutes from the car, then I ran for a good half hour before walking about a mile to this spot. If the lunatic kept walking deeper through the trails, he could be nearby. Kelly has no doubt called the police. They probably found my car. I'm not moving a muscle until I see a uniform. I'd guess that my distance to the parking lot is nine miles or so. Yikes. That's far.* She stood fully erect and stretched the aches from her legs. She walked to a patch of ferns, knelt beside them, and drank the dew from their leaves. *Now I wait and pray that crazy Keith isn't around.*

~~~~~~

The detective was thorough. After questioning Kelly, Laura and Tom, he knocked on the doors of several other apartments to pose similar queries. He then called Mr. and Mrs. Gardener in Detroit.

"We'll find your daughter, Sir. My guess is that she either sustained an injury or lost her bearings last night as the sun set. I've requested dogs to facilitate the search. My advice is to stay put for now. I will call you this afternoon." The conversation continued for a while longer until the detective put a quick end to it. "Sir, I need to hang up this phone and do my job. I'll contact you this afternoon. Please stay home until you hear from me again."

Detective Harmon departed with Esther's photo and her blue sweatshirt.

The K9 unit authorized Hazel, a stocky and serious bloodhound, and her partner, Lieutenant Gerard, to search Moshannon Park for the missing college student. Two police officers were waiting at parking lot 4 for the team to arrive.

"Her description worries me a bit. At just five-feet two-inches and one-hundred-four pounds, I'd call her scrawny. And a library science major. Not your typical rugged hiker if you ask me. We've got to find her today, Kent." Ron was the worrier of the two. A cop in University Park for just a year, he had yet to handle a vicious crime against a college girl. He hoped this wouldn't be the first.

"Harmon says that her roommates were emphatic about her tough spirit. If she's as headstrong as they say, then my bet is that she simply lost track of her direction and is waiting us out somewhere in that park. Remember that if a woman keeps her head straight during an initial confrontation with an unarmed attacker her chance of escape is about thirty percent. If the guy has a gun or knife, well, those are a different set of stats." Kent turned to see the squad car pull into the lot. "There's Harmon with the dog people."

A quick round of introductions were made while the two police officers studied Esther's photo. Detective Harmon distributed trail maps and water bottles, and then dictated the orders. "You two will take the trail that heads eastward over there, and I'm going with Gerard on the north trail. If you find the girl, shoot your pistol once. If you find evidence, such as size seven running shoe prints or an article of women's clothing, indicate your findings on the trail map. I have a team searching the trails that connect to parking lot 5 and the trails that connect to lot 3 as well. We will search until we find her."

~~~~~~

Unable to sit still, Esther found a maple tree and climbed into its top branches. Perched nearly forty feet up, she could see a fair distance around her. While scanning the area she replayed the attacker's description in her mind. *He has light brown hair, brown eyes, and is about five-feet nine-inches. He is thin. He wore tan shorts and a gray sweatshirt. He's about forty years old. He said his name is Keith. He teaches high school history somewhere in Philadelphia. I want to go home . . .*

After nearly three hours on the hunt, Hazel began barking frantically. Dragging the detectives behind her, she was overcome with the instinctive knowledge that the search was over. Gerard knew that the scent must be strong; the dog was nearly uncontrollable. When he unhooked the leash from her collar, she bolted ahead into the woods and stopped at the base of a large tree about two hundred yards east of the trail. The dog sat hard onto her haunches and howled with pride.

"Hiya pooch! What took you so long?" Esther shimmied down the tree, careful to keep her grip and balance. Breaking a leg at this point would be a really bad idea. She hopped onto the ground and wrapped her arms around the slobbering bloodhound. Harmon and Gerard raced to the pair with hearts and expressions full of relief.

"The photo doesn't do you justice young lady; you're a lovely sight for sore eyes. I'm Detective Harmon and this is

Lieutenant Gerard; your tracker's name is Hazel. Are you hurt?"

"No, Sir, and I want to go home. A man attacked me and I can describe him for you, but I want to shower and eat first. Do my parents know about this?"

Detective Harmon gave her a water bottle and then held his finger up in a just-a-minute motion. He walked several yards away from the tree, removed the pistol from his holster, and fired a single shot into the air. Returning to Esther, he replaced the pistol. The detective was surprised to see her in such a stable emotional state. *What sort of crisis has this girl been through already that such an ordeal hasn't frightened her into hysteria and tears?*

"I spoke with your father this morning. Did the attacker harm you in any way? Did he have a weapon?"

"No, Sir. And I don't think he carried a weapon. I ran away from the bastard. My guess is that if he'd had a gun he would've shot me because I seriously pissed him off."

Her crass statement put grins onto the faces of the detectives. "We'll follow you back to your apartment and you can call your folks. An officer will be posted at your apartment this morning while you take care of business. He'll then bring you directly to the police station where you'll describe your attacker; perhaps we can get a sketch out of it. We'll probably keep a patrol car near your apartment building until you're back in Detroit for the summer—or until we catch the guy." Detective Harmon loved his job today. He'd love it real well if he could put the maniac behind bars.

~~~~~~

The last few days of school were booked solid. Adding two trips to the police station to review mug shots put Esther into an overdrive mode. Despite the fact that the composite sketch was a pretty good likeness of her attacker, none of the photos she viewed matched the guy. After the horrific experience she realized her vulnerability in the big world. She hated being wary of every stranger she encountered lately and hoped the underlying fear would subside over time. Esther refused to walk alone around campus; Kelly, Laura, and Barry took turns bodyguarding until the day arrived for her departure to Detroit.

"I'm gonna miss you so much, Es. Please be careful driving home. Stop only at places where there are lots of people around. I'll be here one more night so call me as soon as you get home." Kelly wasn't usually a crier, but today was different. She'd nearly lost her precious friend last week and now she wouldn't see her for three months.

"Love you, Kelly. I'll miss you too. Call me if you want to visit the cabin; we'll be there in July. Can you believe we'll be seniors in the fall?" The girls embraced tightly and then let go for the summer.

~~~~~~

Lavender Lane had never looked so good; but did it have to keep appearing smaller each time she returned from Pennsylvania? Mom had planted the pink and purple petunias around the boxwoods again and they looked nice. Her car wasn't in the garage; the woman didn't know how to sit still. Esther was anxious to see Joseph and stepped into the house with trepidation.

"Joseph?" He was sleeping in the recliner with the newspaper draped across his stomach. *Just like dad.* He sounded bad and looked worse. His breathing was raspy and he'd lost a good amount of weight. *Why Joseph, dear Lord? Why someone so smart and kind? Why do healthy lunatics run around in this world while honorable people are burdened with pain and suffering?* She knelt beside her brother and laid her head on his arm to continue the prayer. He woke slowly from the sleep.

"I've missed you terribly. How're you feeling? You look a bit wore out." She smiled outwardly while pangs of grief struck her heart.

He coughed until the spasms subsided and then sat upright. "It's good to see you, Es. I feel okay but take a nap every day to replenish my strength. I want details on the park incident. Mom said you outran a crazy guy." He offered the crooked grin that she adored and then stood to greet her properly. They walked into the kitchen together and he sat at the table while Esther put water in the kettle for tea.

"I want the scoop on you first. I can't believe my little brother will be a high school graduate. Does mom have any cinnamon tea left?" Esther rummaged through the cupboard to find the box of tea.

"Got my cap and gown a few weeks ago. Graduation will be a blast. Sarah is having a party next Saturday and she asked if you could come. I already told her you'd be there."

"I'd love to go."

"Bought you a present, Es. It's in your bedroom." Sitting up and sipping his tea, Joseph's color had improved.

"You're the graduate; I should have one for you." She strode to her room and stopped abruptly to admire the gift that lay gleaming on her bed. A guitar. She pulled it onto her lap before strumming it clumsily, then returned to the kitchen with the instrument in her hand.

"Thank you. I'd never have thought to get a guitar for myself." She bent down to hold her brother in her arms. *Thank you, God, for this young man.* "I'll learn to play this summer and by September you'll be humming campfire songs."

Agatha had been to the music store. "You look wonderful, Es! I haven't stopped worrying since the call from Detective Harmon." With tears of relief, she clutched her daughter tightly and handed the bag full of sheet music to her. "I cleaned out the folk music section. I think you'll have everything you need."

"Thanks, Mom. And this makes me even more confident about the decision I made about my final year of college." Esther sat down at the dinette, arms stretched out against the familiar maple wood.

"Are you going for a Master's?" Joseph was perplexed.

"I'm staying here in Detroit for a hiatus. I've decided to start my senior year in 1983 because I want to be home with my family now."

"You will not put your life on hold for me, Esther. I refuse to let you do that. This isn't about a stupid hiatus and you know it." Joseph was fuming, "It might take me three years to die. You gonna wait around here that long?"

Agatha put an end to the tirade, "We'll discuss this another day. Both of you are too strong willed to debate this issue without an arbitrator, and I'd be no good because I agree with both of you. Let's sleep on it and then bring dad into the discussion."

The summer of 1982 whizzed by like a movie reel in fast forward, starting with Joseph's graduation. The Gardener family members were nearly inseparable throughout the summer. Strawberry picking, a July 4th party, a week in Arcadia, walks in the park, a symphony in Detroit, fishing, barbeques, and church socials. In between the family outings and Joseph's tune-up at the CF center, Esther managed to complete twenty guitar lessons. Joseph became her biggest fan and declared that when she strummed even the simplest tune he felt her spirit whisper straight into his heart.

At summer's end, Joseph was the victor in the back-to-college battle. A minor war was waged between the siblings in August. He growled and slammed doors at the sight of his sister. He refused to let her touch him, and then posted on her bedroom door a long list of the events she'd sacrificed throughout her childhood because of his disease. Joseph dared Esther to add "delay college graduation" to the list. After two days of wrangling with her brother, she caved in; she couldn't bear having him so angry with her.

~~~~~~

In Pennsylvania, another battle had been won. Unfortunately, the composite sketch of the suspect hadn't matched any of the past graduates from Penn State or the University of Pennsylvania. That would've been too easy. During the months of June and July, Detective Harmon spent hours of personal time comparing the police sketch of Esther's attacker to faxed copies of every high school teacher in Pennsylvania. He found a perfect resemblance in the Lancaster High School yearbook and sent the photo to a Detroit police station.

On August 11th, Esther drove to the Detroit station to check the photograph of Mr. William Keith Dubois. "That's him." She'd walk the campus this fall without holding her breath and vowed to never hike alone again.

Spring ~ Autumn 1983

"What're you doing here at seven o'clock in the morning?" Mitch had a final review meeting in a few hours and was duplicating the blueprints for sign-off, a tedious job that didn't demand much patience unless the person had to replace the roll of mylar, which was the case this morning.

"The exterior design of the Jefferson Avenue building has become more of a challenge than I had anticipated. I've walked the avenue, explored the surrounding buildings, and studied my consultation notes ad nauseum. I envision a simple and traditional feeling for the building and am grateful that the structures in the area aren't ostentatious. Yet they're almost too ordinary. I want a substantial window framing, but that's got me stumped as well." Daniel stepped away from his drafting table to grab the jar of cashews from his filing cabinet. He'd forgotten to eat breakfast again. "I'm leaning towards window arches and detailed cornice work along the roof line to reflect aspects of the older buildings in the vicinity."

"Check the concrete catalogs for ideas. The precast moldings can lend a lot of character to a simple structure. I know you want to align your building's exterior with the nearby structures, but also remember that you can incorporate the Jacobson genius into the interior layout and design of the lobby as well." Mentoring the young architect through his intern development program (IDP) the past year had been a great learning experience for Mitch and Daniel both. They were fast becoming a fortuitous design team.

"I designed the lobby with a two-story ceiling. The stairway wraps up the west wall above the elevator and then turns to become the second-floor hallway. The first section of that hallway will overlook the lobby until it proceeds into the actual office spaces. The ceiling beams, stairway and railing, and lobby floor will be oak; the steps will require a padding to minimize sound. The investment group might balk at the cost of oak flooring, but it's worth a shot. I'm meeting with the brick and stone supplier this afternoon and hope to come away with some inspiration for the exterior facade." Daniel set down the cashews and began rummaging through a stack of architecture magazines and catalogs.

"Relax. I wouldn't have twisted your arm to work for me a year ago if I didn't have confidence in your design ability. Next summer I'm changing my company's name, by the way. How does 'Smythe & Jacobson Design' sound to you?" While Daniel's mouth dropped open and the duplicator hummed through its printing task, Mitch headed into the break room to make a pot of coffee.

"You want to make me a partner next summer? Are you joking? I still have a year of IDP to finish." Daniel was on Mitch's heels.

"You're brilliant with guts and integrity, and you easily passed the first round of AIA exams. You'll have certification after the AR next summer. We're a good team and I don't see the point in waiting two or three years to make you my partner when you'll be ready in one." Mitch pressed the coffeemaker's red button to start the brewing.

"I don't know what to say. I'm a bit stunned, actually. I've simply showed up here every day and applied my education to the realities of an architectural practice under the guidance of a genius." Daniel smirked sideways, "Brown-nosing out of the way, do you think we'll ever get a chance to bid on a Chicago project?" He now grinned exuberantly.

"With your design talent and our combined determination, I believe that someday we could have a structure in the windy city, my dear boy. It might take a decade or two, but anything's possible." Mitch poured a coffee, slapped his protege's shoulder, and ventured back to the blueprint duplicator.

~~~~~

"It's nearly thirteen-hundred square feet of living space, plus the attached garage for extra storage. The building is only six years old, Mr. Jacobson, and all appliances stay. This is a good part of town as well. Another bonus is that it's move-in ready; the current owners vacated the property two weeks ago." Margaret was your typical realtor—mid forties, great shoes, and perked on caffeine.

Daniel stood on the balcony that extended from the master bedroom on the second story of the condominium. The view was tranquil and he liked the floor plan. The fireplace downstairs would be nice in the winter; the living room provided sufficient space for a decent-sized social gathering. Both bedrooms were upstairs with a laundry room and second bathroom. He'd put a drafting table and futon in the second bedroom. "Can we walk around the neighborhood?"

Amid blooming crabapple and lilacs, the pair strolled through the well-maintained grounds of Spring Creek Condominiums. He liked what he saw and felt that the time was right to take on a mortgage. *Am I crazy to tie myself down in the north? I hate the cold weather, but I'll be a partner in an architectural firm here...* "Let's make an offer, Margaret."

They shook hands and set a time to meet in her office the following afternoon. The walk back to his truck was pleasant; April had certainly done its job of providing showers. The trees and blooms throughout the city of Grand Rapids were glorious. Daniel hoped that Margaret could set the closing date to match his twenty-fifth birthday. He'd give her a call this afternoon.

~~~~~~

"How's med student life, Dennis?" Daniel was glad that his brother had picked up the phone; Dennis' schedule was so hectic lately that he was difficult to reach during the day.

"Counting the days until summer break. You build any skyscrapers lately?"

"Not yet. But I bought a condo last week and will move in next Saturday; I'm up to my eyeballs in clutter today. I don't do well in a chaotic environment so thought I'd better call you as a distraction. How's your GPA this semester?"

"It's probably hovering around 2.5, but I'm cool with it. I scored well on the Step 1 USMLE last year so I'll be okay. Making time to study this semester has been rough because I started attending night time hospital rounds. I've learned to get by with five hours of sleep at night and am sticking to a healthy diet. Whoa, that sounded way too mature."

"I'm proud of you. Come spend a weekend here in Grand Rapids this summer. We could drive over to Lake Michigan and generally chill out. How's Marcy? Will she see Jared this summer? I can't believe he'll be two in June."

"Remind me to show you his recent picture the next time you're here; he's a brown-eyed version of Marcy and a very cute kid. His adoptive parents invited her to his birthday party next month. They've been good to her. She's spending this summer with her folks in Bloomington where she'll volunteer in the summer school program at the high school. She's happy as a clam about that. My girl loves school."

"Glad the news is good. I'll call mom later to see if they'll be at Pete's wedding, and I'd like the scoop on Amy's schedule." Daniel knew better than to take up more than a few minutes of his brother's precious time. "Keep up the good work, doc."

"Ask about the puppy." Dennis chuckled.

~~~~~~

Restless was stuck in his mind. He'd been in Grand Rapids for a year and had purchased a new truck, became a homeowner, and was promised a partnership. His weekdays were busy and satisfying, but the weekends had become a monotonous regularity. He'd finished Douglas Adams' Hitchhiker books and was now in the middle of *Day of the Minotaur,* a novel that one of the draftsmen had recommended. Daniel craved social activity tonight. He'd dated two reasonably nice women the past year but neither relationship clicked and he felt a stab of loneliness. Pete and Minh were getting married in Ann Arbor next month; he swore it had been the longest engagement in human history. He jotted a note near his calendar to call Pete about the tuxedo.

He wandered to the dining table and opened the newspaper to check the theatre listings and circled *Sudden Impact*. A guy just couldn't go wrong with a Clint Eastwood flick. He'd see the eight o'clock showing and then grab a beer at O'Malley's Pub. Neil, the bartender and owner, was a thoughtful man. He and Daniel frequently exchanged rounds of sagacious banter; if the pub wasn't busy tonight they could resume their discussion on supply-side economics.

Neil was emptying ashtrays when Daniel dropped onto the barstool. "What's new, Neil?"

"Not much, Dan. Need a beer tonight? What're you working on these days?"

"Make it a scotch. I have three home additions and a two-story medical building on my table. No skyscraper yet, but if we're ever awarded a high rise project the celebration is happening right here."

O'Malley's was the sort of place where a blue collar crew might stop in after a day's work for a good sandwich and cold beer. Women rarely ventured inside. And on the right night a crude joke might earn a guy his beer. Opposite the wall of the restroom doors sat a rugged jukebox. It was full of the standard hits from the seventies. Neil's handwritten menus offered sandwiches, fries, and onion rings.

"I saw the new Eastwood film up at the Town Commons. It was a bit darker than the other Dirty Harry films but I'd still recommend it." Daniel took a swig of the scotch and winced from the burn; he wasn't much of a drinker.

"Don't turn around, kid. Two pretty creatures just strutted through my door; I wonder if they're lost." Neil darted to the center of the bar hoping that the women might actually order a drink.

"What can I get for you ladies?" Neil arched his eyebrows and tightened his lips to keep from grinning like a fool. It didn't work; he blushed like a ninth grade boy talking to a pair of senior girls.

The haughty brunette spoke first, "Two gin and tonics." She gracefully removed a bill from her wallet and tossed it to Neil. Her friend sat at the end of the bar and winked provocatively at Daniel.

After serving the tonics, Neil snuck back to his friend and leaned his forearms onto the bar, "I think they're after you, Mr. Hollywood."

"Messing with a blond like that would only bring trouble; I wouldn't survive a week with a bird like her. I've been out in the world long enough to know that a quiet sparrow is more my type." He gulped the scotch and asked Neil to bring a beer and bowl of pretzels. After the pair reviewed the Detroit Tigers' roster, Daniel stood from the barstool and headed into the restroom. When he returned to the bar, the blond was perched atop his stool.

"Hey there. Just thought I'd keep your seat warm. Hope you don't mind." She extended her hand, "I'm Jenny." Turquoise eyes and a dazzling smile numbed his sensibilities.

"I'm Daniel. Nice to meet you, although it appears that you deserted your friend."

"Natalie and I saw you walk into this place twenty minutes ago and wanted a closer look, Mr. Daniel." Jenny crooked her finger towards Natalie, who moved to take a seat on the barstool beside her friend. Neil assumed a position across the bar from the women. With introductions formally made, the party of four bantered for a few moments to share jokes and small talk. Neil reveled in the situation; Daniel was cautious.

"Do you always get what you want, Jenny?" Daniel gave a discerning look before popping a pretzel into his mouth.

"Some things are tougher to get than others, but in the end, I usually get whatever I pursue. What do you do for a living?"

"I'm an architect."

"Oooh. Interesting occupation. Where'd you go to school?"

"Penn State. I'm from Chicago originally but landed a great opportunity with a designer here in Grand Rapids. How do you pay the rent, Miss Jenny?"

"I'm a model. Mostly clothing catalogs. I hope to move to Los Angeles next year."

Daniel had heard enough to know that it was time to dodge a bullet and get a good night's sleep. "Thanks for the fine beer, as usual, Neil. I'm homeward bound. Nice to meet you both." He fished a small ring of keys from his pocket and headed to the door. Jenny slid down from her stool and reached for his arm.

"Wanna have dinner sometime?" Jenny implored with an angelic face.

"I don't see myself in California and wouldn't want to start something that couldn't be finished." She was beautiful and tempting; his heart thumped.

"Here's my number—we could have ourselves a real fun evening."

"Sure. See you later." Daniel slid the small piece of paper into his pocket without looking back.

~~~~~~

Daniel had met Minh two winters ago and knew instantly that Pete's choice was correct. She was smart, energetic, a little bit shy, and adored Pete. Minh soothed the restlessness in him; he was a calmer and saner man these days. And he doted on his fiancé with tender caresses and gentle smiles. Minh had been very surprised at the time that Daniel had no girlfriend.

"You are so handsome and smart, just as Peter tells me. But you have no girl to love. You are busy with college studies now, but when you're settled somewhere and working, you'll need a nice girl to come home to." Minh's observation was heartfelt.

Daniel shrugged off her comment two years ago, but now it rang true. He was at his best friend's wedding without a date. He'd taken Jenny out to dinner twice but wasn't ready to start a serious relationship just yet. Her beauty simultaneously attracted and repelled him. Hearing the words, ". . . until death do you part" at the end of the ceremony, he felt a panic rise. *What if I never find the right one?*

After dinner and several toasts, Daniel moved from his seat with the wedding party over to his family's table. Dennis and Marcy already seemed married; so in love and at ease with each other. The pregnancy and subsequent adoption they weathered nearly three years ago had bound them together tightly. Dennis had reached a maturity far beyond what Daniel thought he was capable of. He was confident that his younger brother would indeed be a doctor some day. And Amy barely had a moment to converse; she was enjoying the attention of a young man at the reception. Daniel decided that when she sat down again he'd be the next to ask her for a dance.

"Tell Daniel about the puppy, Mom." Dennis scooted his chair away from the table and settled in to hear the story.

Sandra rubbed her palms together and leaned forward to weave the story while John rolled his eyes. "We went to the pound a couple months ago to find a dog. With you two on your own and Amy around only in the evenings, I wanted some company on the days I was home alone. And I figured a puppy would force me to take walks and get into shape." Sandra laughed loudly and John promised to cut off her wine.

John continued the story. "Once we got into the pound your mother wandered to the puppies. There were hound mutts, a lab mix, and breeds that were too mixed to identify. In a cage near the end, a big-footed tan puppy was yelping a mournful cry. I asked the attendant if she knew its breed."

Sandra jumped in, "It was a Great Dane. I told your father that a dog that size didn't belong in our house; I wouldn't be able to lift the bags of dog food into the car trunk. I had my eye on a beagle puppy while your dad hooked a leash onto the yelper. We walked the dogs around the building for a few minutes. My little beagle hopped around politely and sniffed the trees and grass. Guess what the big-foot did?"

"Ran into the street?" Daniel pictured his dad chasing the puppy between fast-moving cars.

"Nope. He lifted his leg and peed all over your dad's shoe." Sandra giggled and cued John to finish the story.

"I took it as an affront and challenge. I tightened the grip on his leash, marched that puppy back into the pound, and filled out the paperwork to take ownership of the little monster. But your mom wouldn't give up the beagle."

Sandra provided the finale, "We have two dogs now. Brutus and Charlie. They're a lot of fun and get along quite well together. You'll like them, Daniel."

Daniel gave his mom a thumbs-up before tapping Amy's hand when she finally took a seat at the table. "You and I dance to the next slow song, okay?" She nodded. And when Nat King Cole began to sing, the pair strode to the dance floor.

"Dennis will be in Grand Rapids for a short visit in two weeks. Come with him, Amy. It'll be a fun time. You can see my home and office. I have access to a nice swimming pool and there's a great Japanese restaurant that you'd really enjoy. As Dennis advances through medical school, scheduling summer getaways will become difficult. And you'll have a serious beau soon whom you won't want to leave for a weekend." He poured on a convincing sort of charm.

"It'd be nice to get together and reminisce. Let me think about it. I heard you're dating someone; tell me about her."

"Aw c'mon. Mom's probably hearing wedding bells and I've only seen this girl a few times. Her name is Jenny and she's a model. We saw a movie a couple weeks ago and went out to dinner twice. I'm not confident she's the one for me at this point, but who knows."

"A model. Why doesn't that surprise me? I remember how girls swooned over you in high school. I hope she's the one."

"How's the job at the accounting firm?"

"I'm happy there. I like being a secretary and the people are very nice. I know you guys wanted me in college but it wasn't a good fit for me. After I'm married I'd like to work for just a few years and then raise a family full-time. I'll be very content to take my children on picnics, read bedtime stories, and sew Halloween costumes." Amy rested her head on Daniel's shoulder as the song neared its end.

"Do you have a guy in mind yet?"

"No. I believe that when the time is right our paths will cross and it'll somehow be obvious that we're supposed to be together."

"That's throwing fate into the wind, dear Amy."

"Yup."

~~~~~~

The foundation and framing of the Jefferson Avenue building was complete in late September. During the first week of October, Daniel worked closely with the building contractor as the exterior stone was being placed. After touring Grand Rapid's Heritage Hill District, conducting extensive materials research, and surviving several late-night deliberations, Daniel finally chose a tan Arriscraft Renaissance Stone for the building's exterior. The choice would reflect the relationship between materials, texture, and color already established in the area without duplicating designs found in nearby buildings. And his client had agreed to oak flooring in the lobby. He was a kid all over again and couldn't sleep some nights because visions of the completed structure would excite him to alertness. He was anxious to see the final window arches.

And then there were evenings when Jenny threatened to complicate his life . . .

"You have to spend the night, Daniel." Jenny became furious while he tied his shoes before leaving. "We've been dating for three months and you have yet to spend the night with me so we can share breakfast. I'd make you a wonderful omelet."

"That's something only married couples should do. Heck Jenny, what we do here should only be done in the confines of marriage." He put his jacket on and sat beside her. "I've got a big day tomorrow and I want to wake up in my place with my own shower and my own kitchen."

"When are we getting married?" She pulled his hand against her cheek and bent to kiss his palm.

"I dunno. Thanksgiving isn't too far away. Want to come to Chicago with me? You'd like Dennis and Amy. Of course, the dogs might give you a bit of trouble initially but they'll leave you alone after a few tasty bites." He stood to depart.

"Chicago sounds wonderful and I imagine the shopping is fabulous." Jenny was confident this was a step in the right direction. *If his family likes me then perhaps they'll bring up the idea of marriage... an engagement ring for Christmas would be a grand prize.*

~~~~~~

She was more beautiful today than when they'd first met in June. Her Calvin Klein jeans appeared to be painted onto her long legs, the blue cashmere sweater accentuated her eyes, and her blond hair begged to be touched. "Good grief, we're only staying two nights, Jenny. This suitcase weighs at least forty pounds."

"I packed a hairdryer and two curling irons, plus two nice outfits and two casual outfits. And four pairs of shoes; a woman can never have too many shoe options when traveling to such a fine city." He lugged her suitcase down to his truck and tossed it into the back.

"Why aren't we driving my car? It's much more comfortable and less noisy." She gave a pouty look.

"I can park the truck in your garage and we'll drive your car, I suppose. There's no snow in the forecast so that might be just fine." Daniel hauled the suitcases out of the truck and over to her new Mercedes Benz. He wondered for a moment if he'd ever said "no" to her. Probably not. She looked too darned good to refuse any request that she made of him. He wasn't so sure that was a good thing.

"I'm driving because I can handle Interstate 94 in Chicago. End of discussion." Daniel stared her down and she kissed him hungrily before he pulled onto the street. "And you will not do that while I'm driving." His full lips offered a crooked grin as he sank into the leather seat of the fine German car. Jenny turned the radio dial and stopped on a Billy Joel song.

"And we're not listening to that music." Daniel turned down the volume.

Jenny crossed her arms and sighed, "Then let's talk about something. How about you start?"

"Have you read Isaac Asimov?"

"Never heard of him." Jenny pressed her head against the back of the seat and closed her eyes.

"He's a prolific science fiction writer who's famous for his robot anthologies. They illustrate relations between humans and robots from the time that the first robots were created until the time when computers basically take over the progress of mankind. It's really quite cool."

Jenny sighed as she dug through her purse in search of gum, "I don't read much. I like TV instead. Do you watch *Dynasty* or *Remington Steel?* Those are my favorites."

"I usually watch the news, although I do like *Hill Street Blues*. Saturday morning cartoons are great with pancakes. I prefer to read though, and if I need entertainment beyond my books I hit O'Malley's Pub."

She found an emery board, began to file her nails, and hummed a popular tune.

Daniel focused on the road and enjoyed the Mercedes ride. *I'm bringing Jenny to meet my family. What will mom and dad think of her? Is this a good idea? Am I serious about her? If I'm not really serious about her, then why am I doing this? Help me, Lord.*

~~~~~~

Brutus was standing, literally standing, at the back gate when Daniel parked the Mercedes in his parents' driveway. Front paws and large jowls hung over the fence top as he barked with a puppy joy. More human toys.

"What kind of dog is that? You didn't tell me there would be something so large here." Jenny clung to his arm as they approached the gate.

"He's a Great Dane with a teddy bear heart and jaws of steel." Daniel chuckled as he patted the beast on the top of its head. He wanted a dog once he got into a house with a large yard. *I won't build a house until I'm married, and it'll be something we create together.*

"Welcome, both of you." Sandra embraced her son warmly and offered a tentative hug for the beautiful blond. John's voice nearly caught in his throat when Daniel introduced Jenny. The first impression she made on Daniel's father earned high marks. Coats were quickly hung and suitcases dragged in from the car. Dennis was at the hospital until later in the night but Amy was home to welcome her brother and his guest. The family assembled with coffee and a tray of light appetizers in the living room.

Amy broke the ice, "Is this your first time in Chicago?"

"I drove through the city several years ago with my family on our way to the Wisconsin Dells, but we didn't stop. It's such a beautiful city; do you go downtown often?"

"I didn't go much as a kid, but my friends and I like to go for lunch and shopping occasionally. And riding the El is pretty cool." Amy relaxed into the recliner. "Daniel went downtown every chance he got when he was young. Whenever grandpa visited from Indiana, he and Daniel would spend an entire day walking the streets and gawking at buildings." Amy loved to boast about her older brother.

Daniel ambled into the kitchen, "What's cooking tonight?" Six years away from home and he still missed Sandra's home-cooked suppers.

"Meatballs, mashed potatoes, coleslaw, and biscuits. There's strawberry ice cream for dessert." Sandra was mashing potatoes.

He took the masher from her hand to finish the task. "What do you think of Jenny?"

"Well, she's very beautiful. I imagine she'll earn good money if her modeling career takes off. She seems smart and nice. What do you think of Jenny?"

"She's planning a move to California. I like her and she's a lot of fun, but Jenny likes to get her way and I think her appearance opens a lot of doors." He scooped the potatoes into a serving bowl while Sandra loaded meatballs onto a platter.

As the Jacobson family sat down for dinner, Dennis waltzed into the house. "Hi! Smells great, Mom." He quickly washed his hands and took a seat next to Amy. Daniel introduced Jenny to his brother.

"How is it that such a beautiful woman would be with a fastidious and compulsive architect?" Dennis winked at his brother as he spoke.

"Daniel is the most wonderful man I've ever met and I hope to be with your brother for a very, very long time. I think he'll be a wonderful father." Jenny peered into Daniel's eyes affectionately.

Sandra choked on her biscuit.

Spring ~ Summer 1983

The ringing phone jarred the women from a sleep that had just begun. Esther groaned out loud and checked her clock, which read 12:17. If Tom were calling she'd give him an earful on telephone etiquette the next time he was at the apartment.

Kelly staggered loudly into Esther's room and insistently shook her shoulder, "It's your mom, Es."

"I'm up. Hang on a second." Before her bearings had a chance to tumble into place and align her with reality, she bolted upright and knew instantly the purpose of the untimely call. *Joseph.*

"Mom? What's going on?" Panic seized her and the adrenaline forced her heart rate to a triple-time pace.

"I booked flight 247 for you out of Philadelphia at six o'clock this morning, honey. You need to come to Detroit; he's real sick."

Her face went numb and the phone in her hand felt sixteen pounds heavier. She was going to throw up. "Will you pick me up at Detroit Metro? Is he at the hospital?"

"Rent a car at the airport and drive to Beaumont Hospital, Es. Do you have your credit card?"

"Yeah. I'll see you when I get there."

Kelly remained at Esther's side without offering a word; she stood as a solid form to be leaned into or bawled on. Esther did both, but just briefly, before wiping away her tears and marching into the shower to begin the journey. After the girls packed a suitcase, Esther scribbled a list of her course names and their locations. She instructed Kelly to tell her professors that she'd be out of school until further notice.

Kelly coaxed her morose friend into drinking a few sips of tea before departing into the campus darkness.

At two o'clock in the morning there was no pink haze of

dawn to indicate a new day had begun. The grass was damp and the tree leaves rustled faintly to assure Esther that some things in the world wouldn't change. Spring will always arrive, daisies will bloom, and only God knows when the timing is just right for each of these events to occur. It was Joseph's turn. The parking lot was illuminated by just two streetlights but it was enough to spot her small car. Her chest felt heavy as she inserted the key into the door. She tried to inhale deeply but the muscles wouldn't expand; she pulled a tissue from her pocket and wiped her eyes instead. She knew this was coming; it was long overdue. Joseph had lived years beyond the lifespan he'd been assigned by the doctors. A hint of a smile crossed her face as she realized that this meant many more memories of him to enjoy as she traversed her life path without him. *Thank you, God, for those eighteen years.*

~~~~~~

Unfortunately the sight was familiar. Esther had seen him propped on a steel-frame bed enough times to know that scenes of Joseph's hospitalizations weren't fading from her mind any time soon. She stiffened as she entered his room and knew immediately, without prayer and without a word from any doctor, that this day was the end. This was the day she would hold her baby brother one last time. This was the day she'd caress his forehead, kiss his cheek, and speak lovingly to him as he departed. This was the good-bye day. And so ironic that it was May 16th. That warm spring day eighteen years ago had been one of the best in her life; the baby was home. She remembered fondly the book she'd created for her baby Joseph so many years ago. The smiling faces, the sunshine, the wagon. Her mother now kept the book in a cardboard box wrapped with a blue ribbon.

Esther set a chair beside Joseph's bed and staunchly refused to weep. The tears would come later. Oh, they'd come. But she wouldn't waste the final precious moments of his life crying. Ken and Agatha stood from their seats and moved nearer to

Esther; her father squeezed her shoulders gently. Her mother's cheeks were wet with salty tears.

At home two weeks ago, when he knew for certain that his life would end before summer arrived, Joseph had demanded that his parents keep Esther away until the last possible moment. He loathed the idea that his death might interfere with her college graduation. And he wanted her memories to comprise the living part of him, not the dying. Additionally, and as important, he'd insisted that his morphine drip be kept minimal once admitted to the hospital. He wanted a reasonable state of coherence during his good-bye with Esther. His parents had complied with both requests.

"Es?" Joseph whispered her name and turned to face her. His lips curled into a dry and crooked grin.

"If I could trade my life with yours now, I'd do it Joseph. You're a courageous and brilliant young man. You've given so much to me; I wish that I could repay you with my own body so you'd experience life on this earth without CF. I want you to know that I am me because of you. And you taught me more about life than I'll ever learn from another person. I love you."

"Love you, Es. You're a great person—stay who you are. Thanks for giving so much to me." Her ear was inches from his mouth to gather the strained words.

"I pray for you every day, Joseph. It keeps me close to God and that's a really good thing. You're a constant vision in my thoughts and you'll forever remain a part of whom I am."

"If I get to heaven and you keep praying, maybe I'll hear your voice. Sing some prayers with your guitar. That'd be nice." He gasped weakly for a breath and then stilled, finally able to submit to the eminent suffocation after having seen his precious Esther one last time. Their gazes locked for just a moment before he clutched her hand and turned away.

After several long minutes of silence, the blood oxygen monitor sounded its alarm; his lungs were drawing final breaths.

A doctor strode into the room and noted Joseph's condition before solemnly turning to the family who stood beside the boy. "I can make his departure painless," was all that he said.

Ken nodded and then bowed his head to brace against the wave of grief that swept across the room. The doctor adjusted the morphine drip and left quietly.

Esther stood to press her face against Joseph's chest. His breathing had become unrestrained and barely audible. After thousands of prayers, the answer had finally come. *Dear Lord, Let him breathe without pain.* She sat back down and took hold of her brother's hand. Ken and Agatha laid their hands over hers.

Joseph passed away at 2:10 p.m. And Esther's tears came.

~~~~~~

The funeral service, sullen gathering on Lavender Lane, and return flight to Philadelphia hadn't even registered in her mind. It's not that the memories were merely vague; they didn't exist. She attended the final days of her college courses in a catatonic state, literally bumping into walls and forgetting which days she worked at the library. For more than two weeks, remorse and shock had pulsed through her veins; it had been causing excruciating headaches and nausea lately.

Esther's perspective on life now spiraled in a bizarre direction. It seemed that her insides had collapsed into a tiny speck and she was left with a cavernous void. Unable to express laughter and cheer, she wasn't sure how to cope with the celebratory atmosphere that permeated the campus. The loss she'd just suffered was taking a toll. Her bones ached and her skin was constantly chilled from an anguish that had taken residence a week ago. The memories of her childhood were encased by visions of Joseph; she'd been his rock for most of her life and now she had nothing to support.

Esther was glad her parents were in University Park for the graduation ceremony. It forced them to climb out of their despair for a few days. She'd met them at their hotel earlier in the day to share a quiet breakfast. They'd celebrate tonight, in a dazed fashion, with dinner and champagne at the Stillwater Grille. Kelly's folks were planning to join them. Esther would return to Michigan in a week and restart her life as a college graduate. She'd give herself a year to recover on Lavender Lane, work a decent job to save up some cash, and then move to Arcadia next spring. *Thank you, Lord, for the cabin.*

Heather, Steve, Tom, Barry, and Laura stormed the apartment. Everyone hugged everyone. Smiles were framed in laughter and tears.

"Esther, you look ravishing my little darling." Barry scooped her up like a child and twirled her around the room.

She wrapped her arms around his neck and squealed, "Put me down crazy man, you smell like beer!" She couldn't help but offer a grin. And then solemnity tapped her on the shoulder as a reminder that she'd probably never see some of these people again. Adding comic relief to the scene full of mixed emotions, Kelly yanked curlers from her hair while twirling through the craziness.

Barry pulled Esther into her bedroom and closed the door behind them. "I'm sorry, Es. I know that Joseph is a part of who you are, but promise you won't mourn for too long. Rebuild and look forward; cherish the memories but don't wallow in self-pity. Okay?" He swallowed hard and then locked onto her eyes, "I'll miss you for a long time, despite the fact that we never got past first base." He ruffled the top of her head and chuckled, "You're an infinitely kind woman; the only one who could've talked me into a church. I hope your life is amazing and the man you marry is perfect." Pressing her face between his palms, Barry kissed her tenderly, knowing it was their last.

~~~~~~

The Stillwater Grille was a popular post-graduation spot. The Gardener and McGowan families were seated at a table away from the rowdy center of the restaurant. Agatha had spoken with Kelly on the phone many times and she was glad to finally meet Esther's roommate. "Will you teach in this area, Kelly?"

"I submitted my application to the Philadelphia school district for an intern position; I requested elementary, but they'll assign me where I'm needed. I hope to teach either first or second grade and will relocate outside of Pennsylvania if the offer is right." Kelly looked forward to working directly with young students in a classroom environment. She had spunk and loved children; her career path was a perfect fit.

Doug McGowan, a high school history teacher, had recently traveled with his senior class to Washington D.C. He and Ken were engrossed in a conversation. Because Ken hadn't seen the capitol city, he was an eager audience as Doug highlighted the best points of the capital tour.

Sheila McGowan was delighted to meet her daughter's roommate and parents. She knew that Esther had had a very positive influence on Kelly during the past few years and she felt somehow indebted to her. "Kelly mentioned that you own a cabin in Michigan, Esther. Sounds interesting."

"I inherited the property from a friend two years ago. It's in Arcadia, which is on the northwest edge of the lower peninsula on Lake Michigan. The atmosphere there is very serene and even whimsical at the right moment. I don't know that I'll ever put my library science degree to use up there, but I intend to move into the cabin next summer. I have to trust that the Lord gave the cabin to me for a reason." Esther smiled half-heartedly as she offered additional details of Arcadia. . . lovely beaches, quaint restaurants, marinas, and such.

"I tried to talk her into working somewhere like Philadelphia or Boston, but her heart is set on that little town." Kelly wrapped her arms around Esther, "Be sure to call me from that cabin as soon as you have a phone number."

"I'd love for you to visit; promise we'll stay in touch?" The roommates clinked champagne glasses to seal the deal.

~~~~~~

The summer crawled along forlornly like a tired freighter on the lake. Esther hadn't yet moved from her crossroad; she felt caught between her life as it had been and life as it would be. The bakery job kept only her hands occupied on weekdays from six in the morning until early afternoon. This morning she was perusing her old algebra book when the phone rang. *Why didn't I help him with this? I was too selfish and absorbed in my stupid life.*

Esther laid on the bed to gather her concentration and focus him sharply in her mind. His face was clear; she could see him at the kitchen table, scribbling solutions and chewing on the end of his pencil. She worked up a strong image of Joseph in her mind several times each day; she had a chronic fear that he'd fade and she refused to let that happen. The persistent depth of her yearning for him was overwhelming sometimes, and she couldn't deny the consuming grief that had left puddles of tears in her mind. *Will there ever be joy in my life again?*

Agatha stepped from the kitchen into the hallway, "It's Karen on the phone."

"Hi, honey. How are you?" Karen hadn't seen Esther since the funeral in May but felt certain that her young friend was still in shock.

"I'm sad and lost. There are days I feel my life won't continue without him because a part of me is dead." Tears brimmed and then tumbled down her cheeks.

"Oh, sweetie. Cherish your memories and don't let go of your own life. I'm calling because I have some very interesting news, and you of all people will truly appreciate it. First of all, do you remember that Velma left a substantial amount of money to the City of Frankfort to use for a library expansion?"

"Yes, I do. Have they done anything yet?"

"The money she donated three years ago wasn't enough to pay for the entire building project. But after years of fund-raisers and private donations, it looks like the library will finally get its expansion next summer. Isn't that wonderful?"

"That's great. A grand library is such an important part of a community." Esther was sincerely delighted that the project would finally take off.

"And now my second piece of news. A woman by the name of Annette Carlson is the Frankfort librarian." Karen barely contained her excitement, "I saw her at the post office the other day and she's retiring next year to move to Florida with her sister. We'll need a librarian and if you decide to move into the cabin, I bet that job could be yours."

"Are you serious? I'd love to be Frankfort's librarian." Esther hadn't experienced a positive outlook in months, and now it was literally filling her up; she was at last feeling a warmth that came from within.

"The Blueberry Festival is soon. How about getting away from Detroit and coming up here for a week or two? I'd introduce you to Annette and she could show you around the library. I mentioned a northern trip to your mom and she was open to the idea. I can have the electricity turned on in your cabin and air it out some; or the three of you can stay here with us. Think about it for a few days and call me back. And Esther?"

"Yeah?"

"You're going to be okay, honey. The pain will lessen and he'll remain in your heart. You've lost his body but not his spirit."

"You're a wonderful friend. I'll call you in a few days."

~~~~~~

An endless soliloquy played inside of her. The beauty of the beach was merely a backdrop to the dark curtain of pain that cloaked her heart. Thundering waves broke onto the shore, seagulls circled overhead, and brilliant white sand surrounded her. These were soothing visions to many people, but none of them matched the comfort she found in Ken's grip. Agatha was lying against his body while he clung to her tenderly. They'd made the drive north, hoping that the tranquility of the lake could erase some of the grief. But Arcadia brought a flurry of memories instead that intensified the wounds. They would stay another day and then return home. Esther decided to stay the entire week; she'd return to Detroit via Greyhound bus.

Esther strolled along the water's edge toward the dunes, eyes open wide as she searched for flat stones. After skipping each one, she scanned the water to catch a glimpse of the sailboats dancing along the horizon. The anger and shock were finally making their exit. She was healing and knew without a doubt that this would be the place where her life without Joseph would begin. She looked forward to another week near the lake, and was anxious to meet Annette on Monday.

~~~~~~

"I'm sorry your folks couldn't stay longer, but I truly understand. I lived in a fog for six months after we lost Brian." Karen still sunk into a grieving period during the week of Brian's birthday in August, but decided against sharing this personal information with Esther.

John had hired twenty pickers this year; his and Karen's personal work in the fields now totaled just twenty hours each week. John was supervising the crew today and Karen had the day off. She and Esther were headed to the library; Karen chatted ceaselessly about the new shops that had sprung up in town. Frankfort now boasted an art museum, a sporting goods store, and a delicatessen. And two of the Victorian homes near the downtown area had been converted to bed-and-breakfast enterprises.

"I could live here for a hundred years and never grow tired of the view that this stretch of M-22 offers." Esther was prone in her seat, head lolling on the headrest. "Can you believe that I've visited Frankfort a dozen times yet never once stepped foot into its library? Do you really think I've got a shot at the librarian position?"

"Are you kidding? You're probably the only person within a hundred-mile radius who has her degree in library science. Who else would they offer the position to?" Karen chuckled before continuing, "I know that Annette wants to stay at least through the planning stages of the new addition next summer, but she wants to be in Florida by the following October."

Karen parked on Ninth Street so they could walk to the library on Main Street. Lining the sidewalks were mostly maple and young elm trees. The tiny lawns were groomed with great care and a wide variety of flowers had been lovingly planted around several of the houses. Summer in Arcadia was brief and the gardeners cherished each day they could tend to the outdoor plants. Esther thought of the Bentley oak tree on Lavender Lane and smiled easily.

The library was a very small structure with a squat brick face. Brushed aluminum letters conveyed the building's name and purpose. A group of thirsty geraniums hung from their flowerbox near the entrance. Karen walked inside and Esther followed beneath the bell that jingled above the door jam.

Karen greeted Annette immediately, "Good morning. I'd like you to meet Miss Esther Gardener."

The amiable librarian gently grasped Esther's outstretched hand, "Welcome home, Esther."

"Thank you, Annette. Nice place you've got here."

Summer 1984

The pangs of guilt grew stronger in her stomach the farther north they drove. Esther's father pulled a small U-Haul trailer behind the Buick and she followed in her Toyota. Her back seat was full of her clothing, guitar, and a few favorite plants. The Gardeners were traveling to Arcadia for the Memorial Day weekend. Esther would stay and her parents would return to Detroit on Monday. One of her main roles in life seemed to wither away after Joseph's death a year ago. She subsequently assumed a new role as supporter and comforter for her parents during the past year; and now she was leaving them.

Esther had attended numerous grief counseling sessions, which helped immensely in reassembling her emotional state and outlook on life. But Agatha's sorrow continued and Ken became immersed in his law practice, often spending sixty hours a week at the office to cope with the loss. As she gained psychological strength and began sketching out her future, she realized it was unhealthy to linger on Lavender Lane.

Lying on her passenger seat was the notebook that she and Joseph had taken to Arcadia almost four years ago. It was open to a blank page where she jotted down tasks that randomly popped into her mind. *Get a washer and dryer. Install a telephone. Ask Annette about the preschool story-time program. Repair the screen door on the side of the cabin. Get the cabin chimney cleaned.* And so on.

They turned onto Glovers Lake Road at last and she'd be home soon. *Home. My home.* Karen would be just minutes away and Carl's family and farm would be her neighbors. She could stroll along the lake every day of the summer. She'd see the autumn glory for weeks on end. And the winters would be exhilarating and harsh. She would invest in a pair of cross-country skis, improve her guitar playing skills, and become a more proficient chess player while stuck in the cabin during the winter weekends.

As they pulled into the driveway, her mental movie reel replayed a picture of Uncle Clem on his cabin porch more than a decade ago, her first summer in Arcadia. She parked alongside the Buick and jumped out to begin unpacking her belongings into the small home. Ken immediately began to inspect the cabin's exterior and overgrown yard. Agatha cried at the thought of losing her daughter to the remote hideaway and wondered at what point in her development Esther had become an isolationist.

The cabin was situated on the southwest corner of the ten-acre parcel and a small log shed stood about twenty yards behind the cabin. The long gravel driveway that turned off of Glovers Lake Road led to the side entrance of the cabin. Years ago, Velma mowed a small area surrounding the cabin every week. A visitor wouldn't have guessed that fact by the sight of the property today. The other nine acres hadn't ever been hacked by a human tool. It held deer trails, rabbit families, fox dens, wildflowers, white pine, birch, maple, oak, wasp nests; and a small pond full of turtles, frogs, and thousands of other tiny creatures. This summer Esther would discover several piles of large fieldstones stacked throughout the property. Velma had planned to haul them to the cabin for use as flowerbed borders, but never got around to actually doing it.

"Once we unpack, I'll inspect the shed for yard tools. If there's a mower you and mom can get gasoline tomorrow after grocery shopping. I'd like to clear out an area around the cabin for you before we leave on Monday." Ken was impelled to stay busy.

Earlier in the month, Karen and John had the cabin's well, septic, and plumbing inspected; the electricity turned on; and the propane tank filled. They'd performed these springtime chores the previous two years to prepare the dwelling for summer visits from the Gardener family. But this year, Karen had done much more. She scrubbed and polished the cabin's entire interior, washed all the windows, cleaned out the fireplace, and washed every dish and utensil in the kitchen cupboards and drawers. Working four to five hours each day, it had taken her three weeks to accomplish the chores. The interior now glistened and exuded a clean, oil-soap aroma. It was her housewarming gift to Esther.

When the Gardeners stepped inside the small home, the flowers on the counter and tray full of granola bars welcomed them. Esther smiled deeply, "Karen."

~~~~~~

The Red Owl market was a surprisingly well-stocked grocery and drug store. Although kiwi and fresh gingerroot were absent, the basic fruits and vegetables were plentiful and fresh. The store offered a good deli and fresh bread as well. Because she'd already purchased bags of supplies and kitchen staples in Detroit several days ago, Esther's shopping cart was not substantially full this morning. While she and Agatha moved items from the cart onto the checkout counter, Esther thought of the fun they'd have stocking and organizing the kitchen. After a visit to the lake, of course.

"How're you today?" Charlotte began scanning Esther's order.

"Very happy. I moved to Arcadia from Detroit yesterday and this is my first shopping trip." Esther hurriedly emptied the last few items onto the counter.

"Welcome home. I'm Charlotte. Whereabouts in Arcadia do you live?"

"On Glovers Lake Road, just east of the elementary school. I'm Esther Gardener and this is my mom, Agatha."

"Nice to meet you both. Are you in Velma's place? You're such a young thing. Why'd you move here?"

"Yes Ma'am. I'll work with Annette at the library for a year, and when she retires next fall I'll be Frankfort's librarian." Esther counted out a few bills to cover her purchase.

"You look like a fruit and vegetable sort of person. Would you like to work in our produce section a few nights a week?"

Charlotte's eyes wore a hopeful expression.

"I don't have produce experience but I'm a quick learner."

"Talk to James at the service desk; he'll give you an application and let you know about wages and such. Have a nice day, Esther and Agatha."

After picking up the job application, loading groceries into the trunk, and pumping a gallon of gasoline, mother and daughter settled into the car for the scenic ride home.

"You belong here, Es. Your energy is admirable and I'm very proud of you; Dad and I look forward to spending time with you here. Perhaps we'll start a tradition this fall; we could make a weekend trip to Arcadia every October and tour the area with you. I bet the colors are spectacular this far north." Agatha's face assumed a melancholy expression at the sight of a young boy casting his line into the Betsie River.

"I like that idea. Don't look so glum, Mom. I'll be in Detroit for Thanksgiving and Christmas; we'll still see each other quite a bit. I'm just five hours away."

"I planned to pack the quilt you made but just couldn't part with it. Do you mind if I keep it for a while?" Agatha's eyes were brimming with tears all over again.

"It's yours. I'll sleep with it when I visit. Sit back and enjoy the pretty drive. Then let's hit the lake and tackle the kitchen chores."

~~~~~~

Esther ordered a Kenmore washer and dryer from the Sears catalog; they'd be delivered to the cabin next week. In the meantime, she brought her laundry into Frankfort on Tuesdays and Fridays before starting her shift at the library. Cowering beneath a bush at the side of the laundromat today was her future roommate.

"Hey little guy." She put the laundry basket down, sat beside the bush, and tentatively reached for the shivering dog. As she rubbed his dirty brown head he whimpered with such a pitiful whine that Esther's throat tightened in sympathy. *Good-*

ness sakes, I seem to be making everyone cry these days. He gingerly crawled from his spot and climbed onto her lap; grubby paws smeared dirt on her khaki skirt. Looking up and down the sidewalk, she saw no one who might be missing a dog. Hoping that the little fellow would follow her inside, Esther marched into the laundromat. He was right under her heels as she sorted laundry into two piles, measured detergent, and inserted handfuls of quarters to start the wash cycles. She plopped onto the floor and he made himself at home again on her lap.

"My guess is that you don't have a home, but I'll make a few signs at the library today to post around town in case someone is looking for you." Esther was pulling items from the dryer when Cindy arrived.

"Morning. Are you vacationing this week?" A middle name like Chatty would be entirely suitable for Cindy, a convivial woman with a knack for banter. Her quick wit, natural blond hair, and Betty Boop figure made her an automatic enemy to many women. But today was her lucky day. She was about to meet a pure-hearted girl who needed a friend.

"I moved to the area a week ago. I'm Esther and this is a lost dog."

"I'm Cindy Cullen. I work in the Mayor's office and just moved into my own place at Bayview near the beach a few months ago. My family has been here forever. Do you live in Frankfort?"

"I live in Arcadia but work four days a week at the Frankfort Library. I might start part-time work at the Red Owl, too."

"How'd you choose this area?" Cindy was glad to see a friendly twenty-something face.

"That's a pretty long story and I'd share it with you, but I'm due at the library in ten minutes. Will you be doing laundry here again sometime? We could visit then." Esther didn't want to appear pushy.

"Are you serious? We don't have to visit in this place." Cindy dug a business card from her purse, scribbled her home number, and handed it to Esther. "Call me tonight, we'll go to dinner sometime. Have you eaten at the Cabbage Shed yet? It's a fun place on Fridays and I can introduce you to lots of people."

Butterflies filled her stomach and Esther was grateful she didn't have her own washer yet. "I'd like that very much. I'll call you." She hauled her clean laundry out to the car with the beagle on her trail.

~~~~~~

Annette suggested that Esther work in the capacity of a library clerk for the first several weeks to become acquainted with the facility, its programs, and the library patrons. She enthusiastically performed her tasks and, in doing so, earned Annette's respect and friendship. Through mid July she would supervise the circulation desk, check materials in and out, type overdue notices, shelve books and periodicals, update patron records, and do general housekeeping duties.

Esther burst through the front door at ten o'clock sharp and, nearly breathless, approached her colleague. "As long as I'm working in this library, I will never again ask the question that I'm about to ask." Her pleading tone demanded attention.

"Well, now you've got my curiosity piqued. What's the question?" Annette removed her eyeglasses and leaned her gray head forward to better hear the query. Although it had been weeks since a cool breeze swept through the town, Annette kept a cardigan draped over her blouse. She was self-conscious of her expanding waistline and until she had more time to walk, the sweater stayed.

"May I bring a lost dog into the library today?" Esther wasn't posing a query, she was begging.

"As long as I'm working here this will be the only day that I allow a dog inside of the library. If the dog is large, I have the right to refuse his entry." Annette offered her gruffest expression but hid a smirk beneath it.

"You're wonderful. It's a beagle and I found him near the laundromat. If no one claims him, then he'll live with me." Esther dashed from the library and returned with the stinky pooch under her arm.

"Lovely. Put him into my office and then meet me at the magazine shelf; we need to go over the subscription renewal schedule for the periodicals. Later today we'll review the library's budget, which isn't much by the way." Annette had replaced her eyeglasses and stared across the top of them at her protégé, "I'd like you to attend the budget review meeting with me this fall; next year you'll be on your own with the City Council members."

As expected, the day dragged for the young librarian. In between training sessions with Annette, sporadic book shelving, and circulation desk duties, she visited with the beagle and made *lost dog* signs to post around town.

An hour before closing, Annette shooed Esther home, "That dog needs a bath; go ahead and leave early, and be sure to pick up a bag of dog food at the market on your way home. I'll ask my neighbors tonight if they know anyone who's missing a beagle." She cleared her throat and returned her attention to a cart full of children's books.

"I owe you an hour. You be sure to leave early on Friday and I'll close up." Esther scooped up the dog, which she instantly named Bentley, and hurried to her car before Annette changed her mind.

~~~~~~

It never failed. The phone rang when she was either eating or elbow deep in something. Esther pulled Bentley from the bathtub, wrapped him in a towel, and jogged to the telephone.

"Hi! I'll call you back. My arms are full of dog." She balanced a wet Bentley in her right arm and a phone beneath her left ear.

"It's Karen. May I help with something?"

"Definitely. Come on over."

Karen arrived after Esther had fastened a new blue collar around Bentley's neck. "He's adorable. Where'd you get him?" Sitting on the couch, she pulled the freshly shampooed dog onto her lap.

"He was at the laundromat this morning. Annette let him stay in the library for the day. Can you imagine? I posted a few signs around Frankfort before coming home, but secretly hope that no one claims him."

"I brought some chardonnay. I'm in the mood for cribbage and wine with my best friend and her new dog." Karen rummaged through a kitchen drawer to find a corkscrew. "Did you name him yet?"

"What do you think of Bentley? The name popped into my head at the library." Esther set two wineglasses on the counter, pulled the cribbage board and deck of cards from her bookshelf, and sat at the maple dinette. Bentley's toenails clicked across the floor until he collapsed beside his hero's feet. "I met the nicest girl today. Her name is Cindy and she works for the Mayor. Do you know her?"

"That's Ralph and Lisa Cullen's daughter; they've been in Frankfort for nearly twenty years. Ralph is a police officer and Lisa has three kids at home. One of their boys will start Michigan Tech in September. Cindy is the oldest of five; she bought a townhouse just a few doors down from where Velma used to live, if I'm not mistaken." Karen brought the wine and some crackers to the table and sat down. "I really like this maple dinette. How old is it?"

"Mom said her parents bought it when she was in grade school. She just turned forty-eight, so I'd guess it to be about forty years old." Esther rubbed her palm across the worn and scratched top. "I can sit here sometimes and drum up memories that I didn't even know were in my head. Having it here with me is a blessing and it fits perfectly in the cabin." Although she occasionally experienced bouts of doubt and anxiety, the cabin acted as her guardian, wrapping her in its warm walls of comfort.

"How are you getting along at the library?" Karen shuffled and dealt the cards.

"I'll be able to locate a shelved book blindfolded by the end of the summer. This library is much smaller than the Pattee at Penn State; it'll be very manageable for me alone next fall.

Annette has a preschool story-time program that she runs during the school year, but says it's not well attended. I'd like to mail flyers to persuade more young children and parents to become frequent patrons. I'd also like to see the elementary school classes visit the library more regularly. Annette suggested that I request a new line item in next year's budget for mailings and supplies to benefit those programs." Esther fanned her cards and sipped her wine.

"Has James called about work at the Red Owl? Working there a few evenings or weekends a month will be a good thing for you. It'll get awfully lonely in this cabin when winter sets in and I worry about your being alone. You're independent, I know, but you need to spend time with other young women and meet some nice men as well." Karen moved her pegs forward on the cribbage board.

"We've had this discussion already. I'm not worried about loneliness; God has me here for a reason." Esther played a card and grinned.

"Has he dropped any hints?" Karen fingered her cards before discarding one.

"I don't think that's his style. Perhaps I'm here to influence someone, or to be influenced myself. Or maybe I'm supposed to meet someone who needs only what I can give. Even if my purpose here is not monumental, I accept this station until He points me in another direction."

Karen was touched by the young woman's determination; "You have a bunch of faith in that little body."

"My dad likes to call it stubbornness."

~~~~~

She inserted her timecard into the AccuPrint time clock as the official start to her first day at the Red Owl market.

"You need to keep your hair tied back and wear this smock. The crates and loading docks are dirty and this thing will protect your clothes from grime and grease. We'll have an employee badge printed up for you this week." James pointed to a row of silver hooks in the break room, "Hang your smock here at the end of your shift, and if you bring a lunch it goes in that refrigerator." After Esther donned the oversized brown smock he led her into the produce section of the store.

"We have two crates of strawberries, a box of five-pound potato bags, and a crate of grapes from Dole to put out this afternoon. Let's bring the discard bin to the floor; some of the lettuce and cabbage look brown around the edges." A stout Irishman, James had gentle blue eyes and a soft belly. There wasn't a gruff thing about him. Although she heard that he'd previously held an upper-management position in an auto company, Esther couldn't picture him in a well-manicured conference room. She did guess, however, that he wore a wide-brimmed hat when he mowed the lawn or ventured to the beach to protect his very fair skin.

James and Esther strolled to the receiving dock. He pointed out the discard bin, receiving schedule, and the small lift cart she'd use to haul produce crates into the store. A large refrigeration unit held boxes of bagged vegetables, such as celery, carrots, and radishes. She'd be responsible for keeping an eye on the expiration dates of the bagged items on the floor. James would remain in charge of inventory control. "Any questions?"

"No, Sir. I'm ready to get started." They wheeled out the large bin and stopped at the lettuce. They sorted the heads, tossing those that were questionable. "How long have you lived in the area?"

"Ruth and I moved here from Detroit about ten years ago when the kids were young. I was a manager at GM putting in fifty-hour weeks and dealing with shenanigans from the line guys, associate managers, and my own boss. I just grew tired of it all, I guess. We rented a place on Crystal Lake a dozen summers ago, and drove into Frankfort one day to see the lighthouse and do a bit of sightseeing. Ruth and I fell in love with the place. We called a Frankfort realtor the following summer, sold our Detroit house, and bought a home here at nearly half the price of our Detroit property. I've been at this market ever since. I'll be the first to tell you that this job doesn't challenge me much but I'm content and am able to spend plenty of time with the children. Let's move to the cabbage."

Esther pulled the bin behind her and stopped to realign the rows of misplaced banana bunches. "People say that I'm foolish to live in such a quiet town but I can't imagine being anywhere else at this point in my life. I've always been one who's happy with a book or a walk outdoors. I might be simple-minded, but I agree with your point on the subject. There's peace in my heart and I believe that's because I'm supposed to be here right now."

James grinned at the innocent young woman. *Lord, Protect her from harm and send along plenty of happiness.* "You'll do just fine here, Esther."

~~~~~~

"This salad looks yummy. What's in it?" Cindy poked around the cooler in search of a snack.

"Besides the macaroni, I added a bunch of chopped celery, tomatoes, cucumbers, and olives. A little bit of Parmesan cheese, too. I want to eat something besides chips and marshmallows tonight. The bowls and spoons are in that yellow bag." Esther spread blankets onto the beach while Bentley sat beneath the big umbrella, grateful that the sun would be setting soon.

"Let's look for marshmallow roasters. Scott and Daphne are bringing firewood but they won't have skinny sticks." Cindy pulled a sweatshirt over her head and dashed up the sandy cliff into the woods near the Sunset Motel. Esther and Bentley romped behind her. Returning to the beach several minutes later, they found Scott arranging logs in the fire pit while Daphne inserted kindling pieces. Kevin arrived shortly thereafter with a bag full of campfire junk food and a kite. As usual, Kurt was late but carried a cooler full of soda and beer so the infraction was quickly forgiven.

Esther knew Scott, Daphne, and Kurt from the Cabbage Shed get-together a few weeks ago. She hadn't yet met Kevin. (Earlier in the day, Cindy had described him as a normal dentist who'd moved to the area a year ago.) Esther wondered whether dentists played Frisbee; after all, might they get whacked in the teeth? She giggled to herself. Cindy formally introduced the dentist and librarian before pushing them down together on the blanket. Kevin's shy glance into Esther's eyes made them both blush. *Is he my destiny?*

After a few rounds of Frisbee toss and kite-wrestling maneuvers, the group settled down to eat the salad and snacks. Behind them, the sun sank into the water's edge. They drank a boisterous toast to celebrate their friendships, both silver and gold, and the long days of summer. Huddled around the bonfire now, they watched the flames toss sparks into the sky; its globe of light made an orange reflection on the faces encircling it. Lake Michigan thundered its dark waves onto the shore. Kurt tickled Cindy until she dropped her marshmallow in the sand.

"You dingbat! That was a good one." He leapt from the blanket and ran down the beach; Cindy hopped from her spot to pursue her beau in the darkness. The couples remaining near the fire heard muffled laughter and squeals from the distant pair at the water's edge.

"Without a moon tonight the stars are magnificent. Do you see the Big Dipper over there?" Kevin pointed up to the darkness, leaning his face beside Esther's so she could follow his fingertip into the sky. "And there's Orion, the rectangular constellation with a group of stars in its center."

"I missed the night sky while growing up in a big city like Detroit. And I don't recall any stargazing sessions in Pennsylvania. Seeing the sky now makes me think of how it might've looked after God made everything and saw that it was good." Esther leaned back to capture the twinkling canvas and then collapsed onto the sand; the beer had relaxed her leg muscles. Kevin and Bentley plopped down beside the tipsy girl.

"What's it like living in a cabin so far from civilization? And what made you choose that lifestyle?" Kevin posed the questions with a concerned expression.

"Destiny. The Lord set the path before me and I'm simply walking on it. C'mon, let's get some marshmallows." She rose clumsily before walking to the wood pile in search of a long stick. A bewildered dentist and tired beagle kept an eye on the librarian, each for a different reason.

Pulling a crisp marshmallow from a stick, Kevin whispered to Esther, "The Manistee Theatre is playing *2010*. Want to see it and maybe grab dinner at the Chop House next weekend?"

"I'd like that. You'll need directions to my cabin." She pulled Bentley onto her lap and rubbed his ears.

"It's a small town; I know exactly where your cabin is. I can call you next week after checking movie times. Deal?"

"Absolutely." Esther inched closer to him hoping for sparks to fly, or perhaps a heart-rate acceleration. Nothing yet. *Maybe after the movie next week . . . that's when it'll happen.*

~~~~~~

"I'll bring my beach umbrella, guitar, and Bentley." As she and Karen planned the day, Esther stared out her kitchen window. The sun had dropped low into the clouds, turning the evening sky into a layer of cottony pink tufts. In the daylight the fields were full of life and colored by a dozen different hues, but now, beneath the cloaking evergreen shadows, everything blended together into a sandy gray tone. "What time are we leaving?"

"We'll pick you up around eight-thirty. I bet your granola will be popular this year, Es. See you tomorrow." Karen promised John this summer that she'd be a festival vendor for just another year or two, and then it would be time to retire. Fifteen years was long enough.

Esther took the scissors from her pencil cup and walked purposefully out of the cabin. Bentley perked up when she slipped into her shoes and then bolted out the door to scamper into the field. She cut Black-eyed Susans, Queen Anne's lace, ferns, chicory and Indian paintbrush wildflowers. The large bouquet was full of tiny insects so she shook the flowers to set them free; a distant rustling sound stopped her motion. She dropped to her knees and fell silent for a minute to wait for another sound. Bentley jogged to her side and she grabbed his collar. The buck dashed out in a flash and roared past her on thundering hooves, missing Esther by just a meter or two. He was magnificent. She stood to watch him burst across the field and dart onto Glovers Lake Road. Bentley howled and romped to the trail to catch its scent.

~~~~~~

"Those sunglasses won't do much to protect your nose and cheeks; put this sunscreen on your face." Karen squeezed a glob of the lotion into Esther's palm. "How'd the batch turn out?"

"They're a bit crunchy for my taste; I think they baked too long but the maple flavor kept its strength." They were the first granola bars Esther had made without assistance. She hoped to sell all hundred bars today.

"Hello there, Karen." It was Lynn. She and her husband owned the Iron Anchor restaurant in town. "How's the Holsten orchard faring this summer?"

"It's a good harvest; I just picked these yesterday." Karen smiled and peeked out from under the wide brim of her hat.

John stood from his seat to greet Lynn and offer a small cup of blueberries. "Where's Richard these days?"

"He's at the marina with Glen and Earl. They're planning a fishing trip tomorrow and I bet they'd like a fourth man on the boat if you're not in that orchard." She removed her sunglasses and extended her hand to Esther, "I'm Lynn Connor. Is this the Esther I've heard so much about?"

Esther rose to complete the handshake, "Yes, Ma'am. Have I done something to cause a stir?"

"No, no! I had lunch with Annette the other day and she had many kind things to say about you. Welcome to Frankfort. Is this the dog you rescued?"

"Yes, this is Bentley. Would you like a granola bar?"

"My daughter and her three children are visiting tomorrow, so I'd like a dozen, if that's okay. And two quarts of blueberries from you, Karen."

The Saturday floated away like a breeze that caressed the beach and then merged into the water without warning. In the early afternoon, Esther strummed her guitar, softly humming tunes that wove into the mood of the festival. Drawn to its simplicity and eloquence, people stopped to listen. She ended the song when visions of Joseph materialized. His baby smiles, their neighborhood walks together, and Christmas mornings. She recalled his unyielding courage and faith. *He's without pain now.*

At five o'clock, Karen, John, Esther, and Bentley finally packed their gear and headed to the car parked a block away.

"Was I introduced to every Benzie County resident you know today? I probably shook thirty or forty hands." Esther recalled that Scott and Daphne stopped to visit, and she saw several faces that were now familiar to her. She was glad to have her days and weekends full at the library and market. Her spirit was blending into the community and she was growing in so many ways. In just ten weeks, she'd made several friends, moved effortlessly with the rhythm of the town, and joined a church in Arcadia. And the cherry on the sundae today: all hundred granola bars were sold for a nifty profit of fifty dollars.

June 1985

Jack Dawson strolled into the library on his way to lunch, "How's cabin life these days, Esther?"

"Hi Jack. It's much more pleasant now without the wind and snow seeping between the crevices." She'd met the Mayor last summer and liked him instantly. He was attentive and solicitous. Esther guessed he was in his mid fifties; he had two grown children, one in Colorado and the other at Michigan State. His wife, Audrey, was an avid gardener with a spectacular array of ever-blooming perennials; bird-watching was her second favorite hobby. If a person wanted to attract a particular bird to his yard, Audrey could tell him which seed to scatter.

Despite his casual attire, Jack assumed a businesslike tone, "I know that you were in Detroit last week when we met with the first design group; can you attend the meeting with the other group tomorrow? They'll be up from Grand Rapids and we're meeting at ten o'clock in the City Hall building. Annette Carlson and Bob Brigham will be there, too. The architects will of course need to tour the library before they can design the addition; perhaps you can walk them through after the meeting. And they'll want to see the building site as well."

"I'll be there. My shift at the market tomorrow doesn't start until two o'clock. Isn't this exciting? It'll be fabulous for the kids to have a bigger place to gather. I'd love a dedicated room for preschoolers and early readers. . . a few fairy tale paintings could adorn the walls. And a reading couch as well." She looked forward to the meeting; her head was full of ideas.

"Yup, but let's get the building done first, eh? We'll see you tomorrow then, Esther. I'm meeting Earl at the diner for lunch. Tracey made a batch of Traverse City cherry pies and I hear they're terrific."

Esther returned to her card catalog duty. The library didn't experience much traffic during the summer so she was realphabetizing the cards that had been improperly filed. Now in the *H* drawer, she needed to accelerate her pace before the library saw an increase in patrons this September. She peered out the window for a glimpse of the glorious day ahead for Frankfort. Perfect for weeding around her bean plants. She was proud of her first garden; it appeared already that the cucumber vines might overtake the other vegetable plants. She hoped to pick a barrel of tomatoes for canning in August. She made a mental note to ask Carl about quantity pricing for oats. Of course, she first had to devise a marketing plan so shop owners would actually put her granola into their stores before she invested in a ton of oats. She'd make a fresh batch of granola for his family this weekend. *What is his wife's name? Jackie or Jamie?*

The phone rang as she wiped a smudge off a faded card. "Frankfort Library, Esther speaking."

"Hey, Esther, it's Cindy. Mr. Dawson wanted me to ask if you'd make some oatmeal snacks for the meeting tomorrow. He didn't want to ask you personally; I mean, I know he was there to see you this morning, but he thought it might be too much. Could you bring some?"

"Sure. I'm making a panful to bring over to Carl's on Saturday. Would you happen to know the name of Carl's wife?"

Cindy's smile of relief was revealed in her voice, "Awesome. I'm pretty sure it's Jackie. You know she's pregnant again? I think Davey just turned two last month. They work so hard in those fields that it's a wonder where they find the time to raise their two kids. Hey—speaking of over-ambitious, when was the last time you went out? We've missed you at the Cabbage Shed the past few Fridays. Daphne said that Scott's cousin will be here this weekend. You remember the guy who brought the case of Heineken to the July 4th bonfire last year and fell off that raft like two-hundred yards from shore?"

And on and on she talked. Esther wondered how it was that she hadn't been blessed with a chatty gene. She so preferred her books and garden to the social hazards everywhere these days. She hadn't bothered updating her wardrobe in years because it just didn't seem worth the effort when she only went out once a month. "I've been busy with the cabin and garden, and I'm making improvements to the granola recipe. Plus the Friday afternoon shifts at the market keep me tied up. I'll catch up with you guys next week."

"All right then. But I swear, Esther, you're going to die an old maid in that cabin of yours and no one will know you've expired until you miss two Sunday services in a row." Cindy couldn't help but chide Esther; her best friend and always so sensible. She kept Cindy grounded and thoughtful, much like Pinocchio's conscience, Jiminy Cricket.

Back to the card catalog. The library door opened for the second time today and she glanced to the entrance as she heard the familiar jingle from the bell above the door. She spied two boys, probably about eleven years old. "No guys. Out of here with the ice cream cones. You finish them on the bench outside, and *then* you come in." Esther judiciously enforced the no-food-allowed rule.

With sticky hands and satisfied bellies, the boys cautiously waltzed back into the library a few minutes later. "We need a book on how to build kites. Not just regular kites, but really huge ones. We wanna fly them by the lake when we have our party next weekend."

Esther smiled, smoothing out her denim skirt as she rose from her seat. "Let's check the craft section. We'll probably find something between the birdhouse and paper airplane books."

Like a pair of curious elves, the boys tagged alongside her until they reached their destination near the back of the library. Esther fingered the book spines as she searched for the big blue craft book. "Aha. Here it is." She shuffled with the boys to a nearby table, opened the book to its first page. "We'll first check the table of contents. See if there's something on kites in here." She turned the book to the blond boy, who slid his grubby finger down the list.

"This says *Kite Building* right here and it's on page 127," the boy declared. He turned to the page where they found small diagrams of several kites. Each type of kite presented its own set of numbered steps. More pages of drawings and detailed instructions followed; there seemed to be dozens. The search continued until the boys found a satisfactory kite design.

"Can we take this book home? My dad's gonna help us build this weekend and he'll need to see all of this." Esther asked if either boy had a library card, but both shook their heads.

"I'm supposed to get a signature from a parent before giving you a library card; you're not sixteen yet. But I'll sign for you today." Esther dug out two application forms and held out the pencil cup. She was absolutely beaming. Watching the boys hurriedly fill in names and addresses gave her a grand feeling of accomplishment. They handed her their applications and she signed them in an exaggeratedly professional manner. Next, she grabbed the stack of blank library cards, sat down at the typewriter and created two brand-new cards for the boys.

"Mr. Tom and Mr. Doug, these are your keys to knowledge and adventure. Keep them in safe places and cherish them always." Another great part of her job. She stamped a new date on the craft book's *Due Back* card and wrote Tom's card number and the book title into the *Books Loaned* ledger. "You are ready to build. Good luck and I'll see you in two weeks." Tom was thrilled to have the whole process done and the book in his hands.

"Thanks. Maybe you'll see our kite flying if you're at the beach next Saturday." The boys dashed from the library, hopped onto their bikes, and pedaled away with purpose.

Esther heard the pendulum clock chime; it was five o'clock already. She loved the library but was glad to click the deadbolt lock when she left at the end of each day. She was tempted to run across the street to the diner for a piece of Tracey's pie, but then remembered she had the box of Mackinac Island fudge in the refrigerator from her parents' recent visit. It'd provide plenty of sugar for the next few days.

Her blue Toyota was the only car in the gravel lot adjacent to the library; she was immediately glad she'd left the windows rolled down. It was blistering hot in the car and the vinyl seats nearly burned her legs. Strapping herself under the seatbelt, she looked forward to her commute. The fifteen-minute drive south on M-22 to her cabin in Arcadia was resplendent. Rolling hills flourished with pine, birch, maple, and fragrant wildflower fields. Randomly dispersed along the highway were tiny white cottages with flower-boxes full of red geraniums. And of course, as the road veered down into town, she had the spectacular view of Lake Michigan. This afternoon the water sparkled in crystal waves beneath the cloudless sky. If she had enough time after supper and chores, she and Bentley might go for a romp on the beach. They hadn't been to the lake since Sunday.

~~~~~~

Bentley hurled himself onto her bed and whimpered like a baby. Esther made an opening in her quilt so he could crawl in beside her. She rubbed her eyes and listened to the morning unfold. A quick wind was whipping off the coast and the sound of thunder rumbled miles away from the cabin. She scratched her head and thought seriously about heeding Cindy's beauty advice. Her friend insisted that Esther get her hair straightened so it'd be at least slightly more manageable. The humidity was going to wreck havoc on her hair today. The clock read 7:04—plenty of time for a quick run before her shower and breakfast.

She gave the dog a kiss and ear rub, then slid out of bed to fetch him a biscuit. With Bentley settled down, she quickly brushed her teeth and threw on her running gear. No headphones this morning; she wanted a soothing run before her busy day. Besides, if it decided to rain she figured that wearing an electronic device might be a fatal mistake.

She ran her usual route. First, a half mile down Glovers Lake Road, then across M-22 and into downtown past the post office, fire station, Finch Park and historical museum on Lake Street. She paused briefly at First Street to catch a morning view of the lake and thought of Joseph. *Dear Lord, Let him breathe without pain today.* How many times had she uttered that prayer as a kid? Thousands. She pictured him now with his ever-chapped lips and chestnut brown hair. Truly a gift from God, that's what he was. As her return run neared its end past the elementary school, she heard a resounding thunder clap and decided to pick up her pace to get home before the downpour.

Bentley's hysterical barking twisted her stomach as she approached the cabin. *Oh rats.* She immediately saw the squirrel on top of the refrigerator when she opened the door. The poor dog was running in frantic circles around the kitchen table while barking to keep the pest at bay. *I have to trap it in something and then carry it outside.*

After locking Bentley in the bathroom, she remembered the big fishing net her dad had left last week. "You never know when something like this might come in handy, Esther, especially living in the country." Well, howdy doody. How did he know she'd have a squirrel in her house five days later? Gotta love that man's logic.

Esther fetched the net from the shed and ran into the cabin before the squirrel had a chance to hide. There it was. Scampering across the floor to the couch. She slammed the net over the squirrel but he squirmed out from under the rim. Phooey. Now it was under the couch. She poked the net handle under the couch until the blasted rodent dashed out and headed to the fireplace. Slam! She got him. *Oh dear, it's just a baby. Now what? If I lift the net, he'll run out again. How was it that Joseph caught those butterflies with his net?* She remembered. He'd slide a piece of cardboard under the net and then lift the entire contraption.

There was a shoebox in the closet, but that was several feet away. She slid the net-encased squirrel slowly across the floor until she was in front of the closet door. Then, while standing on the net handle, she reached up to the closet shelf and grabbed the box. She quickly flattened it with her other foot and then placed it beneath the little varmint. Voila! With a tight grip on the cardboard and net, she tiptoed to the door, kicked it open and threw the whole enchilada outside. She definitely had to fix the kitchen window screen.

It was nine-thirty by the time Bentley had calmed down and she'd eaten breakfast and showered. Her hair wouldn't get any attention this morning; it simply wasn't in the cards. She did some finger combing, massaged a glob of gel through it, and sprayed the curly tendrils so they wouldn't stick out too badly.

The rain began pelting furiously onto her windshield as she turned onto M-22. She'd barely make it to City Hall by ten o'clock.

~~~~~~

Jack turned to Esther when she entered the meeting room, "Good morning; did you have to paddle to get here?"

She laughed, "Nah. Just a few waterlogged spots on the highway." She set the plate of granola bars onto the table and nodded to the others before taking a seat beside Annette. Esther was pulling her hair away from her face when he walked into the room.

"Now this is real coffee. Did you guys heat this up from last week's council meeting?" Daniel grinned at the group gathered around the table. His eyes briefly rested on Esther. "I don't believe we've met yet; I'm Daniel Jacobson with Smythe & Jacobson Design. My partner, Mitch Smythe, couldn't be here today, so it's just me."

Esther's heart pummeled to her stomach as she stood to greet the architect. She'd never seen a more stunning man in her life. Ever. *Wait a minute. It's the guy I tackled on Allen Street.* The image of his face had engraved itself in her mind five years ago when their eyes met for the first time. There was no mistaken identity here. This was the Daniel she thought she'd never see again.

"Hello, I'm Esther. I'm a librarian here." Daniel reached for her hand and she set her palm against his; it was warm and strong. Her mind somersaulted as she fought for clarity.

Jack spread out the Frankfort Library blueprints and laid down the photos of the building. He succinctly described Frankfort's recent growth and the City Council's approval of the library expansion. Based on the dimensions of the lot adjacent to the library and parking requirements, he guessed the addition would not exceed twelve hundred square feet. He additionally proposed a working budget.

Bob posed several questions about the building phases and project timeline. Daniel summarized the key phases with a rough schedule: site survey and prep; footings and foundation; framing; exterior walls; roofing; duct work; bricklaying; interior work, such as drywall, molding, door hanging, and carpeting; and landscaping. The listeners nodded approvingly.

Finally, Jack nodded to Esther, "Tell him how this expansion will be used."

Daniel watched her shuffle through a folder and pull out a crude drawing with marginal notes written in red. As she expressed her ideas for the added space and defined the rooms' purposes, he was captivated by the enthusiasm flowing across the table. She was so excited about this project. Watching her animated motions, his mind wandered. *She's radiant. An angel.* A strange emotion flickered across his chiseled features, and his heart lurched in response to her obvious innocence and delightful voice.

Esther continued her presentation, describing a separate activity room for community events like seminars and book sales. She stressed the importance of natural lighting and desire for large windows. She then described a preschool room large enough for rocking chairs, several child-sized reading tables, and shelving along two walls. "Well, that's about it, I guess."

She rubbed her nervous palms together and abruptly sat back down. She sipped her thick coffee then glanced to the area in front of Daniel. He hadn't taken a single note. Esther supposed he either had an incredible memory or wasn't interested in what she had to say about the addition. She was suddenly irritated by the handsome architect. She wished for a magic wand to transform him into a homely little man for a day. He'd see the world much differently then, and it might smack that cocky smile off his face.

After Esther's spiel, Annette volunteered further information on the size and use of the rooms. She then mentioned that additional bathrooms would be unnecessary; the two restrooms in the library already had two stalls each.

Bob was the note taker of the bunch. As the City Council representative, he meticulously tracked the discussion so he could relay the information at the next council meeting. It was his turn to make an important point, "We have a good construction crew in this town, Dan. Henry Gillman heads up the team. In addition to about a dozen houses they've built recently, they did the update work on the post office and built the new high school gymnasium. I think they're working on a theatre project in Manistee now, but that's supposed to wrap up in about a month. Do you want Henry at the next meeting?"

"Definitely. If you have his number I'd like to call him once I'm back in my office to discuss the schedule. Thanks, Bob."

"Ahem." Esther rose from her seat. "Did I mention a skylight for the central area? Natural lighting is far superior for reading than fluorescent lighting. You might want to add that to your other notes there, Mr. Jacobson." She peered surreptitiously at Daniel as she took her seat once again.

With arched eyebrows above seductive blue eyes, Daniel smiled boldly. *A feisty angel.* Esther blushed and set her hand over her eyes.

Bob requested details on how the addition might connect to the existing library, "Will there be a breezeway or must an entire wall be taken down?"

After describing the options, Daniel walked to the green slate on the back wall. He inquired, "Jack, do you have chalk?" Jack hurried to the telephone desk in the corner and rummaged in the drawer until he withdrew a piece of white chalk.

"I have a very preliminary idea for this library's addition. Let me show you." Daniel sketched the existing squat, flat-top library, and then continued with the addition.

As he sketched and spoke of the design, Esther was soothed by his voice. She wondered what it'd be like to wrap her arms around his sturdy waist and lay her cheek against his broad chest. She shook her head back to reality in time to see that he had included everything the committee members had described.

Daniel stepped away from the board, "What do you think? I'm just brainstorming at this point and it's obviously quite crude. I certainly can't develop any design until I see the actual library. But do you get the gist of what I'm going for here?" The four locals nodded their heads in unison.

Jack spoke up, "Bob and I have to return to our offices right away; could you spare an hour to walk Dan through the library and building site, Esther? You mentioned that you're not scheduled to be at the market today until two o'clock."

"Oh, Jack, I'm so sorry, but I have to get to the hardware store before my shift. My kitchen window needs a new screen. A squirrel managed to get in this morning and it was crazy. And I forgot that Cindy and I had planned a lunch date today. Annette? Can you give Mr. Jacobson a library tour?" She hoped she didn't sound rude, or worse, in an obvious state of hyperventilation.

"I'd be happy to. Daniel can follow me back to the library."

Esther sighed with relief, "Well, then I guess I'll see you all later. Nice to meet you, Mr. Jacobson. We look forward to seeing your design. Thanks again, Annette, and thank you so much, Jack, for inviting me to the meeting." She shuffled out the door and ran to her car as Daniel iterated the items he'd bring to the design review meeting.

By the time she parked beside the hardware store Esther's pulse had returned to normal. She could definitely walk without stumbling now. The bell jingled as she opened the door and waved to Mrs. Carnahan. *Bells are big in this town.*

"Do you sell rolls of screening, Mrs. Carnahan?"

"Sure do. Do you want metal or plastic?"

She replied quickly, "I'm replacing the screen in my kitchen window—whatever you think is best."

While Mrs. Carnahan bagged the screen, Esther dug through her purse to find the cash she'd slipped into her checkbook that morning.

"Your face looks flushed, Esther. Did you run here from the library?"

"No, no. It's just one of those hectic mornings. You know

how it is, lots on my mind and busy, busy." Esther hoped that Mrs. Carnahan wouldn't detect the nervous tone in her voice.

"You take care, Esther, and be sure to stop by next week to pick up those stepping stones you ordered."

Esther waved good-bye before jogging back to her car. She tossed her purse and the screen into the back seat, and then opened the glove box. Thank goodness, it was in the car. More comfortable than her favorite slippers and as soothing as chamomile tea. John Denver. She started her car and pushed the cassette into the tape player. By the time she parked in front of the pizza shop on Main Street, the image of the architect had been replaced by a vision of the bespectacled folk singer with shoulders drenched in sunshine.

~~~~~~

After sharing a vegetarian pizza with her friend in Father Marquette Park, Esther was refreshed and ready to face the produce at the Red Owl market. She'd been careful not to mention Daniel and definitely didn't tell Cindy what his eyes did to her brain. If Cindy knew how Esther felt about him, she'd get hold of his phone number, call him, and tell him to get back to Frankfort and take care of her twenty-four-year old virgin friend.

"Hi, Charlotte." Esther waved to the cashier and then strode to the employee room to fetch her brown smock. A glance in the mirror gave her quite a startle. Did she have to look so wild when her insides told her she was a little fraidy cat? What would a man like Daniel possibly see in someone like her? Why was she still thinking about him? She had to do something to clear him out of her head. She hoped that Claire needed potato salad for the deli counter. Mixing ten pounds of potatoes into mayonnaise and onions would turn a woman's head to mush. It might be just what she needed.

She remembered that the Dole shipment of pineapples and bananas had probably arrived this morning. She grabbed the wheelie-majig (her name for it) and loaded a crate of pineapple onto it. Once she got the prickly fruit onto the produce floor, she searched for a place to stack it. While shuffling around the bags of apples, a finger tapped her shoulder and she turned around quickly. *Oh dear.*

"Hello, Miss Gardener. Nice to see you again."

"Oh, hello, Mr. Jacobson. I'm moving these apples over to make room for the pineapple." *Brilliant Esther. Just brilliant.* "Are you on your way back to Grand Rapids?"

"Not yet. I thought I'd get some fruit before taking a walk around town for an hour or two to get a feel for the community and its architectural style. It helps me establish a set of design concepts before I sit down to my drafting table."

"That's a swell idea. We have a special on Traverse City cherries this week. Of course, then you'd have to deal with the pits. The old standby always works for me. How about an apple or banana?" She pointed to the section of Macintosh and Granny Smith apples.

"An apple sounds great. By the way, I enjoyed the granola. And the library tour with Annette was very helpful; it's obvious you need more space. Have a great weekend Esther." *Where've I seen her before today?*

Esther clasped her fingers around the cool metal edge of the produce table until her knees stopped quaking and she regained control over her palpitating heart. *No need to fret. He's gone for a couple of weeks. There is no way I'm attending the design review meeting. Jack and Annette can see the design without me. I'll suffer a stroke for sure if I see him again and then my parents will never have grandchildren. It's definitely the Daniel from Penn State. What should I do? He certainly doesn't recognize me. Why would he?*

The rest of her day was quiet. Not a single fruit or vegetable cracked a joke about her reaction to the stranger who had ruined what might've otherwise been a perfectly normal day.

~~~~~~

Esther had just shoved a spoonful of Raisin Bran into her mouth when the phone rang. She quickly chewed and swallowed a big chunk of the cereal before answering. "Hello."

"Morning, Esther. This is Jackie. How're you today?"

"I'm fine. Just finishing up breakfast and then on my way to church. What's up?"

"The children devoured your granola snacks yesterday; they're delicious. We were wondering if you could do us a favor Wednesday afternoon if you're not at the library. Aunt Millie will be visiting my folks in Manistee, and Carl and I would love to see her there and enjoy dinner without the children. Do you think you could babysit for a few hours?"

No good deed goes unpunished. Who said that? Churchill?
"Sure. I only work until two o'clock on Wednesdays. May I bring Bentley and my Frisbee along? He loves children and doesn't see them except when we're at the beach."

"That'd be fine. Can you be here around three o'clock?"

"Sounds good. Have a great Sunday."

Well. This actually isn't a bad thing. Perhaps the kids will exhaust me into a deeper sleep Wednesday night. Anything would be better than sleeping with visions of him. . .

Setting her bowl into the sink, Esther sighed into the warm breeze that pushed through the new screen. She hoped that it wouldn't be too warm this morning. Pastor should've been serving rounds of lemonade during his sermon last Sunday, it was <u>that</u> hot.

She opened the cabin door and called for Bentley to come in. After pulling her hair back into a loose braid, she closed the bathroom door and looked briefly into the full-length mirror. Her youthful skin was clear and smooth; a suntan radiated a healthy glow. She pulled the long sundress above her knees and was suddenly swarmed with a distressing feeling, despite the great legs that appeared in the reflection. *Is it time for me to purchase an easel and paint, Lord? In time I might become a fine seascape artist.*

July 1985

John entered the kitchen noisily and slid off his dusty boots. "They need another two weeks to ripen but I hung the bird-chasers because we won't be in the field much." Karen nodded and smiled. It was only July 2nd so he was probably right. She loved the way her husband pulled off his cap and brushed the top of his arm across his forehead. Just something masculine about it. After nearly forty years of marriage she still felt a rush when he stood near her.

"You ready for lunch?" Karen knew his answer but asked out of habit. "We have about a half-pound of Earl's smoked trout; it'll taste good with my bean salad."

Before she bustled to the refrigerator, John drew her against his chest for a brief bear hug, "Love you."

She responded warmly, "Love you too, babe."

After filling plates and pouring coffee they sat down together to discuss local happenings and whatever important news John had gleaned from the Detroit paper.

"I hear that Jack has his eye on the Grand Rapids firm for the library addition; he says the architect is straightforward and will design something that's right for the town. Karl overheard a young fella at the diner last Friday asking Tracey lots of questions about the library and whether people meet there for seminars and such. Turns out the curious guy was that architect. And he was apparently talking to people all over town. Now ain't that the darndest thing you ever heard?" John's quizzical grin creased his hazel eyes.

"That's a wise man. Our library project might be relatively insignificant for his company, yet it sounds like he wants this add-on to be a grand improvement for Frankfort." Karen set her fork down and continued, "I think Esther attended the meeting last week with that design firm. Funny she didn't mention it to me when I saw her at the market Friday night."

"Well, whoever lands that job might need an outside construction crew at start-up if Henry's group doesn't have the theatre done by August. I suppose a crew from Manistee or Cadillac could be hired temporarily. That'd be an awfully big daily commute from Cadillac though, and those travel expenses would get added to the budget. Glad to have just the boat business and the orchard to worry about, eh?" John slouched in his chair and sipped the last of his coffee.

The couple finished lunch and then rinsed their dishes; Toby's ears perked up. The dog was fine company, not to mention a great roving scarecrow for the orchard. A squirrel never lived to tell of an encounter with the great brown-faced Toby. Karen tossed the dog a piece of bony fish and patted his wrinkly nose before he returned to the sunny spot near the couch to finish his nap.

~~~~~~

Sunday afternoon with the newspaper on the porch rejuvenated Karen for the drudgery of the orchard inspections that she and John would start this week. The heat wasn't bothersome today and the dry spell meant fewer mosquitoes. She always read the front page first, then the editorials, and finally the Ann Landers column. But something else caught her eye today. The Fifth Annual Expo for Small Michigan Businesses was being held in Traverse City this year. *This might be an opportunity for Esther to publicly introduce her granola bars.* Karen grew excited as she read more about the Expo. *If a few food-store owners sample the granola... well, perhaps one or two would want the treats on their shelves. And the Expo would be a great place for Esther to experience a bit of city life; meet new people and partake in conversations outside of this small town.* While scrutinizing the ad for details, ideas brewed in her mind.

John planned to work at the boat shop in Cadillac the following weekend. She'd call Cindy and Esther to see if their Saturday nights were free. They'd make a batch of fried chicken, and she and Cindy would convince Esther to attend the Expo in September.

~~~~~~

More than a week had passed since the meeting and subsequent encounter with Daniel at the market. While weeding her garden, Esther estimated the number of jars she'd need to can her tomatoes and pickles; the freezer would be filled with green beans in another five weeks. As she continued digging around the vegetable plants, she was swept into a melancholy mood. She loved her cabin and enjoyed exploring the parcel of land. Her flower garden was lovely; she couldn't resist the smooth pastel stones she found while strolling the beach and had arranged them into small piles in her flowerbeds around the cabin. In the midst of the bold colored zinnias and geraniums, the pretty stones made their own subtle mark. To Esther, they were like God's fingerprints.

Despite her fulfilling job as a librarian, not to mention her work on the Blueberry Festival Committee this year, Esther found herself frequently repressing a hollow mood that threatened her usually positive outlook. There wasn't a gaping hole; rather, it was more like a craving that neither friends nor chocolate could satisfy. She wanted to share her life with someone. Bentley enjoyed beach walks and car rides into town, but he'd never fully appreciate the way the lake looked at sunset or the sight of the bright green cornstalks against a chicory blue sky. She shared plenty of good times with Cindy, and sipping iced tea with Karen on her back porch always put Esther in good spirits. But her friends didn't *really* belong to her. They didn't *really* know her dreams and innermost thoughts. Esther wanted someone she could open up to and who understood all of her idiosyncrasies. Someone to love and cherish her. Someone tall and strong. *Darn that Daniel Jacobson for throwing a wrench into my previously blissful and orderly life.*

She stood slowly, holding her trowel in one hand and pushing against her tired lower back with the other. Bentley traipsed alongside her into the cabin. She washed her hands in the sink and then splashed cool water over her face. She paused for a moment after drying her face and then eyed her bookshelf. Memories roared like a wave. She could recall nearly every trip she'd taken with Joseph and her mom into the old Detroit bookstore years ago. She was a book hound. She loved the classics, and the older the better. Although Joseph had at least twice her brainpower, he preferred the pulp fiction. Westerns and science fiction were his favorites. She slid *East of Eden* from the shelf and blew off the dust. It was time to read her favorite again.

~~~~~~

After suggesting minor revisions to the stairway location and design, Mitch approved Daniel's site plan, floor plan, and design drawings for the Frankfort Library addition. Daniel was hopeful that the committee would like it. He wanted the facility to be more than an extension of the existing library; perhaps a meeting place for friends and community events, as well. His design included a surprise element that increased the proposed budget by about seven percent, and this had him worried because he'd have to sell the idea to the purse-string holders. It was vital that the committee catch his vision of the concept through his drawings, and if they did, he assured himself they'd approve the entire project, surprise included.

Daniel liked Frankfort. The proximity to Lake Michigan and slower pace of the town made it very attractive. The place beckoned him now and he looked forward to the review meeting.

"Hello, Jack. This is Dan Jacobson. How are you today? Is Frankfort getting its share of the rainstorm?"

"Hi Dan. We're definitely getting a bit of it up here, but we need the moisture and it's good fishing weather so I suppose we're happy with the precipitation. How's the design coming along?"

"Well, that's why I'm calling. I have a site plan, exterior perspective, floor plan, and three interior perspectives for you to review. I contacted a construction crew in Cadillac. Five men are willing to commute to Frankfort; they requested three-day weekends, however. Based on Henry's theatre schedule in Manistee, it looks like we'd only need the Cadillac crew for the site prep and foundation pouring. I'll bring a rough timeline for the project when we meet. Do you want to call me once you set a meeting date with your library committee?"

"Sounds good. We look forward to seeing your design. We haven't received word yet from the other bidder, so yours will be the first. I'll call you tomorrow with a meeting date."

Sleep wouldn't come that night. A mystery gnawed at the back of his mind, like hearing a song from years ago and trying to remember the name of the band that played it. Daniel crawled out of bed and wandered into the kitchen to pour a shot of whiskey. He tossed a few ice cubes and water into the glass and began to muddle over a solution. *Think. Where have I seen her before?* He probed his memories with determination. He recalled the places he'd lived and worked, one city at a time. She definitely wasn't from Chicago. He tried to remember the girls he'd seen in Grand Rapids during the collegiate summers he worked for Mitch. Had he met her in college? He thought of the women he knew at Penn State, and then tried to recall the faces of his teammates' girlfriends. None matched. And then it struck him. *She was the runner who nailed me by the dorms.* Hoping the drink would cloud his thoughts, Daniel emptied the glass and headed back into bed. Beneath the sheets a minute later, the blushing Esther returned, dressed in a brown smock and stacking fruit at the market.

~~~~~~

Fried to a crisp and greasy perfection, the chicken was divine. The three women sat at the kitchen table rubbing their stomachs and burping in between sips of 7-Up. They'd each drunk a glass of sangria with supper and the atmosphere was frivolous and relaxed. As Karen poured another round of the sweet wine, Cindy remarked on the occasion, "It's an evening in heaven to kick off my shoes and let my hair down with you two." The camaraderie the trio shared was in full bloom. Subtle gestures, the right words at the right time, bouts of silliness, and sincere empathy were key ingredients in their friendship.

"There's an ulterior motive behind the chicken and wine." Karen winked at Cindy. "I read an interesting article in the paper the other day and you came to mind immediately, Esther."

"If it involves wearing a red skirt, then it's not happening you guys." Esther recalled her embarrassing Valentine's Day nearly a decade ago and winced.

"Hear us out, Es. I think it's a fabulous idea. You need to get away from your cabin and this town for a little while." Cindy's enthusiasm made Esther nervous.

"For the past few years the Michigan Business Council has sponsored a formal social gathering and exhibit day for small business owners in the state. It gives the owners an opportunity to show products and make connections with other businesses. For example, a hobby shop owner might meet a woman who designs paint-by-number artwork and then make a deal with that artist to sell her kits and share the profit. Or a specialty food storeowner might meet a woman who bakes gourmet muffins. It would be a perfect opportunity for you, Esther; the Expo is in Traverse City this year." Karen searched Esther's face for a reaction.

"But I have neither a product nor a shop. Why would I go?" Esther hadn't the slightest idea where her loony friends were going with the idea.

Cindy grabbed the large jar of granola from Karen's countertop and set it onto Esther's lap. "You make fabulous granola. If you bring this to the Expo and a food-store guy samples it, then you've got yourself a business, babe."

"You're joking, right? I don't have any way to mass produce this stuff. If someone decides they want my granola, how am I gonna make hundreds of granola bars each week in my cabin? My work at the library and Red Owl keeps me busy enough. You guys are totally nuts." Esther rose from her chair to pace around the kitchen in an irritated and excited sort of way.

"We'll cross that bridge when we come to it. You're always working on that recipe and you talk about growing oats in your fields someday. If your granola sales boom, you can quit the Red Owl job. I'll buy all the ingredients you need to make a few hundred granola bars for the Expo." Karen was intent on getting the young librarian to Traverse City in September.

"I don't even have a business card. And won't I need a professional display or something? I can't just set out baskets of granola bars; I'd be mistaken for a wacky peddler."

"A table display would be simple and nature photography is my hobby, Es. My photos are hanging in the Iron Anchor Restaurant, two gift shops, and even in your library." Cindy stood to interrupt Esther's pacing routine, "Taking pictures of wholesome around here is a cinch. We've got kids on the beach, the blueberry orchard, wildflower meadows, and wheat fields against a blue sky. You'll write the marketing text. There's an art supply store in Manistee, and you can get business cards printed anywhere; you don't need a logo. Please say you'll do this." Cindy hoped her pitch would work.

Esther was walking in circles now, ideas churning through her mind. *It would take a few days to make hundreds of granola bars, but the exposure could actually result in a business deal. The experience alone might well be worth the effort and perhaps I'd meet some interesting people.*

"Let me think about it. I'm definitely interested and it sounds like a cool adventure. I'm not so sure about the social gathering though; crowds give me the jitters, especially when it's a big group of people I don't know."

Karen jogged to her bedroom and returned with an ear-twitching grin and bag in her arms. She removed the pink flapper dress from the bag and draped it over Esther's arms, "Remember this?"

"Of course. You want me to wear this to a party full of inventors and professional business people?"

"That's a sassy look, Es. Go try it on." Cindy could barely contain her excitement. The thought of pulling Esther out of her cautious and conservative shell for a weekend was more than she could stand; she took a big gulp of sangria.

Esther waltzed back to the kitchen looking more like a movie star than a librarian. The dress fit her more snugly now than when she was a teenager; it appeared custom-made for her figure. "How would I wear my hair?"

"Don't put it up." Cindy elaborated on the hair idea, "You should go to a salon once you're in Traverse City and have a stylist do her magic with some highlighting and straightening. Leave your hair flowing and untied. Gosh Esther, you should have been a model."

~~~~~~

"You'll be here Friday morning, right?" Annette peeked around the aisle to where Esther was shelving a stack of biographies in the 920 section.

"Of course. I'm cleaning the reference area and then digging up some preschool books for story time on Monday."

"Jack wants us at a review meeting; the Smythe & Jacobson group has a design ready. I'll call him back and let him know we'll be there at ten o'clock." She shuffled back to the telephone.

"Wait Annette." Esther hadn't even thought about how she'd excuse herself from the meeting and hoped that an idea would simply roll off the tip of her tongue. But she was a terrible liar. *Do I confide my dilemma?*

"I really can't go to the meeting. I'm sure the design will be great and you can tell me about it."

"You've been singing about this addition for weeks; you're now telling me that you can't go to the review meeting? What's going on, Esther Gardener?" Annette removed her eyeglasses; a perplexity indicator.

"He's too overwhelming and I lose my head. There. It's out." She blushed and wrung her hands.

"More of a reason to go then, young lady. Confront your fear head-on. He seems like a nice young man and I personally think you should be there to see the design. I'm retiring in a few months and you'll be the one who'll live with it. Be brave for goodness sake." Annette dialed the number to the Mayor's office. Esther felt like running away.

~~~~~~

Five members from the library committee attended the Friday morning meeting at City Hall. Bob Brigham and Terry Wagner were the City Council voices, Henry Gillman was the construction voice, Annette Carlson represented the library staff, and Jack Dawson headed the meeting. Mitch and Daniel spread out the site plan, floor plan, and perspective drawings before starting the presentation.

"Are we waiting for the other committee member to arrive?" Daniel was hopeful that she'd walk into the room at any moment.

"Miss Gardener called this morning and apologized. She has a stomach virus so won't be with us today." Annette nervously twisted her pen cap and frowned with regret.

Mitch began, "First of all, I'd like to thank you for the opportunity you've given our firm to create a design for your library addition. As usual, Daniel went overboard on research before defining a structure to satisfy your present and future needs. I believe you'll find his solution appealing and functional. He'll present a site plan, an exterior perspective, an interior floor plan, and three interior perspective drawings. We'll then review the project phases, timeline, and budget."

Daniel first presented the site plan and exterior perspective, "The footprint of the add-on structure will be twelve hundred sixteen square feet. The exterior face of the addition will have a very similar architectural style to the existing building to ensure cohesiveness and visual continuity. I'm suggesting the parking lot be placed on the south side; a tiered rock and perennial garden will wrap around the south and west sides. We will use the same type and color of brick; however, part of the new roof will rise above the current building by fifteen feet to accommodate a second-story reading area." Daniel paused to observe the initial reactions.

"This upper-level reading area will add four-hundred eighty-four square feet and open up main floor space for additional reader seating, displays, shelf space, or whatever the community might desire in the future. I suspect you'll have a computerized card catalog some day, and perhaps much more by the year 2000. You'll need space to accommodate that growth." The approving nods from the committee members indicated a positive response to the upper-level idea; he elaborated further, "Thirty percent of the upstairs wall space will comprise windows to allow for plenty of natural lighting and offer a contemporary edge to the current rooftop."

He continued with the interior floor plan, "The central portion of the space will be an 18 x 32-foot area and contain shelving along its walls to hold two thousand books. There will be space for six 4-foot square tables and chairs." He pointed out the skylight, windows, rear exit, and lighting fixtures. "You'll access the multi-purpose room, preschool room, and stairway to the upper-level area from this central space."

Daniel propped up another drawing, "The 18 x 20-foot multi-purpose room will seat up to sixteen people comfortably at a 6 x 10-foot table. Without a table, you can easily place five rows of eight chairs to seat forty people for meetings and seminars. This room will have two floor-to-ceiling windows and an emergency exit door."

Daniel now wished that Esther were present as he held the next drawing for the committee to view. "The 14 x 20 preschool room will contain wall shelving for six hundred books, accommodate three 3-foot square tables, a small couch, and two rocking chairs. Total seating capacity for this room would be around fourteen. This preschool room will have two 4 x 5-foot windows and an emergency exit door. Building codes today require an exit door in all floor-level rooms of a public facility."

Next, he displayed his drawing of the 22 x 22-foot upper-level space. He described his vision for the area, providing details on its floor plan, shelf locations, stairway, windows, railing, and lighting. The committee grew enthusiastic over the idea of adding nearly five hundred square feet to the originally planned twelve hundred that the footprint provided.

Finally, using several photographs to convey his design choices, Daniel described the architectural style and detailing of the interior windows and molding, the skylight and ceiling lighting, shelving units, and floor covering.

The committee members were duly impressed. The drawings presented a casual and utilitarian design, yet they were each a work of art. The detailing, fixtures, and color scheme were perfection. The group engaged in a question-and-answer session to discuss safety issues that related to the stairway, railing, study partitions, bookshelves, and emergency exits. A few minor changes were immediately discussed and agreed upon. The enthusiasm that permeated the room was thick.

Henry announced that the theatre construction was humming along ahead of schedule; he anticipated that his crew would be done by August 9th. Mitch and Daniel exchanged glances; a definite plus for the schedule and budget. A resident crew for the duration of the project would make Daniel's job much easier and he voiced his thanks, "That's great news, Henry."

Annette offered refreshment refills and a tray of sandwiches while Mitch assumed Daniel's spot at the head of the table to present the project's timeline and budget. As he spoke, Daniel distributed copies of a preliminary schedule.

"The project begins with today's design review meeting and makes several assumptions. First, it assumes that the site survey and preparation are complete by August 1st, and that we're granted the building permit by August 8th. I'll schedule the building materials to be delivered the day after the concrete is poured to ensure framing starts immediately after slab inspection. We included a few extra days to accommodate bad weather, but more than four days of hard rainfall during the framing and roofing phases will definitely impact the schedule." Mitch made a few notes before addressing Henry.

"It'd be great to have your crew available in early August, Henry. The current budget includes two weeks' worth of commuting expenses to cover the Cadillac crew. Keep us posted on your exact availability date." Mitch turned to the group, "As we're all aware, health issues dictate that Henry supervise the site only two to three days per week this summer. Daniel has agreed to manage the site on the days that Henry cannot. Additionally, Smythe & Jacobson would seek reimbursement for only one-half the lodging expenses that Daniel accrued on the days he'd be here in Frankfort."

Mitch finally presented the project budget, which he'd created with input from his suppliers and Henry. It itemized the costs for design revisions, site survey and clearing, concrete, framing, electrical utility extension, interior carpentry, bricklaying, roofing, driveway/parking lot, landscaping, and inspection fees. "I currently estimate that the upper level, which adds four hundred eighty square feet to the building project, increases your proposed budget by about seven percent."

"Then we'll have to forego the second level," Bob was the Eeyore of the group and believed finding that amount of money in a town of fifteen hundred people was an impossible task.

Annette rose from her seat, poised to fight for the extra space. "The second level stays. If we do the math, gentlemen, that budget overrun comes to about eight dollars per Frankfort resident. I'd be willing to bet my entire IRA account that residents will happily donate that amount for this design."

"I happen to agree with Annette." Jack felt strongly that the expanded library would increase usage of the facility and, in turn, strengthen the community. "We had already planned a construction loan to cover the anticipated shortfall of funds available for this project. I'm confident the townspeople will rise to the occasion and raise the extra money. If we choose the Smythe & Jacobson design, we'll submit a press release to the newspaper; it'll include a few of Daniel's drawings and a detailed description of the addition. It'd certainly stir interest and excitement in the project. We'd then request donations; money collected would go to the principal of the construction loan."

After a satisfactory level of heckling had been reached, the meeting finally wrapped up. The group agreed that, if Daniel's design were chosen, they'd meet again on July 20th.

Annette dashed back to the library. She couldn't wait to call Esther and tell her about the design.

~~~~~~

Her stomach was fine but her conscience was a mess. Esther had driven to the library after ten o'clock to tackle the jobs she'd promised to do. She jumped when the bell jingled.

"Esther? What're you doing here? Where's the virus?" Annette found her colleague pulling preschool books.

"I'm okay now." She apologized for missing the meeting and began explaining herself further when the bell jingled again. It was Daniel. She bolted to the reference shelves and began dusting in earnest.

"Hi, Annette. Would it be all right if Mitch and I did another walk-through of the library and building site before heading back to Grand Rapids?"

"Explore whatever you need, gentlemen. I have a cart of books to reshelf and overdue notices to address. Holler if you have any questions." Towing the cart behind her, Annette strolled to a non-fiction aisle to begin her task.

Mitch went outside to explore the building's exterior and adjacent lot.

Daniel walked further into the library after spotting Esther cleaning a row of shelf tops. She'd slipped off her sandals and was standing on her bare toes atop a wooden stepladder. He quietly strode in her direction and then stopped beside her.

"How's your stomach?"

"Oh!" She teetered on the ladder, nearly losing her balance. He quickly grabbed her waist to steady her. Their gazes locked and she forgot to breathe. *I don't know this man. Lord, help me.*

He immediately released her. "Sorry I startled you. I brought my partner to see your library and building site." His ears felt warm and his chest tightened.

She hopped down from the ladder, landing just inches from him because he hadn't budged from his spot. She slipped her feet back into her sandals and then eased around the handsome architect to gasp for air in the main aisle. "You can inspect whatever you need and you're welcome to check the property as well. I have work to do in the children's section." She took a deep breath and quickly strolled away from the man causing an inferno in her lungs.

"Just a second, Esther."

She turned around to find him standing directly beside her again. "Yes?"

"Were you at Penn State in 1980 or 1981?"

She was stunned by the question. "Yes."

"I got tackled by a girl on campus and you look just like her." He stepped back and made a visual appraisal, trying to recall if she indeed was the runner. His throat swelled as a craving for the young woman pulsed through his heart.

The memorable collision replayed across her mind and she was thrilled that he'd actually remembered her. "I'm sorry about that. How odd that we literally bump into each other again in Frankfort." *If I don't turn away this instant I'll say something totally stupid and humiliate myself into wishing I were a mouse. A red-faced mouse.*

Daniel's heart pounded and an urge to reach out and touch her hair nearly dissolved his sensibilities. "I'm not sure whether *odd* is the right word. Would you like to see the drawings?"

Esther swallowed the fireball of fear, "Sure. You can put them on that table if you'd like."

As he described the design and second-level concept her eyes sparkled with awe. She praised the drawings and posed several good questions about the design's details. She had never enjoyed a conversation more and was disappointed when Mitch interrupted. Daniel introduced his partner to Esther, and then left the table to walk through the library to take notes and photographs of the interior before returning to Grand Rapids. And with those notes and pictures, he exited the Frankfort Library with a vivid image in his mind of the timid librarian.

Esther returned to the reference section to complete the dusting task. Annette wandered back to the busy girl, "How's your pulse rate?"

~~~~~~

Their relationship had been crumbling for quite some time. Daniel initiated several break-ups over the past six months, but Jenny would call weeks later to insist they were meant to be together and that she couldn't live without him. And he'd cave in to her tears. Now he knew for certain that he had to extricate himself from the relationship for good. She wasn't his girl. The sparrow he wanted was a librarian in Frankfort. He'd seen her just three times, but that was enough.

Driving to Jenny's apartment, he hoped she didn't keep a gun in her nightstand drawer. *This isn't going to be pretty, but neither is the surgery that's required to remove a tumor.*

~~~~~~

"Got a minute?" Mitch closed the door behind him before dropping onto the armchair in Daniel's office.

Daniel was bent purposefully over his drafting table. Mechanical pencils, pens, a calculator, and triangles were strewn around him. A large window filled the west wall; his drafting table consumed most of the southern side of his office. Above his horizontal filing cabinet hung a large bulletin board. Pinned in neat rows across the board were twenty-seven postcards from his Aunt Amelia, each from a different city. The cards displayed the world's most beautiful skyscrapers, from the Chrysler Building in New York City to the Kasumigaseki Building in Tokyo.

"Sure. What's up?" He remained hunched over his work but tilted his head in Mitch's direction.

"I hope you have a decent set of books to read and appreciate small-town diner food." Mitch tapped his partner's head with a triangle, "The Frankfort Library committee wants your design built, Mr. Jacobson. They unanimously approved it without even seeing your revisions and the blueprints. Your design apparently blew the competition out of the water."

Daniel now leaned back from his work, "You have no idea how much that project means to me. Absolutely no idea." He rose from the stool and shook his partner's hand with exaggerated force.

"Where are your Jenny photos?" Mitch scanned the room to find the portraits of the gorgeous blond he secretly coveted, but there were none.

"Tossed 'em. She's not my type." He gazed out the window and smiled when he realized he'd be working part-time in Frankfort for the next five months.

August ~ September 1985

On August 7th, just six days after the application, site plan, blueprints, and site survey report were filed with the City of Frankfort, a building permit for the library addition was issued. Bob Brigham faxed a copy of it to Daniel, who immediately phoned Henry Gillman to discuss site preparation tasks. On that same day, the mercury climbed to ninety-two degrees, the local seagulls wisely waddled beneath shade trees in the parks, and John sent the berry pickers home early.

After watering her wilting vegetables, Esther left Bentley at Karen's house before heading up to the library; she didn't want him cooped up in the warm cabin all day. Her pulse quickened as she crossed the Betsie Bay bridge, just minutes before reaching the library.

Like unpainted soldiers with pink ties, the surveyor's stakes stood proudly around the site. Esther imagined tiny mouths on the faceless soldiers and nearly heard them shout, "The building is coming! The building is coming!" Her thoughts turned to Daniel before she pulled into the library parking lot. *Will he be here today?* Annette's car was alone. *Rats.* She was in the middle of a telephone conversation when Esther walked into the library. After stowing her purse and lunch in the office the young librarian organized a cart of books for re-shelving.

"That was Mr. Jacobson on the phone. They have the building permit; the site preparation will start next week. He'll be here Tuesday to consult with Henry on footings, whatever that means."

"It's happening so quickly. I can hardly believe we'll have the new space before Christmas." Esther was cheerful the remainder of the day, humming through her tasks and twirling between the bookshelves like a kid on the first day of summer.

They stood at the edge of the cleared building site. Reading the prints rolled out on the hood of his truck, Daniel was most concerned about the connection point.

"The new foundation slab will include a 12 x 10-foot section that connects to the existing library foundation. You'll bolt a steel angle-iron from the new slab to the existing one. We need to remember that this connection, no matter how strong, depends on good soil conditions and footings for strength. According to the surveyors, this soil is sandy. The slab beneath the existing library was stabilized with piers at eight-foot intervals. That means our slab must have piers." Henry nodded as Daniel spoke. "Study these for a minute while I go inside to work out a telephone arrangement with the librarians."

Daniel strode into the library, jingling the bell above the door before wiping off his dusty boots. Esther was at the front desk.

"Good morning. Terrible heat wave, isn't it? The temperature hasn't dropped below ninety since Friday. But the forecast promises cooler weather tomorrow." She looked like a brown-eyed pixie beneath large eyeglasses.

"I didn't know you wore glasses." He was staring.

"It goes with the territory." She smirked and fumbled with the pages of her ledger. "May I help you with something?"

I need to touch you. "Uh, yeah. As the project gets under way I'll need regular access to a phone. Do you have a public phone here, or one that I can use without disturbing anyone?"

"Your best bet is the office phone. Annette and I don't use it often and you can close the door for privacy. Its number is different from the main library phone so you won't tie up the public line." Esther walked from behind the desk and waved at Daniel to follow her, "C'mon, I'll show you where it is."

He appreciated the view offered by her lightweight skirt as she led him around the corner to a small office.

"That'd be great, thanks." *Those are definitely runner's legs.*

Leaving him to use the telephone privately, she walked to

the children's section to investigate the current activities and subdue her nerves.

"Hello, Jane and Luke. What kinds of stories are you borrowing today?"

"Hi! We want Curious George and mom can't find them." The kids were glad to see the librarian.

"Margaret Rey is the author of those stories so we need to check in the *R* section." Esther scrunched down to better see the contents of the small shelves and then fished out three monkey books. "Will you be here for story time next Monday?"

Their mother replied, "Will you bring your guitar again? The children enjoyed the story last week, and I heard several positive comments from parents about your performance. The music keeps their attention so well."

"Sure, I can bring it along; I'm working on a Jack and the Beanstalk mini-musical. I'll be at the circulation desk when you're ready to check out."

~~~~~~

Dust flew everywhere while the crew made a twelve-foot opening at the base of the library's south wall; the tarp caught only half of the rubble that scattered around the demolition area. The addition would connect at this point in the foundation via a breezeway. Daniel had been purposefully steering clear of Esther to better focus on this crucial phase of the foundation work. However, there wasn't much for him to do this morning besides wait for the delivery of the pier and footing materials. He decided that a chat with the girl who'd been starring in his dreams lately might do some good. She was reading the newspaper at the front desk when he approached.

"Good morning, Esther. Is it the duty of a good librarian to be informed of current events?"

"Hi. A lull around town usually occurs after the Blueberry Festival, so we've been slow this week. It's exciting to watch the building changes begin and I'm glad it's cooled down for you." There it was again. Her pounding heart and dry mouth would expose her secret crush if she wasn't careful. *Fainting is not a possibility.* His t-shirt was damp and his chin and neck were covered with dirt. And he looked spectacular.

"Have you always lived in Frankfort?"

"No, well, I live in Arcadia, which is about fifteen minutes south of here. I grew up in Detroit, went to college in Pennsylvania, and moved to this area last spring."

"Why a librarian in Frankfort, and what sort of training do librarians require these days?"

"I have a Library Science degree and worked at the university library for three semesters. This library is quite a bit smaller than the Pattee at Penn State."

"Why choose Benzie County if your family isn't here?"

"That's a fairly long story. The cliff notes might be something like, girl visits Arcadia with family, meets friendly blueberry growers, spends a few summers with blueberry growers, inherits a cabin and land, and here I am." Esther's pulse settled back down. He was surprisingly attentive and seemed genuinely interested in what she had to say.

His forearms were crossed and pressed onto the desk as he leaned toward her to hear the softly spoken words. She spoke quietly for two reasons. One, standing next to him made it difficult to breathe; and two, it's a librarian's nature to whisper.

"You live full time in a cabin? You don't look tough enough to manage that kind of lifestyle, although it appears to suit you quite well. Do you live alone?" The more she talked, the more her eyes and voice engaged him.

"I live with my beagle, Bentley." She crinkled up her nose and grinned.

"Well, Miss Librarian, tell me about this wonderful town called Frankfort." Daniel hoped the answer would be lengthy; he didn't want to leave the desk. His tender eyes bore into her soul.

"You mean a mini history lesson?" Her query wasn't rhetorical and he nodded with a positive response.

"A man by the name of Frank Martin came here in 1855 and made a temporary residence in a trapping shelter on the north side of the Betsie Bay. The strong winds off Lake Michigan piled snow and sand around the Martin residence. So Martin and his friends built a wall of logs and brush around the north side of the place to protect it. They called it 'Frank's Fort'. This was the inspiration for the name of the town when it was officially organized. The population today is roughly fifteen hundred, although it's more populous in the summer with tourists. It was mainly a lumber town years ago and served as a railroad stop with car ferry service to other port cities on the Great Lakes. It's basically a fishing town and resort area now." She tilted her head and smiled as she reveled in his attention.

"Hey Dan! We need you outside pronto." A worker from the south wall hollered the urgent command.

"Gotta run. See you later."

"Bye Daniel." *Oh brother. I'll never get to sleep tonight.* Until his appearance her life had been simple and predictable. But he had stirred a persistent thrill and ache. She'd developed a craving for the giddiness that filled her when their gazes collided; his presence gave her sustenance.

~~~~~~

Even after showering the day's grime away, Daniel still felt wiped out from the hours spent in the afternoon heat. His back ached and he wanted to be in his own bed. The crew was doing well; no major setbacks and they were a good team. Henry gave him lip occasionally, but that was fine. The guy was experienced and smart and Daniel appreciated his opinions. His thoughts turned to Esther. *His* Esther. What was it about her that kept him walking into the library to catch a glimpse of her? It felt right to be near her. She blushed so easily when he nodded her way or said "hello". She was a tiny thing with a grand attitude. Intelligent and amusing without pretense. He'd enjoy sitting on the beach with her and watching the seagulls fly by.

~~~~~~

She had expected this. Wide awake at midnight with thoughts of him rewinding in her mind. The way he set his right knuckle against his waistband while studying a blueprint. The way he nodded in her direction whenever he strode by the front desk. The sound of his voice when he talked to the crew. It was confident and stern. Every glimpse into his eyes clouded her self-control and made her want to crawl into his arms. Just a few moments with him this afternoon had jumbled her thoughts. Esther knew that when tomorrow came the desire to press her lips against his mouth would still be there. She wanted to leave him numb and aching just as he'd been doing to her. It was only fair, after all. But it was out of the question. He was breathtaking and most certainly one of America's national treasures. She was plain and simple, lived in a log cabin, and got way too dirty when she worked in her vegetable garden. She was falling in love with the wrong guy.

~~~~~~

Daniel had been in Grand Rapids while the foundation cured, a seven-day process. He returned to Frankfort on the last day of August to meet with the inspector. If the foundation passed inspection, framing would begin immediately. Since the site work started three weeks ago, Esther and Daniel had experienced a plethora of emotions. New moods emerged and silently bound them together. They were physically separated by their jobs, but each felt the other. And then he was gone. Their time apart intensified mutual, hidden desires.

Esther dropped her armful of books when he plowed through the door the day he returned to the library. Daniel stopped in mid-step when he saw the befuddled librarian. Their gazes locked for a moment before she bent down to gather the books from the floor. Both hearts fluttered but neither of them revealed the pleasure.

He spit out the question before he lost his courage, "Wanna go for a walk on the beach tonight?"

"What time?" She rose from the puddle of books.

"How about five o'clock?" He pushed his hands into his pockets to calm his jitters.

"Okay. I have a blanket in my car if you'd like to sit on the beach for a while. If you like milkshakes, we can pick one up at Tracey's diner."

"Sure." Daniel left the library and returned to the crew.

~~~~~~

"Were you purposefully avoiding me today? You turned away whenever I approached you. You didn't stand near me at the diner, you stared out your window during the entire ride here, and now your eyes are watching the lake. Have I done something to offend you, Esther?"

"It hurts my stomach to look at you and your eyes. My guts shake, my heart pounds, and my mouth gets dried out," she replied solemnly. Esther glanced at the tiny stones she'd mindlessly gathered into her palm as he'd posed the questions. "I'm a sparrow and you're a quetzal. And you're amazing and heaven knows how many beautiful girlfriends you've had. I suffered a broken heart years ago; it hurt real bad and the mending process is far too long. I'm not doing that again."

He'd get this woman to look in his direction if it killed him. "Then you leave me no choice. I'm taking off my shirt right here in front of you, and I know darn well, Miss Gardener, that you'll peek. And if you don't peek, then there are plenty of lovely ladies strolling down the beach who will be more than happy to take a gander."

"Oh dear. No, please don't do that . . ."

But it was too late. He'd jerked himself upright and yanked off his shirt with a flick of an elbow.

Esther looked up to him, squealed with delight, and began laughing hysterically. "I'm, I'm, so. . . so. . . sorry!" She couldn't contain her giggling, "But you're white as a ghost. Your neck and arms are bronze and then. . ." more giggling, "You're pale as a baby's bottom."

She fell back onto the blanket and kicked her feet into the

sand, still laughing and holding her stomach. "Oh dear. Oh goodness sakes. You're not perfect after all. You, Daniel Jacobson, have a flaw. A miniscule flaw, but a flaw nonetheless."

He had to touch her. Her small face scrunched up in laughter and those long, smooth legs caught him off guard. A heated surge pulsed through him and he couldn't stop what he was about to do. He quickly knelt down, collected the bundle of girl energy and brought her onto his lap. "You are unlike anyone I've ever met. I feel my entire body smile when I see you carrying a stack of books or cradling the phone to your ear at the library desk."

His lips descended to her precious mouth and she reached her hands around his neck to receive the kiss as if it were a delicacy to be savored. Sliding her tongue to meet his, she closed the kiss. He formed her mouth into his, drew her body closer to deepen the kiss, and fell into an oblivion of pleasure. Esther abruptly put an end to it. She leaned onto his shoulder, nuzzled against his solid chest, and forgot to breathe. *Thank you God for bringing him to me. I realize that someone like Daniel could never be mine, but I'm so glad for this moment.*

"It's getting late and I'm canning tomatoes tonight." She felt rubbery and leapt from his lap.

"Can we walk out to the lighthouse? C'mon, I don't see anyone else on the boardwalk." Clasping her hand tightly he pulled her across the beach. They didn't make it ten yards down the boardwalk; she shivered nervously until her legs wobbled like a marionette. He gripped her shoulders and turned her to face him; his eyes bore through her.

"You're definitely not cold. Are you upset?" He drew her against his chest, pulled his hands through her hair, and let his fingertips slide down her neck.

"NO! I want to go home. I think you're here because you feel sorry for me and wanted to kiss a plain girl. And I know for sure that you're going home to Grand Rapids in a few days to spend nights with your pretty girls and not even remember my stupid name. So just go!" Esther ran across the beach and into the parking lot to hide her tears. And then she realized that if she wanted to get back home, Daniel would have to drive her to the library so she could get her car. *Why am I such a loser?*

With head down, she walked to his truck and then watched him fold the blanket and amble to the parking lot.

"It's unlocked Esther, go on in and buckle up." They drove back to the library in silence. Once there, she withdrew her purse from under his seat, stepped out of the truck and walked to her Toyota. He sped away, and that, apparently, was the end of that.

~~~~~~

"Hi Es. How about lunch today in Manistee? And we'll pick up the art supplies for your Expo table. It's a nice morning for a drive; if we leave early enough we'll beat the afternoon rain. Did you see Cindy's pictures yet?" Karen hadn't seen Esther in a while, but saw Annette at the market the other day; she'd voiced a concern over the young librarian's recent glum mood.

"What would I do without you? A day trip would do me wonders. Cindy brought them to the library on Thursday; they're propped on my table now and look absolutely fabulous. There are five, all sized at 8 x 10—you can see them when you pick me up. I'll be ready in thirty minutes."

After art supply shopping, they ordered hot fudge sundaes for lunch and split an order of onion rings at Charlie's Deli.

"I think the earth tones will work perfectly as the background color scheme; granola doesn't seem pastel to me. I'll ask Cindy tonight if she can work on the display with us tomorrow after church." Esther was now glad to be traveling to Traverse City in a week. The recent tension at the library and construction site was nearly unbearable. Daniel spoke to her only when necessary; she regretted what had transpired at the beach but wasn't certain she should apologize. *I'd have only been a summer fling.*

"How's the construction going?" Karen had seen the recent progress but wanted to hear Esther's opinion.

"The framing is on schedule, I guess. There's no roof yet, but that'll happen soon."

"You don't seem as excited about it now as you were a month ago. Does the noise and sawdust bother you?"

"Am I that transparent? You read me as well as my mom; I can't mask emotions around either of you. I'm ecstatic about the addition; it's the architect that'll put me into the funny farm. I think I'm in love with a man who could have any woman his heart desires. For a while I had the impression that he was interested in me. Fat chance."

The women left money for the tab and tip, and headed back to the car. Karen linked her arm through Esther's, "We have a long ride home, start at the beginning and perhaps we can solve this puzzle together."

The raindrops splattering on the car window contributed to her already bereft feelings. She pressed her fingertips to her temples, took a deep breath, and then spilled out the details of her encounters with Daniel over the past few weeks. Karen acknowledged Esther's fragmented sentences with reassuring mumbles.

"Sounds like a situation that's beyond your control, Es. You insisted years ago that Arcadia was your destiny. And now a handsome and intelligent architect appears in this little town and literally plops you onto his lap. He'll be here through November. A mutual attraction may be what the Lord has planned for you two. Open yourself up to the idea. You'll know it when love gets a grip onto your heart; it's much, much stronger than desire." Karen grasped Esther's hand and squeezed it gently. "Just remember to breathe and keep an open mind."

~~~~~~~

Someone had a horrible cough. Esther furrowed her brow at its hoarse and raspy sound. *Whoever that is should be home in bed.* She checked the clock and hurried back to the office to retrieve her guitar for the Princess and the Pea story on her agenda today.

"Daniel?" He looked terrible and probably felt worse. "Are you the guy coughing this morning?" She instinctively reached out and rubbed her hand against his shirtsleeve to offer comfort.

"Yup. My only choice is to stay because Henry's out and the crew needs direction." He put his head down, coughed deeply, and then fiercely blew his nose.

"I have ten minutes before story time. We have an electric kettle and I'll make you some tea. Stay right there." She pressed her palm against his forehead just the way she'd done a hundred times to Joseph. "No fever."

Daniel sank deeper into the chair. *I need you, Esther. Please believe that.*

She was back shortly with a cup of steaming chamomile tea, "You should stay inside for a while. Do you have any medicine, like a decongestant or something?" She knelt beside his chair and probed his eyes with raw concern.

"I don't need medicine and I'll be fine. Thank you for the tea and attention, mother Esther." He sneezed and coughed, nearly spilling the contents of the cup.

"You're a stubborn mule. Go ahead to your darned work. When I finish my story I'll fetch you something from the drugstore and shove it down your throat." Esther marched out of the office with guitar in hand and a steamy halo atop her wild, brown hair.

Daniel smiled at the feisty woman. *She's perfect.* He drank the tea, which admittedly, improved both his sinuses and outlook. Departing from the small office back to the crew, he was impelled to stop and listen to the story. She sang the words of the princess, strummed her guitar melodically between the scenes, and spoke the parts of the frustrated prince, queen, and king. The children absorbed the tale and watched her performance with saucer eyes and wide smiles. As she finished the story, Daniel released a resounding sneeze; it was a comical exclamation point to the tale's ending.

"Excuse me." The embarrassed architect jogged from the room and out to more familiar territory; the librarian and her listeners giggled at the red-nosed man.

After stowing away her guitar and slipping into a jacket, she approached her colleague cautiously, "Annette, I'd like to take an early lunch; I promise it'll be short." Esther had her purse strung over her shoulder and car keys in hand.

"Go on ahead. The second graders won't be here until one o'clock." Annette was poring over the budget to prepare for the meeting next month and barely glanced up from the paperwork.

~~~~~~

A bag of medicine in one hand and a styrofoam bowl full of vegetable soup in the other, Esther with attitude wobbled through the piles of debris towards Daniel. He saw the little librarian marching his way and thought he'd better head her off before she built up enough steam to blow up at him. *Would she smack me if I kissed her?*

"You need to come into the library and eat this soup and take this medicine. Please Daniel, we can't have you getting sick on us." Her eyes wore a pleading expression, "I have Sudafed, cough medicine, and some Tylenol." She put the bowl of soup into his hands and pulled him with her into the building.

They sat at a table near the reference section to share lunch; Esther was blatantly breaking the no-food policy but felt that the situation dictated a bending of the rule. Daniel needed nourishment in a relaxing place, and the office would be much too intimate. From her own sack she withdrew a sandwich, granola bars, and a banana. Esther put half a sandwich and a granola bar beside Daniel's soup bowl.

He put his face over the steaming soup, "This smells good."

"Where'd you grow up? Do you have siblings?" Esther wanted to know more about the man who had designed her building and was starring in her dreams. She continued posing queries before he'd even had a chance to reply to the first two. "Where are your parents? What's your favorite season?"

Between slurps of soup, he described Chicago, his family, and his early interest in architecture. "I like autumn because Halloween was my favorite holiday as a kid." He sneezed, coughed, and apologized for the symptoms.

"I'm sorry about the beach." Esther looked down at the crumbs left by her sandwich.

"Me too. Maybe we could go for a walk around town." Daniel tilted his head to engage her eyes with his own.

"When you're feeling better I'd like that very much." She discarded the banana peel and wrappers into her lunch sack and rose from her seat. "There's a second grade class coming for a tour in little while. You should leave early and get some rest."

"Thanks for the soup and medicine, Esther."

~~~~~~

The tour was done, the budget was finished, and the repair guy had fixed the photocopier. Peeking around the building site, Esther was dismayed to see Daniel still working; it was nearly three o'clock and she hoped he would have left early. *I can't physically drag him out of here, I suppose.* The bell jingled to announce a patron.

"Hey, excuse me. Where can I find Dan Jacobson?" The request was hissed in a haughty tone. Esther looked up from her ledger to see a lovely blond behind pricey sunglasses.

Esther gulped, "He's probably around the back with the crew. May I help you?" *How about a swim in the lake with a weight around your neck?* She removed her glasses and sat straighter to appear less mousey.

"I need to do this myself, thanks." The bombshell strutted out the door and headed directly to the construction area.

Okay, I was right. There's a stable of stunning women in Grand Rapids. Looks like she's not his flavor of the month. Good grief. What does the one he picked look like? Esther pressed her hands over her eyes when the beautiful woman began to scream. The diners across the street would be talking about this altercation until Thanksgiving.

"I've been totally depressed and stressed out since you called it quits! But now I've got a powerful bunch of hate and you're gonna hear me out, Dan!"

"Whoa, Jenny. Let's do this someplace else." Daniel removed his hardhat and nervously wiped his brow. He tried to steer her to his truck, but she pushed his arms away and started punching at him with a violent disgust.

"I hate your stinking guts! You strung me along and you were never going to marry me, were you? How many women have you done this to, you filthy creep? This hurts, Dan. It really hurts. I gave more than a year of my life to you. Why did it take so long for you to figure out that I wasn't the one for you, huh? I hope your life sucks, I really do. I hope you fall red-hot in love someday and then she dumps you on the side of the road. And then I hope you rot in hell for eternity! Have a nice freakin' day!" Jenny stomped away from the construction site, hopped into her sporty Mercedes, and peeled down Main Street. Dan watched the tail-lights disappear, scratched his sweaty head, coughed loudly, replaced the hat, and returned to his task.

He peeked up to the howling crew, "Okay, show's over, let's get back to business. A round of beers on me at five o'clock, all right?" More yells from the men. And then a sudden sigh of relief when he stepped over the crowbar that hadn't been lying more than six feet from where crazy Jenny had been standing.

"Did you hear that?" Annette had walked from the office to the circulation desk where Esther sat.

"A real heart breaker that Daniel." Esther swallowed the lump in her throat.

"Did you see that woman? She looked straight out of Hollywood if you ask me, and she had money too. Wonder what his new girl looks like." Annette shook her head slowly as she shuffled back to the office.

Esther looked back to the ledger but tears clouded the numbers. *If a girl like that can't keep Daniel, why do I think he'd be interested in someone like me?*

September 1985

As a registered Expo exhibitor, Esther had to be at the Spring Hill Marriott by Friday afternoon to set up her display table. This weekend was costing her a small fortune, plus travel expenses. Preparing for the outlandish trip was more time consuming than she had anticipated; she hadn't been in the library since Tuesday. But she clung to what Karen asserted the other day, "If just one store owner decides to carry your granola, then the trip will be a success."

Mingled with her feelings of excitement about the show were thoughts of Joseph. She thought about the trip they'd made to Arcadia together five years ago. It was on that journey that she'd further discovered his astounding depth and brilliance. Proof yet again that only the good depart from this earth while far too young.

Oh rats. The traffic swarming on M-37 had screeched to a halt. Despite having learned to drive in Detroit, she wasn't a confident driver and immediately appreciated the lightly populated streets of Arcadia. She turned up the volume to hear Simon and Garfunkel; the melodious pair always delivered serenity. Thoughts of Daniel crossed her mind and she hoped he'd recovered from the nasty cold. She finally turned onto Center Drive and then pulled into the hotel parking lot. Now she was nervous.

With help from Karen and Cindy, she had a professional-looking foldout for her small display table. Cindy had done a great job with the photographs and artwork, Karen designed the background and color scheme, and Esther wrote the text and coordinated its typesetting. For amateur marketeers, the display look darned good; they had successfully projected a natural and wholesome theme. And Karen had provided several antique baskets for holding the granola samples. But Esther had no logo and the address on her business card matched the one on the rusty mailbox in front of her cabin. Yet Karen assured her, "Sweetie, they won't know it's a cabin. And besides, that makes the whole product even more down to earth." *Gosh, I don't even have a way to mass produce the stuff. What if I run out of granola before five o'clock tomorrow?*

She hadn't slept much the past few nights; she'd been up past two o'clock making the samples. She'd planned to make about four hundred granola bars and ended up with four-hundred-and-thirty. Now, just smelling them in her backseat made her want to puke; she was <u>that</u> sick of oatmeal and maple. Exhausted and nauseous, she locked her car doors and walked into the lobby to begin the adventure.

With the help of a porter, she had her belongings and granola settled into the hotel room in just a few minutes and, by midday, she had the display table ready for the morning show.

Cindy and Karen had insisted last week that she get her hair done professionally before the party tonight. "Put your beautiful self out there, Esther. You might meet a rich businessman."

Esther definitely wasn't planning a romantic encounter this weekend. Nonetheless, she appeased her friends by contacting a Traverse City salon and scheduling a hair appointment for today. After washing her face, she headed to the front desk for directions to Heidi's Salon. As luck would have it, the place was just three miles north of the hotel with all right hand turns. Karma?

She hadn't stepped foot into a salon since her cousin's wedding last year. Now that was a memory to be erased. The guy she was conveniently seated next to at the reception had been an obnoxious letch. After he groped her rear twice during a dance, she moved to a table with the blue haired relatives. Then she drank too much champagne and was sick the entire next day. Esther made the decision that day to have a small, innocuous wedding; too much could go wrong at the big ones.

"Good afternoon, Ms. Gardener. I'm Michelle. What can I do for you today?" Michelle's hair, nails, make-up and outfit were chic and savvy. Esther couldn't comprehend how women spent so much time on their appearances *every single* day. She had to admit though, the woman looked great.

"My friends suggest that you trim, highlight, and then straighten my hair with an iron, but I'm leaning towards an elegant up-do design."

Michelle sat Esther down into the chair and finger-combed her thick, sable hair. "Honey, hair like yours doesn't walk into this salon every day. Are you getting this done for a wedding?"

"I'm attending the Business Expo party tonight at the Marriott."

Michelle's eyes lit up after she shot a glance at Esther's bare ring finger; her styling gears kicked in, "Tell me about your dress."

"It's a vintage 1925 dress with shaky fringe around it. It's sleeveless, light pink, and above-knee length. It fits snugly but is actually quite flattering."

"Esther, my dear, you'll strut out of here drop dead gorgeous. Those Marriott janitors will be working overtime to mop drool from the floor of that party room. Look at you. You're a size four with long legs, magnificent hair, and a pixie angel face. My job is easy. You'll need a bodyguard tonight."

"I was going for pretty but gorgeous might be fine." Esther blushed and glanced into the mirror to catch Michelle's mischievous smile.

Ninety minutes later, she saw her reflection and couldn't help but laugh aloud. Tears filled the corners of her eyes and she nearly cried. Michelle had trimmed just a bit off the ends of her long hair and added highlights to create a subtle, sun-lightened look. Then she had straightened the curly mane into a shiny cascade. Once straightened, Michelle used a curling iron all around Esther's head to give the hair bounce and waves. Esther rose from the chair and hugged the stylist, "Thank you."

"Knock 'em dead, gorgeous."

~~~~~

From one hotel room to another. Daniel just wanted to be home. Of course, home right now was a lonely condominium in Grand Rapids. He was definitely glad that Jenny was out of his life but didn't know what to do about Esther. He had worked in the library only two days this week; she hadn't been there either day. Annette explained that the young librarian had an entrepreneurial streak and was working on her granola recipe for an important meeting. He knew zilch about the granola; it was so like Esther not to boast of her accomplishments. She was different from anyone else he knew. Not just her simple lifestyle or her selfless nature. Well, she was a beautiful and splendid woman; there was no doubt about that. But she possessed a spirit that he connected to, something in her that he needed and felt strengthened by.

Snapping shut his overnight bag, he chastised himself for allowing the librarian into his thoughts so frequently. He wasn't even sure if the attraction was mutual. Perhaps what he needed tonight was the touch of another woman to erase Esther's smile from his thoughts.

He'd brought his best suit to Frankfort so he could drive directly to Traverse City today, check in, shower, and head to the party. Mitch was bringing the display materials and brochures from Grand Rapids late tonight; one less thing to worry about. He picked up a sandwich from Tracey's diner, gassed up his truck, and headed away from Lake Michigan and east to the city. What he really needed was an evening in front of a fireplace with her. Wine, music, soft lips, a blanket . . . Visions of such a night sated his mind as he made the drive to the Expo. He couldn't wait to see Esther at the library next week and hoped she'd wear the short blue skirt again; her legs were incredible. He regretted that autumn had come so quickly.

~~~~~~

Esther awoke with a start. *It's seven o'clock!* She intended to read just a few minutes but had fallen asleep. She immediately thought of Elaine and didn't want to disappoint her. The women had met a few hours earlier in the hotel restaurant. Elaine Simpson, an interior designer from Lansing, was also an Expo exhibitor. They conversed over salads and promised to find each other at the party tonight; neither wanted to go stag. But the party had begun and Elaine would be looking for her.

She leapt from the bed and went into the bathroom to wash her face, put on her dress and shoes, apply some make-up, and switch a few items into her tiny pink purse. *Wow.* She'd nearly forgotten what Michelle had done to her hair.

Grabbing her room key from the dresser put her stomach in knots. *Should I really be doing this? How long will I have to stand in these heels? Is granola-making a real business? Just go, Esther. You think too much. Lord, help me.*

~~~~~~

Daniel arrived promptly in the ballroom at seven o'clock. Without Mitch he'd have to mingle alone for the evening. There was a decent sized crowd that appeared trendy; he hoped the topics of the murmuring conversations were at least somewhat colorful. He ordered a scotch from the bar, dished up a plate of appetizers, and sat down to enjoy his small meal. While indulging in the cheeses and meats, he saw that the crowd was comprised mostly of men; only a few women showed up this year.

A small group of gentlemen near his table had been speaking amicably; after Daniel finished his appetizers he meandered in their direction in hopes of becoming part of a decent discussion. Then she walked into the room. He didn't know whether to cry or shout with joy. Esther didn't see him and he thought that was probably a good thing. He chimed into the mutual fund debate while his eyes roved the room looking for her. *That's the most stunning creature I've ever seen. How is it that she's an enchanting child one moment and an alluring woman the next?* Other guests noticed the woman in the pink dress enter the room; many nodded and stared approvingly.

She appeared to be looking for someone and Daniel surreptitiously ducked behind a heavy guy so she wouldn't see him.

She spotted Elaine and immediately walked over to her, "Sorry I'm so late. I fell asleep in my room; it's been a crazy week."

"No problem. Jake has been wonderful company." Elaine linked her arm through Jake's and continued, "The bar is over there and a table full of tempting appetizers is beside it."

Esther grew suddenly uncomfortable with the dozens of eyes leering in her direction. Although the stares boosted her ego significantly she felt like a lamb amongst wolves. *Why am I wearing this slinky dress? What would Daniel think of me now?*

A well-dressed businessman from a circle of orators approached her. He introduced himself and gently cupped her elbow into his palm before guiding her to the bar. Daniel watched the scene and clenched his fist when the letch touched her arm. Esther disguised her discomfort and carried herself gracefully while the guy waltzed from the bar with her to a nearby table as if holding a coveted prize.

Daniel sauntered to the bar and ordered another scotch. He drank this one quickly before dodging into the restroom to regain his composure. *What's going on? I've known her for just two months. She's timid and distant and I can't draw her out.* An idea suddenly struck. He recalled checking *quetzal* in the dictionary after her insult on the beach last month. It was an exotic bird in Mexico. He'd break the ice with a quip about the bird, and only Esther would understand the joke. He hoped she would smile. Wiping his face with a damp towel, he blinked hard a few times to bolster his clarity, and then re-entered the room to find her.

An ogling letch was vying for attention on either side of her now. Still lacking a sufficient amount of courage to approach her, he ordered a third scotch and took a few healthy swigs. His heart pounded and his neck felt sweaty as he took the first step on a mission to sweep this woman off her feet.

"Hello there. I'm quetzal." Daniel aggressively grabbed Esther's hand from her lap and pulled her up from the chair. *So much for clever and suave.*

Her head jerked up quickly to see a very irritated Daniel.

"Hey man, what's your problem?" The bulky Italian guy stood from his seat and stuck his chin towards Daniel's face.

"Just taking my lady friend for a little walk into the fresh air; please, excuse us."

Esther grabbed her tiny purse from the table before Daniel hauled her to the door. He held her hand tightly while her heart leapt in fright. "Fancy meeting you here. Where are we going?"

He didn't answer immediately, but instead wrapped his arm protectively around her shoulders, steered her into the lobby, bolted out the main entrance, and turned left to the dark side of the building.

Now she was frightened.

He finally stopped and pressed her against the brick wall. Loosening his grip on her shoulders, he began to speak, "You have driven me to the brink of insanity. It takes me hours to fall asleep at night. I think of you every time I see anything remotely connected to what might possibly exist inside of a library. Whenever I eat an apple I remember the day I saw you stacking fruit at the market. And I swear that if I don't kiss you now, then I might just consume you right on the library circulation desk when I see you Tuesday morning."

She couldn't breathe. There. He was doing it to her again. He smelled of whiskey and she wondered how many drinks he'd had. Her knees felt rubbery and he slid his hands beneath her arms to bring her against him. His touch sent tremors down her spine.

"Is this really happening?" She wrapped her arms around his neck and tilted her mouth upward, daring him to resist.

He pressed his mouth against hers and then opened her lips gently. She acquiesced shyly and her teasing motions drove him into a frenzy. He opened his jacket, tightened his grip around her slender waist, and aligned her against him. The kiss drained her body of all resistance; they fit together perfectly and a mutual wanting arose. He urgently drew her into him so fiercely that she panicked and immediately ended the kiss.

"Esther, come to my room tonight. I want you. I'll bathe you in the morning and then keep you by my side during the day so that I can touch your hair and kiss you whenever the impulse arises. And then I'll repeat it all a thousand more times because I love you."

"I love you, Daniel." She looked away before speaking again, "I'm afraid."

"Afraid? You believe I won't love you forever? Is that it? You're an alluring and unique woman who has changed my life; I can't go back to a world without you in it, Es."

"I don't know how to do this and I'm not supposed to feel this way until I'm married. But I've never had my body get so mushy. My temperature rises at the sound of your voice. And now we're here at a hotel where the temptation is just too great to ponder." She surrendered to another passionate kiss and they both became even more dizzy with need for the other. His touch was numbing her conscience.

"We have to stop. I'm completely serious, Daniel. This is totally new territory. My conscience is screaming *no* but my body wants to drag you up to my room."

His glazed eyes studied her alarmed expression. *There's something that she's not telling me. I've had whiskey but not too much to know that this girl is hiding something. Wait a minute.* He grinned deeply, reluctantly released her waist and stepped back a few inches.

Daniel murmured huskily into her ear, "Are you a virgin, Esther?"

"Um. Yes. Pretty much. That's pretty much it."

He spun around and whooped exuberantly. After cheering again he put his finger beneath her chin and tilted her head up to look at him. She was blushing. "I am the happiest man on earth at this very moment in time, and you, my darling Esther, will marry me. And you will never cease to surprise me, and I'll give you such pleasure that you will ache for me on the days we're apart."

"I never said that I'd marry you, Mr. Jacobson." She snatched her purse up from the sidewalk, flipped her luxurious hair over her shoulder, and proceeded to march her cute body back into the hotel lobby, leaving Daniel breathless and bewildered.

~~~~~~

Esther ordered a glass of chardonnay from the bar and found Elaine and Jake. She approached the couple and graciously joined their conversation. A hotel crew was busily clearing tables from the dance floor while a DJ set up his station. Daniel quickly found Esther and possessively set his palm against her back.

"Elaine and Jake, this is Daniel Jacobson. He's here from Grand Rapids representing his architectural design firm, Smythe & Jacobson. We met in Frankfort this summer."

The small talk resumed. Daniel was on fire and standing next to her was a risk. An uncontrollable impulse threatened to overtake him—the kind that would embarrass him right into a dark corner. The music started in the nick of time.

"Dance with me, Miss Gardener?"

Before she could reply he led her to the wooden floor and took her hands into his. Their eyes locked and the world was obliterated. He had never, ever felt this out of control in his life; what she did to him was indescribable. A slow song played and he drew the curves of her body against him. She laid her cheek onto his chest and he wrapped his arms around her. The pair swayed rhythmically together around the floor, unaware of anyone else in the room. His heart pounded against her ear.

"Daniel?"

"Hmmm?"

"Will I see you again after you finish the library?"

"You think I was kidding out there? You will be the sun around which my life will revolve, little bird."

September ~ October 1985

He hadn't slept. Thoughts of her invaded his mind and had spread throughout his body overnight. It felt like an insanity, almost like he was losing himself to her. He wanted Esther, both physically and emotionally, and suddenly had to know whether she liked jelly donuts. Not that it would matter. He simply wished that he knew everything about her. Did she prefer beaches or meadows? What did she look like when she brushed her teeth? Daniel swung his legs from beneath the covers, planted his feet onto the floor, and set his head into his hands. *She's the one.*

After showering and shaving he called Mitch to ask what time they'd meet for breakfast. "Good morning, partner. You ready for some eggs?"

"Give me about ten minutes. Go ahead and get a table, and turn my coffee cup over. I'll need a large dose of caffeine to survive the morning; I don't sleep well without Angela and I'm gonna be grumpy today."

"You got it." He slid the room key into his sport coat pocket and thought about what Mitch had said. *How long has he been married? Perhaps twenty years.* He could appreciate how Mitch felt. Lying next to Esther every night and waking with her wild hair and soft face was something he now longed for. He hadn't ever thought of spending an entire night with a woman, not even Jenny. But he belonged with Esther now.

He dug out the display floor map from his guest packet to check the location of her table on the Expo floor. The tables were organized by business type: designers and builders, landscapers, computers, household appliances, food products, hobby products, and so on. He realized then that he hadn't even asked her about the granola last night. Heck, last night he wouldn't have cared if she'd been peddling Bic pens. He scanned the map for the name of a healthy snack. *Aha. Outrageous Oatmeal Bars. Darn it, her table is on the northeast corner of the room and ours is slated for the south side.*

The restaurant was crowded for seven o'clock in the morning. Daniel recognized several faces from last night's party. The waitress poured two coffees and set down the menus. *I wonder what she likes for breakfast.* Mitch arrived just as he had conjured up a vision of Esther eating a sticky donut; she had icing all over her lips.

"How was the party last night? Did I miss anything exciting?" Mitch looked lousy and in dire need of coffee. Daniel shook his head and smirked a crooked grin.

"What'd I say? Do I have something on my face?" Mitch rubbed his cheeks.

"No. It's me. Remember the librarian in Frankfort? The shy girl with the beautiful hair? Her name is Esther."

"Sort of. What about her?"

"She's here at the Expo. I saw her at the party last night."

"What did you two do last night?" Mitch leaned closer to Daniel for details.

"I kissed her. And we danced. And we talked. Then she went to her room at the Marriott, and I came here to mine. And I didn't sleep."

"So what's the big deal about that Jacobson? She's cute and you kissed her. For crying out loud, you've kissed dozens of cute girls."

"I'm marrying this one."

Mitch nearly choked on his coffee. "You? Married! After a dance and a kiss? Does she know you're marrying her?"

"I asked but I don't think she took me seriously." Daniel was frowning now.

"Well, let's look at this from her point of view. You asked this woman to marry you after having just met her two months ago. Did you two date in Frankfort?"

"We talked a few times and walked on the beach. She bought me some decongestant and soup, too." He stared blankly across the room as he recalled the kiss on the beach.

"Let's eat, I don't believe what I'm hearing. And what's really frightening is that you sound completely serious." Mitch wasn't so sure he liked the new Daniel that sat across from him.

~~~~~~

The Smythe & Jacobson team had their table set up by nine-thirty. Mitch headed for a pay phone to call Angela. When he'd left Grand Rapids last night his daughter was complaining of a sore throat and fever; his world wasn't right when his wife or one of the kids were sick.

Daniel strolled the Expo floor in a northeast direction. He found her table but she hadn't yet arrived. He smiled inwardly at the granola display; it projected a peaceful feeling, sort of like looking into her brown eyes. He ventured into the main lobby in hopes that she'd need help carrying stuff from her hotel room.

His heart thundered when he finally saw her emerge from the elevator area holding a large box; baskets hung from her forearms, swaying and bumping against her hips as she walked. She wore a navy skirt and white blouse, and her hair was Esther again—wild and soft. A man followed her with a second box; they appeared to be together. She was merrily chatting at him about something. *Who is that?* As the pair approached, Daniel ground his teeth.

"Hi. Let me get that box." Daniel took the load from her arms and positioned himself within inches of her as they made their way to the display floor.

"Thanks, Daniel. How are you? Did Mitch arrive last night?" Esther posed the queries in a formal tone.

"I'm fine and Mitch is here. Our table is on the south side of the floor. Who's the guy carrying the other box?" He spoke through clenched teeth and was agitated before she could even respond.

"I dunno. He offered to help while I was struggling with the baskets near the elevator upstairs." Finally at her display table, she turned to the other man and thanked him for his assistance. She then met Daniel's gaze and quickly closed her eyes to descramble her brain, "I couldn't sleep last night." Leaning closer to him while whispering the confession, she touched his shoulder to unleash a tremor in his groin.

Daniel made an urgent request, "Want to take a short walk around the building? We have some time to kill before the doors open to the public." They meandered back to the lobby and then out the front door.

The morning was cool and cloudy. Summer still had its grip on Michigan but autumn would be loosening that stronghold in another week or so. Traffic hadn't yet begun to pulse through the city streets; it was Saturday morning and many residents were still enjoying corn flakes and coffee at home. Daniel took hold of Esther's small hand and squeezed it tightly as they walked along the path that led to a well-groomed flower garden.

A marble bench beneath an oak tree beckoned them to sit. He led her to the seat, sat down abruptly and pulled her onto his lap. Wrapping his arms around her, he pressed her head against his shoulder. *This feels so right.*

Esther initiated the kiss. First his neck, then rugged jaw, then his clean-shaven cheek. She finally pressed her lips ardently against his mouth. His response was fierce and he drew her tightly into him. The kiss was electrifying and she put him on the edge of panic when her hands slid beneath his jacket. She curled her fingertips over his shoulders; he wanted to pull her inside of him and never let go.

Esther sighed with frustration, "My body wants something that I mustn't have. It's improper and I'm sorry." Her face grew warm; she clung to him and shuddered.

"Marry me, Esther. I want you near me every day and don't want to wait." He posed the question with an underlying fear that if she refused then nothing else would matter. He'd never be able to design or build again. But with her at his side, it'd all be so easy. Without her? Unimaginable. "You're the angel that I never thought I'd find." The tenderness in his eyes took her breath away.

"Let's get back to Frankfort. I need my cabin and dog; this is moving too quickly and I don't have my bearings." She kissed him extravagantly once more and ignited a raging desire within him.

He set her off of his lap, stood from the bench, and then impulsively drew her near him again, "We should get back inside. Will you have lunch with Mitch and me?"

"Yes." She responded with a wide smile.

He took her hand, pressed it against his lips and kissed her palm tenderly. The pair glided into the lobby still aglow from the lovely flower garden.

~~~~~~

"At least a hundred of the granolas are gone already. And nearly half of my business cards were taken as well." Esther was delighted that there was an interest in her product.

Mitch caught an eyeful as he ate his pastrami sandwich and fries. He'd never seen Daniel so enamored. If he had a magic lens, Mitch swore he'd see little stars swirling around his partner's head. And that's precisely how he felt during the first six months with Angela. His wife still drove him crazy; he adored every inch of her. Mitch only hoped that Esther had strong feelings for Daniel. If she didn't? Then Smythe & Jacobson Design would be in for one heckuva bad autumn.

"Where does one learn to become a librarian, Esther?" Mitch wanted to know more about the girl who so enthralled his partner.

"My earliest and most favorite memories are of reading. I worked very hard to learn to read so that I could tell stories to my little brother when he was sick. As I grew older, I wanted to share that passion with other people; a library holds a key to so much. I have my Library Science degree from Penn State."

Mitch's jaw dropped as he turned to Daniel, "You went to the same college; that's a strange coincidence, isn't it?"

Esther set her hand on Daniel's arm, "He graduated a few years before I did. And Daniel tells me that he didn't do much work in the Pattee Library. Our paths crossed just once, but it was incredibly swift." She blushed.

The lunch continued with polite conversation and subtle gestures. Mitch liked Esther. Jenny had been far too high-strung and snobby. There was a purity and depth to Esther that was immeasurable; Daniel realized her value and it appeared he wasn't going to let her go. Mitch was happy for the couple and by the end of the hour, it was obvious that the match was meant to be. Had it been something divine that led Smythe & Jacobson to bid on the Frankfort project? Mitch believed that that indeed was the case, and he looked forward to sharing the love story with Angela.

~~~~~~

The addition's frame was finished on September 23rd. The exterior wall sheathing and the roof sheathing would go up during the next several days. Henry had already given Daniel a grumbling earful about the skylight. Daniel pacified the carpenter by reminding him that the window size fit precisely between the trusses, and roof rafters would not be cut. To further minimize the carpenter's complaints, Daniel promised to personally assist with the framing of the light-shaft wall. Despite the occasional grunts, he appreciated the skills and leadership that Henry provided; and the men on his construction crew were diligent and precise. When they promised to have something done on a certain date, he could count on it. They'd work on the sub-flooring soon and then have the drywall hung by late October.

Annette worked only two days a week at the library now; she was preparing for the move to Florida and had her house on the real estate market. Despite Esther's busy schedule working as both a librarian and produce assistant at the Red Owl, she made time to prepare a king-sized pot of minestrone soup one evening. Afterwards, she called Karen, "Do you have blueberry bread in your freezer?"

"Sure do—four or five loaves. Why?"

"I made a huge pot of soup for the crew tomorrow and thought your bread might taste good with it. Would you be willing to part with two loaves? Daniel will be at the library tomorrow and I'd really like you to meet him. Interested?"

"I have to give up two loaves of bread to meet your beau? I dunno, Es."

Esther felt Karen's smirk through the phone, "Oh, c'mon!"

"All right, but you'll owe me a few hours of berry picking next summer."

"Deal."

Dressed in flannels, sweatshirts, and knit caps, the workers stormed into the rear of the library the next day when Esther announced that lunch was being served.

"You all wipe those boots on that gray rug before marching in here. And take off those hats!" She stood over two crockpots situated on a reading table that she'd covered with a beach towel; their plugs were stretched across the floor to an extension cord. Esther ladled the bowls with soup to the brim and offered plates full of blueberry bread and cheese. Daniel made sure he was last in line and, after she poured his soup, he set the bowl down, stepped around the table and picked her up into his arms.

"I love you, Es. Dinner at the Cabbage Shed on Tuesday was great and the walk through downtown on Wednesday night was cool. The soup smells fantastic." He pulled her into a non-fiction aisle and smothered her with fervent kisses. She pressed herself deeper into his arms when he pushed his rough hands up beneath her sweater to caress her back. "I've seen the beaches, the Betsie River, your market, and the restaurants. When will I see your cabin?"

"I love you and don't trust us alone there. We need to stay in public places if I'm to remain pure. Besides, this might simply be a summer-to-fall fling and you might not be the man I marry. And then what would I tell my husband?" Esther liked to tease him; she flashed her mischievous eyes before kissing him unabashedly and then dashing back to the soup table.

Karen walked from the office with a handful of plastic spoons as the young couple reappeared in the soup area, "Is this our architect?" She extended her hand, "I'm Karen Holsten, an old friend of Esther's. She's told me so much about you."

"Yes, Ma'am. I'm Daniel Jacobson. It's nice to meet you. Thanks for bringing the bread." He excused himself and took his bowl and plate to the table where Henry and the crew sat.

Karen and Esther ate their lunches in the office.

"How do you concentrate on your work with him here? He's so good looking and is obviously quite smitten with you."

"We work in two different ends of the library. The time flies when he's here and I have so much energy now. Is that part of being in love? It seems that I don't need to eat or sleep as long as I see him."

"I do recall that feeling years ago when John and I met. And over time, if the love is true, it doesn't slip away. The excitement and energy eventually simmer down a bit. It evolves into a strong friendship and dependency, and it matures to become comfortable and warm like a favorite sweatshirt. It's reliable and durable. There will be days when you'll wonder what it was that drew you to Daniel, but something will always happen to remind you just how special and important he is."

"I'm afraid to jump into an engagement too quickly. Why would such a dashing man want me?"

"Daniel is wise, Esther. You're a pretty woman who doesn't flaunt her outer beauty. But there's no need for that because your most precious part is the wellspring of delight that flows from you into those you care about. He's been touched by that."

"But we've only known each other for a few months and there are so many things that I need to tell him. He knows I had a younger brother, but doesn't know he died from CF. I don't want to hide anything from him but I fall to pieces when I talk about Joseph. And what if I pass the disease onto my children? Would that be fair to Daniel if we really do get married?"

Karen suppressed Esther's concern, "Your mom and I had this discussion when your parents visited in June; it must've been the night you were working at the market—they spent a few hours with John and me that evening. I'm surprised she hasn't mentioned CF testing to you."

"It never came up, I guess. I hadn't thought about being a mother until just a few weeks ago. What's CF testing?"

"There's a genetic blood test to determine if a person is a CF carrier. Both parents must be carriers to produce a child with CF. If you're a carrier of the CF gene and your husband has a normal test result, the chance that your baby will have CF is very, very small. If you're both carriers, then the chance of having a child with CF is about twenty-five percent."

The serious conversation was interrupted when Daniel peered into the office. "The crockpots and plates are empty. Everyone enjoyed the meal and they thank you both; it's a treat to eat a homemade hot lunch." Daniel kissed Esther on the forehead before retreating to the work site. She followed him down the short hallway and then jumped in front of him.

"My folks will be in Arcadia this weekend. We're planning a drive into Beulah and around Crystal Lake to see the autumn colors. Will you be in town on Saturday? Would you like to join us?" Esther hoped she wasn't pushing him into something he wasn't ready to do. She stepped slightly away from him as if to apologize for her bold invitation.

"I'm supposed to finish a few drawings in Grand Rapids this weekend for a bid presentation next Thursday. Mitch might hang me for staying in Frankfort, but I won't pass up the opportunity to meet your parents, Es. I'm at the Dune Valley Motel."

"No. Don't jeopardize your job to meet my folks. That's a bad idea."

"I can leave Frankfort on Sunday and work on the drawings Monday and Tuesday. Working a pair of ten-hour days isn't difficult for me, especially when I'm designing. Henry can supervise the sheathing and sub-flooring without me. As long as I'm back by the middle of next week, I can still help with the sky light." Daniel drew her against him.

"Should I give you my phone number?" She pressed her forehead into his chest, realizing fully now that Daniel had literally reached inside and stole her heart to claim as his own. She was afloat with contentment and there was no denying her love for this man.

"No. I'd like directions to your cabin so that I can sneak into your window and climb into bed with you tonight." He chuckled at her startled reaction, "I'm just kidding. Of course I'd like your phone number. May I call you tonight before I go to sleep?"

~~~~~~

After hanging a new bird feeder in the yard and scattering corn on the ground for the blue jays, Esther walked into the cabin and slid out of her jacket before answering the ringing telephone.

"Good evening, beautiful."

"I was going to call you in a few minutes. I searched the newspaper for weekend events in the area and found a few interesting choices. Do you like jazz music?" She posed the query with crossed fingers.

"Ah, Duke Ellington, Herbie Hancock, Miles Davis, John Coltrane. I like jazz music very much. Come to Grand Rapids with me next weekend and we'll listen to my jazz collection."

"I'm not so sure we'd hear much of it if we spent a weekend alone at your place. That wouldn't be a good idea. Stay on track with me, Mr. Jacobson. There's a jazz festival Saturday afternoon at the Kresge Auditorium in Beulah. My parents are huge jazz fans. How does that sound to you?"

"Count me in. What're you wearing?"

"Red wool socks and a white flannel nightshirt with yellow cats on it. I'm doing a crossword puzzle on the couch and watching the embers glow in my fireplace. It's very cozy. I'll probably read a bit of Emily Dickenson before I go to sleep."

"Sounds like a fairy tale. My heart beats faster when I hear your voice, Es. I wish I were there."

"Me too. Sometimes my stomach hurts when I need to touch you but can't. It's tempting to invite you here but it'd be a mistake; please let's change the subject. May I bring a lunch for us to share in the library tomorrow? Do you prefer mayonnaise or salad dressing?"

"Mayonnaise, definitely."

"Me too. Good night."

"Good night, little bird."

"Henry?" She walked through the entryway of the addition. The smells and sight of the new structure were intoxicating. Sawdust, glue, tools, and fresh concrete. While she spent her day in a world of books and whispering voices, Daniel designed and oversaw the noisy construction of buildings where people worked and lived. And this one was for her. It would be filled with the things she cherished. *Thank you, Daniel.*

"I'm up here, Esther." Henry called down from a scaffold.

"I'm leaving in twenty minutes and need to lock up for the weekend. Daniel left with the other key at four o'clock; he had a four-thirty phone conference scheduled with Mitch, but you probably already know that, huh? You guys need to leave with me tonight."

"Yup. We'll wrap it up by five o'clock, Esther."

As she headed back to the main library, Chuck jogged to her side. "Got plans for the weekend?"

She was caught off guard, "My folks are in town and we're driving out to Beulah tomorrow. And we're picking apples on Sunday. What are you doing this weekend?"

"I'll be wishing that we were together, Miss Esther." Chuck propped his arm over Esther's shoulders.

Before she could react, Henry stormed to the scene, "She's Daniel's girl so you'd better back off."

"Just being friendly, Henry. No need to stir up trouble." Chuck winked at Esther and strolled back to the work area to tidy up.

"Sorry about that. I'll talk to the crew about proper behavior around a pretty lady; please don't be offended." Henry's face wore an agitated expression.

"It's all right, Henry. Thank you. I've got a few things to put away, then I'll get my coat and we'll get out of here."

The strong northwest wind threatened to pull the leaves from their branches before they hit peak color. Esther enjoyed the changing landscape while driving home and thoughts of the autumn season's festivities crossed her mind. She'd ask her dad to dig out the scarecrows from her shed and set them onto the front porch of the cabin tomorrow. Next week she'd bring autumn decorations to the library; Indian corn, pumpkins, pots of chrysanthemums, and baskets of apples. Maybe she'd perch a little witch somewhere in the library this year. She'd bake apple muffins for the construction crew, too. But Esther wasn't looking forward to her second winter in Arcadia. She shuddered to remember how many times she had shoveled a path from the cabin door to her car. And the wet snows were back breaking.

Seeing her parents' Buick parked at the end of her driveway instilled an overwhelming sense of gladness. Although they had tentatively planned a second summer visit to Arcadia in August, Ken and Agatha instead took a cruise to Alaska. It was Agatha's birthday gift from Ken, and they returned from the trip with a renewed marriage, a positive outlook, and a peacefulness that resonated even through telephone lines. They were alive again. *Dear Lord, Thank you for the love and grace you've bestowed upon my parents. Your works are indeed astounding.*

She burst through the door to find them snuggled on the couch. "Welcome. You both look terrific."

Her parents brought a roast and fresh vegetables; Agatha had obviously put them into the oven hours ago and the aroma made itself at home in the cabin. Hugs and chatter filled the living room while Bentley jumped and howled around the edges of conversation. Ken shared photos from their summer trip, and Esther described the library addition and current events in town. After supper Ken built a fire in the hearth and the threesome reminisced of past summers in between bites of granola.

"There's a jazz festival in Beulah tomorrow; would you like to go? The weather should be decent and we can get a fish supper afterwards."

Agatha leaned her cheek dreamily onto Ken's shoulder just as Esther had seen her do a thousand times before. It warmed her heart. "That sounds like fun; when will we meet your Daniel?" Agatha winked at her now blushing daughter.

"He's in Frankfort tonight and we'll pick him up on the way out. We can leave here around noon." Esther skipped upstairs to the phone in her bedroom.

~~~~~~

"Hi, Daniel."

"Hello, beautiful. What time should I be ready?" He dog-eared the page he was reading and dropped the book. He needed both hands to cradle the phone when he spoke with her.

"Is 12:15 okay? We can pick you up in the lobby. We'll eat lunch at the festival and then find a seafood place for dinner."

"Sounds fun. I'll bring along a few jazz tapes if your dad has a tape player in his car. Hey Es?"

"Yeah?"

"Don't do anything to your hair. It's too nice to tie up." He closed his eyes to feel her smile into the phone.

"Okay, I won't. Daniel?"

"Yeah?"

"Do you prefer hamburgers or hot dogs?"

"Burgers."

"Me too. Do you like scrambled or fried eggs?"

"Fried."

"Me too."

"Would you rather go ice skating or sledding?"

"Sledding."

"Me too."

"Esther, what are you doing?"

"Just curious. Did I tell you that I have a younger brother?"

"Yeah. You read stories to him when you were a kid. Is he here with your parents?"

"Joseph died two years ago; he was eighteen." Tears spilled down her cheeks and her throat tightened.

"Oh man, Es. I'm so sorry. Was there an accident?"

"Cystic fibrosis took him. I just want you to know that. And I still miss him every day. I have a picture of Joseph to show you tomorrow."

"I'm glad you told me. If your parents are asleep and you need to talk tonight, just call me. I love you and I'll see you in fourteen hours."

"I love you, too."

~~~~~~~

The morning's autumn breeze was brisk but by midday the sun had warmed the air and dried the dew. The maple, oak, and birch trees dazzled the hills and valleys with waves of breathtaking color. It would be a resplendent drive from Frankfort to Beulah. Ken dictated the seating arrangement; Agatha moaned over his request that the guys ride in the front of the car and girls ride in back. "That's like Barney and Fred Flintstone, Ken."

"That's just fine, Wilma. You and Betty visit back there; we'll all have plenty of time to yak it up together this afternoon." (It was Ken's prerogative to interrogate the young man who had so charmed his daughter.) Daniel scored big points when he set the Miles Davis tape onto the dashboard.

"Nice music." Ken nodded at the younger man.

"Great music." Daniel grinned.

"Esther tells me you designed the library's addition; I'm looking forward to seeing the site tomorrow. I don't hear of many architects who remain involved through the construction phase. Doesn't that usually fall into the lap of a building contractor?"

"Yes, Sir, that's typically the case. But the foreman of this particular crew couldn't be at the site every day of the week so we worked out an arrangement where I'd supervise the site ten days each month. The crew is doing a great job but my presence and site management role are important, not to mention the fact that I enjoy rolling up my sleeves and working with the guys. We've been lucky so far; the library project hasn't interfered with my design work in Grand Rapids. I'm in Frankfort just a couple days each week, and it's only a four-month time frame. I'm not usually here on the weekends; Esther invited me to join you today." Daniel was less nervous during his AR exam two years ago.

"Did you grow up in Grand Rapids? How long have you been with the design firm?"

"I grew up in Chicago and met my partner the summer after I graduated from high school in 1977 when he . . . "

"You're a partner in the firm?" Ken mentally chalked up another good-impression point.

"Yes, Sir. I was made a partner last summer. Mitch and I comprise the design team; we have one full-time and one part-time draftsman as well. I worked for Mitch out of high school and then during three summers while I was at Penn . . ."

"You're a Penn State grad?" Ken was befuddled, "Did you and Esther meet in college?"

"It was an extremely brief encounter, Sir."

And so the drive continued, boys bantering in front and girls giggling in the back. The couples paired up once they stepped out of the car.

Daniel felt both comfort and an accelerated pulse rate when he grasped Esther's hand and pulled her against him. "Your hair smells nice." He brushed his palm from the top of her head to the middle of her back, feeling the wavy texture of her hair.

Daniel insisted on purchasing the show tickets. Ken graciously thanked him and made it clear, "The dinner tab is on me."

After enjoying plates of Cajun food and California wine for lunch, the couples were seated for the show. The musicians provided splendid performances of great jazz titles, which included songs from the 1950s and 1960s as well as music from contemporary albums. The music was invigorating and soulful. Of the three listeners, Esther had the least experience with jazz; a taste, she realized, that had to be acquired over time. Despite her preference for the acoustic guitar she found herself moved by the rhythms and sounds of the unpredictable music.

Back in the car with plenty of time before dusk settled in, the party of four circled Benzie County in search of a whitefish supper. The music they'd shared that afternoon eased them into a cool and dreamy mood. After finding a dimly lit diner the group swaggered inside to a bluesy sort of beat. They'd each taken a sip from their martini when Daniel initiated a round of small talk, "How did you two meet?"

Ken liked to tell the story and it had been a few years since he'd last shared it. "It was June 1959 and I had just landed my first position out of college in a decent-sized law firm in Detroit. My brother roped me into a strawberry-picking excursion with his wife and kids on a Saturday. He insisted it would do me good to get dirt under my fingernails and berry stains on my knees. A church group was picking berries in the row of plants beside us, and one of the chaperones was a gorgeous blond wearing a red skirt and straw hat."

Agatha chimed in, "Ken followed me around the orchard and kept trying to get my attention. When we finally made eye contact, I saw how handsome he was. The kids in my group filled their buckets before Ken's family was finished, and when I walked from the orchard into the barn to have the berries weighed, he followed me inside. When he stood beside me and I got a chance to look into his eyes, my heart lurched and my throat swelled up. Then he introduced himself and, after talking for a few minutes, we learned that we both lived in Detroit. He asked for my phone number and called that night to ask me out."

Ken wrapped his arm around Agatha and drew her close to him, "I proposed to her in July and we were married on September 7th. I knew she was the one immediately."

"Great story. Did you pick out a ring together?" Daniel's mind raced with scenarios.

Ken held Agatha's ring finger, "I bought the ring myself and gave it to her when I proposed. It's been on her hand for more than twenty-five years."

"Just one more question, Sir."

"Please call me Ken."

"I have just one question, Ken." Daniel swallowed nervously, "I'm driving back to Grand Rapids tomorrow and I won't see Esther again until Wednesday afternoon. May I sit beside her during the drive back to Frankfort tonight?"

"Permission granted, Mr. Jacobson."

November 1985

The library addition was winding down to completion; only the paint, carpet, molding, and bookshelf installation were left to be done. Even without these final interior elements, walking through the new building took her breath away. Before the structure had even come alive, Esther's feelings for its creator had a stronghold on her heart. She was wholly impressed with his diligence and fortitude in guiding the construction process. He had leapt over innumerable obstacles and pacified indignant men without resentment. Daniel had been the living representation of the new structure, and she felt that he had breathed a part of himself into it. His dedication in ensuring that all steps were precisely executed became nearly intoxicating to her. The finished building was magnificent and far exceeded the expectations of many people. Esther knew the coming days would be tortuous without him. He wouldn't return to Frankfort until late November for the final building inspection, which was scheduled for the Wednesday before Thanksgiving.

It was Saturday morning and the library was closed. The trunk of her car was filled with paint, brushes, a roller, masking tape, paint trays, and tarp. Esther plied her long hair into a braid and dressed in gardening overalls and an ancient t-shirt. She initially planned to paint the preschool room one wall at a time over the course of the coming week, but wanted to bring the room to life all at once. Henry had given her the go-ahead to paint this weekend and she was anxious to get started. She grabbed her radio and headed out the door.

~~~~~~

Supervising the library project meant driving through Arcadia every week to access highway M-22 into Frankfort. For the past four months, Daniel didn't realize that the small cabin amid a cluster of towering pine trees on Glovers Lake Road was hers. When he was in Frankfort early last week it finally dawned on him to search the telephone book for her address. The old mailbox perched on the roadside verified that the cabin was indeed her property. The scarecrows were still sitting on the front porch but the pumpkins and flowerpots were gone. He looked forward to the day he'd walk through that cabin door and be greeted by open arms and a barking beagle. He dare not knock on her door today; it would spoil the surprise. His truck was loaded with the supplies needed to paint her preschool room. Daniel wished he could be in the library on Monday morning to see the look of surprise on her face.

Turning into the library parking lot, he was shocked to see her Toyota. *Why is it that she's always the one to surprise me?* Daniel's heart quickened when he realized that they'd be alone in the library. They hadn't seen each other in days. He jogged to the front entrance. She had locked the door. He silently inserted his key into the lock and, while opening the door, remembered that the darn bell would jingle to announce his arrival.

He quickly perused the building and didn't see her immediately, so stepped stealthily to the addition. A radio was blasting country music; Esther sang loudly right along with it. Daniel desperately hoped she hadn't heard him because she'd stop singing. The commotion came from the preschool room and he strode to its doorway and peered inside. As long as he lived he'd never forget the vision that burned into his heart the moment he saw her. As she steadily rolled paint onto the walls in time with the music, he saw that her overalls and arms were speckled with pale yellow paint. It would be a pity to disturb her so he simply allowed himself the pleasure of watching her fulfill the task.

Her voice was a lovely soprano. Curls stuck out everywhere from her braid, and her round derriere, visible even beneath the baggy pants, had alone been worth the two-hour drive. She stopped suddenly and put the roller into its tray. She then set her face into her messy hands and began to cry. His heart broke into a million pieces and he ran to her.

"Esther?"

"Daniel!" She turned into him and wrapped herself around him until he gasped for air. "I've missed you so much. What're you doing here? I hate that you're not in Frankfort anymore. You live far away and we have separate lives and what are we going to do?" Her face was now covered with streaks of yellow-tinged tears.

Daniel held her tightly, stroking her hair until she was sated in his arms, "I miss you too. I came to paint and here you are. Let's get some soap and water on your face, then we'll talk and finish the painting together." After fervent kisses and a dozen reassurances, the couple headed to the bathroom to clean up.

"Come to Chicago with me for Thanksgiving. I want you to meet my family; my parents will love you. Amy will adore you and Dennis will declare me the luckiest man alive."

"You so easily assume that we're getting married. But what if we don't? What if something happens and one of us decides it's just not right?" She began to cry again.

He felt the blood drain into his feet. It pulsed back into his head to stir a potent anger, "We're getting married!" Now it was his turn to be scared. *Has she changed her mind? What if she doesn't love me?* "We'll work everything out. There are libraries all over the state. I don't have to live in Grand Rapids. I can design in a home office and check in with Mitch a day or two each week. I'd be happy in the cabin, Esther." Before his legs buckled beneath him, Daniel sat on the floor.

Esther walked to him and plopped onto his lap. "I don't want you to give up your world for me. You're a brilliant architect with enough passion to fill this room. How would you glean inspiration from a cabin in Arcadia?"

"You're my inspiration and we're supposed to be together. By some weird set of circumstances you ended up here and my design was chosen for your library. We can live in a town between Frankfort and Grand Rapids. I know how much you love it here and I don't want to take you away from it. But darn it, Es, the world is just going to have to work around us." He pulled the tie from the end of her braid and then pulled his fingers through her wavy hair to set it free. "Come to Chicago.

You've never seen the city and I want you to meet my family."

"I'd like that. " She sighed deeply as her heartbeat slowed to a normal rhythm.

"We'll leave from here Wednesday afternoon; I have to be in Frankfort for the inspection anyway." Relief filled him as they rolled paint and planned the Chicago trip. By early evening the room was ready for its molding, carpet, and shelving.

"I wish you could come with me to the cabin but I'm finding you especially irresistible today; supper alone together would be a disaster. Any ideas?"

"How about a nice hotel room? We could shower together and then order room service."

Her heart leapt through somersaults before dismissing his idea, "Don't do that to me."

"A&W? We'll eat a quick supper, say our good-byes, and I'll return to Grand Rapids before temptation consumes me."

Esther clung to him, "It's only the 12th and you won't be back here until the 23rd. It'll be the longest eleven days of my entire life. If I really, really need to talk with you next week during the day, may I call your office?"

"Yes. Call me there. Mitch already thinks of you as Mrs. Jacobson." As they walked out into the chilly afternoon Daniel slid his business card into her coat pocket, wondering why he hadn't given his office number to her a month ago.

~~~~~~

Henry and Daniel paced around the empty addition waiting for the inspector to complete his job. The inspection report would pass or fail each point of the building—roof, exterior, interior, heating, cooling, electrical, insulation, and even lot grading. Esther supposed that what Daniel felt might be akin to a mother having her infant inspected and weighed during its monthly check-up. As she replaced the November magazines with December's issues, she heard an exuberant roar.

Daniel jogged to his librarian, "Esther my dear, grab your suitcase and dog; we're heading to Chicago. The building passed all inspection points. We're cool with the codes! I'll apply for an occupancy certificate after the holiday and then have Henry wrap up the punch-list tasks by mid-December." He beamed with pride as he lifted her into the air with ease.

~~~~~~

"Are you sure your folks won't mind that I'm bringing Bentley?" The beagle sat with a stoic attitude between the couple in the front seat of Daniel's truck.

"Charlie and Brutus will show him a good time. You'll dig Brutus; he's big as a house but occasionally considers himself a lap dog. If you sit on the floor you might end up with a Great Dane on top of you.

Esther pulled from her purse the compatibility test that she and Joseph created years ago, "I have some questions for you."

"Yes, I've been with other women. But I love you and don't care about anyone else."

"That wasn't one of the questions, Mr. Jacobson. But since you brought it up, how many?"

"I need my lawyer." Daniel patted her knee, "A few. Do you want names?"

"No. Chocolate or vanilla ice cream?" And so the twenty-five question test began.

After she imposed the test, Daniel shared his thoughts, "I don't think about those things, Esther. Why those questions? Why not something like, 'Are you a Christian?' or 'Do you believe in capital punishment?' But whether we agree on ice cream flavors; that's not so important, is it?"

"Many philosophical issues can be debated and someone might even be convinced by another person that electrocution is okay. And as far as religion goes, there are Jews marrying Catholics every weekend in America. But all the tiny decisions and rationalizations we make every day are indicators of who we are underneath the face we put on every morning. A man might have to pretend that he's enjoying lunch with his boss, but he at least orders his meal truthfully, which is based on his innate preferences. There's no faking that stuff. Joseph and I made this test when we were teenagers and I promised to give it to the man I fell in love with. So there it is. Perhaps you're right, but I still like the idea of a compatibility test."

"How did I do?" He was nearly afraid to ask at this point.

"We matched twenty-two out of twenty-five answers." Esther unhitched her seatbelt to kiss his cheek, "I think we might do all right together, Mr. Jacobson. However, the idea that you prefer French fries to onion rings boggles my mind; I suppose that I'll have to overlook that flaw." She scooted back to her side of the seat.

They drove in silence for a while, comfortable with each other's presence while Bentley whimpered in his dreams between them. Esther decided that another moment couldn't pass without presenting the CF facts and statistics before the relationship advanced further.

"Do you know anyone with cystic fibrosis?"

"No, Esther."

"Can I tell you about it?" She was twisting her scarf fringe as she spoke nervously.

"Absolutely."

"CF is a genetic disease that creates mucus in the lungs, which makes breathing difficult and leads to infections. It also causes pancreatic insufficiency, which leads to digestive problems. People with CF take lots of medicine every single day, and they cough a lot and their health tends to deteriorate as they grow older. Some cases are worse than others. Someone born this year with CF will survive twenty or thirty years. Joseph was born in 1965 and doctors gave him about ten years; he survived to eighteen. A carrier of CF can pass the disease to her child." She felt as those she'd just exited the confessional at church; all at once cleansed and freed after having passed the troubling information from her soul.

"Are you a carrier?" Daniel knew where this was headed.

"I dunno, I haven't been tested. If both the husband and wife are CF carriers, there's a one in four chance that they'll give birth to a child with CF. If that's our case, would you stay with me?"

"Now those are the kinds of questions I'm talking about. We'd get married and adopt kids. And it might even make sense to take the chance one time to have our own child. Do you want to meet with a genetic counselor or get tested? Are you worried?"

"I wouldn't have traded my childhood with Joseph for anything in the world. But his suffering and the crushing pain I've carried since losing him is wretched and extremely difficult some days. I don't know that I could live through it all again."

"I believe that God brought us together, Esther, and I think we'll have a family someday. Only He knows who our children will be." Daniel reached around the dog and pressed his fingertips against her cheek.

"You're a moral and intelligent man. You should have your own biological sons and daughters because the world needs more people like you in it. If by some extreme long shot we're both CF carriers, you and I need to think long and hard about our future together." Her eyes watered and she quickly wiped them with her scarf.

"No one in my family tree had or currently has cystic fibrosis. So the point you're making is moot. I appreciate your explaining all of this to me, but I'm not a carrier. It's nearly lunchtime; let's find a place that serves onion rings. If I'm going to live with you for the next hundred years I'll need to acquire a taste for them."

"I love you Daniel."

"It's you and me forever, Es. I love you too."

~~~~~~

"Dinner was delicious, Mrs. Jacobson. It's been a blessing to spend the holiday with all of you." Esther stood from the table and began clearing plates to take into the kitchen. When Sandra rose to help, Esther insisted that she stay seated and enjoy the time with her family. Amy rose to assist in the clean-up effort, and the young women wandered into the kitchen.

"I've never seen my brother so happy; there's an aura of peace about him now. How did you two meet?" Amy tied an apron around her waist and offered one to Esther.

Esther unraveled the long love story while Amy enjoyed hearing the tale that ended in the yellow room of the library addition. In turn, Amy shared with Esther her favorite childhood memories of her eldest brother while she filled a plate for Dennis and stashed it into the refrigerator.

"I've come for pie. Sandra says there's whipped cream in the refrigerator but I don't see a spinning cow in here." Grandpa Jacobson moved a bit more slowly now, but his wit was sound.

"I'll bring plates and forks to the table and you can carry the pies, Grandpa." Amy found the whipped cream on the counter, retrieved utensils from the drawer, and handed napkins to Esther before they regrouped around the dining table for dessert.

"Penn State is a good school, Esther. I understand you graduated a couple of years behind Daniel. Did you grow up in Arcadia?" John wanted to learn more about the unique woman who had an obvious hold on his son's heart.

"I grew up in a Detroit suburb with my brother and parents. They recently spent a weekend in Arcadia with me to pick apples and attend a jazz festival—and to meet Daniel."

"Did your brother choose an out-of-state college as well?"

"Joseph passed away two-and-a-half years ago. He finished high school but didn't get to college. Cystic fibrosis is a terrible disease, Mr. Jacobson."

"Oh dear, I'm so sorry Esther." Sandra's expression turned mournful and her apology was genuine.

"It is a vicious disease. My niece's first child died of CF at the age of six back in 1963." Grandpa looked knowingly at Esther.

"I remember that, Dad. Daniel wasn't even in school yet. That was Aunt Paula's daughter. What was her name, Becky?"

John held his fork in the air while searching his memory for details of the child.

Grandpa closed his eyes and responded, "Her name was Beth and she had beautiful blue eyes just like Daniel's."

Esther blacked out momentarily and nearly toppled off her chair. She dropped her fork to the floor, spilling its scoopful of pumpkin pie. "Oh! Let me get a cloth to clean this." She strode to the kitchen in a panic and Daniel followed on her heels.

"You cannot cry about this, Es. CF is a rare disease because both parents have to be carriers. We have a nice weekend planned, and when Dennis gets home we'll play Parcheesi and drink the wine I brought. Then you'll camp in Amy's room tonight, and you and I will dine downtown tomorrow." He sat at the small breakfast table and pulled her onto his lap. As he began to smother her in soothing kisses, Dennis rolled in from his hospital rounds. His schedule was wildly unpredictable and the Jacobsons had learned early not to plan around it.

"Hi there. That's a fine supper you're holding onto, Dan. Where's the turkey?"

Esther jumped from Daniel's lap and extended her hand, "I'm Esther and you must be doctor Dennis."

"If I survive the next three years of medical school and a year in hospital scrubs, that'll be my title. Very pleased to meet you, Esther. Marry her Daniel; the love that's steaming in this room is thick enough to choke on." Dennis marched past the couple and into the dining room to greet the rest of his family.

"I knew Dennis would like you."

~~~~~~

"My parents took me to the Signature Room for dinner on my eighteenth birthday. The view of the city is incredible and the salmon is to die for. I can't believe Daniel didn't tell you anything about it. I'll not say another word because he might want to surprise you." Amy was pulling dresses from her closet and holding them up to Esther. "I'm taller and wider than you, but my mom can do magic with a needle and thread, if necessary.

May I fix up your hair?"

"This hair has a mind of its own and Daniel doesn't like it tied up. But if you want a challenge you can take a curling iron to it and smooth out a few kinks." Esther liked the jade green dress; its color paired nicely with her sable brown hair. "If I tighten this belt around my waist . . . voila! An instant fit." She had never been fashion conscious and wasn't about to start now. As long as the clothing fit well and didn't itch her skin, Esther wore it. She didn't own a formal dress and was grateful that Amy had been gracious enough to loan her one.

"Mom has a great pair of shoes to go with that dress, and her feet are closer to your size." Amy dashed to the other room to get the shoes and returned in a moment. "The outfit is totally complete. Do you wear make-up?"

"I'm wearing just blush and mascara. Is that enough?"

"You have lovely skin and don't need much. How about we add just a bit of eyeliner and lipstick when we finish your hair?" As Amy wrapped a long hair strand around the curling iron rod, Daniel strolled in.

"Touch her hair and I'll tickle you to the ground and make Brutus sit on you."

Esther took an appraising look at her dashing beau in his dark gray suit and, as usual, felt weak-kneed. "Is my hair okay like this for the Signature Room?" Esther bit her lip.

"You're a stunning creature, library girl. Let's go. The reservations are for six-thirty and it'll take a while to park. Are you ready to walk through my magnificent city?"

"As long as you hold my hand."

Amy quickly pulled Esther away from her brother and pushed him out of the room. "She'll be ready in two minutes."

~~~~~~

Bringing her into his city proved to be a thrilling ordeal for Daniel. Just walking a half block to the building and riding the elevator with her had lifted his spirit into the upper echelon of elation. He hoped to never forget the evening and yearned for it only to become better.

Seated in the elegant and tastefully adorned dining area of the Signature Room on the ninety-fifth floor of the John Hancock Center, she was thoroughly delighted. "It's breathtaking, Daniel. I've never been in such a grand building. Thank you." The wine had subdued her nerves and Esther absorbed the atmosphere like a child in a circus; she was simultaneously astounded and bewildered.

Daniel saw nothing and no one else in the room but the woman in front of him. *Share your life with me. Marry me.* He squeezed the small velvet box in his pocket and decided to wait until their dessert was served.

"I used to imagine designing a structure like this one when I was a kid. I should show you the skyscraper models I built fifteen years ago; you'd get a real kick out of them. My oldest memory is of downtown Chicago. My parents said I was three-and-a-half when they took me into the city for the first time. They walked me down South State Street to see the Palmer House Hotel and Lytton Store building. Although they're only twenty-story structures, they seemed ominous as a little kid."

The couple savored the meal while the fire that had ignited between them during the summer continued to burn into a loving friendship. They opened up completely to each other and rose far above the small-talk stratosphere. Each felt as though they'd been absorbed into the other. Their discussion was briefly interrupted by the waiter who brought champagne and an extravagant strawberry mousse.

"Champagne! This meal will cost you a week's work, Daniel. Please don't order another item."

After they'd each tasted the dessert and sipped their drinks, Daniel removed the box from his pocket, pulled her hand into his, and set the box onto her palm. "Open it."

She carefully peeked inside to expose a brilliant solitaire diamond set in a delicate silver band. "It's beautiful."

"Will you be my wife, Esther?"

"Yes."

His chest swelled, "It'll be a sweet life; I hope you like the ring."

He took the ring from the box and slid it onto her finger. She was his. "Until death do us part, little bird. Do you think we can swing a December wedding?"

Esther with attitude walked around the table and plopped onto his lap. "The ring is lovely and my feet haven't touched the ground since you shook my hand in June. Let's leave. We've got some kissing to do."

~~~~~~

The City of Frankfort granted the occupancy certificate for the library addition on Thursday, December 1st. Esther was invited to meet with the City Council members on Monday to plan a dedication ceremony before Christmas. Amid the excitement of organizing books for placement into the addition, training a part-time library clerk, planning the ceremony, and arranging her wedding, an underlying fear gnawed in her chest.

To assuage her concern, Daniel offered to be tested for the cystic fibrosis gene. He assured Esther that it would only confirm what he already knew, "I'm not a carrier so stop fretting." He had blood drawn in Grand Rapids the day after they returned from Chicago. If his prediction was correct there'd be no need for her to get tested. But when they spoke this morning he hadn't mentioned the test results. *It's been four days since his test. How much time does the lab need?* She pushed the anxiety to the back of her mind and pulled the book cart to the east side of the library.

There it was again. Esther stole a glance at the ceiling. *Joseph? Is that you?* She finished shelving books in the non-fiction section and now stood silently poised with perked ears. Determined to find the source of the cough, she slowly strolled around the library. It was a young girl, perhaps nine or ten years old. She was with her mother and they were sorting through a stack of poetry books.

"May I help you find something? I'm Miss Gardener." *I'm Mrs. Jacobson.*

The woman looked up from the small table, "Hello. My daughter enjoys poetry and we'd like to find something she hasn't yet read. I'm Miranda Klaussen and this is Melissa."

"Nice to meet you both; I'd be happy to help. I indulge in poetry myself and there are some days that I simply must read Frost or Dickenson before I go to bed. If you've already read the books in that stack, might I suggest a title or two by Walter de la Mare? Have you read any of his works, Melissa?"

"No Ma'am. I don't know his name." She coughed mightily to clear her lungs. Mrs. Klaussen withdrew an inhaler from her purse.

"I'll be right back with a few books for you." *The girl has CF. Dear Lord, Help her breathe freely today.*

Esther returned shortly with <u>Peacock Pie</u> and <u>Book of Rhymes</u>. "These were written in the early 1900s. Mr. de la Mare was a writer and poet who lived in England. One of his most popular works is the story of Thumbelina, which he wrote in 1921."

"Wow! That's a long time ago." Melissa accepted the books, "Do we need a library card?"

"You do need a valid card to borrow these books. Are you Benzie County residents?"

Mrs. Klaussen answered, "We moved here from Lansing two months ago. We bought a Victorian house on Leelanau Street and are converting it to a bed and breakfast inn. We hope to open on Memorial Day."

"Welcome to the town. That sounds like a fun and challenging project. Let's go to the front desk; I'll make a card for each of you."

They followed her to the desk where they completed application forms. "When were you diagnosed with CF, Melissa?"

"How do you know about CF?" Melissa was puzzled; most people thought she had asthma or bronchitis.

"My brother was born with it." It was the first time she'd mentioned Joseph without having an ache tighten her throat.

"Melissa was diagnosed with CF when she was a year old; she's ten now. We're grateful for the medications that alleviate her symptoms. But as you well know, it's a struggle." Mrs. Klaussen handed the forms to Esther. "That's a gorgeous ring, Miss Gardener. When is the wedding?"

Esther spoke as she typed, "Thank you. My fiancé picked the ring; I couldn't have chosen one more lovely. We hope to be married by May. Daniel and I have to settle our living arrangements before we set a date." She offered the cards to the new residents and checked out the de la Mare books. "We're planning a dedication ceremony for the new library section. I'm sure you'll see something in the newspaper about it—I hope you can join us."

~~~~~~

"Maria?" Esther strode into the new preschool room where the library clerk was framing posters to hang on the wall. "I'm taking an early lunch to run to the hardware store for picture hangers and bird seed. I haven't filled the feeder in my yard for days and the birds are starving. See you in a few minutes."

"I'll be fine so take your time. If the new tables arrive while you're out, is it okay if I sign for them?" Maria, Esther's new assistant, had just recently become confident in her role.

"Sure. If they come today have the men carry them into the central area of the addition." Walking to her car, Esther was privately pleased with the recent snowfall. It had softened the crusty brown edges of the land and lightened the atmosphere of the town. She didn't mind a few inches of snow; it was the batten-down-the-hatches snowstorms that left her anxious. As usual, her thoughts turned to her architect. The days without him were horrendously lonely and she looked forward to his arrival tomorrow. He would finally see her cabin and they'd share two days together before he had to return to Grand Rapids. *It's improper to have him spend the nights in the cabin, but I can't help but wanting him with me, even if he's on the couch.*

The hardware store was nicely decked in holly and garland. Tool sets covered in red and green bows were displayed around the front entrance and a festive jar of candy canes stood beside the cash register.

"Hi, Mrs. Carnahan. We're hanging posters in the library and need wall fasteners. I also need some bird seed." Esther followed the shop owner to the aisle that contained small hardware.

"If the posters are framed with glass tops, they'll be quite heavy, but if the tops are plastic, then these will work." Mrs. Carnahan pointed to the row of hangers and then spotted Esther's ring. "Oh my! Are you and Daniel engaged?"

Esther blushed, "Yes, and we hope to have a spring wedding. I think we'll have the ceremony in Arcadia, even though his family is in Chicago and mine is in Detroit. I'm a member of the Trinity Church and this is where we met."

"That's wonderful news." Mrs. Carnahan rang up the purchase and dropped a candy cane into Esther's bag. "Come back and see me if you need holiday decor for your cabin or the library—we have a good selection this year."

~~~~~~

When she returned to the library, Esther found Maria admiring the newly framed posters.

"Where'd you find these pictures? They're timeless. And such great depictions of the fairy tales; I think the Little Red Hen is adorable."

"When Mrs. Kelly was here with her second grade class I asked to borrow her supply catalog and ordered these posters from it. My favorite is the Three Little Pigs."

After hanging the posters the women loaded carts with the preschool and early reader books. Esther hoped to finish the preschool room before Daniel showed up tomorrow. "Daniel made a dozen wooden bookends that he's bringing with him. They'll look terrific holding up the seasonal books."

The loquacious women spent several hours moving and

shelving books. The yellow room had come alive and achieved the appearance that Esther desired. It would beckon mothers and children to come inside and read together. By one o'clock Esther shook from exhaustion and her head pounded. She sat in a rocking chair to press her fingertips into her temples and ease the pain. *If the world would just stop for a moment and let me catch my breath. Please Lord, let Daniel's test result be negative.*

"Are you okay?" Maria patted Esther's shoulder as if waking a small child from a bad dream.

"Having my mind so full has me feeling pretty drained. After I soak in a hot bath tonight the headache will subside."

"Why don't you go home now? We can finish clearing out the old bookshelves tomorrow. I have all the returned books logged in and the re-shelving isn't a big deal. Go ahead. I'll only be alone here for a few hours; I can handle it." Maria insisted that Esther get a good amount of rest so she'd be ready for the workload tomorrow. "I know how to lock up, and besides, your checklist won't let me forget a thing. Go home."

"I suppose you're right. I'll see you tomorrow morning, Maria. Thanks." Esther retrieved her coat and purse from the office and traipsed out the door. The powdery snow had become tiny ice pellets during the early afternoon and they now stung her cheeks. After starting her car and scraping its windows, she hopped in and pulled off her snowy mittens. She pressed the ring against her lips. *I need you Daniel. Do you think about me as often as I think of you?*

Thin rays of sunlight penetrated the thick cloud covering to draw glittery lines in the snow along Glovers Lake Road. She was glad to be home and decided to make a fire in the hearth before taking her bath. Bentley whined and pranced in circles as she pulled off her winter gear and stowed away the large bag of birdseed.

"Hey, little boy. Did I surprise you?" She squatted beside the fireplace, opened the flue, placed kindling and logs onto the grate, and lit a newspaper stick to ignite the kindling.

As the fire grew Esther saw that the smoke wasn't rising into the chimney. *Uh oh. I wonder if the opening is blocked.* She quickly donned her coat and ran outside to check the chimney; only tiny traces of smoke were rising from it. She hauled the ladder from her shed and propped it against the cabin. Once on top of the roof, she discovered that a large pine branch had fallen onto the chimney top. With one hand grasping the stony chimney she reached up with the other hand to pull the branch off. *Got it.* She tossed the heavy branch to the ground, losing her footing and falling from the roof onto the snowy ground below.

~~~~~~

A box of treasures sat beside him in the truck. Brightly painted bookends for the preschool room, Christmas ornaments, fudge from his mother, and a pink cashmere sweater for his sweetheart. She had no idea he was arriving a day early. Mitch had given him a stern lecture, but Daniel was impelled to get to Esther today. His work tomorrow would've suffered anyway because the yearning had pushed everything else out of his mind. He felt the full brunt of love's power and could do nothing but give in to it. And he was anxious to see her surprised expression when he walked into the library this afternoon.

After driving west on Glovers Lake Road for several miles, he glanced down the right side of the road to catch a view of her cabin. Surprised to see smoke coming from the chimney, he pressed the brake pedal to reduce his speed. *That's her car.* He stopped quickly to turn into the driveway, realizing immediately how much he had missed his lovely sparrow. He dashed from the truck to the side door and froze in his tracks. "Esther!"

Kneeling beside her he screamed her name again and nearly collapsed from fear. He drew her up close while she whimpered; the horror and anguish whirled through his core in a maelstrom of emotions. "I'm here, baby. Can you hear me?"

She groaned without opening her eyes, and then reached for him. He scooped her up and carried her to the truck; her hands and face felt frozen. After laying her on the passenger seat, he slid behind the steering wheel, removed his coat, draped it over her body and set her head onto his lap.

A seizure of panic gripped him, "Esther, please stay with me. We're going to the hospital." She began to tremble. Daniel turned up the heater and skidded out of the driveway. *Dear Lord, don't take her away from me. Not Esther.*

December 1985 ~ Part 1

Engaged for just a few days, he was grasping for the first time the pain that so often accompanies love. The nurse had shooed Daniel to the waiting area five minutes ago. A doctor promised to speak with him after Esther's examination and x-rays were done. Consumed with an aching desire to comfort her, he pressed his back against the wall and tapped his head into it. Perhaps the rattling would erase the frightful picture of his injured girl. It worked. He recalled the fear he'd felt last winter when he learned that his grandpa had suffered a heart attack. Relief after that episode wasn't realized until he spoke with his grandpa on the telephone two weeks later. Wrapping his arms around that feeling a year later, he could now only describe it as being struck by a bullet and thrown off kilter. He now felt drenched in tension and anxiety at the thought of losing Esther. *She had asked for Karen . . .*

Daniel hurried to the receptionist. "I need a pay phone, Ma'am. Do you have a phone book?" Without lifting her nose from the paperwork scattered in front of her, the administrator withdrew a telephone directory from a small bookshelf, set it onto the corner of her desk and pointed to the east hallway. He plunged his hand into his pocket to grab a dime.

"Frankfort Library, Maria speaking."

"This is Daniel and I'm at the Paul Oliver Hospital. When I got to Esther's place she was on the ground beside her ladder. She was barely conscious so I brought her here. They're doing x-rays now and a neurologist is due shortly to examine her. She asked for Karen, but I don't know where to find her. I don't even know Karen's last name. Does she live in Frankfort?"

"Oh mercy heavens. Is she going to be all right? Oh Esther. What was she doing up the ladder? Karen Holsten lives in Arcadia. I'll call her from here and send her to the hospital.

Call me as soon as you get a report from the doctor."

"Sure thing. Thanks, Maria."

Daniel returned to the drab waiting room outlined in unfriendly vinyl chairs. Randomly placed tables held skewed stacks of over-used magazines. A TV mounted in the corner of the room had been shut off for lack of viewers; a seemingly endless row of lighthouse pictures provided the only visual entertainment today. He hadn't done any serious praying in a year; his world could be pretty much summed up as a bowl of cherries. But now this. His life had evolved to become more purposeful since the library project had begun. He felt bound and indebted to Frankfort and its people. Esther filled his thoughts and it bothered him to be living alone in Grand Rapids without her. *Dear Lord, I realize I've been walking around on this earth with life going mostly my way. And I really do appreciate that. But if you're thinking I need a train wreck of some sort to strengthen my faith and character, ah, could you do something like zero out my bank account balances? I beg you, Lord, to help Esther. She's precious to so many.*

Fraught with fear, he set his head into his hands and took a few deep breaths to calm his nerves. *If I smoked then I'd at least have something to do with myself.* A hand tapped his shoulder and he jerked up in a daze.

"Hello, Daniel."

He stood immediately to find Karen at his side and shook her hand in a tentative and frightened motion. Daniel recognized her, but couldn't place where they'd met.

"I'm Karen Holsten. We met at the library when Esther brought soup in for the crew. How is she? What happened?"

"I'm glad you came. She fell off a ladder near the cabin. They're doing x-rays now and then will check for head trauma and internal injuries. If they suspect an organ or brain injury they'll send her to Traverse City for an MRI." His voice trembled and his eyes moistened; Karen handed him a tissue.

"This is more serious than I thought." She sat on the edge of the worn vinyl seat and turned to him like a mother to a distraught son.

"Oh man, I hope it's not serious." Daniel leaned forward in his seat and set his head back into his hands.

"I mean you and Esther—look at you. This has certainly become much more than a summer-to-winter romance." Karen set her hand atop his shoulder, "She'll be all right; Esther is a tough woman. The ground around that cabin was covered in a blanket of snow and it probably softened her fall. And she couldn't have dropped much more than twelve feet. Does she know how you feel about her?"

"Have you seen her since we've been back from Chicago?"

"John and I just got back from Ohio on Tuesday; the last time I spoke with her was before Thanksgiving."

"We're engaged. What if she's not okay?"

"Congratulations. Sparks fly when you're together. Let's not fret about Esther's accident just yet. I have a lot of confidence in that little girl; she's going to be all right, Daniel." They sat silently in separate thoughts while sensing that they'd each just made a dear friend.

~~~~~~

"Are you Esther Gardener's family?" Dr. Koytzen approached the pair to impart the news they'd been waiting for.

Daniel replied quickly, "I'm her fiancé."

"Esther has a grade 3 concussion, but sustained no internal injuries or bone fractures that we can detect at the moment. Her skull and spinal x-rays are clear. Esther's vital signs are stable, her vision and hearing are in the normal range, and her reflexes are normal. She's experiencing a sensitivity to light as well as dizziness and nausea, but neither vomiting nor extreme fatigue, so that's a good sign. As a matter of fact, she wants to go home. However, because we don't know whether she was unconscious for five seconds or ten minutes, we want to run a CT scan and keep an eye on vital signs overnight. She has an IV in place as well. Any questions?"

"May I see her?" Again, Daniel responded immediately.

"That would be fine. She's settled in room 148. I need one

of you to complete these forms as best you can, and then contact her family. Esther's coat and clothing are in her room but she doesn't have identification with her."

Karen volunteered to do the paperwork and call Agatha and Ken in Detroit. Daniel clutched her hand in a subtle thank-you gesture before marching in the direction of Esther's room.

She was lying motionless in the stark room; a purple bruise had risen on her forehead and her long, wavy hair laid in tangles over the white pillow. Her eyes were closed when she heard Daniel enter; a desire to have him near heightened her senses. Esther opened her eyes and spoke shyly, "How'd you know to come a day early, Superman?"

The sound of her voice brought such a flood of relief that he gasped for air. With a tightened throat and trembling hands, he rushed to her side, "How're you feeling, little sparrow?" She opened her arms. He pressed his body against hers before burying his head on the pillow beside her. She was delicate and frail, like a bird. She pulled her fingers through his hair and drew tiny zig-zags around his neck and shoulders.

"I'm staying here tonight and they can't make me leave." He pushed himself up and then cupped her small hands into his. "You scared me, Es. What if I hadn't come? Why were you on the ladder? You could've frozen to death." Daniel quaked inside as other what-if scenarios played in his mind; the thought of never holding her again put him on the brink of tears.

She scooted higher up onto her pillows, "The fire!"

"What fire?"

She furrowed her brow, pressing fingertips at her temples, "I made a fire in the cabin. That's why I was on the ladder. A branch was stuck in the chimney and I pulled it off. What if my cabin is burned down? And Bentley? Ouch, my head hurts." Esther reached for him.

Daniel settled her back onto the pillow. "If you cleared the chimney then your cabin is in no danger. I'll check Bentley and the cabin. Marry me tomorrow at the courthouse, Es." He gripped her shoulders and eagerly pressed his mouth against hers. The kiss began tentatively and grew hungry with need. He ended the kiss to touch the bruise on her head.

Neither had heard Karen come into the room. "The church in Arcadia is a much nicer place for a wedding."

With an extravagant grin on his face, Daniel fetched a chair for Karen and placed it beside the bed.

"May I see the engagement ring?" Karen was delighted that her darling friend had found love. "It's beautiful and I'm happy for both of you." She bent down to gently embrace the bruised girl.

"I'll compromise. A January wedding, then?" Daniel grinned with anticipation.

"Oh Daniel—it's December and we just met in July. We need to wait until the spring at least. You have a one-track mind; please check the cabin for me."

He nearly came unraveled at the thought of not being able to live with her for another four months. Good grief. He'd never make it. "We met in June."

"And we barely exchanged a dozen words that day..."

"Then when did you fall for me, huh? Let's start there."

"When I ran into you at Penn State."

Daniel's cheeks reddened, "Are you serious?"

She grinned like a little girl with a secret. "Yeah, that's pretty much when it happened. And when you walked into the City Hall conference room five months ago, my heart nearly stopped."

Daniel's chest swelled as the love he felt for her consumed him all over again. He wanted her home. In *their* home.

It was Esther's turn to ask the question now, "When did you know that I was the one?"

"When I saw you stacking pineapples at the Red Owl market. You were blushing and adorable and I wanted to touch your pretty smile."

"I still think we should wait until spring." She closed her eyes to the light that came in through the window. Her head pounded now.

"Let's get her out of this hospital before you make wedding plans. I talked to your mother, Es. I told her what the doctor told me, and I gave her your room number. Your phone should ring any second. We'll step into the hall for a minute so you can chat privately with her."

Karen clutched Daniel's shirtsleeve and yanked him into the hallway. She knew what he was thinking.

"First of all, non-family members cannot stay overnight in her room. So you're not staying. Second, do you have to get back to Grand Rapids this weekend?"

"I'll be here through Saturday, but I have to return to my office Sunday afternoon to finish a perspective. I also have a draftsman working on a project; I need to personally review his work and make revisions by Monday afternoon. Will you be here Sunday afternoon and Monday in case she needs something?"

"I'll definitely be here, and Esther's parents might drive up as well. She won't be alone while you're gone. If Ken and Agatha can't make the drive, she can stay at my house on Sunday. I'll call Charlotte at the market and let her know that Esther needs a few days off. I spoke to Maria and she'll work alone on Monday and Tuesday. Are you okay with all of this?"

"No, but I don't have choice, unless I sneak in through the window of room 148."

Karen walked to the drugstore to buy a brush, toothbrush, and toothpaste for Esther. Daniel headed directly to her room.

"My mom wants to drive up but I told her that I'm in great shape and nothing is broken. They were just here a couple months ago anyway. Daniel, please get to Arcadia and check the cabin for me."

"I'm on my way, bird." *It's killing me to leave you here. Every bone in my body wants to stay.*

"The door should be unlocked. Um, while you're there would you mind letting Bentley out, giving him some supper and putting seed into the bird feeder for me?"

"I'd be absolutely happy to." He sat on the edge of the bed again to kiss her forehead, cheeks, and mouth. "I'll go ahead now before it gets dark. Karen went to the store to get a few things for you; she'll be back in a minute."

While Daniel shrugged into his coat, Esther described where to find the dog food and bird seed. He couldn't believe she was worried about the birds but decided to appease her rather than instigate a debate.

"I'll be back tomorrow morning to bring you home, okay? Do you want me to bring some different clothes?"

"I'll be all right. Besides I don't think it's a good idea for a man to be rummaging around a woman's undergarment drawer, do you?" Her eyes twinkled up at him.

Daniel blushed at the thought. He was just being polite. They exchanged another kiss before he was out the door for the evening.

~~~~~~

Bentley barked when Daniel turned the doorknob of the unburned cabin. *Esther said he wouldn't bite but there's a first time for everything, I suppose.* A rush of anxiety caught him off guard as he realized he'd be stepping into her private world. He would see the things that were dear to her and touch things that had perhaps, in some small way, helped shape her into who she was. With trepidation he opened the door and immediately felt her presence surround him. Bentley hopped up to him and begged for an ear rub; he squatted down to let the dog nuzzle his hand. The room smelled faintly of smoke so he opened two windows; the cross-ventilation would clear the air in a matter of minutes.

"Hey there, fella. Run out and take care of your business."

He opened the door and watched the beagle trot into the yard. Turning back into the living room of the cabin, he'd never seen anything like it. His world comprised contemporary smooth lines with coordinating furniture placed at proper angles. An oak entertainment center with a TV, stereo, and alphabetically arranged cassette tapes; glass-top end tables; glistening countertops; and beige carpeting filled his condominium living room.

But this. This was a Goldilocks-and-the-three-bears sort of thing. An old crocheted afghan was slung over the back of a blue plaid couch, a black iron skillet full of apples sat on the kitchen counter, a dusty braided rug covered a worn-out wooden floor, and a refrigerator that would barely fit a case of beer displayed notes held by apple-shaped magnets. A bookshelf stuffed full of ancient books stood against the wall in a spot where a TV belonged. *There's no TV.* This was so Esther.

The main floor of the cabin was fairly small; Daniel guessed about six hundred fifty square feet. He admired the stone fireplace and thought about sitting in front of a blazing fire with her. Underneath a blanket. Clothing tossed onto the couch. Whoops. . . too far.

He crept into the cozy kitchen and felt an urge to eat pancakes. It was tidy and extremely modest. Cupboards were installed only above the sink and beneath the countertops. The knobs and handles were wrought iron. A stainless steel teakettle stood like a round-bellied watchman atop the old gas stove. An antique dinette and its matching chairs sat near the kitchen counter. A few books, basket of stationery, and a stack of folded clothes covered the tabletop. *No bedrooms downstairs; probably on the second floor.*

He admired the stairway, fully appreciating its raw beauty. It was a remarkable piece of craftsmanship that could nearly be categorized as a functional sculpture. The rails were simply sanded logs and the steps were log halves, placed flat side up. The effect was earthy and beckoning. Daniel stopped himself from climbing up to her bedroom. *Nah, there might be a baby bear sleeping on an itty bitty bed.*

He'd promised to put seed into the bird feeder but felt anchored to the cabin floor. It was as though he had stepped into the home he'd been missing for years. Closing his eyes, Esther appeared in the kitchen. She wore a white flannel nightshirt; her hair was awry and she was spreading jam on warm wheat toast. *Now what kind of vision is that?* If she were there, he'd sneak up behind her, spin her into him, kiss her deeply, and then carry her up to the bed for . . . *Time to fill the bird feeder.*

Darkness crept around the cabin and below the pine boughs as he jogged with the bag of seed into the yard. Bentley greeted him and skipped in a way that only a beagle can do when full of delight. Daniel couldn't help but smile down at the happy dog, and then struck up a conversation, "Esther took quite a tumble this afternoon. She'll be back home tomorrow so don't fret. I'll feed you supper and tuck you in tonight, pal." The dog replied with a howl.

He spotted the feeder in a birch tree near the small shed. The feeder was a long tube with a scattering of holes and a cymbal-shaped top to keep the squirrels from burglarizing the contents. Once he'd finished the task, he leaned against the snow-covered picnic table and scanned the now dusky yard. He spied a fifteen-by-fifteen-foot fenced-in area. Although now covered in a layer of snow, he knew immediately that it was her garden. It'd be no surprise if her cupboard held rows of canned vegetables. Another vision materialized. He saw her picking tomatoes. Bare feet, straw hat, and fabulous legs. He'd sneak up behind her, pick her up, spin her around, kiss her deeply, and then drag her upstairs . . . *Whoa. Time to feed the dog.*

~~~~~~

Did she truly love him? Did he love her? Did the engagement happen too suddenly? She didn't think so. She saw them together with crooked hands and ugly shoes in sixty years. They'd enjoy homemade soups and make applesauce in the fall. *Where will we live? His life is in Grand Rapids and mine is here. What if I'm a CF carrier?* The worries tumbled around in her mind like dozens of little wet mittens in a dryer. Her head began throbbing but she couldn't rest until some of these issues were resolved. The nurse waltzed in to save her from the mitten fiasco.

"I need to get your blood pressure again, Miss Esther. How are you feeling?"

"My body feels good. But I have a headache and feel tired; it's been a pretty rough day."

"One-fifteen over seventy-five; that's a good reading. What's on your mind, Missy?"

"How many times have you been in love, Loretta?"

"Once. Still am. Lewis and I have been married nearly thirty years now. I still look forward to seeing his old face at the end of the day. We hold hands during movies, I don't nag about his socks on the floor and he don't nag about my toothbrush on the bathroom counter. We honeymooned for a decade."

"How'd you know he was the one?"

"When I first saw Lewis thirty years ago, my bones tingled, my mouth dried up, and my knees went rubbery. That went on for five years. Our engagement was short, just three months, but it was all we needed. That's a gorgeous ring on your finger. Is the handsome man who was here this afternoon your fiancé?"

"That's my Daniel. I love him so much that I sometimes psyche myself out and worry that it's all a dream. I got it bad, Loretta."

"Settle down and stop analyzing it all. When God puts forth a plan it's best to just keep your feet on his trail and open your ears to the hints he drops from the sky."

Esther was a born second guesser, no doubt about that. A sub-conscious analysis had been churning at the back of her mind for days. She and Daniel were just too well paired. She had a premonition of doom but couldn't define it; the sensation lurked as a shadow, and the darn thing was growing.

~~~~~~

He called Esther at the hospital to let her know Bentley and the cabin were in tip-top shape. She insisted that he spend the night there, and he was more than happy to oblige. As Daniel settled in, he discovered that her couch was a real comfortable place. He'd found a bag of biscuits in the cupboard and spread them with peanut butter and homemade jam. He then ate an apple with a chunk of cheddar cheese, enjoyed several granola snacks, and was now covered in the afghan. The music of James Taylor streamed from the speakers that sat on top of her bookshelf. He looked forward to Esther dreams and a sleeping beagle at his feet. This far surpassed any hotel accommodations and his condo didn't even come close, despite its trendy decor. *When will I tell her that I'm a CF carrier?*

December 1985 ~ Part 2

Pushing his bride-to-be out the hospital door in a wheelchair, Daniel vowed to never let her near a ladder or rooftop again. He settled Esther into the truck and covered her with the crocheted afghan. She smirked to herself as he fastidiously fussed over her. The drive to the cabin was quiet and unrushed; the empty highway wove between uneven banks of snow that were splotched gray with mud from slushy tires. Random snowmobile paths criss-crossed around white-capped houses and barns. They grinned while passing the chubby snowmen that peppered the elementary school playground on Glovers Lake Road.

She smiled broadly when they parked beside the cabin, "Look at the lovely cardinals at the feeder." She unfastened her seatbelt and stepped into the snow, "Seems like I've been gone for more than just a night—it's good to be home." He held her arm as they walked to the cabin door.

After Bentley greetings, Daniel insisted that she rest on the couch while he prepared lunch. He returned to the truck and collected the groceries he'd bought that morning.

He became suddenly nervous. *She's keeping a vow. Is spending the night a good idea?* "I picked up some ground beef and potato salad so we can have a burger lunch, if that's okay. My mom insisted I bring a batch of her fudge along, and I bought a bag of marshmallows to roast over the fire tonight."

"Sounds delicious. What do you think of the cabin?"

"It fits you to a *T*. And I slept like an old bear on your couch last night. One can't help but get a good night's rest in a cozy space like this. I spent a lot of time admiring that stairway; it's a fine piece of work. Didn't venture upstairs though. How big is it up there?"

"About four-hundred-fifty square feet. Just my bed, dresser, and a rocking chair are upstairs so there's plenty of room for other furniture, perhaps even an entire office."

"May I take a look once these burgers are in the pan?"

"My feelings would be hurt if you didn't. Let me first check that the bed is made; I don't want you to see that I'm a messy housekeeper." She shuffled up the steps to find the room in order and pulled up the shades to let the midday sun stream in. Daniel entered the bedroom as she stepped away from the window.

"This is quite spacious. The beam ceiling is very earthy and the wood has aged beautifully." He stood at the center and roamed the space with his eyes to absorb its charm and beauty. "An office near that window would be great. I'd probably wire the upstairs for a few more electrical outlets, and I'll definitely insist that you leave the room when I need to work because you're an awful distraction, Mrs. Jacobson." His eyes locked onto hers as he crossed the room to her. "I'd give anything to lay beside you on this bed for the rest of the day."

Esther's heart lurched at the velvet roughness in his voice; his seductive eyes scanned her with adoration and desire. The need for his touch was urgent and her vow teetered on the edge of her conscience. Then she smelled smoke. "Lunch is burning!"

She ran downstairs, pulled the smoking pan from the stovetop, leaned into the counter, and giggled with relief. "How'd you know I like my burgers crusty on the outside?" Daniel joined her laughter and they finished preparing the first meal they'd share in the cabin.

"Besides setting the wedding date we have a lot of decisions to make, Es. Should I sell my condo and move here? Do we live in Grand Rapids? Or a city between the two places? Even if we don't live here year-round, this cabin will be a great weekend and summer destination . . ."

"Daniel?"

"Hmm?"

"Did you get the test results back yet?" She was afraid.

"Yup. It just so happens that I'm a CF carrier."

"No." She nearly gagged on the crunchy beef. The room spun around her and she chewed furiously to regain composure.

The dark shadow had taken form, slashing her heart in a mocking motion.

"Yes. And it doesn't faze me a bit, little bird. God wouldn't have gone to all the trouble of putting us together if we're both carriers. Case closed."

"Would you object to my getting the test?"

"Not at all. Have you composed any new fairy tale tunes for your story time?"

"You're a CF carrier and the disease killed my brother. Let's skip the fairy tale discussion and delve right into reality for just a second." She closed her eyes briefly to shut out the headache that began pressing into her forehead, then finished her point, "A monster crawled out from under your bed and I'm not ignoring it."

"Don't go there, Es."

"I'm going . . ."

"You're jumping to a conclusion without all the facts. I'm not venturing into what-if territory today. We just got back from the hospital, you have a concussion and need to rest, I love you and we're not halting marriage plans because there's a blip on the radar."

Esther was locked in a rock-hard fear and hadn't heard a word he said. "This is the lightening strike. It's the deal breaker. What obstacles have you encountered in life thus far? Any car wrecks? Bullies? Thieves? Diseases? Back stabbers?"

"A vampire punched my lights out." Daniel hoped a bit of comic relief would return them to the bliss they'd shared just moments ago.

"Huh?"

"It was a Halloween episode."

"Let me rephrase this . . . When have you <u>not</u> gotten what you wanted? You set goals, you worked hard, and you received your rewards, time and again. There's been no tragedy in your life. You've paid no dues for two decades and now the jig's up. Your number has been called." Esther was in a full blown panic.

"I don't see obstacles in life—only challenges."

She swallowed her irritation, "That's a cliché, Daniel and it won't work with me."

"What about you, Es? Standing next to you, Pollyanna looks like Charlie Brown." He'd pressed a button and now watched her seethe in response. A stab of regret hit him when she rose from the chair and ambled to the couch. Dropping into its corner, she pulled a pillow against her chest to block out the raging turmoil and curled her feet up underneath her.

"I love you. But now what? Do we take this as a sign?" The fiery anguish kept her eyes dry.

"A sign of what? How about we see this as the first hurdle we face together? You're melting down prematurely, Esther. We don't even know what the odds are that you'll test positive for the CF gene. Either way, and in the end, it's you and me. Think of the sort of life we'll have marching down the road as Pollyanna and Hercules. . ."

"Hercules?"

"I dunno the name of Pollyanna's male counterpart. Hercules popped into my head without warning." His reasoning and humor abated her anger.

She laughed out loud to further dissolve the friction. "It irritates me that you're not upset about this, but you're probably right; we'll stash the monster into the closet for now. But I intend to pray real hard about my blood test." His single, silly sentence had soothed her nerves and she felt mushy staring up at him now.

Daniel drew her into his arms from the couch and carried her upstairs, "You thrill me to the verge of insanity, little bird." He laid her onto the bed and sat down. After a long and tender kiss, he posed a question to which he already knew the answer but had to ask anyway, "Can we sleep together tonight if I don't touch you?"

"Bedtime isn't for another ten hours. And I'm pretty sure that sleeping together is against the rules." Her eyes closed to shut out the desire. *Dear Lord, Turn my body off.* "We'll end up in a heap of temptation if we don't get away from this bed."

"Sleep is the last thing on my mind, Es." He found an ounce of willpower and clung to it. "We've got a tree to decorate; you rest here while I string the lights. Then we'll hang ornaments and neck on the couch."

~~~~~~

Esther spent Sunday with Karen and John stringing popcorn, playing Scrabble, and being pampered like a spoiled little girl with the measles. Her headache had completely disappeared by suppertime. But back in her own cabin that night, she found it quite necessary to fret over the CF gene crisis, which resulted in a stiff neck and perturbed mood. Warm cocoa, a few pages of Robert Frost's poetry, and Bentley's cold nose provided a sufficient dose of serenity to ease the pain and allow sleep to finally come.

That same Sunday in Grand Rapids, Daniel had spent nine hours in his office designing and drawing. Details flew from his pencil as he drew like a crazed artist at a blank canvas. He had energy galore. Abstinence and love combined created a serious adrenaline rush. It was like drinking two pots of coffee every day without the side effects. *This must be the love potion people write about.* The sidewalks were clear around his neighborhood and he looked forward to a long run in the cold air tonight. He made a mental note to ask Esther to run with him sometime soon; he bet she had a great stride. Heck, she'd probably outpace him in a distance race.

~~~~~~

As she shoveled a narrow path to her car on Monday, Esther realized that living in the cabin year-round wasn't practical. The twists and turns of M-22 were treacherous in the winter and it was difficult to maintain a seventy-degree temperature in the cabin. She looked forward to the upcoming weekend with Daniel in Grand Rapids. Her schedule for the week was full so the four days to Friday would pass quickly. This morning she'd meet with the City Council members and then go to the hospital to get blood drawn. On Tuesday morning, she and Maria would move more books and furniture into the addition; they'd decorate the library for Christmas in the afternoon. She was having lunch with Karen and Cindy on Wednesday. And Thursday was her afternoon shift at the market.

Maria had called Sunday night to insist that Esther stay home and recuperate for another day, but Esther convinced her that Monday was a day that she simply couldn't miss. After a weekend of pampering, her head felt fine; the bruise was ugly but fading fast.

Her nose and fingertips were still cold from shoveling and scraping her car when she walked into the City Hall building fifteen minutes later. Cindy squealed and ran to Esther, "A bumped head and engagement in the same week; good grief, Es. That bruise looks nasty. Show me the ring!"

She pulled off her wool mittens and held out her left hand, "Daniel chose it for me—isn't it wonderful?"

"It's gorgeous. Have you set a wedding date?" Cindy embraced her friend.

"It'll be April, I think. We have living arrangements to work out yet. I'm seeing his place in Grand Rapids for the first time this weekend. I feel nervous though; isn't that strange?"

"Nah. The anxiety will disappear as soon as you lay eyes on him. We're still on for lunch on Wednesday, right?"

"You betcha."

The meeting attendees scheduled the library dedication ceremony for December 17th; Esther was assigned the advertising and catering tasks. There wouldn't be a full-course meal, just appetizers, and she'd enlist Maria to help. The members of the Ladies Club planned to handle the cake, coffee, tableware, flowers, and tablecloths. Two council members offered to order champagne and Jack Dawson would prepare a speech. The group agreed to meet again in a week to finalize the details.

~~~~~~

Esther rattled like a kite in a windstorm while filling out the medical history form that afternoon. Minutes later, she was ushered into a nurse's station where her left arm was bound tightly with a rubber strip. The nurse stabbed her vein and drew blood into the vial that would be sent to a laboratory. She mumbled a silent prayer as she eyed the glass tube holding her dark red blood. *Dear Lord, Please calm my fear; help me accept the result of this test, whatever it is.*

"When will they know?" Esther's voice was a whisper.

"It usually takes the lab four days. You can call Friday morning or we'll call you, whichever you prefer." The nurse put a band-aid over the needle mark on Esther's arm.

"I'll call you." She felt faint with fear so stood quickly to return to the comfort and safety of her library.

~~~~~~

Lugging and stacking books for six hours on Tuesday left Esther with weary arms and an aching back by the end of the day. Too tired for a bath, she simply washed her face before slipping into her pajamas and robe after a light supper. She built a small fire and felt a pulse of excitement when she moved the pair of long sticks away from the hearth. Feeding gooey marshmallows to each other had become an erotic game last Saturday, which resulted in Daniel taking yet another cold shower. She hadn't slept well that evening knowing he was so near, and awoke in the middle of the night. She had tiptoed downstairs to watch him sleep, and recalled the prayer she uttered: *Keep him safe, Lord. He's the most precious thing to me and I love him with all my heart.*

The phone rang and she assumed it was Daniel; he usually called after supper. "Hello darling."

"Good evening. My name is Grant Whelan. I'd like to speak with Esther Gardener, if she's available."

She gulped before turning beet red, "This is Esther."

"How are you this evening, Ms. Gardener?"

"Just fine, Sir. What can I do for you?"

"I own a coffee and gift shop in St. Ignace. I serve simple edibles such as pastry, croissants, gourmet coffee, and candy. I enjoyed your granola in Traverse City this past September and brought several snacks back with me. The customers responded positively. Do you offer quantity pricing? What would the shipping cost be for a box of fifty?"

"Um, yes Sir. I do offer quantity pricing." Esther stretched the phone cord to its limit and grabbed the pricing chart from the bookshelf. "One box contains twelve snacks, and the cost for one to five boxes is $6 per box; six to ten boxes would be $5 per box. I could ship you four boxes for $24 plus shipping, which would come to $31."

"Do you accept telephone orders? Will an invoice be sent with the order or will the shipment arrive C.O.D?"

"I do accept telephone orders and can include an invoice with your shipment."

"Then I'd like to place an order for forty-eight granola bars, Ms. Gardener. How soon can you ship them?"

"Is next Monday soon enough, Mr. Whelan? You'd receive the shipment on Wednesday."

"That will be fine. If my winter patrons consume twenty-four bars every week, then the summer visitors will probably consume a hundred each week. Will your facility accommodate my summer orders?"

"I'll have to get back with you on that next week, Mr. Whelan." Esther jotted down his shipping address before wrapping up the conversation. "If you have any questions or don't receive the granola by Wednesday, please call me. Thanks so much for your order, and I hope your customers enjoy it."

Esther felt an emotional upheaval coming on. *How will I tell Daniel that I'm making forty-eight granola bars this weekend? What if more people call? What if five people call and they each want fifty granola bars? Why did I listen to Karen and Cindy?*

~~~~~

Maria and Esther were eating gingerbread in the library office Wednesday morning after decking the halls, so to speak. They had propped Christmas books on display tables, hung holly over door-frames and around the stair rail, and decorated a small Christmas tree beside the stairway in the new central area. Esther quickly dabbed her mouth with a napkin before answering the ringing telephone.

"Frankfort Library, Esther speaking."

"Miss Gardener, this is Mitch Smythe. How're you today?"

"I'm well, thank you. How may I help you, Mr. Smythe?"

"Congratulations on the engagement—it's terrific news."

"Thank you, we're both very happy."

"I'm hoping that you can help me with a problem. Daniel has been distracted lately; his patience seems to have vanished and I've caught errors in his drafting work. And this is from one of the most compulsive guys I know. Any idea what might be upsetting him?"

"He didn't seem disturbed last weekend, although you've known him much longer than I have." *It's either lack of sex or concern over the CF test.*

"When you're here this weekend would you talk to him or do whatever it is a woman does to put a guy back on track?"

"I guess so. I'll do what I can, Mr. Smythe."

She scratched her head and frowned. *What a weird conversation.* Esther wasn't sure how to interpret what just transpired and a tremble scared her into a nauseous state. *Is Daniel having second thoughts?*

The library bell jingled and Esther crept to the front to see Mrs. Marland walk in. Making time for a break this week was becoming a challenge.

"Hey Esther, I need a book on the War of 1812; Stan has a report due next Friday. Got anything?"

Esther was glad for the interruption and the request had a simple solution. "Follow me to American history." *Remain calm. Do not panic. He loves me.*

The three friends met in the overly decorated diner for lunch. Tracey had draped red and silver garland around every window. From the light fixtures she hung long red ribbons that held whimsical ornaments; the kissing polar bears were real smile makers. Holly wreaths greeted restroom visitors. And on the radio above the cash register, Elvis sang about a hound dog. Go figure.

Karen and Cindy were sipping Cokes when Esther plopped down beside them.

"I've got a problem, I think."

"You're perfect, Es, you don't have problems. Well, a few hair issues, but really nothing an iron can't fix."

"I know you're serious about Kurt and I need to ask a very personal question."

"Oooh. This is gonna be good."

"Did you guys have sex yet?"

Karen covered her ears, "Count me out of this conversation, girls. I got married decades ago."

"For crying out loud, I'm twenty-three years old. Of course."

"Well, you know I haven't. Ever. And I won't do it until we're married."

"You're engaged to a Greek god, Es. Are you kidding?"

"The Bible is very clear on the issue and Daniel is okay to wait until April. Well, he tells me he's okay, but I just talked to Mitch, his partner in Grand Rapids."

"Mitch called you? About sex?"

"He said that Daniel's fuse has been short and he's making mistakes at work. But Daniel is a perfectionist to the core. My guess is that it has to do with his needs and my vow of abstinence. What do you guys think?"

"You're heating the man up and then sending him away for a week. Good grief, he's frustrated. You're seeing him this weekend, right?"

"Yeah. I'm leaving Friday afternoon."

"Take care of him, Es. He's drop-dead handsome and a man who looks like that is NOT a virgin. Besides, you're engaged so it's cool."

"I'll think about it." Esther drummed her fingers on the table.

Karen had an opinion on the issue, "Stick to your guns, Es. Daniel obviously loves you and has respected your decision so far. If you have sex before your wedding night, I think you might both regret it at this point. You've held off this long."

"I'll consider both suggestions. Item number two." Esther slurped her Coke loudly before sharing the news. "I got a granola order this week and I'm shipping four boxes to St. Ignace."

"Way to go girl." Cindy put her palm up high and the three slapped their hands together. "Onion rings are on me."

~~~~~~

This would be her life-changing day. Esther had survived the hectic week and even reveled in its busy pace. Christmas music played at the market and a general feeling of holiday cheer wafted throughout Benzie County. The cashiers at the market wore Santa hats, colored lights decorated the town, rooftops were covered in snow, and she was reeling in love. But her world could turn upside down after a simple exchange of words during a single telephone call. The nurse suggested she call Friday morning. It was Friday and it was ten o'clock. Only Daniel knew she'd taken the blood test; it had been too frightening to discuss with anyone else. She sat in the library office with the phone in her hand and insides quaking. Someone picked up after two rings.

"Hospital lab, Karla speaking."

"This is Esther Gardener. I'm calling to request the results of my blood test."

The nurse asked for Esther's social security number and birth date. "I need to get your file from another department; this blood was sent to a different lab for genetic testing. Could you please wait just a moment?"

Minutes passed without a sound. Her heart was pounding. She tapped her feet, closed her eyes, and uttered a prayer. *Dear Lord, Please give me the strength and faith to accept the results. Amen.*

"Miss Gardener?"

"Yes, Ma'am."

"The laboratory did not detect a CF gene."

Esther couldn't believe what she was hearing and thought she had misinterpreted the statement, "What does that mean?"

"Negative, Miss Gardener. You're not a CF carrier."

"Thank you, Karla. Have a wonderful day." She placed the phone into its cradle and let the tears of relief flood from her eyes. *I need to work on this crying thing.*

December 1985 ~ Part 3

"Need anything else, Mitch? It's close to quitting time and I'd like to get a few things done at home before Esther shows up." Daniel was itching to wrap his arms around her. "My Monday afternoon is open if you need me to check Mark's blueprints; just let me know."

"I'm ready to start the weekend myself. I hope Esther can work the kinks out of your system, Daniel. You've been out of touch the past few weeks. Get between the sheets and relieve that pressure before Monday, eh?" Mitch chuckled and arched an eyebrow.

"You're a caveman. It's not happening and my sex life is none of your business, by the way."

"It's 1985 and you're engaged, Dan. You mean to tell me that the two of you haven't slept together yet?"

"Not until the wedding night. Don't mess with me on this."

"So we have to put up with your frustration the rest of the winter?"

Daniel clenched his jaw before responding, "If I push Esther hard enough, she'll succumb. But I'd hate myself and she'd regret it. We're doing this right."

"Then you need to harness your tension somehow because this firm will not suffer while you gnash teeth and break pencils. Shape up, Dan."

"I didn't know it was obvious. Sorry. But I'll tell you what, Mitch ol' boy, when I'm back from the honeymoon you'll be looking for a Superman cape underneath my shirt."

~~~~~~

He'd put a pan of chicken into the oven ten minutes ago. A bouquet of white roses sat on the dining table and he'd bought a floor length flannel robe for Esther earlier in the week. The skimpy one she wore last weekend in the cabin hadn't covered her well enough and he'd probably suffered an aneurysm while watching her move around in the thin garment five days ago. If she was completely covered this weekend the temptation might not be so great and his heart would get a much-needed break. He had changed into his favorite jeans and Penn State sweatshirt and was slicing tomatoes when the doorbell rang.

"C'mon in, lovely girl."

She dropped her purse and jumped into his arms. "You feel so perfect." They savored a long kiss before he shut the door and ushered her inside. He laughed out loud when he removed her coat and saw they had dressed identically.

"Nice place—and decorated very tastefully. I'll leave my old furniture in the cabin if we live here."

"Lab test?"

"Negative."

He swept her from the floor so quickly she lost her breath. "Thank you, God!" He set her down just as fast to press her against the wall. Plunging his fingers into her hair, he covered her small frame with his and kissed her with desire and relief.

"I love you, Daniel. Take me to your bed."

"No. We're waiting until the wedding night. Besides, I started running last week to keep my libido in check; I'll be in great shape in a few weeks. I might even pick up a pole next spring and vault again."

"But Mitch called and he said I should take care . . ."

"This is NOT his business and I'm sorry he did that. Mitch is NOT your conscience and he won't call you again; he'll have a T-square lodged in his throat."

"All right. Let's be happy. Show me your place and the room where I'll be sleeping." He walked her through the living room where she admired the fireplace; then into the kitchen, where she rubbed her hand over the clean oak cabinets; and finally upstairs to the bedrooms. He watched her plop onto the futon like a kid at a slumber party. And then she pulled off her sweatshirt to reveal the most delicate and exquisite figure he'd ever laid eyes on. And she had saved herself for him. He'd never been with a virgin. She would be his bride in a few months and it was more than he could handle in a single moment.

He ran downstairs to the kitchen hoping to erase what he'd just seen. No such luck. He steadied his breathing and opened the refrigerator to count something. Anything. One pitcher of orange juice, two tomatoes, four beers, milk, salami, six eggs . . .

With her shirt back on, Esther tentatively approached him, feeling ashamed of her boldness, "Am I going about this totally wrong?"

He closed the refrigerator door, "You're incredible. I was just surprised, that's all. I'm mentally prepared to wait until our wedding night. You made an important vow and it's the right thing to do; has someone convinced you otherwise?"

"But I want to take care of you." She tugged at his arms and pushed his hands beneath her shirt.

"Let's think about this for a night, Es. I want no regrets." He lifted her onto the countertop and embraced her tightly. "I think the chicken is done. I'll get some plates while you grab the salad from the refrigerator."

~~~~~~

The flannel robe had been a good idea. Both survived the night; Daniel had taken yet another cold shower and locked his bedroom door. Morning arrived just a few hours after he finally dozed off and he awoke to a brand new smell. He stayed in bed for a few minutes to guess what she was making in the kitchen. *A pastry? Pancakes?* He pinpointed two elements in the aroma: maple and nuts. Curiosity got the best of him and he pulled on his jeans before clamoring downstairs.

Good grief. How will I keep my hands off her once we're married? With her hair clipped in a fluffy ponytail, snug fitting denims, an old flannel shirt that had probably once been her father's, and dainty bare feet, she looked irresistible.

"What're you making?" He scratched his messy hair and yawned.

"Good morning. You're beautiful without a shirt."

He walked behind her and pulled her into him, "Granola for breakfast?"

"I'm shipping forty-eight bars to St. Ignace on Monday. A man placed an order and I'll make twenty-two dollars." She spun around proudly.

"You don't have to do this, sweetheart. I earn a fine salary." Daniel spooned a chunk of dough into his mouth. "This is good. Where'd you get the ingredients?"

"You ate raw dough, silly. I brought everything with me and kept it in the car overnight. And money isn't the point, Daniel. This is what I do. I'll make twenty-four bars this morning and twenty-four tonight. Then I'll wrap them properly Sunday night in my cabin. I'm sorry I didn't tell you last night, but it didn't seem to fit into any of our conversations."

"It's all right. The coffee smells good." He poured himself a cup and leaned into the counter to watch her press the batch of uncooked oatmeal mixture into a large pan. "What time did you get up, Mrs. Jacobson?"

"Around seven o'clock. I hope I didn't wake you. How'd you sleep?"

"Terribly. You?"

"Like a baby. I dreamt of you all night long. This is a good house; I could live here."

"Really? We'd change the furniture if you want something different. And you can do whatever you like with the kitchen. What about the Frankfort Library and your cabin, Es?"

"We'll figure something out. We'd use the cabin a lot during the summer. I'll miss Arcadia and the library though; the addition is so beautiful. I can visit Karen and Cindy every few weeks; they're just two hours away. It's best for you and your career to stay here in Grand Rapids. This city is large enough to accommodate another librarian, but I'm not confident that Benzie County needs a prodigious architect."

"Know what?" He set his cup onto the counter and drew her into him until her head was tucked beneath his chin.

"Hmm?"

"Valentine's Day is on a Saturday. Wanna tie the knot in two months?"

"Yeah. April is too far away."

~~~~~~

The night she returned to Arcadia, Esther phoned Pastor Wrigley. Another wedding was scheduled for February 14th at two o'clock, but Pastor assured her that he could certainly swing a small ceremony at five o'clock as well. She called Daniel to share the news, and the couple decided that Esther would immediately order the wedding invitations in Frankfort so they'd be ready for mailing in January.

Esther phoned Agatha to fill her in on the recent change of plans, "We're getting married on Valentine's Day, Mom. When Daniel and I visit for Christmas, let's shop for a wedding dress."

Agatha was delighted. She'd been eminently pleased about the engagement last month. "Honey, that's wonderful news and the shopping will be fun. I sent a package to you a few days ago—it should arrive by Thursday."

"What is it?"

"A black dress and shoes for the dedication ceremony. I know that you don't like to shop for such things, but when I saw the dress it seemed to have been made just for you."

"Thanks, Mom. I hadn't even thought about what to wear Saturday night. I'll take lots of pictures. Should we have a bridal shower on Lavender Lane? The wedding is so small; I'd like the shower to be kept very informal and intimate, just Aunt Gail, grandma, Linda, and our closest neighbors."

"Having it here will be fine, Es. Let me know which weekend in January works best for you and I'll make the arrangements. I think a lunch would be nice; quiche and salads?"

"Sounds great. Mom?"

"Yeah?"

"I miss him. He and Daniel would've been pals."

"Absolutely. Joseph would most certainly have approved of your Daniel. I miss him too, Es. A part of me passed away with him. But let's keep our chins up; there are a lot of good things on this earth to look forward to."

~~~~~~

After work on Monday, Esther phoned Kelly and Linda to insist that they set aside the February 14th weekend for a trip to Arcadia. Kelly would attend the wedding with her husband. Linda promised with great enthusiasm that she'd be there and, only as a favor to her best childhood friend, agreed to assume the role of "date" for Daniel's friend, Austin.

The library dedication ceremony was only days away. Esther had ordered an impressive array of gourmet appetizers, including brie and raspberry stars, roasted tomato bruschetta, scallops in bacon, pear and Roquefort squares, and bacon wrapped sirloin. Two sheet cakes would provide dessert for the attendees. The Ladies Club would also provide three large fruit bowls and spend Saturday morning decorating the library for the ceremony, which would begin at four o'clock.

While her head spun with dedication ceremony tasks to tackle, she made a wedding to-do list—flowers, cake, dress, shoes, and catering—to post on her refrigerator. She'd delve into those tasks after Christmas. A compulsive planner at heart, Esther felt waves of anxiety as she thought of all that had to be done in just eight weeks' time. The trip down spontaneity lane was certainly becoming an adventure. She hummed a little ditty to keep from fretting, "Something old, something new. Something borrowed, something blue." *Do I have something blue? What should I borrow? Where will we spend our wedding night?* The phone rang as she chewed the eraser off her pencil.

"Hello, wife."

"Hi. How was your day?"

"Mildly busy with home-addition drawings. Mitch pulled some strings and it looks like we'll get to develop a design and proposal for a six-story office building on the riverfront. It'd be a huge project; the investors want to see the design in March."

"I'm glad you gave me the office tour last week; I can picture you at the drafting table. You're brilliant; I'm so proud of you."

"I have an idea that I want to throw at you. Call me an idiot if you'd like, but I'm going to suggest it anyway."

"You don't have bad ideas."

"I think that the best place to spend our wedding night is in the cabin."

"Yes! That's what I want but was afraid to ask. Daniel?"

"Hmm?"

"I hope that I don't disappoint you."

"Sleeping with you for the first time, Mrs. Jacobson, will be an indescribable pleasure."

"Getting through the dedication ceremony on Saturday without dragging you into the reference section for kisses will be an extreme challenge. Good night, Daniel builder."

~~~~~~

She dressed leisurely after a languid bath. Esther pulled the silky dress over her head and black undergarments; the fabric settled over her skin like a breath of air. When she strode across the room to step into her shoes the dress shimmered with each step. For the first time since the Traverse City salon visit, she spent more than a few minutes putting order into her hair. After a few dozen hot-iron pulls, her locks were shiny and smooth. She wanted Daniel to see 'sexy' tonight so she used a heavy hand with her lip-gloss and mascara. She grimaced at her reflection for a moment . . . *too much? Nah. He'll love it.*

This was the day a cop would bust him for speeding. He'd been fifteen miles over the limit for the past several miles on Bear Lake Road. But Daniel refused to lift his heavy foot from the accelerator because he didn't want to be late for the ceremony. During their nightly calls the past week, Esther had spoken animatedly each time she'd mentioned the event. The appetizers sounded great and her new dress sounded even better. His vivid imagination pictured slinky black fabric wrapped around her figure over barely-there lingerie. He wished now that she'd never taken off that darn sweatshirt. *Focus on driving.*

He turned onto Main Street just ten minutes late; the library lot was full so he parked the truck on Ninth Street and jogged to the library. He ran his fingers through his hair, straightened his tie, and pushed the door open. Jack Dawson spotted him immediately and sauntered in his direction.

"Daniel Jacobson, the man of the hour. The building is spectacular and you managed to complete the project on time and within the allotted budget. You'll be the first architect we contact when the City of Frankfort needs a new building. Congratulations, by the way; Esther is a gem."

Audrey Dawson came to her husband's side to rescue Daniel from further pontification. She subtly looped her arm around Jack before nudging him in another direction, "I'm sure he wants to see his fianceé, dear." Audrey then turned to Daniel, "Esther is upstairs in the reading area. She's visiting with a group of teachers."

"Thank you, Mrs. Dawson. Where will I find the champagne?"

"You'll see the table in the central area of the addition. Enjoy the evening. You've certainly earned it."

He picked up two drinks and walked up the steps to find his bright bird. During the two-hour drive to Frankfort he had promised himself to remain cool when he saw her. He'd fight the urge to sneak her from the library and into his truck where heaven only knows what he might do. He spotted her as soon as he stepped onto the second floor. *Wow.*

"Daniel." She walked to him gracefully. "I'm glad you're here." She kissed his cheek gingerly and accepted the glass he offered. He wrapped his free hand around her slight waist and suffered a string of thundering heartbeats.

"You look great, Mrs. Jacobson. Happy with the addition?"

"We love it. The children enjoy the yellow room, and the junior high teachers plan to bring their classes here after the holidays for a re-introduction to the library. I'm working on a reading list for them. It'd be great to see a rise in patronage among the younger population. The new space is better than we could ever have imagined; thank you."

"My pleasure, Es. Can we speak privately somewhere?"

"Sure. The office is locked so no one will be there." Esther quickly introduced her fiancé and then excused herself from the discussion.

Alone in the small office, Daniel wasn't sure he could put a lid on his libido, but he'd give it a real hard try. "I'm feeling insanely in love with you right now and we need to make an adjustment to our evening plans. My willpower seems to be at an all time low tonight. If we spend the night together in your cabin I guarantee that your vow will be broken."

She giggled and scrunched her face at him, "Are you serious? Do you like my dress?" Holding her arms away from her sides she spun in a circle to model the enticing garment.

"It's incredible." He emptied his champagne glass and closed his eyes in an attempt to erase the vision of her in black lingerie. But the picture gained clarity so he quickly opened his eyes to focus on something else. *Her hair probably looks great at dawn after tumbling through a night of sleep.* "I'll definitely need a hotel room without you in it tonight. And a cold shower, no doubt."

"I have an idea. Stay with Karen and John tonight. They'd be happy to have you as a guest. John can teach you to play cribbage and Karen will feed you a fine breakfast. They're here somewhere so let's go find them."

Before departing from the small office, Daniel pressed himself into the black dress and buried a groan into Esther's hair. She pulled his face to hers and they shared a long and sensual kiss. And then another, and another. "If my heart can survive the next fifty-nine days, Esther Gardener, I will live to be a hundred years old." They emerged from the office flushed and frustrated in search of Karen and John, who were glad to have Daniel as an overnight guest.

By eight o'clock the last guests were saying their good-byes. Audrey Dawson found the young couple at the front desk chatting with Henry Gillman. She had news that she simply had to share before she burst, "I hear that the wedding will be in February. Marilyn and I came up with an outlandish idea, but we both agree that it suits you so well we simply must suggest it for consideration."

Daniel and Esther exchanged puzzled glances and offered curious stares.

"The Elk Lodge isn't much of a place for a party, even when it's decorated. What do you think of holding your reception here in the new library addition? I understand that your guest list is small and the central area of the new building would easily accommodate a group of twenty people. After all, isn't it the addition that brought you two together?"

The Wedding

The Gardener family shared a quiet Christmas on Lavender Lane. The women had baked shortbread in the morning to enjoy as a sweet ending to their relaxed dinner. The fire crackling in the hearth subdued the evening conversations and provided the only light in the living room.

"Cherish your holidays together, you two. In twenty years they'll come and go so quickly you'll feel as though they're just weeks apart. I was handing out Hershey bars to goblins just minutes ago. In the blink of an eye I'll be digging out the springtime wreath for the front door." Agatha sighed in a middle-aged and motherly sort of way after offering the sagacious advice.

A bulb on the string of lights around the Christmas tree had burned out an hour ago, leaving the tree as nothing more than a conical shadow dressed in ornaments and candy canes. (The lazy foursome had unanimously agreed to wait until morning to hunt down and replace the expired bulb.) The drowsy mood and warmth from the fire had long ago sent Bentley to his blanket in the kitchen corner; he was snoring now. Yawns exchanged erratically until Ken and Agatha finally stumbled into bed, leaving the young couple to share the end of their first Christmas together privately.

Esther shuffled to the couch and dropped beside Daniel. She cozied up against him, laying her arm across his chest and head against his shoulder.

"Your parents are great, Es. It's been a good holiday."

"I'm very lucky." She kissed his cheek before wrapping both arms around his neck.

Before indulging in her affections, he expressed his uneasiness with the sleeping arrangement, "I'm uncomfortable spending the night in Joseph's room. I can't explain the qualm, but it's there. If your parents aren't okay with it, I'd be more than willing to camp in the pink room with you. Or crash here with a blanket and pillow."

"They're fine, really. I think that a different person in Joseph's room for two nights might be a blessing because it provides added closure for all of us." Esther plucked her fingers through his hair before shifting her legs onto his lap.

"Fifty-one more days until the wedding night." He kissed her forehead and let his fingers graze her knee before sliding his hand beneath her sweater and around her bare waist. Her body tensed and she wanted more but both knew the caress dare not go further. He lifted her from his lap and set her down beside him; Esther in the current position would most certainly cause insomnia tonight.

She yawned in a catlike stretch and whispered in a titillating voice, "Merry Christmas, Daniel builder. I'm going to bed to finish this scene in my dreams."

Caught up in the tenderness of her sleepy brown eyes and sultry cartoon voice, he drew her face against his cheek and murmured quietly, "You'd better lock your door; the temptation to lie with you tonight will be nearly impossible to subdue." They temporarily quenched their mutual desires with a brief kiss.

~~~~~~

"This is too formal. A simple winter gown without lace and frills is what I'm looking for, Mom." Although she'd only tried on seven or eight gowns, Esther was already frustrated, "They're all so full of layers and lace, and my kid-sized bust hasn't filled any of the dresses I've tried on so far."

"We have four more shops to check and I'm confident you'll find your gown, honey."

Three shops and fourteen dresses later, she did. The unique, form-fitting gown featured a sweetheart neckline accented with a row of tiny beads. The long sleeves were finished with delicate satin buttons and more of the tiny beading. The bodice was accented with twisted ivory cording in a subtle floral pattern, and each flower was hand beaded with tiny pearl and opal beads. Once the seamstress had pinned the gown to fit Esther's petite frame, it was absolutely stunning on her. (Esther was privately pleased that the gown was closed with a single zipper down the back; Daniel wouldn't have the patience to endure a row of thirty buttons.) She refused to try on veils because she intended to clip wisps of baby's breath flowers in her hair. Daniel admired and touched her hair often and she didn't want it covered on their wedding day.

The seamstress promised that the dress alterations would be done by January 27th. Agatha and Esther were grateful; the bridal shower date was set for January 28th and Esther wouldn't need to make a second trip to Detroit for a final fitting. Mother and daughter literally skipped from the shop into the cold December wind with a mission well accomplished. Next on Esther's list: shoes. But first they'd grab a bite to eat and linger over a cup of coffee during one of their final lunches together as the Gardener girls.

~~~~~~

The forty-five minute drive into Ann Arbor was meditative for Daniel. He'd kept the radio turned off and waded through his pool of thoughts instead. His world was in order for the moment and he felt secretly glad to be settling in Michigan. The driving distances to his friends and family would be short, he and Esther could take several weekend trips each year to the Arcadia cabin, and the down-to-earth nature of Midwest folks was refreshing.

Following Pete's directions into the neighborhood near Stadium Blvd., Daniel saw why his friend chose an Ann Arbor residence. Well-established neighborhoods, plenty of shops and restaurants, a diverse downtown area, a beautiful university campus, and reasonable walking distance to the football stadium were all great pluses. Pete heard the car pull up and met his friend at the door.

"Nice place. How's the law practice?"

"C'mon Jacobson, we both know you're not here to talk about my career as an attorney. Let's have a beer." Pete offered a drink to his friend before taking a seat at the kitchen table.

"No thanks, I don't drink before lunch." Daniel put the unopened bottle on the table and sat down.

Pete poured a cup of coffee and sat it across from his friend. "We don't have time to skirt the issues, so I'll make my point before you even finish half of your coffee." Pete swigged his beer before continuing, "I have trouble picturing you as a married man. Ravishing women pursued you for a decade. You've dated a model, physicist, artist, and there's a doctor in there too, I think. And six months ago you end up in a speck of a northern town and fall head-over-heels for a timid librarian who lives in a cabin. I spoke with Esther only briefly in Chicago last month but I did sense that she's right for you. I'm certainly not doubting your choice but why rush into marriage? A long engagement is a good thing. Learn about each other before making the commitment."

"The commitment is already there, Pete. I could never, and will never, live without her. The days I don't see Esther are nearly hellish at this point, and the February wedding date isn't soon enough. There's an enrichment I experience with her. It's indescribable, really. She's a beautiful and soulful woman; there's no sense in waiting. It's the wedding night that has me anxious."

"Problems in the bedroom already?" Pete leaned onto the table and lowered his voice, "Our wedding night was fantastic. Be sure not to drink too much."

"I've never been with a virgin."

The admission blew Pete out of his chair and over to the sink where he finished choking on his beer, "I thought only high schools held the world's virgins these days. How old is Esther?"

"Twenty-four." Daniel took a second sip from his coffee. He hadn't realized the depth of his underlying anxiety until voicing it out loud.

"You're telling me that you two have done nothing more

than kiss for the past six months?" Pete was incredulous, "Not even a quick feel?"

"Nope. We're living proof it can be done. It's not easy but it's possible. Esther made a vow and isn't breaking it. I give her a lot of credit because I'm sure there were temptations in college too, but her faith is undeniably strong. I'll be glad when the cold showers come to an end, though. And doubly glad to hold her beside me every night."

"You two will be fine. My first was in high school. You remember Abbey Dillon? It was awkward to say the least but we managed all right. Abbey said it hurt a lot so you might want to tuck that piece of news into your head."

Daniel grimaced before closing his eyes briefly, "Yeah, I've heard that."

"Have you decided where you'll live once you're married?"

"She's moving into my place in Grand Rapids. Her cabin is great, but we both think that Grand Rapids is the better of the two places for establishing roots and raising a family. She feels strongly that she lived in Arcadia only to meet me. Esther claims that destiny led her to the cabin and the Frankfort Library."

"She's right. If she had traveled to Arcadia only for an occasional vacation you two never would have met. Doesn't she have some land there?"

"There are about ten acres around the cabin; she kept about a half-acre mowed and the other nine acres are untouched. It's very nice. Esther kept a decent sized garden as well. Remind me to give you a tour in February if the snow isn't too deep." A frown appeared across his face.

"What's wrong?"

Daniel stood abruptly, a physical reaction to the chain of distressing thoughts that lashed across his chest. "Esther's giving everything up! She's rearranging and relocating her life to meld into mine."

"She's still got the cabin. And Grand Rapids is closer to Detroit; that's a good thing for her folks."

"No! She spent nearly two years in Arcadia, making friends,

establishing a home, starting up a small business, running the town library. There are no deer around the condo, she won't have a garden, and her library..."

"Whoa, Dan. You're giving up quite a bit for Esther..."

"Nothing changes in my life, except that it'll get better with her in it. She doesn't belong in a condominium. She's a meadow-strolling, tomato-canning, granola-making sort of girl." Daniel sat down and pressed his hands flat against the table.

"Esther will be Esther whether she's in Dallas, Texas or Grand Rapids, Michigan. Good grief, Dan. Settle it down. Find a nice piece of land outside of Grand Rapids and build her a house. She married the right guy." Pete took a long swig of his beer, satisfied that he'd arrived at a sensible piece of advice.

"Man, I've got the jitters; February won't get here soon enough." Daniel rose again from his seat as Minh ambled into the kitchen with a bag of groceries. Her kind smile momentarily erased his tension.

"Congratulations, Daniel. We're so happy for you." She set the bag onto the counter and took his hands into hers as a warm greeting.

Stepping beside her husband, Minh whispered, "Peter, could you please bring in the other grocery bags for me? I'll heat some vegetable soup for your lunch today, and I bought some nice deli meat for sandwiches."

"Marriage is a fine thing but chores do come with the territory." Pete pulled Daniel into the garage.

After hauling groceries and eating lunch, the friends conversed through the early afternoon about high school days, college pranks, home improvement ideas, and plans for the new year. Pete saved what he considered the best news for last, "I have a new airplane design downstairs. Want to check it out?"

~~~~~~

Maria was already wringing her hands in anticipation of her colleague's last day of work on Thursday. "Running this library without you will be a nightmare, Es. You're so efficient. When people ask for a title you know the author's name without checking the catalog. You're a bona fide library scientist and I'm a part-time clerk."

"You'll do fine, Maria. You've checked books in and out, done lots of overdue notices, rotated the periodicals, and know the general layout of the library. Re-shelving might take you a bit longer than it does for me, but time and experience will take care of that. Remember, I'll be here two Wednesdays each month for a while, and you can call me in Grand Rapids any time. Not to mention you'll have my help for an entire weekend in October to work on the budget, too."

"You're a great teacher, Es. Thanks for the Dewey Decimal chart; it'll be worn out in two weeks. I'll post your Wednesday story-time dates so parents can mark their calendars."

~~~~~~

On the evening of February 13th, Karen, Cindy, Audrey and Marilyn decorated the library addition for the intimate wedding reception that would take place the next evening. Wreaths with tiny white and red hearts now donned doors and entryways. They placed dried berries and flower arrangements in white, silver, red, deep violet, and green all around the central area. They strung tiny clear lights around the windows and the edge of the cake table. A winter wedding wouldn't be complete without snowflake decorations, so they scattered snowflake placemats around the four guest tables. As a surprise, Karen set out twenty snow globes engraved with the bride and groom's names and the wedding date. Cindy left several boxes of fine chocolate in the shape of hearts and snowflakes for the newlyweds and their guests. Jack and Audrey Dawson's gift to the couple were small decanters filled with Irish whiskey for after-dinner drinks.

Esther had arranged the reception to be catered by the Iron Anchor restaurant in town. The menu would include salmon in dill sauce, steamed vegetables, scalloped potatoes, and a green salad with walnuts and cranberries. Tracey planned to deliver the cake tomorrow morning; a bonus to small town living was the freedom to leave the library key with the cake-baking waitress across the street.

~~~~~~

Although the Trinity Church in Arcadia was far from crowded on the afternoon of February 14th, all nineteen guests who'd been invited to the wedding were there. After fussing over their son, Sandra and John were now seated with Dennis, Marcy, and Amy.

Standing just outside the door of the ladies' lounge, Esther held Karen's wristwatch in her palm; she'd walk down the aisle at five o'clock. Ken and Agatha doted on their daughter with a bountiful shedding of joyous tears. Agatha, usually never short on words, was speechless. Esther's happiness was so apparent that she literally glowed. In Agatha's mind, neither comment nor compliment were necessary; the body language exchanged between mother and daughter spoke volumes; all was right and all was good. Ken, on the other hand, couldn't stop babbling. He knew that Esther had been only a temporary gift to raise into adulthood, but she'd been a delightful blessing and letting go was breaking his heart into a thousand pieces. Her departure from their lives was just minutes away and he was impelled to fill their last bit of time together before she took her husband's name.

Karen finally separated the threesome. After shooing Agatha to her pew, she briskly led Ken to the back of the church and instructed him to wait until 4:55—then he'd walk to the sixth pew and wait for his daughter. The ceremony would start in ten minutes.

Daniel and Pete sat in Pastor Wrigley's office. "I thought that I'd be more nervous but I'm actually quite calm. You know the feeling that comes when you look down a tranquil beach at daybreak and decide to take a walk alongside the waves? That's the one I've got." Daniel shook his head quizzically at Pete.

"Let's get into that church and wait for your bride, Mr. Jacobson."

Her heart skipped a beat when she checked the watch. *I'm coming Daniel.* Before stepping out of the lounge, she peeked around the corner to find everything in place and shuffled quietly to her father. "I love you, Dad."

Ken clenched his jaw to fight the emotion that tightened his throat. He kissed his daughter's cheek and pressed a finger against his watery eyes. "He's a good man, Es. Are you ready?" Esther nodded and Ken quietly strode to his place near the front of the church.

Once Ken assumed his position, Esther appeared at the end of the aisle and the organist began to play.

She has flowers in her hair. Thank you, precious Esther. Daniel fell more fervently in love as he watched her step toward him. He vowed to cherish her until the end of time and nearly lost his breath when Ken placed Esther's hand into his. *Dear Lord, Help me to be a good husband.*

~~~~~~

After the bride, groom, and wedding guests had piled their coats onto the front desk of the library, the out-of-towners insisted on a tour. Esther, radiant in her white gown, and Daniel, dashing in his tuxedo, led the guests on a walk through the addition. Hand in hand, the couple pointed out their favorite details of the new structure. The skylight, tall windows, yellow preschool room, and extravagant stairway that led to the upstairs reading room. It was as though they were bringing friends into their own home. And indeed, the building had come to life as the love between the builder and librarian unfolded. Moments that led to their falling in love were woven into the structure itself. Their mutual attraction began with the foundation, and they were engaged just two days after the building passed its final inspection.

While Ken and John poured champagne for the guests,

Tracey and Audrey arrived to assist with the meal service and clean-up.

"Do you have seating arrangements in mind, Es?" Kelly was bursting with joy for her friend and knew the reception would be pleasant, regardless of whom her tablemates would be.

"Each of those tables will comfortably seat five or six people. You and Andrew can sit with Cindy and Kurt, and ask Amy to sit with you, too. The five of you will hit it off real well, trust me." Esther embraced her friend warmly, "I'm glad you came; Andrew is so nice and you both look very happy. I still can't believe you got married in Vegas."

"Andrew is definitely a dream guy. Let's be sure to have a long visit after dinner. And I'd like to get a few pictures of the two of you. You're a stunning couple, Es." Kelly bent closer to Esther's ear, "How did you manage to keep your vow? He's very good-looking. Where are you spending the night?"

"We'll be in the cabin," Esther snickered, "It's perfect."

Champagne flowed and the guests raved over the meal. Ken, Agatha, John, and Sandra had met for the first time last night and now carried on as if they'd been friends for years. They were pleased to have become family through the union of their children.

Pete, Minh, Austin, Linda, Dennis, and Marcy shared another table. Dennis hadn't spent any serious conversation time with Pete and Austin since starting college and relished the updates they provided. He insisted that it was Roger's injury in Riverside Park that pushed him into medical school. The cozy and energetic atmosphere provided the perfect backdrop for flirtations to rise between Austin and Linda.

Mitch, Angela, Karen, and John were the lucky guests who shared their meals with the bride and groom.

Angela recognized the faraway look that crossed Karen's face more than once, "You're going to miss her, aren't you?"

Karen sighed, "More than I thought was possible. I've known Esther for a dozen years and watched her grow into a woman. She's been a blessing in my life. It almost feels like I'm losing a daughter."

"Nah. You're gaining a son, Karen." Angela's kind comment just barely eased the pain of Karen's heartache. "I understand the snow globes were your idea. They're a very nice touch."

"Thanks. Be sure to take one home with you. It looks like Tracey and Audrey are preparing the cake for cutting." Karen tapped her glass with a spoon and stood to offer a toast. She stepped between the newlyweds and hugged them together briefly before speaking.

"To a whirlwind romance and a fire that grew into a loving and remarkable friendship. Daniel and Esther, may your lives be rich with blessings and God's grace. May you boldly embrace the challenges that life will surely bestow upon you so that your relationship grows even stronger. And may the two of you always find something to cherish in each other as long as you live." Karen raised her glass to honor the couple.

~~~~~~

Pete had kept a hidden eye on the newlyweds and began to wonder whether Daniel would ever move further away than fifteen inches from his bride. He'd seen plenty of young love-birds over the years, but this couple had it nailed. He checked his own emotions for envy, but dismissed that possibility. The break finally came after the cake was served; Dennis had pulled Daniel away from the crowd to chat in a quiet corner. Pete strode quickly to Esther.

"Very nice reception, Mrs. Jacobson." Pete murmured in a wry tone before setting his hand across the top of Esther's chair. He gently caressed her back and then leaned near her cheek, swiftly touching it with his own.

She turned to meet the whisperer's eyes and was startled to find Pete hovering over her. She immediately stood from her seat. "Thank you. There are many people to whom I'm very grateful; I certainly couldn't have pulled this off alone."

Pete gently nudged her away from the table and indicated that he had something of great importance to impart. "How did you manage to capture his heart, Esther? The man you married has been pursued by the most beautiful and intelligent women in the Midwest. He has very high standards; you're either an angel or an extremely talented actress."

Initially stunned by the lash of his caustic tongue, Esther replied boldly, "I'm neither of those, Mr. Peter Lyons. I am a child of God who's been blessed with a fine family, friends, contentment, and tragedy. I strive to do what is right and hope to never harm another person intentionally. I will love and respect Daniel until my dying breath. And I'd never dream of saying to someone what you just said to me."

"Well, I surely hope that your goodness will keep him home at night. Heaven knows how many women are waiting for the bliss to wear off." Pete smiled openly, not unlike a con man who'd just made a nice profit on a cheap watch. Esther attempted to swallow her disgust, but was unsuccessful. *Forgive me now, Lord, for what I'm about to say, but I simply cannot hold . . .*

"Hey Pete." Daniel slid his arm around Esther's waist and deftly kissed her cheek. "It's great to see my best friend and wife spending quality time together and becoming better acquainted. Did you like the salmon?"

"It was delicious. Minh even gave it a great review and she's not usually a seafood fan." He moved back a step, "I understand there's Irish coffee being served. Congratulations again to you both. Nice chatting with you, Esther."

Before she could recover from what had just transpired, the couple was interrupted by yet another guest. And so the evening continued with jovial conversation, much laughter, and very few private moments for the newlyweds.

But during the past hour, Daniel had become overtly nervous and couldn't wait another moment to confide in Esther what Dennis had relayed to him earlier, "We need to go into the office for a second, Es."

"Take me, darling." She giggled.

Behind the closed door, he spoke in a solemn whisper. "I want you to know what Dennis told me earlier tonight. Apparently, Pete's carrying around a barrel of anger. He confided in Dennis that he's not ready to be a father; the pregnancy was a mistake. Second, Pete's still brewing over a major legal battle he lost last month. And there's gasoline on the fire: Dennis saw him using cocaine in the bathroom."

"Oh dear. I'm so sorry." She leaned into her husband to offer solace and comfort.

"Did he say or do anything strange to you while I was with Dennis an hour ago?"

A dilemma on her wedding day. Not married yet for twenty-four hours and God had thrown a challenge to them already. *Do I mention what Pete said? But it was the drug talking; that wasn't the real Pete an hour ago. Was it? I don't want to harm their friendship and I definitely don't want to injure Pete's character. But I won't lie to my husband.* "His behavior was odd, Daniel. Definitely not the same guy I met last Thanksgiving in Chicago."

"I think I'll pay him a visit in a few weeks; maybe I can convince him to get some help. The baby is due in a month and he's got to straighten out." Daniel's pulse raced as his thoughts turned to the evening in the cabin. "It's nearly ten o'clock. Let's start the good-byes and head to our honeymoon suite, Es."

"I'm afraid." Esther felt goose bumps erupt beneath her satin gown.

"C'mere little bird, it'll be fabulous." He drew her against him while his throat swelled with emotion. Her warmth seeped through his shirt and his senses became saturated with her touch. They kissed deeply, her sweet and receptive mouth hinted at what she'd give tonight.

~~~~~~

After politely withdrawing from the edges of the reception and offering many thankful embraces, the couple left the library amidst rounds of cheering and applause. Daniel proudly tucked his bride into the elegant sedan he'd rented for the week and headed south on M-22.

"The reception was beautiful and I bet the guests will stay for at least another hour to finish the coffee. Linda and Austin spent most of the evening together; I wonder if they'll go out tonight after the reception. And the women did such a nice job transforming the addition into a reception hall. I must send each of them a box of granola." Without energy for further comment, Esther sighed contentedly and turned to Daniel; the sight of his handsome silhouette made her far too aware of her own plainness. *He's too good for me.* Butterflies filled her stomach.

He turned to meet her eyes and nearly cringed at the terrified expression she wore; it erased what he was about to say. He quickly retrieved another thought so she wouldn't know that he'd discovered her fear, "A bottle of '78 chardonnay is packed in my suitcase. Austin brought it back from a California winery he toured years ago and promises we'll enjoy it." He clasped her hand into his and thumbed the ring on her finger. "I didn't have much champagne tonight. It'll be nice to share the wine with just you, Mrs. Jacobson."

Daniel's overwhelming desire got them to their rustic honeymoon suite in less than fifteen minutes; a record time when driving the winding winter roads in the dark. He left her in the car briefly to unlock the cabin door and prop it open. He returned to claim his bride and carried her up the snowy step and across the threshold. Bentley hopped up for ear rubs.

"He's not sleeping with us tonight, Es."

She laughed out loud, both from the champagne and the disgruntled look on her husband's face. "Bentley is afraid of the stairway and won't venture to the bedroom unless I carry him. Are you ready to put me down?"

He set her onto the couch and quickly took a seat at her side.

She pulled his palms to her face, "You appear to be more nervous than I am." She kissed him lightly to dispel her own butterflies, "I'll light some candles upstairs; would you like to pour the wine?" Esther slipped off her shoes, strode quietly into the kitchen, withdrew two goblets from the cupboard and set them onto the counter. When she turned to meet his gaze from the dimly lit room, she appeared angelic against the backdrop of sturdy dark cabinets. The white flowers still clung to her hair and framed her fair skin.

"There's a dreamlike quality to all of this, Es. Almost like the fog that surrounds you after waking from a deep sleep in the early morning darkness. And tomorrow morning we'll share those minutes for the first time. I've never spent the night with another woman. My first will be with you." Daniel saw that she was obviously pleased with his confession as he held her eyes with his own. "I'll never forget the way you look tonight."

He watched his bride ascend the steps in her lovely gown. *She's probably scared. I'm scared.* He removed his tie and tux before pausing in the kitchen to rein in the scattering of thoughts and joys that were consuming his clarity. His decisions, dreams, and doubts would all be shared now. He was filled with a rush of relief because he knew that Esther was the right one and, with the Lord's guiding hand, had found her in a most unlikely place.

~~~~~~

The newlyweds sat on the edge of the bed and sipped the fine wine; her right hand entwined in his left.

"Should we get undressed together?" Esther wanted desperately to make the night perfect for her husband. She was simultaneously consumed with timidity and fervency, and the conflicting weight it caused in her chest allowed only small breaths to pass. Her pulse rate quickened at the thought of his touch in places no one had ever seen. She drove away an underlying fear as she watched him set their glasses on the nightstand and then turn to face her . . . *He loves me.*

His eyes captured hers while he unbuttoned his shirt and dropped it to the floor; her inhibitions tumbled down with it. She stood urgently to press her cheek against him but before she could take a step, Daniel swept her off the floor and into his arms. He swayed with her to the motion of the flickering candlelight around them. His lips finally descended upon hers to initiate their first night together.

He laid her across the bed like a fragile doll, placing his arms on either side of her face. Whispering kisses along her neck and into her wavy hair, he spoke huskily, "Once this dress is off I cannot promise that I'll be able to control my desire to touch every inch of you from head to toe. Don't be afraid, Es."

He reached behind her back and pulled the zipper down, grazing her skin with tantalizing pressure from his fingertips. Grasping onto the sleeves, he easily slid the satin gown from her shoulders, down her waist, and off of her legs to reveal her small lithe body in white lace. She lay taut as a wire and held her breath with expectant eyes. Her camisole rose well above her stomach to reveal a slender torso and delicately curved hips. His heart pounded at the sight of her. *Slow down.* "You're stunning." He nearly choked on the realization that he was the first man to see her unclothed.

His sensual mouth seized possession of hers in a stirring kiss that left her trembling. He caressed her shoulders then let his fingers glide lower until his strong hands covered her breasts. Roaming back to her arms, he pulled the camisole over her head and gasped at her smooth and delicate curves; his need became even more intense. With warm lips and fingers, Daniel touched her flesh gently and relentlessly. She writhed in an unbridled ecstasy as he trailed kisses along her throat and shoulders. She pulled his face to hers with a fiery insistence and pressed her mouth onto his. His tongue coaxed her lips open and the thrust sent shock waves of pleasure through her body. He wanted her desperately but the desire to give her pleasure before the eminent pain was greater. Knowing that their lovemaking tonight would be hardly pleasant for her, he vowed to put her mind and body into a languid state before the union.

Esther submitted completely. He soothed and excited her until she seemed unable to tolerate another caress. "Let me touch you, Daniel." She was dazed and had reached an exhilaration that spun her into a whirlwind of excitement.

He pulled off his trousers, lied down beside her now trembling body, and guided her hand. She wrapped her fingers around him and aligned her body against his. He bit his lip to keep from screaming; no other touch had been so electrifying. Caressing him shyly she nuzzled his neck and chest with a dozen tender kisses.

With bodies pressed together tightly, her fingertips slid across his stomach as she dared to say what he'd been waiting to hear, "I'm not scared." She warmed his mouth with a fairy tale kiss.

Daniel rolled her beneath him and tasted her lips once more before penetrating the fragile barrier that broke her vow. She screamed and clung to him. Pressing his mouth against her ear, he whispered repeatedly, "I'm sorry, Es."

Warm tears spilled from her eyes and fell onto his cheek. Pushing gently, he stopped with each whimper and soothed her with barely-there kisses, nearly hating himself for loving her so much.

When the initial waves of pain subsided she succumbed to a dreamy haze of passion. Rising to deepen their union she felt his tentativeness finally escape. Sensations he'd never experienced rushed through him as they exchanged rhythm and pleasure. All feelings of awkwardness fluttered away and a primal need took hold. Their lovemaking became frantic until Daniel cried out, consumed by an agonizing shudder. Their breathing slowed while the rhythm abated. Physically drained yet bursting with emotional energy and a lightness of being, their eyes locked to linger in the precious moment.

They lay joined together, hearts still beating wildly yet sated after the union. The flowers from her hair had spilled all around them and were now confetti on the pillows.

Gliding down from the heated passion, Daniel exhaled and trembled with joy. "I love you and won't ever hurt you again; I promise this will soon be a good thing for you. It's never been like this for me, Es. Never." Daniel rolled to her side and saw tears on her cheeks. He groaned at the sight of blood on her thighs and felt a stab of guilt. "I'm sorry. Please don't cry."

"They're happy tears; I love you so much." Unable to express the emotion that filled her she decided that further words might dampen the exquisite moment and remained silent.

Daniel pulled her over his arm and onto his chest to realign her curves against him. He wasn't confident that he'd sleep well with her lying so near him all night (or for the next few nights, for that matter), but he'd squelch his own desire until her body had time to heal. His past had just been completely erased and he knew now that this is what mattered. Life with Esther mattered. He wanted her again almost immediately; making love with her was right and real. But he'd wait for her to ask him.

They laid with limbs entwined for a long while before he finally spoke, "After we do this a few times it won't hurt you and we'll share what I felt tonight. Let me know when you're ready, okay?"

She turned to face him before resting her chin on his chest. She kissed him sumptuously and blushed, "I'd be too embarrassed to ask you, Daniel. Besides, people don't do this every day, do they?"

"That won't be enough for you and me, little bird. If you're ever too shy to ask, then write me a note."

"I bet making love outside would be wonderful." Esther squirmed against his sturdy frame.

"In the snow?"

"Of course not. When spring comes let's take some blankets into the meadow after dark. And we'll bring flashlights . . ."

"Say no more, Mrs. Jacobson. I'm taking that thought into my dreams."

~~~~~~

A reluctant dawn roused the newlyweds from a heavenly sleep and they wakened together to an opaque light that dusted the room. Brown eyes smiled at blue before they reached a silent agreement to snuggle deeper beneath the comforter and revel in their first morning together as husband and wife.

"Your hair is a lovely mess, young lady."

"Your face is scratchy and handsome, Daniel builder."

"I'm starving."

"Me too. I'll make some breakfast. You can start a fire in the hearth if you'd like; it'll be cold downstairs."

Esther donned her flannel robe and ventured downstairs to let Bentley outside and assemble ingredients for pancakes and scrambled eggs. She then wrote a note to place beside her husband's coffee cup.

Just a few notes . . .

Frankfort and Arcadia are resplendent lakeshore towns on the northwest edge of Michigan's lower peninsula. My family and I spend a week in a log cabin there every summer. We climb dunes, fish for trout, swim in the lake, visit the lighthouses, comb the beach for lovely stones, enjoy dinner at the Cabbage Shed, and go rafting.

The actual name of Frankfort's library is the Benzie Shores District Library. And the City of Frankfort does indeed host a Blueberry Festival every August. Arcadia and Frankfort residents will find that I took many liberties with the names and locations of several businesses in these towns. I hope you overlook these liberties and enjoy the story as a work of fiction.

To accurately portray Joseph's illness, I researched the symptoms and treatment of cystic fibrosis as it occurred thirty years ago. If you personally live with CF, or love someone with CF, and find inaccuracies in the depiction of Joseph's condition, please accept my sincerest apologies.

In reality, Esther and Daniel could not have taken the CF blood test in 1985 because the CF gene wasn't discovered until 1989. Scientists continue to make astounding progress in developing medication and treatment plans for CF patients. Children diagnosed with the disease today live relatively normal lives into their forties. For more information about this disease, please visit www.cf.org.

If you'd like Esther's granola recipe, please send a request to lilli@pagemasterpublishing.com. Look for my sequel, coming soon, *The Arthur Road Cabin* (hint: Alaska!).

Lilli

Acknowledgements

For editing several chapters, providing great grammatical and compositional adjustments, and offering guidance to improve key parts of the story, many thanks to Frances Ilnicky.

Thanks and blessings to Laura Tillman for spending numerous hours answering "just one more question" and for collecting anecdotal responses from friends with CF.

I'm grateful to Richard H. Simon, M.D., The University of Michigan, for answering my long list of queries about the complications and treatment of cystic fibrosis.

To the hundreds of people and organizations whose websites provided pages full of cystic fibrosis data and inspiration; I couldn't have written Joseph without you.

To my husband, Robert, an 18-foot pole vaulter, mathematician, and logical partner; thank you for creating such a wonderful environment in which to write this story. I love you.

To my sons, Max and Alex, who accepted this book into their lives and listened to my readings with genuine enthusiasm. You're incredible blessings and I love you so much!

Seven brave people read the manuscript in its raw, unedited form and insisted that the story was good. Thanks to my mother, Dixie Kibler; my mother-in-law, Joyce Babits; Ann Kinnick; Margi Evans; Katherine Gerus; Karin Babits; and Cindy Lynn.

And finally, I'm very grateful to Gwenna Davis and Annie Griffin at PageMaster Publishing for believing in this story, designing a fabulous cover, proofreading to perfection, and guiding me through the publication process.

About the author

Lilli was born in Cadillac, Michigan and grew up in a Detroit suburb with her parents and four siblings. After graduating from high school, she moved to California where she married Robert, attended college, and worked as a technical editor and writer for several years. She and her husband relocated to Knoxville, Tennessee in 1990 where their two sons were born. In 2001, the Babits family made Howell, Michigan their home town.

When she's not writing or doing bookkeeping tasks for her husband's business, Lilli enjoys gardening, jogging the local country roads, making jam and granola, reading, watching her sons pole vault, and teaching Sunday school. Her flower gardens are full of pastel beach rocks that she brings home every summer from their Lake Michigan vacations.

Faith is a living and unshakable confidence,
a belief in the grace of God so assured that a
man would die a thousand deaths for its sake.

~ Martin Luther